Includes Bonu[s]
The Train Sto[ry]
BY GAIL SATTLER

To Walk in Sunshine

SALLY
LAITY

BARBOUR BOOKS
An Imprint of Barbour Publishing, Inc.

To Walk in Sunshine ©2002 by Sally Laity
The Train Stops Here ©2002 by Gail Sattler

Print ISBN 978-1-68322-190-6

eBook Editions:
Adobe Digital Edition (.epub) 978-1-68322-192-0
Kindle and MobiPocket Edition (.prc) 978-1-68322-191-3

All scripture quotations are taken from the King James Version of the Bible.

This book is a work of fiction. Names, characters, places, and incidents are either products of the author's imagination or used fictitiously. Any similarity to actual people, organizations, and/or events is purely coincidental.

Published by Barbour Books, an imprint of Barbour Publishing, Inc., P.O. Box 719, Uhrichsville, Ohio 44683, www.barbourbooks.com

Our mission is to publish and distribute inspirational products offering exceptional value and biblical encouragement to the masses.

ecpa Member of the
Evangelical Christian
Publishers Association

Printed in the United States of America.

Chapter 1

The *clip-clop* of the old workhorses' hooves and the crunch of wagon wheels over the dusty road meandering alongside Back Mountain echoed off stone walls that stretched along either side. Behind the cloth flaps of the wagon, hanging pots and tools clinked and rattled together in a distinctive rhythm so familiar to Rosalind Gilbran they lulled her into a daze.

A sudden jolt tossed her against Grandfather Azar on the hard seat beside her. That and the warmth of the June sun on his sleeve revived her, and she straightened, blinking to stay alert.

"One stop more, and we will go home," he commented in his gruff voice, a grin broadening his silvering mustache. "I have hunger enough to eat bear."

"*A* bear," she corrected gently, smiling at the twinkle in his brown-black eyes. He rarely spoke in their mother tongue anymore, so determined was he to fit in here in America. He and Grandmother had made great strides in mastering the English language in the dozen years since they'd emigrated from Lebanon. But Rosalind had to wonder how many more years it would take before the inhabitants of Wyoming Valley would accept her people.

Grandfather offered a friendly wave to an open motorcar chugging toward them from the opposite direction, but the fashionably dressed man and woman in the vehicle merely stared, then averted their eyes as they drove by.

Rosa raised her chin and concentrated on the delicate pink of the mountain laurel adorning nearby rises and rocky outcroppings. For a few moments, she imagined that the wagon was navigating through the mountainous land of Lebanon, whose famed cedar trees were used by King Solomon in the building of his wondrous temple.

Because her family immigrated to America when she was a young child, she barely remembered their homeland. But during her travels with her peddler grandfather, he often pointed out this feature or that in the lush countryside that reminded him of the Old Country. She pressed each scene in the scrapbook of her mind, surmising that Lebanon must be the most beautiful place on earth. There, at least, an olive complexion, dark eyes, and colorful clothing would not be an oddity to passersby.

Ahead, a narrow lane jutted off to the right, and Grandfather guided the team onto it. The supplies in back clanged in loud protest as the rickety wagon lurched over washboardlike ruts in the trail.

Not far off the main road, a tidy wood-frame home nestled in a clearing, its white paint bright against the variegated greens of the trees so abundant in northeastern Pennsylvania. Fat hens pecked the ground within a chicken wire pen enclosing one of the smaller outbuildings, and a nearby garden sported an assortment of vegetables growing nearly as high as the rose bushes alongside the house.

A pair of big gray dogs loped toward the approaching wagon, while a trio of young children on the porch stopped their play and looked up. Just then, a woman emerged from the side door, drying her hands on the apron covering her housedress.

"Who is it, Mama?" one of the youngsters hollered. He and his siblings sidled up to the banister, the threesome so close in age that their heads resembled stair steps.

"The peddler. You kids just keep your distance."

"Hello, Neighbor," Grandfather called good-naturedly as he drew the horses to a stop and hopped down. Immediately he threw open the cloth sides of the traveling store, allowing easy viewing of the goods available. Meanwhile, the family pets sniffed around him and the metal-rimmed wheels.

The woman gave a polite nod, but the guarded look in her

light blue eyes eased only after she glimpsed Rosa.

"Good day, Madam," Rosa said pleasantly. The dogs didn't appear threatening, so she climbed down, adjusting the gathers of her maroon skirt. Moving nearer to Grandfather, she checked the display of needles, pins, ribbons, and laces, then tugged a particularly pretty scarf into prominence before stepping aside. The sun made the glorious colors even brighter than those of the floral-printed babushka she'd tied over her curls and secured behind her ears earlier that day.

She glanced at the children and found them perched almost motionless where they were but intensely curious. She smiled at them and received a shy smile in return.

"We bring new pots today," Grandfather said. "Sharp knives and scissors, good needles for sewing. Brooms and buckets. Books for reading and elixirs for coughs. Come. See."

After a slight hesitation, the woman acquiesced, taking her time in a slow perusal of the wagon's wares before selecting a packet of needles, some stockings, and an egg beater. "I'll have to go inside for the money." She hastened away, stray hairs from the loose blond bun at her neck stirring on the breeze. Within moments she returned with the correct amount needed.

Grandfather dropped the coins into his drawstring leather bag and tipped his head. "We thank you, Missus. Is there anything we can bring for next time?"

She regarded him for a few seconds. "A new strainer, perhaps. Mine's all but worn out."

He nodded. "Will bring many strainers with us. For you to choose." With that, he closed the flaps once more, and he and Rosalind climbed aboard.

When they pulled out onto the main road again, Rosa just had to ask, "Doesn't it bother you, Grandfather, that no one likes us in America? Even people we've seen dozens of times do not welcome us as they do others."

He gave an indifferent shrug. "To God we are all the same.

In time, maybe here, too." He paused and a low chuckle rumbled through him. "They like me more when I have you with me, my Rosa. That is one thing I learn quick. With pretty little granddaughter in wagon, people think maybe I not so bad."

She couldn't help smiling, recalling how young she'd been when she first started accompanying him on his rounds. Since her mama had succumbed to a fever on the voyage to the United States and her father died two years later after being kicked in the head by a horse, most of Rosa's memories centered around the maternal grandparents who raised her. Settling back against the seat, she tucked an arm through her grandfather's, knowing he would soon relate stories about life back in Baskinta, as he so often did on their way through the towns, villages, and farms they frequented on a regular basis.

At last their camp on Larksville Mountain came into sight, perched on a rolling clearing rimmed on three sides by thick forests. Rosa couldn't help but sigh. After the many neat farms she and Grandfather had passed, the tiny settlement seemed little more than a hodgepodge of forlorn shacks, dingy tents, house wagons, dreary sheds, and chicken pens. Here and there, on clotheslines suspended between trees, someone's wash flapped in the breeze. Instead of having a sense of permanence about it, the whole camp looked as if they could pick up and leave at a moment's notice should some inhospitable official ask the lot of them to move on. It happened often enough. Admittedly, many of the inhabitants lived here only temporarily, hoarding whatever wages they earned until they could open a business and become established elsewhere. Rosalind had a few grand dreams of her own. Someday, she told herself, she would live in a real house. Surely that wasn't too much to expect out of life.

A multitude of sounds drifted toward them as they approached camp. The bleating of sheep and lowing of cattle drifted on the wind. Blended together from inside the camp itself came laughter from children at play, barking dogs, music from violins and accordions, and voices—male and female—from people busy with afternoon chores. Rosa had to concede, life on the mountain was rarely quiet.

As they entered the encampment, a swarthy, wiry-haired man carving a flute outside the first shack paused and looked up. The bright red neckerchief tied loosely about the neck of his collarless shirt made his narrow face appear longer than it was, especially with the dark, five o'clock shadow from the undergrowth of beard on his cheeks. "Greetings, Abraham." His near-black eyes shifted slightly. "Rosalind."

She did not miss the slight curl of Nicholas Habib's mouth when his attention centered on her, nor the too-knowing gleam in his eye. Seven years older than she, he made no secret of the fact he wanted to wed—wed her, to be exact—as a replacement for his first wife. No one knew the cause of the woman's unfortunate death. Clinging to the knowledge that her grandparents still needed her, Rosa had convinced them to turn Nicholas's offers down.

Pigheaded as the man was, however, no one expected him to give up, even with other eligible young women of marriageable age available among their people.

Schooling her expression to maintain calm, Rosa gave what could barely be termed a nod as they went by.

Moments later they reached their simple cabin. Built of unpainted wood and situated on the higher end of the camp, it overlooked some of the other dwellings. With the supper hour approaching, delectable smells came from open windows and permeated the air. Rosalind knew Grandmother Azar would be making *Sheikh El Mighshi*, baked eggplant stuffed with lamb, and just thinking of the tasty dish made her mouth water. The fresh berries Rosa had gathered yesterday would end the meal.

Grandfather guided the team around back to the shed, then climbed down and immediately began unhitching the horses.

Before Rosalind could climb out, she heard approaching

footsteps and a familiar smiling face appeared before her. Strong arms reached to help.

"Hello, Cousin," Philip Rihany said. At seventeen, scarcely less than a year younger than Rosa, Philip's close-cropped curly hair, boyish features, and charming smile gave him incredible appeal. His once-skinny frame had taken on some manly contours, thanks to his job at Mr. Serhan's warehouse in the nearby city of Wilkes-Barre; solid muscles bulged in his upper arms as Rosa leaned into his hands. "A good day, was it?" he asked.

"A good one. Grandfather made many sales."

Ebony eyes sparkling, he gave an appreciative nod. Then a grin tweaked the corners of his lips, and he tipped his head toward Nick's place. "Still got his cap set for you, eh?"

Rosa groaned. "He is the last man I would choose to marry. I fear that hot temper, and any wife of his would be treated the same cruel way I have seen him treat animals when no one else is watching. Of course, in front of my grandparents and the other families in camp, he pretends to be kind and gentle."

Philip shrugged. "Yes, I have seen that, too. But it is not always up to us to make the choice, you know. We must trust our elders to know best."

The reminder, even though made lightly, dampened Rosa's spirits, but she straightened to her full height. "Perhaps. But this is America. Things are different here."

"I hope they are, Cousin. For you, at least." He reached into a trouser pocket and withdrew a silver bangle bracelet, which he placed into her hand. "I thought you might like this. I bought it from Mr. Serhan."

"Why, thank you. It is lovely. But you should not be spending your money on me." Nevertheless, Rosa smiled and slid it over her wrist, then admired it from arm's length, liking the way it glistened against her olive skin.

"Who else would I spend it on?"

"Maybe one of the girls who worships the ground you walk

on," she said, counting them off on her fingers, "like Farah, perhaps, or Kamila, or. . ."

A broad smile revealed Philip's strong, even teeth, and he laughed. "With so many, how could a man choose?" He accompanied her around to the front of the house, then headed for his own dwelling next door.

Rosalind watched after him until he went inside. More than just her relative, handsome, curly-haired Philip was her very best friend. And one of these days, she would be sad to lose his attentions to someone else. She opened the door of her grandparents' weathered, four-room cabin and entered.

Not for the first time, she appreciated that what the rustic abode lacked as far as beauty on the outside, it more than made up for inside. Granted, it was a bit cramped, with the kitchen and living room sharing the front half and drapery panels dividing the back into two bedrooms. But red calico curtains at the windows and multihued rag rugs scattered about the floor added cheer, and colorful cushions complemented the horsehair sofa and chairs, promising comfort. An inviting glow from the oil lamps gilded the dark pine table and chair backs, lighting upon her grandmother's endless supply of hanging herbs and the labeled jars on the shelves below them.

"I heard you coming," Grandmother Azar said, removing the baked eggplant from the oven. Turning, she carried it to the table and set it on a quilted pad in the middle, where a bowl of buttered potatoes, a plate of sliced bread, and a pot of strong coffee already waited. Then she put aside the towels she'd used to protect her hands from the hot pan. "We can eat as soon as your grandfather comes in from tending the horses." Brushing her hands down her half apron, she smiled, plumping out cheeks rosy from the temperature of the room.

"That is good. We are starving." Rosalind returned the smile as she went to wash her hands in the basin on the sideboard. "Everything smells wonderful."

The door opened just then, and Grandfather entered, stomping the dust from his boots on the braided mat. "I am home, my Eva."

"So I see," she said as he crossed the room to hug her and kiss her button nose.

Enjoying the ritual played out a thousand times before, Rosalind looked from one guardian to the other. Short and plump like the salt and pepper shakers on the table, the pair went together equally as well, with hair nearly identical shades of gray and the same twinkling sable eyes. Rosa hoped the day would never come when one of them would depart this life and leave the other behind.

"Well, then, Woman," he boomed good-naturedly, "let's eat."

The dreary sky turned the thriving town of Edwardsville a dozen shades of gray, a somber palette broken only by the deep green of the wide variety of trees climbing the rolling hills. Numerous coal companies conducted their operations here and in bordering towns. And always in the vicinity of the collieries, culm banks— black waste heaps of clay, crumbled rock, and slate—grew by the day. Near some of those culm banks, oily-black brackish ponds emitted the smell of sulfur. Wisps of acrid white smoke rose from the banks in places, eerie evidence of fires raging deep within— fires that burned on and on, even through days of drenching rain. At night, the culm banks glowed a dull red.

Feeling every bit as dismal as the surroundings, miner Kenneth Roberts trudged the downward slope leading home from the Hudson Coal Company colliery, clutching his two weeks' pay, or the meager remains of it, in his coal-blackened fist. Miners contracted with the coal company to remove clean coal at a certain price per coal buggy, and the company then deducted the cost of the equipment used to accomplish that job—and the earnings of the fellow laborer, or butty, who worked with them, from the miners' wages. Added to those expenses, Ken's family often had to purchase groceries "on the book" at the neighborhood store.

He often wondered if he would ever pay off the debt his late father had left behind, especially now that the demand for coal was beginning to decline.

Many European immigrants in need of steady work had been lured to northeastern Pennsylvania's growing anthracite industry. Ken's father was only one out of multitudes who signed on to blast and chip hard coal from its seams far below the earth. All of them expected to make a decent living. Few did. If cave-ins and constant accidents didn't claim lives, the disease known as black lung took a huge toll among the miners. But once a man owed his soul to the coal company and the "pluck me" store, he had little means to go elsewhere. Ken had to struggle against the bitter conviction that after scrimping and saving to cross the ocean for a better life, his family was no better off than before they left. In fact, in some ways they were worse off.

He started down his street, a dirt road bracketed by plain company houses positioned fairly close to one another and separated by narrow side yards. Each had a small swatch of grass in front, overlooked by a porch, and a sizeable backyard. Some had a few brave flowers either planted along the base or in clay pots on the porch steps. But all had weathered clapboard siding blackened by the ever-present coal dust. Reaching the next to the last one in the row, Ken went around back, wiped his work boots on the doormat and went inside.

"Hi, Son," his mother said. Slight of build and dressed as always in a crisp, patterned housedress and her faded brown hair pinned in a neat roll, she stood at the counter slicing fresh bread. "We just drew water in the tub. Soon as you wash up and change, supper will be on the table."

"Thanks." On his way across the worn linoleum to the cellar door, Ken placed his unopened pay envelope beside her, then clomped down the steps to the bathroom to bathe, pointless though it seemed. Even after a quick shower in the shiftin' shack—the gathering point for each shift—at the end of his workday, he could never scrub himself completely clean. After eight hours of chipping and hacking at coal hundreds of feet below the earth's surface, black grime clogged every pore in his body. Even when he wasn't near the breaker, he could still smell coal dust with each breath he took. Only on the days when he hiked into the woods and breathed nature's clean, crisp air for a few hours could he forget for awhile that he was a miner.

The bleak cellar housing the bathroom, furnace room, storage space, and coal bin, sported few furnishings. It had a dirt floor except in the furnace room, where a water tank next to the furnace provided a fairly reliable supply of hot water for the house. In the bathroom, Ken crossed the wooden walking plank between the commode and the cast-iron tub and shucked his dirty clothes, then lowered himself into steaming waist-deep water, relaxing momentarily against the back edge of the tub.

His thoughts drifted to green forests and clear-running waterfalls. Oh what it would be like to be truly clean and stay that way. At least tomorrow was Saturday, he reminded himself, and the thought cheered him. He did consider himself fortunate that the mine was still in full production, running two shifts, when mines in many places were closing down. But he also appreciated a little respite from the dreaded duties there. Once he finished the chores around home, he hoped to go up on the mountain for a few hours.

On the floor directly above, three sets of footsteps moved about as his mother and his siblings tended to supper, sounds that brought Ken back to the present. He filled his lungs and exhaled slowly, then reached for the soap and scrub brush.

By the time he toweled off and put on the clean clothes waiting for him on the straight-backed chair, Ken felt considerably better. He combed his damp hair in the dim light of the wall lamp and set the comb down on the shelf below the wall mirror before climbing the stairs to the kitchen.

"Oh, good," his golden-haired sister, Hannah, said, her airy voice more breathless than usual. "You're done." At nineteen and the image of their handsome mother, she turned a fair share of heads whenever she walked down the street to the trolley. Eyes of summer blue sparkled with her smile as she handed Ken the water pitcher. "Be a sport and take this to the table, would you?"

"Sure thing."

"Oh, and don't say anything about Timmy's eye," she added in a whisper.

Ken cast a glance heavenward and shook his head. Hardly a week passed that their twelve-year-old kid brother didn't get into a fight. It had to stop. And there was one way of making sure it did.

He carried the pitcher into the dining room and set it on the table, right in front of Tim. It was all Ken could do not to laugh at the towhead, who, conspicuous in the attempt to keep his freckled face averted, squirmed uneasily in his chair as his older brother and sister took their seats.

"You may say the blessing," Ma said, a pointed frown directed at Ken, and everyone bowed their heads.

"Thank You, Lord, for this good food. And for helping us to triumph over our enemies. . .if we did. In Jesus' name, amen."

Timmy snorted.

Hannah giggled under her breath.

"Oh, really!" Ma huffed. "Let's not start it. Pass the pork chops."

"It ain't nothin' anyways," Tim said, the relief in his voice noticeable now that the tension in the room had eased.

"Isn't," their mother corrected. "And I don't wish to discuss it at the table."

"Yes, Ma'am." Sitting up straighter, he snatched a slice of bread and slathered it with butter.

Ken helped himself to several pork chops when the platter came his way, then filled the well in his mashed potatoes with gravy and spooned peas and carrots beside them. "Looks great, Ma. I'm famished."

"Then you'll love the chocolate cake I just finished icing," Hannah said.

"Only if there's any left when I'm done with it," Timmy countered, heartily digging into his meal.

She wrinkled her nose at him and sliced a chunk of pork, then sampled it.

"How was your day?" their mother asked Ken.

"Same as always. Long. But at least the week's over."

"Somebody told me the other guys call you 'Preacher.' That right?" Tim asked.

"Yep."

"Well, I think it's swell," Hannah said. "They know what you stand for and respect you for it."

Tim turned a puzzled face to him. "How'd you get 'em to do that? Respect you, I mean."

"By not fighting every time somebody says something I don't agree with," Ken replied evenly.

The lad blanched, making his freckles stand out all the more. "It's different there than at school," he muttered.

"Even schoolboys respect a man who has a job," Ken went on. He ate a chunk of pork, then looked up. "There's talk of hiring on more breaker boys."

Their mother dropped her fork and blotted her lips with her napkin. "I'll hear no talk of Timmy becoming a breaker boy," she declared with fervor. "Besides, he's only twelve. That's too young."

"Not if I talk to the right man," Ken said. "Look in my pay envelope, Ma. Look at what Hannah earns at the silk mill. All those hours we put in, and together we're barely bringing in enough money to keep up with the bills, let alone get us out of debt. If the kid can help out a little, I say let him. We don't have much choice."

"I could take in laundry," Ma offered.

"No, you can't. You work too hard as it is. Harder than you're supposed to, according to Doc Peters. After all the years you and

Pa supported us, the least we can do is take care of you now. It's what families do."

"He's right, Mother," Hannah chimed in. "Let us help. All three of us."

Her shoulders sagged, and she placed her hands in her lap. "I just don't feel good about this. I already lost a husband and one son to those mines. I don't know if I can face the possibility of losing anyone else, much less my baby. Someone in this family needs to graduate school."

"Aw, Ma," Tim said, puffing out his chest. "I ain't no baby. And what good is school, when nobody around here can *be* anythin' except a coal miner anyways?"

"I'm hoping the day will come when we can move away from the mines," she said, her eyes moistening. "Your pa and I wanted you all to have a better life. Nobody expected that cave-in that took his and Matt's life. Things just didn't go like we planned."

"So we'll have to make the best of it," Ken replied, purposely refusing to dwell on the cruel past. "We'll have to make enough money to get out of here on our own, and we have to do it while it's still possible. When people started switching to oil and gas heat after the war, the demand for coal dropped. Mines in some parts of Pennsylvania and West Virginia are already closing down. We're running out of time."

She sat quietly for a few seconds, her eyes downcast. "At least let me pray about it. I hate to be forced to make a decision like this—one I've dreaded more than anything in my life—without taking it to the Lord."

"Fair enough," Ken said, watching her rise, pick up her half-finished meal, and leave the room. It wasn't a decision he'd come by lightly himself. But what other choice did they have? Any of them?

Chapter 2

Strolling through the dappled shade of the forest far above the encampment, Rosalind stepped around a cluster of lush ferns to where a patch of sunlight illuminated a growth of dandelion-like coltsfoot. Removing the cloth bag hanging on her shoulder, she knelt among the yellow flowers to gather some of the scaly stalks for her grandmother. The older woman, a trusted healer among the Lebanese immigrants, would make an extract from fresh plant leaves and form it into hard candy cough drops. The dried leaves would be saved to steep when needed for medicinal tea.

Though Rosa enjoyed the noise and activity of the camp, she appreciated the quiet solitude of the forest even more. Grandmother Azar had taught her well how to recognize the many herbs and plants with healing qualities, and now with her advancing years, she was more than happy to let Rosalind keep her sufficiently supplied for her trade.

A gentle breeze whispered through the canopy of leaves overhead, and colorful birds flitted from treetop to treetop, trilling out their cheerful melodies as Rosa continued her search for herbs. Periodically a rabbit or a squirrel would scamper across her path and just as quickly disappear from sight.

Coming upon one of her favorite spots, where a gleaming ribbon of water sliced through a small clearing, Rosa stepped out of her slippers and lowered herself to the spongy ground to rest awhile. She tucked her legs beneath the folds of her skirt and listened to the gurgling, crystal-clear stream rushing by. This had to be one of the loveliest places anywhere, she surmised, letting her gaze drift to the infinite variety of trees all around. She especially liked the ferns growing in such profusion, and the bright wildflowers speckling the ground, lifting their fragile faces toward the rays of sunlight.

From her skirt pocket, she took out a book of poetry and, ever thankful that her people had no qualms about making sure that girls as well as boys received an adequate education, she lost herself in the beautiful words.

Before long, approaching sounds drew her out of her reverie. A forest creature, she suspected and cautiously slid the book back inside her pocket. She kept her eyes peeled toward the rustling coming from the other side of the stream.

But no furry animal emerged into the small clearing. Instead, a sandy-haired man moved into view.

His eyes found her in that same instant, and he halted in his tracks.

Startled, Rosa snatched the herb bag from where it lay beside her and bolted to her feet, instantly calculating the shortest route home.

His voice, pleasantly deep, stopped her before she took flight. "Please don't run away," he said kindly. "I won't harm you." As if to prove he meant no threat, he held his open hands aloft, a gentle smile softening wide-set eyes of palest gray. Beneath straight brows on his square-jawed face, a tranquil quality from within the silvery depths drew Rosa in a way she had never before experienced.

She moistened her lips. A tiny voice inside warned her of the dangers of associating with strangers—particularly those with light hair and eyes, who considered her people unwelcome foreigners. But this one appeared harmless enough. Rosa felt her guard crumble a little.

"I'm Ken Roberts," he said, still smiling as he started toward her. He paused on his side of the water and slid one hand into a trouser pocket. "Are you new around here?"

Rosalind's hoop earrings tickled her neck as she shook her head, but she didn't dare take her eyes off him. In a swift assessment, she noted his manly bearing and quiet confidence, his easy manner, and generous, well-shaped mouth. She watched the corners curve upward into a smile.

"I come here pretty often," he went on in that calm tone, "but I've never seen you before. That's why I thought maybe you were new to the area."

"No," she murmured. "I am not new. We—I—live on the mountain."

"This one? Larksville Mountain?"

She gave the hint of a nod.

"Sure is pretty around here," he said. "God didn't spare the beauty when He made our part of Pennsylvania."

His words, so sincere in their delivery, somehow made her feel she belonged here and put her at ease. She drew a slow breath and relaxed a bit more.

"My family and I live not too far from your camp," Ken continued, "down in Edwardsville. I work at the mine. I come up into the woods to breathe clean air now and again. I feel closer to the Lord among all this evidence of His handiwork." He paused and tipped his head in the direction of her side of the stream. "Mind if I join you?"

"As you wish," Rosa said, hoping she would not regret the rash decision.

He hopped across easily and grinned with satisfaction. Then, withdrawing an apple from his pocket, he sliced it in two with a pocketknife and held out half to her.

Hesitating only a second, she accepted it. "Thank you," she whispered. "My name is Rosalind. Rosalind Gilbran."

"Very glad to meet you, Rosalind." With that, he plopped down beside where she'd been sitting and stretched out his legs as he crunched into his part of the apple.

Rosa couldn't quite find the courage to retake her seat on the ground, so she remained standing while nibbling the fruit he'd given her. But she kept a sharp eye out, lest someone from the camp should happen by. It wouldn't do for her to be caught doing something forbidden. . .like speaking to a miner.

From the corner of his eye, Ken watched the petite Rosalind Gilbran, feeling her unease as if it were a tangible thing. He breathed a silent prayer that God would keep him from scaring her off. When he finished his apple, he tossed the core over to a tree where he'd spied a squirrel busily hunting acorns and other tidbits.

Rosa followed suit. Then she stooped and rinsed her fingers, trailing them in the water momentarily. The full skirt she wore billowed about her in a cloud of red, blue, and yellow, the bright colors adding richness to her flawless olive complexion and sable eyes. A short red bandana with ends tied behind her ears hid a portion of her dark brown hair, but beneath its folds, shiny curls softly caressed the shoulders of her blouse.

Ken couldn't help but be fascinated at the grace of her movements and for a fleeting second envisioned her dancing to gypsy violins, her willowy form swaying like a flower in the wind. He forced himself to rein in his thoughts. "Do your parents know you wander so far from home, Rosalind?" he finally asked, liking the sound of her unfamiliar name.

She turned and met his gaze. "I have only grandparents. And they know I have good reason to be in the forest."

"Ah." Her statement, spoken in soft tones and with the barest hint of an accent, only added to Ken's curiosity.

He'd had few encounters with Lebanese people, a fact he attributed to their apparent reluctance to relinquish the daylight and willingly enter an iron cage that plunged down into the bowels of the earth where they'd have to work in dank darkness. He knew that a few of them peddled their wares in various parts of Wyoming Valley and the Back Mountain area and that others had recently opened businesses of their own. Though at first they seemed to suffer slightly more discrimination than other nationalities, they almost always turned out to be conscientious workers who met with surprising and amazingly swift success in their ventures.

Rising to her feet, Rosa slipped the cloth strap of her herb bag over one shoulder. "I cannot stay. I must go now."

"I hope it's not because of me," Ken ventured, feeling a twinge of disappointment that she would not visit awhile longer.

She shook her head. "No. Grandmother is waiting for the herbs I found."

"Well, take care, then. I'm glad I met you, Rosalind Gilbran. Maybe our paths will cross again sometime."

Her dark eyes met his and lingered for a heartbeat. "Perhaps." Then with a timid smile, she turned and hurried away.

An elusive element in her gaze caught at Ken's heart, and for several moments after she vanished into the greenery of the woods, he tried to analyze it. Surely not fear, as she'd seemed fairly relaxed in his presence. But it might have been sadness or loneliness. Even a deep yearning. He bowed his head, as he so often did when alone in nature's haven, and breathed a prayer for Rosalind Gilbran. He had a feeling the two of them would meet again.

On the return trip to town, hours later, the memory of the young woman he'd met in the wooded hills teased his consciousness. It pained him to picture someone so lovely as she living in the coarse and ragtag gypsy encampment on the mountain. . . yet the stark, dismal company house he called home wasn't all that superior. The last thing he wanted was to be stuck working in the coal mines forever. Maybe they all—gypsies and miners alike—shared the same dream of being able to obtain a better life someday.

As Ken reached the house and went around to the back door, his kid brother came running from the next yard and joined him.

"Guess what! I think Ma's gonna let me be a breaker boy," he announced.

"That right?"

He nodded. "At least she ain't havin' a conniption about it no more. That's a good sign, right?"

Ken tousled Tim's hair, and they climbed the steps and crossed the shallow porch. "It might be, Squirt. It just might be."

"What might be?" their mother asked, looking up from kneading bread dough as they came in. The flour on her hands and nose put the aged and chipping paint in the rest of the cheerless kitchen to shame, but she kept the old counters and floor scrubbed and squeaky clean, as if that made up for its shortcomings. The pale yellow curtains looked like she'd starched them again, too.

"Nothing much," Ken answered, giving the towhead a conspiratorial wink. Having worked in the breakers himself, he knew firsthand the difficulties the boy would face in the days to come. Yet he also knew that if Tim stuck it out and proved himself, he could catch the attention of his supervisor and advance to a better job. Like becoming a nipper, as the boys were called who tended the heavy wooden doors down in the mine shafts that controlled the ventilation for the miners. Or maybe even a mule tender, which had been Ken's favorite duty in his younger years. Of course, there was talk of phasing out those temperamental beasts.

"Well, I'm glad you're both here," their mother said. "The sacks of coal Timmy picked this morning never got dumped into the coal bin before he went running off to play. How about seeing to it now? They're by the shed out back. And after that, I have a few other chores for the two of you."

"Sure thing," Ken said, motioning with his head for Tim to follow him outside, where the slanted storm doors to the cellar were located. The common practice of salvaging whatever free coal they could from the culm banks kept a lot of people going when money was scarce. Most of the women and children had a favorite spot they frequented. And they were careful not to get caught by the authorities, even though no one could explain what was so wrong about putting to good use what coal companies discarded in the first place.

Ken made quick work of the things his ma wanted done and was busy polishing all the Sunday shoes when Hannah came dragging in from her Saturday job of cleaning houses for folks over in Wilkes-Barre who could afford such a luxury.

"Whew! How can it be so hot this early in June?" she asked, dropping onto a painted kitchen chair and kicking off her scuffed oxford shoes. Her faded work dress, bearing stains and smudges from the day's activities, clung to her slender form.

"It's not really that bad," Ken said. "Just feels that way when you work hard."

She gave him a half-hearted smile. "I thought I'd never get done at Mrs. Hughes's. She picked today to decide she wanted her lace curtains washed and stretched and the silver polished. All of it. Even the pieces I doubt ever see the light of day."

"But I'll bet they looked real nice when you were through," Ma said, bringing her a glass of lemonade.

"Oh, thank you. And yes, they did." After several swallows of the cool liquid, she brushed damp strands of hair from her forehead and reached into the pocket of her skirt. "Here, Ma. She and Mrs. MacNamara paid me today."

With a nod, their mother picked up the money and took it to the cupboard, where she put it into the sugar bowl with the other family funds. "We're not doing too badly this month," she said a bit too cheerily. "Barring any accidents or the like."

Ken grimaced. "What we need is to get caught up and get a little ahead, pay down the bill at Murphy's that's been hanging over our heads forever."

"The Lord will provide," she assured him.

"I'm sure He will," Ken muttered under his breath. "If we live so long."

"Kenneth!" His mother planted her fists on her hips. "It's not like you to mouth such disrespectful nonsense."

"You're right, Ma," he admitted with chagrin. How quickly he'd forgotten the time he'd spent basking in God's handiwork.

"I'm sorry. I guess I have a lot on my mind lately."

"We all need to get rested and refreshed," she said, her tone softening. "And we'll get that at church tomorrow. Things always look brighter after services."

After returning home with the various plants she'd found on her jaunt up on the mountain, Rosa helped her grandmother sort and prepare them. Some had to be tied and dried, others kept fresh, and others boiled, their extracts strained and put into small bottles and jars. Once that chore ended and supper was over, the dishes washed and put away, Rosa's grandparents went out for an evening stroll. She stayed behind and settled back against the worn cushions of the sofa to relax.

Much as she tried not to think about the miner she'd encountered earlier that day, the memory of his kind voice and gentle gaze seemed to hover at the edge of her mind all during her tasks. And now that she had some leisure time, she allowed herself to relive the pleasant moments she dared not speak of.

Ken Roberts was not at all like the men her grandparents had warned her about. They considered the Welshmen, Englishmen, and Italians who worked in the coal mines to be loud and boisterous hotheads who wasted every penny they earned in the beer gardens near their homes. Down in the coal towns, it seemed there was one of those establishments for every four or five houses— certainly far more than there were churches. Her people felt it their duty to protect the unmarried young women in the camp from being lured away and taken advantage of by some uncouth coal cracker. Already the parents of many of Rosa's friends had arranged marriages for them with countrymen who met their strict requirements.

Rosa wondered if those girls had also approved of mates not of their own choosing and found true happiness. Surely a marriage union should involve love. She was sure love had come for her grandparents. They often displayed deep affection toward one another and for her as well. She hoped one day to have that same kind of relationship with a man who respected and loved her.

Her musings ceased when her guardians returned from their walk. "Such a moon, little one," Grandfather said, his eyes dark as the night and twinkling like the stars. "You should come, too. The neighbors, they like to see you."

"I will next time," she promised. "I was tired from my long walk today."

"She would be tired, Abraham," Grandmother said. "When you don't take her out on wagon, I send her up in forest."

Rosalind got up and hugged them both. "It's all right. Truly. Neither of you forces me to do things. I love helping out."

"But you should think of being bride soon," her grandmother urged. "Tonight Nicholas, he ask about you again."

A chill tingled along the back of Rosa's neck, raising the fine hairs. "Please do not encourage him. He makes me uncomfortable. I do not like the way he looks at me."

"He is good man," Grandfather said. "Has much money saved for future. He will make good home for wife."

"Then he should have a wife who loves him," Rosa said, turning away. She knew her grandparents had never seen their neighbor's cruel side, yet she did not want to be the one to lower their opinion of him. "I want a husband who will have feelings of love for me, the way you two have for each other. And Nicholas Habib is not such a one."

A strange look passed between the older couple, and they smiled. Grandmother moved to the stove and set the kettle over the hottest portion, while Grandfather took his favorite chair, then leaned back and made himself comfortable. "Not always was love between us," she confessed. "Not at first. I not even know him when his papa an' mine say we to marry."

"But we grow to love," he said. "My Eva is good woman. Good wife."

Rosa barely heard his words. Her insides still revolted against the unsettling news her grandmother had just uttered. She knew that more often than not, it was the way of her people. Even her cousin Philip had reminded her of that fact just yesterday. But still, she harbored the hope that for her it would be different. She could not imagine living with a man who made her skin crawl. The look in Nicholas Habib's eyes made her feel undressed. Dirty. Besides, no amount of money could make up for a temper like his. Rosa pitied the woman who ended up with such a man. After all, who really knew what happened to his first wife?

She swallowed the huge lump of disquiet gathering in her throat and looked at one guardian and then the other. "Please," she implored. "Please, don't ask me to marry Nicholas. I am not ready to marry anyone."

"I know, little one," her grandfather said, patting her knee with his big, callused hand. "And we are not ready to give you up."

"But goldenrod tea is ready," Grandmother said, her smile adding another dab of comfort. "Come to table."

More out of duty than need, Rosa stood and followed Grandfather to evening tea. She could not bear to dwell on the conversation they'd just shared. She needed something more cheerful to help restore her happy mood.

Please don't run away. Maybe our paths will cross again sometime.

Even as the words Ken Roberts had spoken drifted across her mind, Rosa couldn't help smiling. Perhaps he had offered her friendship. Now that so many of her friends had married and moved on, Rosa had no one left but Philip. She could use another friend.

No, her sensible side countered. *Don't be stupid. It is forbidden to associate with someone from the mines.* Worse than that, her grandparents would skin her alive if she dared to do so.

"How is tea?" Grandmother Azar asked. "Is good?"

"Yes. Good." Rosa hadn't even tasted it. She quickly took a sip, scalding her tongue in the process. Using more caution after that, she downed the remainder as quickly as possible, then manufactured a huge yawn. "Oh, my. I'm sleepier than I thought. I will turn in now." Rising, she took her cup to the sideboard, then returned to hug her guardians. "Good night, Grandmother, Grandfather. I will see you in the morning."

"Good night, my Rosa," her grandfather said.

But after she visited the outhouse around back and then changed into her nightgown in her room, sleep was the farthest thing from Rosa's mind. All she could think about was a pair of smiling, silver-gray eyes and an offer of friendship that could never be.

The sun had yet to inch its way into the eastern sky when the steam whistle from the motor house at the colliery announced to the countryside the start of a new workday.

In the small, second-floor bedroom he shared with Timmy, Ken flung his sheet and light blanket aside and got up, then pulled on some clean socks and work clothes. As he dressed, he observed the towhead, who lay sprawled on the other bed sound asleep, one bare leg dangling over the side.

What with his brother's excitement about becoming a working boy, Ken just hoped the kid had dozed off at a reasonable hour. At least the hearty breakfast Ma fixed every day would revive them both—even if they did have to gobble it so fast they hardly tasted it. He shook Tim's shoulder to rouse him.

Moments later, in the kitchen, nobody talked as they wolfed down pork chops and eggs, then gulped the strong coffee Ma had perked and waiting for them. Ken avoided looking at his mother altogether, knowing her uncharacteristic silence revealed her fear and dread of sending her youngest child off to the mines.

But the inevitable could not be put off forever. Before exiting the back door, he and his brother grabbed their work hats and tugged on clodhoppers, then took the metal lunch pails Ma held out to them.

She gave Ken a peck on the cheek and tried to smile. Then

she hugged Timmy hard. "Be careful," she whispered.

"I will."

"Don't worry, Ma," Ken assured her. "Ralph Vaughn's a decent supervisor. He treats the boys fairer than most." A quick squeeze of her hand, and the two of them hustled out to join the stream of men and boys already climbing the hill.

Ken looked down at Timmy walking beside him, knowing the glow of anticipation in his kid brother's eyes would be doused long before this workday ended. "I already talked to your boss," he began. "He's willing to give you a fair shot. But you might as well know, it's not gonna be a picnic working in the breaker. It's hard there. Real hard. And your fingers are gonna take awhile to toughen up."

"Yeah, yeah," Tim muttered. "It ain't like I don't know no boys who work there already. I heard lots of stories."

Ken nodded. "Right. I'm just trying to warn you. A couple of hours from now you might wish you'd stayed in school."

"Humph. That'll be the day."

"We'll see if you feel any different when the quitting whistle blows. Not to mention having to work every Saturday."

They soon reached the breaker, a tall, gloomy structure silhouetted against the sky. There, filled coal cars were pulled by steel cables up the steep incline to the top, where the contents were tipped out into a shaking machine. The coal then rushed down into chutes running from the top of the breaker to the bottom, in a deafening, earsplitting roar that made the whole place vibrate and wouldn't let up until the quitting whistle.

Ken took Tim into the building, conscious of his brother's curious perusal of the dismal interior. He saw the kid's eyes widen at the high walls, the narrow staircase that climbed toward a tangle of blackened beams, and grime-covered windows.

Dozens of boys already sat hunched over on pine boards astride the long iron chutes, picking rock, slate, and other refuse, or culm, out of the coal. As they worked, clouds of coal dust,

SALLY LAITY

steam, and smoke settled over them like a blanket, blackening them from head to toe.

Their supervisor, a short, muscular man, stood off to one side. The broomstick he used to keep his workers alert stood propped against the breaker wall, within easy reach.

Ken steered Tim over to him. "Just tend to your own business," he all but shouted above the racket. "Don't shame Ma by getting mixed up with troublemakers who are always thinking up pranks and making mischief."

His brother looked askance at him, but made no reply.

"Morning, Mr. Vaughn," Ken hollered as they approached the overseer. "This is Tim. He's here to go to work."

Leaving the boy to learn his job, Ken walked out of the breaker and headed for the shiftin' shack. Here many of the miners changed into working garb and, after the shift, showered to remove some of the coal dust before going home. His butty, Tony Valentino, had already arrived and stood waiting for him.

Before heading for the iron cage that would plummet them down to their work site, they moved to the peg shanty and retrieved the brass tags bearing their miner's numbers from the board.

Tony gave Ken a cheerless grin.

"Ready for a bright new day?" Ken quipped, nodding to him and the other workers awaiting the descent.

"Let's hope we get a spot wi' a good bit 'o top coal, for once," ruddy-faced miner Sandy MacNeil said in his Scottish brogue. He and his butty worked on the same level with Ken.

" 'Happy is he whose hope is in the Lord,' " Ken returned lightly.

"Verse for the day, Preacher?" Tony asked, his tone teasing.

"Something like that."

Just then the hoisting engineer brought the elevator rumbling into view as it was hauled up by its thick, greasy cable. A pair of waiting workers stepped inside, joined by Ken, MacNeil, and their two fellow laborers.

A bell rang. Overhead, massive iron sheave wheels began to turn, lowering them into the black depths. Slowly at first, past slimy, dripping, moss-encrusted granite blocks at the mouth of the shaft, then faster, machinery creaking and timbers groaning as they plunged with incredible speed. Daylight became a speck above, then vanished. Only the thin, wavering glow from the electric lamps on the men's hats broke the inky blackness.

They came to a stop at one of the many levels being mined hundreds of feet beneath the earth's surface, and the two extra men exited and were quickly lost to sight in tunnels extending into the darkness on either side. Loaded mine cars standing on a narrow-gauge track waited to be pushed by the "bottom men" into the rails of an ascending cage.

After passing additional levels, the platform slowed suddenly, then jarred to a final stop nearly a thousand feet down. Ken, MacNeil, and their helpers stepped off into the gloom.

Despite the strong, cold downdraft of air at the bottom of the shaft provided by huge fans at the surface, the dank smells of rotting mine timbers and of wet rock and earth assaulted their lungs. The thumping of powerful water pumps in the pump room throbbed in their ears.

The young nipper opened the ponderous wooden door that regulated the flow of air into the mine at their level, and they entered the tunnel, or gangway, extending from the shaft. There were noticeably fewer sounds besides the crunch of their boots on the coal dust. Just the eerie trickle and dripping of water from the nearby Susquehanna River kept at bay, the rumble of distant mine cars, and the occasional explosion set off to jar coal loose from the rich seams.

At the fire boss's belowground "office," the men hung their brass tags on a Peg-Board indicating the exact location in the labyrinth of tunnels and chambers where they would be working. No one ever spoke of the purpose the board served—they needed no reminder that in case of a cave-in, the mine officials would know how many bodies needed to be dug out.

Next Ken checked the slate on which the fire boss had recorded his daily notations regarding the present air quality and any spot where the roof needed extra propping.

A huge rat skittered by, as if detecting enticing smells from the lunch pails each of them carried.

"Okay, you guys know what we're here for," Ken said. "Let's get to it." Lunches in hand, they started the long trek along the irregular tunnels to reach the individual chamber, or breast, where yesterday's tools and gear awaited them.

⚬⚬⚬

Washing the breakfast dishes, Rosa peered out the window at the morning sky, noting several high clouds.

"Do not worry," her grandmother said, joining her. "When clouds are white and scattered across sky and winds are from west, no change comes. And leaves on the trees are not bottom up. It will not rain today."

Rosa just smiled. Her guardian had a saying for every occasion. "Then it will be a good day for making the rounds with Grandfather."

But even as she spoke, the older man came in from the shed, a frown knitting his shaggy brows. "Toby has sore foot from stone. We will not go to peddle today. Maybe not tomorrow. I will rest him."

"Show me the hoof," Grandmother suggested. "I will see if a compress or salve will help."

"That is why I love my Eva," he said, his expression brightening. "Always she can make things better."

"Not always," she said, perusing the various concoctions lining the wall shelves. "But I try." She selected a few small jars and slipped them into her apron pocket.

"Is there something I can do?" Rosalind asked, drying her hands.

"No, little one. Not here. But maybe more berries you can

find up in hills. For supper tonight."

"Of course. I will go as soon as I finish sweeping the floor."

When the older pair had gone, she made quick work of the task, then slipped the strap of her herb bag over one shoulder and a basket for berries over her forearm.

One of the rangy dogs from the camp loped over to her when she stepped outside. "Hello, Maloof," Rosa crooned as she leaned down and scratched behind his shaggy brown ears. "Would you like to come with me to the forest?" He licked her hand, and the two of them started up the incline, the dog bounding ahead of her, prone to checking out any and all distracting sounds and smells.

Many more blueberries and raspberries had ripened since her last visit, she discovered when they reached her favorite berry patch, but they could wait to be picked until after she looked around for herbs and medicinal plants. She hung the basket on a low birch branch and checked to see where Maloof had wandered.

A sudden scuffle in the bushes sent a red squirrel scampering out into the open and up the trunk of the nearest tree, the brown dog charging after it in pursuit. Rosalind chuckled as Maloof gave up and followed his nose elsewhere.

In the swampy ground near an underground spring, she gave wide berth to a sumac tree rather than risk contact, which could cause severe skin irritation and blistering. But the dwarf ginseng growing on the moist edge of the clearing was another matter entirely. She pulled out several of the tubers and tucked them inside the bag. Grandmother could boil those for supper.

The deep pink flowers of swamp milkweed caught her attention next. The plant's juice could be used to treat any number of ailments, so Rosa gathered a handful and added it to the bag.

As she worked, recollections of her last trip into the forest teased her mind, along with the encounter with handsome miner Ken Roberts. The mines were operating today, so he probably wouldn't be hiking in the hills. But the thought held more disappointment than relief. Part of her wished she had stayed longer and gotten to know him a little when the opportunity had presented itself. But her sensible side knew she had made the wiser choice. To leave and return home.

Coming to a drier area, Rosalind sank to the ground and propped herself up from behind with her arms, stretching her legs out in front as she stared up at the fluffy clouds.

What was he truly like? Surely a man as friendly and pleasant as he would have a wife or someone to whom he was betrothed. After all, he did mention his family. Possibly he was married, perhaps with a gaggle of children. But if so, why would he even suggest the two of them might meet again? Unless, of course, he had no principles and was as dangerous and uncouth as her people considered the miners.

Oh well, she had no answers to her own questions. She was wasting time and had yet to pick the berries she'd come for. She gave a sharp whistle, Maloof came running, and the two of them headed for the berry patch.

Halfway there, a rustle from the grove off to her right made the animal's ears perk up. Rosa cautiously eyed the trees. Surely Maloof would defend her if a wild creature should crash out of the growth. Or so, at least, she hoped.

But a square, dark-skinned hand parted the branches.

Nicholas Habib's leering smile greeted her. "Ah. The lovely Rosalind. You have been gone from the camp a long time."

He watched me leave? He followed me? Rosa swallowed the uneasy lump forming in her throat. "Nicholas," she managed. "What brings you way up here?"

"I wanted to make sure nothing had happened to you. That you were safe."

Safe! I felt perfectly safe until your swarthy face appeared. "Well, as you can see, you had no cause to worry. Maloof is looking out for me."

"Yes. Maloof the brave one." Eyes black as an onyx peered

down at the dog in derision and got a low growl in return. "Now *I* will look after you," he said, ignoring the animal as his gaze made a leisurely journey up and down her body.

"Thank you, but as you can see, that is not necessary. We are on our way home, Maloof and I. We have only to pick a few berries before we return. We are to meet Grandfather at the berry patch," she added, hoping the lie sounded convincing. "No doubt he is already there."

Habib seemed to be considering his options. Then, his expression darkened and he cocked his head. "Well, then, I shall go back without you. This time."

Rosalind gave a curt nod. "I appreciate your concern. Good day, Nicholas." She wondered if she would ever find solace in the forest again.

❧

Ken dreaded going home at quitting time and facing Ma after Timmy's first day on the job. His own shift ended at three o'clock—sometimes sooner, if his crew filled their required number of coal cars ahead of schedule. But work in the breaker often went on until six-thirty or later, and he knew Tim would really be dragging when the last whistle finally blew.

A quick shower in the shiftin' shack took off a few layers of filth. The rest he'd deal with in a hot bath at home. Ken changed back into his regular clothes, then went to check on his brother. When he peered inside the breaker, however, the coating of coal dust covering the young workers made it impossible to discern one from the other. Even the handkerchiefs tied over their noses to keep the dust out of their nostrils looked dingy and black.

But one lad did appear to be working a little more gingerly than the rest. Noting the blood mixed in with the sulfur muck on the kid's hands, Ken sensed that one was Tim. His heart crimped, and he closed the door.

Ma would be getting out the goose grease tonight, for sure.

By the end of the first week on the job, his brother's hands were a swollen, sorry mess, the fingers cracked open and oozing blood and pus—a full-blown case of "red tips."

"Why on earth won't the supervisor allow the boys to wear gloves?" The pain of a mother's heart clouded Ma's eyes as she gently bathed Tim's hands in warm water in preparation for the nightly coating of goose grease ointment.

Hannah, fussing with getting supper on the table, looked over and winced, then resumed setting out the utensils.

"Come on, Ma," Ken chided. "It's a breaker boy's sense of touch that helps him to work quickly, picking culm out of the coal while it tumbles down the chute."

She grimaced and shook her head. "What sense of touch can there be in hands that look like these?"

Tim puffed out his chest. "Aw, quit talkin' about me like I ain't even here. It ain't so bad, Ma. I'm no baby. Ken says his hands got just like this when he started working there. Mine'll toughen up just like his did. You'll see."

"All the same," she insisted, "I worry all the time you're at the mine. Both of you. It's bad enough, fearing explosions and cave-ins and flooding tunnels. We all know firsthand about losing loved ones that way, don't we? Now I have to worry that in a split second Timmy could lose his balance and fall into the chutes. I don't want to be like poor Mrs. Polinski, trying to get over having my son smothered under tons of rock and coal. Or like Mrs. Stanitis. She nearly went crazy after little Jimmy fell right into the crusher."

Ken moved in back of her and placed his hands on her shoulders, kneading the tense muscles. "Working at the mine is dangerous, Ma. We all know that. But it's what we do. We have to trust God to look out for us and keep us safe. And someday, when it's His time, maybe He'll provide us with some other kind of work."

She slowly filled her lungs. Reaching up, she covered one of Ken's hands with her palm and leaned her head to rest on it. "I know," she said softly. "I pray every day for the Lord to watch over you. For strength to trust you both in His care. But what if—"

Bending down, Ken hugged her from behind. "Let's not think about what-ifs, Ma. He took care of us yesterday and today. We'll leave tomorrow in His hands, too."

She expelled a heavy sigh and nodded.

"Supper's on," Hannah said with forced cheer. "I hope everyone's hungry."

≈

The chirping of crickets and other night insects blended into the sound of guitars from one of the house wagons as Rosalind and Philip strolled the perimeter of the camp. A half-moon and a sprinkling of early stars grew brighter against the fading sky. She captured a lightning bug in her cupped hands, then opened them and let it fly free.

"It made me so angry," she said quietly, "that Nicholas would follow me up the mountain as he did. The forest was my special place, all of it. Now I feel I will have to be looking over my shoulder every time Grandmother sends me there."

Her cousin tipped his dark head and met her gaze. "Perhaps he was concerned, as he said."

"Ha." Rosa let out a huff. "You did not see his face. The way he stares at me. His eyes undress me." She plucked a blade of high grass and toyed with it in her fingers, bending, twisting, then breaking it in two. "I am afraid of him."

"You may have good reason," Philip admitted after some hesitation. "I have seen him do a few things myself."

Rosa blanched. "What kind of things?"

"Like purposely causing pain to some of the animals when he thought no one would see. It was as if he enjoyed it and wanted to watch them suffer."

"How despicable."

He didn't answer, but glanced in the direction of Nicholas's shack, where golden lamplight glowed from the small windows. "I am sorry I have to leave here to go to work every day," he finally said. "I wish I could stay close and see that no harm comes to you."

"But you cannot. I do have Maloof and Grandfather Azar to protect me."

"Just be careful," Philip warned. "Never let Nicholas Habib see you walk away from the camp by yourself."

Feeling a sudden chill, Rosa shivered.

He slipped an arm around her and hugged her. "You are cold, Cousin. I will take you home."

They walked the rest of the way in silence. Rosa cast a troubled glance at Habib's cabin as they neared it, then as quickly directed her gaze elsewhere. She couldn't fathom how any man could enjoy causing a defenseless creature to suffer.

But one thing she did know. . .she would go out of her way to keep him from catching her alone again.

*

"Are you sure there's nothing else that needs doing?" Ken asked his mother. "I replaced the broken glass in the cellar window and patched the hole in the screen door, like you wanted. The garden's hoed; the picked coal's been dumped in the bin. Do you have any other jobs for me?"

She gave him a suspicious look. "Not that I can think of. I'm surprised you were able to finish so quickly."

"Guess I thought that if I worked fast enough, there'd be time to go hiking in the woods."

"That's what I figured. Here's a couple sandwiches from last night's roast, in case you get hungry." She handed him a sack. "And an apple, too."

"Thanks, Ma. You know me too well." Ken gave her a quick hug. Then he went to the parlor to retrieve his Bible, tucked it under his arm, and headed for the door.

After spending many boyhood years tramping through the woods every chance he got, all of the area within a ten- or twelve-mile radius of home was as familiar to Ken as his backyard. Today he planned to follow an old Indian trail some miles away to a quiet place he frequented, where he could read his Bible and pray without interruption.

Ma wasn't the only one worried about Tim and all the hazards surrounding him. . .and the kid's hands were taking overly long to heal. Still, Ken couldn't help but feel proud of his brother's attitude and his bravery. In true breaker boy fashion, Timmy toughed it out without complaint. He hadn't even disclosed whatever initiation the older boys put him through. He just climbed the hill every morning, head high, and did his job, anticipating next week and his first pay envelope.

A cardinal swooped past Ken, drawing him out of his musings. The bird landed high in the trees ahead, its bright feathers a gentle reminder of the gypsy girl he'd encountered last Saturday.

Rosalind Gilbran had been so timid, Ken doubted she'd return to the grove where they'd met. . .at least, not this soon. But even if they didn't run into each other for a long time, he'd always remember her soft voice, her chocolate-brown eyes, and how beautiful she looked in the peaceful setting of the forest. He breathed a prayer, just as he'd done every night since then, that God would bless her and surround her with His love.

At last he reached the shady glen and the old fallen tree he considered his reading spot—far enough away from roads and houses that no sounds of civilization intruded. There wasn't even a brook to distract him. Just other wonders of God's creation and an endless quiet broken only by the wind and the sounds of nature.

Along the length of the big hollow log, untold seasons of fallen leaves padded the ground. Ken lowered himself to the natural cushion and leaned back against the weathered bark. Then he bowed his head and poured out his heart to God, emptying it of the praises and burdens he'd been carrying all week.

Completely oblivious to time and its passing, he opened his Bible and feasted on its treasures until his eyelids grew heavy, then he rested his head against the log and closed his eyes, completely relaxed.

The snap of a twig startled him. Ken bolted upright.

Not three yards from him, Rosalind Gilbran caught her breath, looking every bit as surprised as he. She wore a skirt of emerald green, with a gathered white blouse. As before, she toted a cloth bag over her shoulder. But her glorious soft curls had no covering today, only a dark green ribbon tied at the crown.

Ken recovered first and lumbered to his feet. "Well, hello. . . again."

"I–I did not know you would be here," she said breathlessly. "This is not the same place as before."

"It's my favorite spot in all the woods. I come here to read." To prove the truth of his words, he raised the Bible aloft.

With a shy smile, she took a small book out of her skirt pocket. "I find many quiet places to read."

"Then we have something else in common, besides enjoying the woods."

"So it would seem."

Unaccountably nervous all of a sudden, Ken rambled on. "So, if you need to know where to catch the best fish, how to find the good swimming holes, or just plain want to enjoy a panoramic view of Wyoming Valley, I'm the man to ask."

She smiled and looked away.

Neither spoke for several seconds.

Ken cleared his throat. "Say, I don't suppose you're hungry. I brought along some sandwiches, and you're welcome to join me. . .unless you're in a hurry."

She studied him momentarily in that cautious way of hers, then acquiesced. "I have no need to hurry."

"Then, may I offer you a seat, Miss Gilbran? The best in the house." With a flourish, he gestured toward the leafy ground.

After a slight hesitation, she took the spot he indicated. "I am called Rosa," she said with an almost smile, then lowered her lashes.

Ken forcibly diverted his gaze from the stunning vision she made and sat a modest distance away before handing her one of the sandwiches Ma had prepared. "I hope you like roast beef."

"Yes. Thank you, Mr.—"

"Ken," he cut in.

Rosalind nodded, then began unwrapping the waxed paper.

"I, uh, always like to say a prayer before I eat. Do you mind? I can make it a silent one in that case."

"I do not mind a prayer." She bowed her head and closed her eyes.

🙣

Rosalind could not have been more surprised over having stumbled once again upon Ken Roberts. In an effort to get away from the camp without being seen by Nicholas Habib, she had taken an entirely different route into the forest, one hidden from view of his shack. It took her far away from the little stream and the berry patch she'd visited so often. Encountering the fair-haired miner here in this shady glen put her in a mild state of shock. She didn't even hear Ken's words as he prayed—but the silence when he finished did penetrate her thoughts. She opened her eyes and bit into her sandwich.

"Out collecting herbs again?" he asked casually, eyeing the cloth bag.

"Yes. Whenever I am not out with Grandfather Azar, my grandmother likes me to find different plants for medicine. She taught me where to find them."

He shook his head. "I don't know a lot about that myself, except when it comes to the nuisance stuff like poison ivy, poison sumac, and the like. We get most of our medicines from the company store or the doctor."

Rosalind liked the sound of his voice. A lot. And she found his eyes particularly fascinating, being so different from the dark brown so common among her people. It was hard not to stare into the light gray depths when he talked. . .yet she knew she should not be so bold. She dragged her gaze away and focused on another bite of her sandwich instead.

"What kind of books do you like?" Ken asked casually.

Amazingly at ease with this man who somehow seemed more than just a stranger, Rosa answered with candor. "The one I brought is poetry. I like the beautiful words. Sometimes I try to write my own poems, but of course they are not as good. My grandfather has many books to sell. He likes me to read to him and Grandmother at night, to help them understand English." Astounded that she was babbling, she paused to catch her breath. "What is your book?"

"This?" Ken held it up. "My Bible. It has some poetry, too, called psalms. They're filled with lots of beautiful words about God. He's a friend of mine."

Rosa nearly choked. "God is your friend?" she asked in disbelief. "That is not possible. God is too far away to be a friend to anyone. Too. . .important." Toying with a fold of her skirt, she shrugged. "What is so loving about taking parents away from a child? I do not even remember my mother, and my father's memory fades more with each day. That does not seem like something a *friendly* God would allow."

But the miner didn't seem at all offended by her remarks. He merely smiled and spoke in the most gentle of tones. "I have no answers for hard questions like those. Many people suffer much heartache and sadness in this life. My father, too, is gone. He and my older brother died in the mines, leaving the rest of my family to face the hardship of life without them. But when I turned to God for comfort and started reading about Him in the Bible, I discovered how much He loves all of us and that His heart is touched by our grief. That helped me to deal with things."

He leafed through the pages until he came to a particular passage. "Look here, in the Gospel of John." He moved a bit closer so she could follow along as he read a few lines underlined in ink. "It says, 'For God so loved the world, that he gave his only begotten Son, that whosoever believeth in him should not perish, but have everlasting life.' It's only one verse out of many that tell us about God's love.

"It says in another place that before we are even born, He knows our name. And He counts the hairs of our head. More proof of His love, His concern for us."

Rosa frowned in puzzlement. "I will have to think about that for a while."

"That's easy enough to do in a place like this," Ken said, glancing around them. "All these great trees He made, the beautiful streams and waterfalls, the wild creatures. He gave us the sun and stars to light our way, the rain and wind to keep us cool. Even the plants and herbs to heal us when we're sick. Everything God made has a purpose and beauty of its own and shows His love. He wants us to enjoy His creation. To want to know Him more."

Rosa considered that concept while they finished the sandwiches and shared the apple Ken halved, chatting about lighter things as they did so. She appreciated the easy way he talked about his family and his work, yet there seemed no real need to keep a constant thread of conversation going. Even the silences between them were comfortable ones.

Finally she glanced up at the sky, where from the position of the sun she could tell it was time to bring the visit to an end. "Well, I must go now." Rising, she brushed the leaves from the back of her skirt, then picked up her bag. "Thank you for the lunch. It was—nice—to see you again."

Ken stood also. "You, too, Rosa. I really did expect we'd cross paths someday—but today was a surprise. Maybe we can talk longer next time."

Rosalind nibbled her lips and checked to see no one else was in the area. "I do not think so. I. . .should not be with you. My people, they. . ."

An understanding smile accompanied Ken's nod. "Well, I come here pretty often. Maybe I'll leave you a message in this old log now and then, if you happen by. And should we meet sometime—by accident, of course—I hope you'll think of me as a friend." He reached out a hand and clasped hers warmly.

But inside, Rosa knew the two of them could never share a true friendship. Not openly. And not even in secret. Sooner or later they would be found out, and that would be disastrous. Withdrawing her fingers from his callused ones, she knew no words could pass the sad tightness in her throat. She raised her lashes and met his gaze for a breathless moment, then turned and started for home.

Chapter 3

During the next several days, Rosalind relived the visit with Ken Roberts many times in her mind. Whether she was occupied with daily chores, helping her grandmother prepare meals or herbal mixtures, or tending to other mundane tasks, recollections of the young man's pleasant manner floated about in her head. Even now, jostling along with Grandfather in the wagon, her spirit remained back in the forest with her fair-haired friend.

She had never deceived her guardians before and did not relish the guilt now pricking her conscience. If they had the slightest inkling that a young and virile man from the mines had approached her in the seclusion of the forest—not once, but twice—they would positively forbid her ever to go there unescorted again. She knew their low opinion of the coal crackers.

Having met one personally, however, Rosa no longer shared the blanket sentiment that the lot of them were hard-living drunkards. Ken, at least, demonstrated a tender side. Who was to say the others lacked that quality when it came to their family relationships? Perhaps those who turned to liquor did so only to help them deal with the uncertainties of that dangerous life. Besides, both encounters with Ken had been accidental. It was highly unlikely there would ever be a third occurrence.

The sun's rays speckled the ground beside the wagon, reminding Rosalind of the way sunbeams slanting through the leaves had painted golden patches on Ken's light brown hair. The silvery brook mirrored the hue of his eyes, and she could still hear the resonant tone of his voice. But one thing about their visit affected her most of all: Even though he, too, knew the deep sadness of losing family members, his eyes held no trace of bitterness, only a compelling inner peace.

Still, she couldn't help pondering his amazing statement about God being his friend. No one in her life had ever mentioned such a familiarity with the Almighty Creator. Unlike some of the other inhabitants of the camp, her relatives almost never went to church. And she knew for a fact that her grandparents didn't own a Bible, though from time to time they obtained one to sell along with the other wagon goods.

"You are quiet today, my Rosa," Grandfather remarked. He turned onto a winding lane that eventually would take them to the home of one of their customers.

"I have many thoughts."

"Good ones, I hope." His dark eyes twinkled.

She fought a blush. "Yes. They are good." She diverted her gaze for a few seconds into the thick trees on either side, then turned to her guardian. "Do you ever think of God as your friend, Grandfather?"

"My friend?" One side of his mustache quirked upward. "Who put such a notion into your head?"

Rosa chose an evasive answer. "You said once that all people are alike in God's eyes. And when I walk up the mountain, all the lovely things I see make me think about Him. That is all."

He gave a grudging nod. "I will speak truth. Long years ago, in Baskinta, missionaries came to talk of God. Many of us believed and turned from old ways we knew. But in America, to make a new life, I am busy. Someday I will think of God again. Maybe He will be friend then."

"Maybe." At least her grandfather hadn't gotten angry. Rosa drew a measure of comfort from that.

The sight of a farmhouse directly ahead rendered an end to their conversation. And as usual, the family dogs came running, while the lady of the house hollered for the children to go inside.

Rosalind stifled a sigh.

❧

Contemplating the more than enjoyable chat two days ago with Rosalind Gilbran in the splendor of the woods, Ken found the descent from the sunny morning into the gloom of the mine particularly depressing. He didn't have it in him to participate in the usual banter with the other men, so he tuned their voices out and concentrated on the gangway they were tromping through.

Feeble beams of light from the electric lamps atop their hats played off damp rock walls and massive timbers crusted with a gruesome white mosslike fungus, occasionally glancing off streaks of coal, which shone like black diamonds. The glittering sparkles brought memories of Rosa's dark eyes to mind. Despite the young woman's hesitance to meet him again, Ken hoped she'd change her mind.

Just ahead, coal buggies blocked their path, and the men stepped into the ditch running alongside the tracks, their boots sloshing through the brackish water until they passed the cars and resumed walking the track bed.

The equipment they toted for the day rattled against their backs with each step: pick, shovel, bar, drill, powder, fuses, ax, and lumber. Since he had to bear the expense for the material, plus pay his helper out of his own salary, he concluded the system was designed to keep miners like him perpetually broke and in debt to the company. Maybe it was time he brushed up on algebra, engineering, and surveying and took the state test for his foreman's papers. Surely there was a better future in that.

The men passed numerous chambers opening at right angles into the coal seams. The fire boss's slate had indicated two spots where the roof needed propping in the breast where they'd be working. Ken halted at the one assigned to them. "This is it, fellas. Let's get busy."

Needing no instruction, they set about testing the roof, knocking down any loose or hanging pieces of rock so they could bolster the weaker places with new props to ensure their safety.

"One o' these paydays, Roberts," MacNeil said between grunts as they wedged the timber into place, "we oughta tip a wee glass or two of moonshine at Riley's Beer Garden. See if we can butter up the foreman an' get us put in some easy spot, where we can just knock the coal off the ceilin'."

"Right," agreed Valentino. "Wouldn't take hardly any time at all to fill up our buggies then. We'd be outta here before lunchtime."

Ken chuckled. "Come on, guys. You know how the people at my church view that stuff. We don't even drink real wine at communion."

"That's the trouble with preacher-boys like you. Ye don't know what you're missin'."

"Could be," he acknowledged cheerfully, "but I'll pass, just the same. Now, who's got the hand drill?"

"Me, Reverend." MacNeil's stocky English butty, Bill Henry, unfastened the tool from his belt, where he'd hung it for the trek to the work site.

"Good. Soon as you drill us some holes, we'll set the charges. Then we can get to loading the cars." Somehow, he sensed they had a long day ahead.

When the shift finally ended and he went home, he found the house empty. Neither his mother nor Hannah appeared to be around, although cooking smells indicated they couldn't be too far away. He clomped down to the cellar for his bath, then changed into the clean clothes Ma had laid out. Knowing Timmy wouldn't be home for awhile yet, he then went to their bedroom for a catnap before supper.

In what seemed mere moments, Hannah's knock awakened him. "Supper's on."

"Thanks. I'll be right down." He hurried downstairs to the table laden with roast beef, browned potatoes, and cabbage salad. "Pass the gravy, would you, Tim?" Ken asked after the blessing.

"What'll ya pay me for it?" the kid quipped. "After all, I'm a workin' man now, ya know. I get paid for doin' stuff."

"How 'bout I don't break your arm? Fair enough?"

"Only cause you're bigger 'n me."

Ken caught the meaningful glance exchanged by Hannah and

Ma. The two had been acting a mite strange ever since he took his place at the table. "What's up? Something I ought to know?"

"Oh," his sister confessed, "Mrs. Jessup's husband had an accident today. He got hurt pretty bad."

"Mike Jessup?" Ken probed. Their next-door neighbor worked on level two at the colliery and had a wife and four kids to support. "I didn't hear the whistle blow."

"It never did. He was walking to the cage to go up top, when he tripped in front of a loaded coal car. It ran right over his arm and cut it right off at the elbow. The other men did what they could, then helped him into the cage. The ambulance wagon brought him home."

The news quenched Ken's appetite. Though Hudson's buggies were smaller than those used at some of the other mines, they held as much as three tons of coal and rock when loaded. Many a man had been killed or maimed for life in one blink-of-an-eye encounter with a coal car. Earlier, Ken had noticed groups of men talking among themselves as he dashed to the shower in preparation for going home, but he hadn't thought much about it. He shoved his half-full plate away.

"We took supper over to the family," Ma said in a monotone. "Agnes looked like she was in a daze. The doctor had just left, said Mike won't be going back to the mine. They don't know what they'll do now, where they'll go."

"Somebody's already been around taking up a collection," Hannah added. "I wish we could have done more."

"I'll go over there and see if there's anything I can do. If nothing else, I can at least pray with them. Trust with them that God will see them through this terrible loss."

His intention was to lend comfort, but inside, Ken knew his own trust in the Lord was being sorely tested. All the hopes that families like his had upon coming to America seemed to be plummeting into holes even deeper than those the men worked in every day.

*

"We must go now," Grandmother said, stuffing her medicine bag with medical supplies, then selecting various herbs from the shelves to add to its contents. "Baby born at full moon will be healthy. And from the way Sultana Zayek carried, I think she will have boy. Big, healthy boy."

Rosalind smiled. More often than not, her grandmother's predictions proved to be right. Better yet, the other women in the camp trusted her tender ministrations in the delivery of their new little ones. "I saw Sultana out walking yesterday. She was anxious for the baby to arrive. She has made many tiny clothes while she has been waiting."

"Yes. Well, first we must see that the wee one comes. You will help again. Someday the people will need new midwife, and you already learn much of my trade." The older woman gathered what she could carry, then started out the door, with Rosa toting the remaining items.

Barely two years older than Rosalind, the young mother-to-be already lay abed when her husband, Kahlil, ushered Rosa and Grandmother Azar into the cluttered confines of their house wagon. Obviously wary of the whole torturous event in progress, the jittery man seemed only too happy to go outside to resume his pacing, leaving the women in charge.

Rosa immediately set about doing her usual tasks, laying out clean sheets and towels and removing the scissors, tweezers, needle, thread, and twine from the medicine bag. Her grandmother, meanwhile, tied on a big work apron and moved to her patient's side.

This would be Sultana's second birthing, having delivered a stillborn infant the previous year. Tension lay heavy in the tiny abode, Rosa noted from the muted voices as she stepped outside to heat water at the fire pit. The father-to-be was nowhere in sight.

Knowing her grandmother always insisted on cleanliness

during childbirth, Rosa carried a basin of hot water and a towel to the childbed for bathing the young mother. The pain-filled ebony eyes that met hers revealed a certain calm confidence over being in good hands, yet Rosa sensed her desperate hope that this babe would live. She gave Sultana an encouraging smile, then returned to her duties.

When the water came to a boil, she inserted the instruments into the pot for several moments, then laid them out on a clean towel and carried those, too, inside. Her tasks now would be comforting ones. . .bathing Sultana's perspiring face, holding her hand, and waiting.

And waiting.

"Good, good," Grandmother crooned encouragingly after each contraction. "I see the head," she announced at last. "He is coming."

Sultana gave a last mighty push, and Rosalind's heart contracted as the tiny, squirming miracle presented himself. A touch bluish, at first, he let out a healthy protest at having left his warm cocoon. Still crying as Grandmother gently wiped his eyes, nose, and mouth of mucous and laid him on his mama's belly, he quickly pinkened.

"He is beautiful," Sultana murmured, her eyes misty and soft with love as she cupped a palm around her baby's velvety black head.

Once Grandmother had tied off the cord and cut it, she handed the slippery little one to Rosa. "Go wash him nice for his mama. I finish up here."

This was Rosalind's favorite part, holding one of God's creations. Testing the water in the basin she'd prepared moments before his birth, she found the temperature just right. She soaped a hand and washed his head and rinsed it, then cleaned the rest of him, marveling over the perfect miniature fingers and toes, the strong little legs curled against his body. After wrapping him in a blue flannel blanket Sultana had made, Rosa carried the new babe to his mama and placed him in her arms.

Grandmother had already rolled up the soiled sheets and replaced them with clean linens. "I will help the girl into clean nightgown," she said to Rosa. "You go tell the papa he has fine son."

"I am happy for you, Sultana," Rosa said, giving her friend's hand a congratulatory squeeze. "He is truly beautiful."

Weary and spent, the young woman managed a small smile.

On her way to the door, Rosalind gathered the various items that needed to be taken home and put them inside the medicine bag. Though she herself would be free to leave once Kahlil Zayek had been told of his son's arrival, her grandmother would remain with the new mama for an hour or two to make sure she and the baby were faring well. Only when she was satisfied all was as it should be, would she make her way home to bed.

Rosa stepped down from the house wagon, only to discover that Zayek still had not come back. She would have to find him before she could deliver the happy news. From where she stood, she scanned the grounds of the encampment. At this late hour, the other dwellings lay silent and dark in the moonlight.

Only one cabin still glowed with light.

Nicholas Habib's.

Drawing a long, slow breath to fortify herself, Rosalind gritted her teeth and forced herself to go there.

The occasional bursts of laughter drifting out the windows infuriated her. To think that a man would leave his poor, suffering wife to endure birth pangs—and possible death—while he gallivanted off to drink and have a good time elsewhere! How callous. When she married, it would be to a man who would stay at her side to welcome a new life created by their love union. *If* she ever married at all.

Striding purposefully to the door, Rosa gave three sharp raps.

Muffled footfalls approached from the other side, then it opened, revealing Nick's dusky face. One edge of his mouth curved up in a leering smirk. "Well, well," he gushed on a breath heavy with *Ahrrak,* his glassy black eyes roaming over her. "The beautiful Roshalind, come to call. Thish is a great honor."

"I am here to see Kahlil," she said coolly, ignoring his slurred words and rude insolence. "Please get him for me."

Blocking the doorway, Nicholas regarded her for a few seconds. Then he yawned and scratched his head.

But Sultana's husband, obviously having overheard, pushed Nick aside. He looked only slightly in better condition than Nick as he lumbered out of the cabin, one shirttail askew, his hair disheveled, as if he'd spent hours raking it with worried hands. "My wife. It is over? She is okay?"

Rosa nodded. "You have a son."

"A son! Did you hear that, Nick? I am a papa." He danced an unsteady jig, laughing as he did so. "We must celebrate. Tomorrow. More Ahrrak."

"As you wish," Nicholas replied, his dark gaze still on her. "You should not be out alone thish late, Roshalind. I will walk with you."

"That is not necessary. Grandmother still needs me. I will go back with Kahlil."

His thick brows dipped into a scowl, and he tightened his lips before closing the door.

"A son," Kahlil remarked, his voice husky with emotion as he started for home. "I am a papa."

"Yes." Rosa had all she could do to keep up with his jubilant strides across the grassy campgrounds.

She could feel cold eyes stabbing her like ice picks, but under no circumstances would she let Nicholas see her turn around and look his way.

Chapter 4

A duet of peaceful snoring from the next bedroom joined with the trilling of crickets and other insects outside Rosalind's window in an irregular and comical pattern. Normally the soothing night sounds coaxed her to sleep, but she lay wide awake as she pondered the events of the evening.

She could still feel the incredible wonder of a tiny baby squirming in her arms, could still see the indescribable joy in Sultana's face after having given birth. Rosa wondered if she herself would ever experience the miracle of bringing a new life into the world.

It had not been so very long since the days when she and Sultana had been the closest of friends, sharing the hopes and fears and secret dreams of girlhood. Yet from the time Sultana's parents arranged for their daughter's marriage to Kahlil Zayek—a man eight years her senior and one whom she barely knew—everything changed. Gone were the special times the girls could spend together to laugh and share confidences. Sultana now kept company with the other married women. Her subdued demeanor gave little indication as to whether or not she was truly happy.

Philip said it was the way of their people, trusting one's elders to make that most important of choices…but Rosalind could not accept that. She would not. What if her grandparents paired her with Nicholas Habib? Revulsion for the man rose like bile in her throat.

There had to be someone else. She turned onto her side, fluffing the goose-down pillow beneath her head to softer comfort. But mentally naming off the families presently dwelling in the encampment, she concluded that other than her cousin Philip, Nick was the only other single, unbetrothed man left. All the others had already married and moved on or were committed to do so. Unless new people came to live in the settlement, her future prospects were, at best, bleak. Yet she would rather stay single until she was too old to marry than to settle for Nicholas the wood-carver.

Better a *miner* than him.

The ridiculous notion brought a smile, but reality snuffed it like a candle flame in the wind. No sense dwelling on something so preposterous, Rosa chided herself, aware of her tendencies toward giddiness whenever she was overtired. Besides, she barely knew Ken Roberts. For all his appearances to the contrary, he could turn out to be every bit as bad as Nick.

But even if he was not, Ken was still out of reach. Forbidden. The most she could ever have of that young man would be day-dreams and sweet imaginings. Surely there was no harm in those…after all, he really was nice to think about. With a smile, Rosa closed her eyes.

⌇

If there was anything worse than a dreary, rainy Saturday, Ken didn't know what it could possibly be. All week long he endured the drudgery of mining, with the expectation of the one day at the end that provided an escape. The one day that enabled him to get out of the dull black culm banks and bask in God's greenery. A small part of him harbored a slim hope that he might have seen Rosa again. But regardless of that happening, his weekly hikes into the woods were what kept him sane.

Now look at this day, he thought grimly, glaring through the front room window at the grayish water dripping in relentless procession off the edge of the shingles. Out in the street, the downward course of the rainwater filled the chuckholes and carved narrow ditches. Trees bowed under the weight of heavy, wet crowns. Even the dog loping by looked stringy and forlorn.

"Nice day for ducks," Timmy groused, his own expression flat. "I wish it would stop and get it over with. Me 'n Freddy was gonna get a game of stickball goin' up in the cow field with the other guys."

"Yeah, well, nothing we can do about the weather," Ken commiserated. "There's probably something Ma needs done anyway, like shining our Sunday shoes."

"Whoopee. Lotta good that'll do, with all the mud we'll pick up from here to church and back."

Seeing the kid's grimace, Ken grinned and tousled Tim's hair, and the two of them ended up on the floor in a brotherly wrestling match.

"What's all the commotion?" Ma called from the kitchen. "Be careful you don't break something."

"Yeah. Me!" Tim hollered. "Ow. Ow! He's killin' me."

Chuckling, Ken released the lad and helped him up. "Come on, Runt. Let's do something worthwhile around here."

✍

A faithful flock of worshipers gathered at Edwards Memorial Church every Sunday, rain or shine. This morning, with the sky above slowly clearing, the interior of the tan clapboard building grew brighter by the minute.

"Let's open our hymnals to page ninety-three," lanky Hugh Pembroke said, tugging his starched collar off his Adam's apple. He peered over small round spectacles at plump Blodwyn Pugh, while beating the tempo with one arm.

She nodded and the lap of her flowery dress undulated as she pumped the organ's pedals. The instrument wheezed into action.

"Rock of ages, cleft for me. . . ."

Ken, sharing a book with his sister as they sang, caught the interested glances Hannah drew from some guys occupying the straight-backed wooden pews across the aisle. She did look kind of pretty in her Sunday dress, one of two she alternated every week. The pale blue against her fair complexion made her look extra feminine and fragile, especially in her floppy wide-brimmed hat and white gloves. But if she noticed those fellows, she gave no indication.

Knowing them from the colliery, Ken sized them up from a corner of his eye. They were probably decent enough, and hard workers as well, but he couldn't help hoping they wouldn't get any ideas about approaching her. Ma still needed Hannah around to help out. And truth be known, he was more than proud to have a sister like her. Any man who came calling on her had better be special enough to deserve someone with a heart as big as hers.

"Please, be seated," Mr. Pembroke said. He returned to one of the upholstered burgundy chairs on the platform, while silver-haired Reverend Newlin rose and stepped up to the dark walnut pulpit, his black suit pressed just so, his eyes warm and discerning in the light filtering through the stained glass windows.

"Good morning." A warm smile broadened his jowled face. "I've entitled today's sermon, 'How to Guard Your Mind.' My text is taken from Paul's epistle to the Philippians, chapter 4, verses 6 and 7. Open your Bibles, if you will, and follow along with me as I read."

During the quiet rustle of pages, he looked out over the congregation filling the small but neat sanctuary. "We're, all of us, plagued at one time or another by troublesome thoughts. Everyone yearns for peace of mind and deliverance from nagging concerns and fears. Why, just this morning I must confess waking up hours early, disturbed by a problem that's been bothering me for weeks, yet doesn't appear to have an easy solution. I'm ashamed to admit it kept me awake.

"But now I realize that was entirely my own fault. The apostle Paul has already laid out the way for us to guard our minds against anxiety. He writes, 'Be careful for nothing; but in every thing by prayer and supplication with thanksgiving let your requests be made known unto God. And the peace of God, which passeth all understanding, shall keep your hearts and minds through Christ Jesus.'"

With chagrin over having often given in so easily to his own anxious thoughts instead of committing everything to the Lord, Ken looked up from the passage.

"Dear friends," the pastor went on, "God never intended

for us to take our burdens to the Cross and lay them down as a temporary measure before picking them up again and going home. He wants us to leave them there permanently, so He can bear them all *for* us. Yet how impatient we are. How faithless. As expressed in one of my favorite hymns, 'O what peace we often forfeit, O what needless pain we bear. . . .'"

Next to Ken, Tim fidgeted in his seat, and Ma, on the kid's other side, squeezed his knee. Ken winked at her and she gave him a small smile, no doubt sharing the remembrance of keeping her older sons in line during services through the years.

He focused his attention once more on the pastor, appreciating a message that spoke especially to him, challenging him to stay in close fellowship to God, to spend time in His Word. Even though he felt nearest to the Lord when surrounded by nature, Ken knew God did not purposely withdraw His presence from His obedient followers. His tender watch and care was just as real in one's daily home life and in the mines as it seemed in the woods.

Ken wondered if Rosalind Gilbran knew that.

"And so, dear ones," the pastor said, his voice cutting into Ken's musings, "we must remember to commit our every thought to God, to trust Him to work all things together for the good of those who trust Him. For as the Bible reminds us in Hebrews, 'He is faithful that promised.' Let us bow our heads in prayer."

The sun and an accompanying breeze had dried the dirt road during the church service, making the homeward walk far more enjoyable than their earlier trip. The delicious smell of Ma's pork roast met the family as they came through the back door of the house.

"Everyone stay dressed nice," she admonished. "After dinner we'll go next door and call on the Jessups, to see how Mike is doing. I noticed Agnes wasn't at church. Oh, and Hannah, we'll use the Sunday tablecloth. I do get tired of looking at that oilcloth all the time."

Rosalind gingerly picked her way through grasses and brush still wet from yesterday. Maloof, in complete disregard of such things, bounded along at her side, his lower half sopping up the moisture as they went. He took after a rabbit the instant the unfortunate creature happened into view.

Summer showers never failed to awaken a new crop of wildflowers, and Rosa admired the rainbow of fragile colors dotting the landscape. Choosing a particularly pretty patch of field daisies, she plucked one near the blossom and tucked it behind her ear. Then, ever alert for specific plants, she kept her eyes peeled.

Considering how hard it had rained yesterday, she suspected that Ken Roberts had been unable to venture to that favorite reading spot of his she'd stumbled on a week ago. And everything was still too drenched for an enjoyable outing, so he wouldn't be apt to show up there today. That was for the best, really. The whole forest was hers. She glanced over her shoulder a last time before leaving the clearing, making sure that no one was following.

Turning forward again at the edge of the meadow, she almost passed right by the spikelike white flowers of colicroot that Grandmother had specifically requested she look for. Sultana would appreciate having something to help colic, should baby Rashad show any tendencies toward that malady. Rosa hung the strap of her tote bag on a nearby tree branch and stooped to dig some plant roots from the wet soil.

Afterward, nearing one of the numerous creeks and streams cutting through the forest, she discovered some fringed polygala. According to her grandmother, when the bright pink flowers were eaten by nursing mothers—or cows, for that matter—milk production would increase. Rosa could hardly believe her good fortune.

She washed the plants and roots she'd gathered and spread them out so the air could dry them a little while she rinsed her hands in the brook. Then she shook out the shoulder tote and replaced everything.

There was no real reason to go deeper into the forest, having already found what she'd come for. But the sun was still high and there was plenty of time before she needed to go back. For some reason, Rosalind felt a desire to go to Ken's special spot once more. She just wanted to see it while he wasn't there. To be there when no one could accuse her of anything wrong. It wasn't very far.

Maloof came crashing back into view, emerging from a tangle of ferns and brush. When he got to her, Rosa patted his sun-warmed head. "You are a good fellow, Maloof. A good friend." He licked her hand and padded along beside her at a more sedate pace.

When she reached Ken's haven and stopped, Maloof sat on his haunches, his feathery tail brushing back and forth on the path while he watched her.

Except for the rain-darkened bark, the big old fallen tree looked the same as when she'd seen it last. The leaves on the ground at its base were now a soggy mess, but no doubt the sun and wind would dry them before Ken's next visit. Rosa's spirit felt refreshed in the thicket's quiet serenity as her gaze made a slow circuit of the area, memorizing the rocky outcroppings and other features. . .and she imagined Ken relaxing there with his Bible.

She didn't dare envision herself with him again.

Glancing down at the log, Rosa knew it was too soon to expect a message from him. For a fleeting moment, she thought of leaving one for him to find, but she had no paper to write on or anything to write with. That did not mean she had nothing, however. With a smile, she removed the daisy from her hair and placed it in a depression in the log's rough bark, then turned and started home.

Grandmother Azar, seated in her favorite chair darning one of Grandfather's socks, looked up as Rosalind entered the house. "Did you find something I need?"

"Oh, yes. Wait until you see." Moving to the sideboard, she

took out a linen kitchen towel and opened it on the table, then emptied the contents of her shoulder tote onto it.

Her grandmother, the old bones noticeably stiff after rainfall, hobbled over to join her. "Colicroot! Good, good. It is right time for it to be in flower. And polygala will help Sultana."

"I found mint, too, for our tea. It was a good day."

"Yes, Child. A good day. Already I have water on stove to boil. I will make us tea now."

Rosa gathered her pickings into a neat pile and shoved them aside, clearing enough of the tabletop for their refreshment. Then she took her usual chair.

Within moments, her guardian brought the teapot and cups to the table, along with a small plate of Lebanese pastries. She set them all down and lowered herself to the seat. Her keen gaze fastened on Rosalind even as she poured the tea. "Something is wrong, Child?"

Rosa couldn't quite meet those brown-black eyes. "No. I have many thoughts, that is all. Of Sultana and baby Rashad," she added before the older woman probed further. "Of the friendship we once had that is no more. I miss her. Now I only have Philip, and even he is always busy." She took a cautious sip of the steaming brew.

"You should have husband, too," her grandmother said matter-of-factly. "You are a woman grown. It is getting time."

Rosa nearly choked. "Not yet. I want to help you and Grandfather for awhile. There is plenty of time before I marry." *Time enough for me to find a man I will love,* she almost added. Wisely she held her silence.

But nothing would convince her that she was wrong.

Chapter 5

Bearing a loaf of fresh-baked bread and a pan of frosted cupcakes, Ken paid another visit next door, as he'd done almost daily since his neighbor's accident. He went around back and up the porch steps, then knocked.

Surprisingly, lantern-jawed Mike himself answered the summons. New lines in his long, angular face indicated he was still in considerable pain, but the bandage on his stump appeared fresh, and he looked rested, if still a bit pale. "Come in, Lad. Come in. I appreciate the visit."

"Thanks. Ma sent these over." Ken set the food items on the sideboard. "You seem a lot more chipper than the last couple times I've come by. Feeling better?"

"Could be worse, I expect. Still aches like the devil, and there's lots I can't do anymore—like dress myself, for cryin' out loud. But if I had to lose an arm, I'm glad it was the left one. Well, come on into the front room and take a load off."

He led the way through the dining room and into the parlor. After gesturing for Ken to take the faded davenport, he settled into his usual overstuffed chair and propped his slipper-clad feet on a hassock. The top magazine on a stack of others lay open on the lamp table next to him, indicating he'd been reading when he got up to answer the door. He leaned his graying head on the crocheted doily adorning the chair back.

"I don't know if I've ever heard this place so quiet," Ken admitted, "considering that lively family of yours." He swept a glance around the room. The simple structure was almost identical to his own, except for the different furnishings and typical clutter kids always managed to leave around.

"Yeah, that's an understatement. The wife's down at the store. She took the young 'uns with her, to get 'em out of the house for awhile. It's been like a morgue around here, everybody walkin' on eggshells." He rubbed callused fingers over his unshaven jaw. "Can't say as I blame 'em. I haven't been very good company since I got carted home on a stretcher that day."

Ken marveled at his friend's improved attitude. "What's. . . uh. . .brought about the change—if you don't mind my asking."

"Naw." He gave a half smile. "Guess I've just had some time to think, laid up in that bedroom with the door closed, the curtains drawn. I sure didn't want this to happen. Didn't expect it. But what's done is done, and there's no changin' it. So I figure since I'm still here, the Lord must have somethin' else for me to do. It's up to me to do it."

Not knowing how to respond, Ken just shook his head in amazement.

"The rent's paid up 'til the end of next month, so the company says we can stay in the house 'til then. After that, I guess we'll move up New York way. Aggie's uncle has a farm there with an empty bunkhouse we can use. He says he'll keep me busy. It'll be a better place for the kids to grow up, too."

"Can't disagree with that," Ken had to admit. "We'll sure miss having you and Agnes as our neighbors, though."

"Same here. Say, I have a bunch of study books upstairs that'll be goin' to waste, unless you want 'em. It's time you got studyin' for your foreman's papers. There's night classes you can take over at the high school, too."

"That's real decent of you, Mike. I don't know when I could pay you for the books, though."

He waved his good arm. "Hey, they were given to me. I'm just passin' 'em on. I'll send one of the kids over with 'em after awhile."

"Thanks. Thanks a lot." Ken stood. "Well, listen, I don't want to tire you out, just wanted to check up on you and see how you're doing. Go back to your reading. I'll let myself out."

Leaving his friend's house, Ken breathed another prayer for Mike and his family, that the Lord would guide their future paths and take care of them. To think they'd be living out in the country in the open air, away from the mines! Something good had come from the accident. . .but not without a price tag.

Low clouds earlier in the week had brought more showers to the valley, but three days of sunshine quickly dried the landscape. Ken had already finished his weekend chores, so his thoughts quickly turned to climbing the hills. He threw a lunch together, tucked a small New Testament into his pocket, and exited the house.

Having been cooped up for two weeks because of the rain, he had a lot of hiking to catch up on. Out of the infinite number of Indian trails dissecting the woods, he chose one of the most familiar, breathing deeply as he strode along.

The humid air was fragrant with the fresh scent of moss and other growing things occasionally mixing with the sweet breath of wildflowers growing at various clearings and swampy places.

Coming to a fork in the trail, Ken nearly took the branch that led to a rocky ledge overlooking a good part of the city of Wilkes-Barre in the distance. But at the last second he changed his mind and remained on the original route. He'd go to his haven and read for awhile.

The lush ferns and underbrush along the way seemed thicker since the rains, lending a refreshing coolness to the trail even in the sunny places. A teasing breeze gently stirred through the trees, and a red-hooded woodpecker pecking for his lunch seemed undisturbed by a pair of goldfinches playing tag among the swaying treetops. Ken enjoyed watching their antics for a few seconds.

With his personal thicket just ahead, he resumed walking, lengthening his stride. How great it would feel to sit down on the spongy ground and rest his tired legs for awhile. His gaze assessed the leaves along the base of the fallen tree on his approach, and to his delight, they appeared dry. At least he wouldn't have to sit on the hard rough surface of the log.

Lowering himself, he braced a hand on the wood for leverage.

His fingers brushed the silken petals of a daisy. The flower was a bit shriveled, as if it had been there for several days. Maybe the wind. . . *No*, he thought, glancing around. There wasn't another daisy anywhere in sight.

Then a slow smile spread across his lips.

Rosalind must have come by one day and left the flower in greeting. Despite being hesitant about spending time with him, she had still left a token of friendship.

For some reason, Ken found it hard to concentrate after that. Trying for the third time to read the passage on the page before his eyes, he finally gave up and closed the small Bible.

In the distance, he detected a faint rustling in the brush. The sound came gradually closer, until a scruffy-looking dog bounded into the clearing.

Ken jumped to his feet in reflex, quickly assessing possible branches within his reach that he might use to fend off the beast, should that be necessary.

The animal's hackles went up, its ears flattened, and strong canine teeth bared with a low growl.

"Maloof. No," Rosalind panted, out of breath after running to catch up to him. She leaned to stroke the furry head with her palm. "It is okay," she crooned. "He is a friend."

Ken watched with no little relief as the animal immediately calmed and nonchalantly loped off into the bushes without so much as a backward glance.

Rosa met Ken's gaze, two bright spots of heightened color cresting her cheekbones. "I am sorry if Maloof startled you."

"For a minute there, I thought I was a goner," he admitted with a sheepish smile.

Her shining curls danced as she shook her head. "He would not hurt anyone unless I was in danger."

"You'll never be in danger from me, Rosalind," Ken said gently, drinking in the alluring sight of her, unable to decide which hue in her multicolored skirt suited her best. He was elated that she had actually showed up. "Would you like some lunch? I have plenty."

She offered a shy smile. "I have brought dessert. Grand-mother made baklava this morning. Honey pastry. It is good." Removing her tote from her shoulder, she reached inside and withdrew a cloth-wrapped package.

"Swell." Motioning for Rosa to be seated, he waited until she was settled, then reclaimed his place a slight distance away. "I didn't expect to see you today," he said, offering her some cheddar cheese and a thick slice of bread.

She shrugged a slender shoulder, her olive skin rich against the whiteness of her blouse. "I did not think I would come."

"I'm glad you did," he heard himself say.

"I am also." She lowered her lashes and went to bite into the cheese but paused and glanced up at Ken, waiting expectantly.

He bowed his head. "Thank You, Lord, for this day, for the food You provided, and for the gift of friendship. May You bless them all. In Jesus' name, amen."

While they ate, Ken tried his best not to stare at Rosa and make her uneasy. "How've you been?" he finally asked.

She stopped chewing and swallowed. "I am well." Then her expression grew soft. "There is a new baby in our camp. He is as beautiful as my friend Sultana, his mother."

Ken doubted anyone could surpass Rosalind's exquisite beauty, but he managed a detached smile. "Another of God's gifts," he said, "like everything else that comes into our lives."

"Do you truly believe that?" Rosa asked, puzzlement making her eyebrows dip toward each other.

"Believe what?"

"That God gives us all things."

"Yes, because He says so in the Bible. Oh, by the way. . ." He reached into his pocket and took out the New Testament, then handed it to her. "This is for you. I was going to leave it in the log if I didn't see you today."

"It is for me?" Catching her lower lip between her teeth, Rosa looked up at him with a heart-stopping smile. "Thank you."

Touched by her sincere gratitude, Ken watched as she opened the cover and perused the inscription he'd written: *To my friend, from yours.* "A good place to start reading is the Book of John," he said. "The ribbon marks its location."

"I will start reading this tonight," Rosa told him. "I was not expecting a gift."

"It's only fair, since you left one for me last time you were here." Ken showed her the daisy he'd found in the log. Even in its wilted state, a fragile beauty remained.

She blushed again and lowered her gaze. "You must have some baklava now." Unwrapping the dessert she'd brought, she handed him a piece of the flaky layered pastry.

Ken bit into it, and the golden sweetness melted in his mouth. "Mmm. This is delicious!"

"I was hoping you would like it. Baklava is my favorite treat." Smiling, she ate her portion.

"I can see why. In my house, Ma bakes a great elderberry pie. She had my pa plant a bush out back so she wouldn't have to go looking for the berries every summer."

"Grandmother makes wine from those berries," Rosa replied. "Do you come from a large family?"

He shook his head. "Since my pa and big brother died in the mines, that leaves four of us. Ma, my younger sister and brother, and me. It's been. . .rough."

"I am sorry. . .about your loss."

With a grudging nod, Ken averted his gaze to watch a squirrel stand upright and peer around before scampering up a tree. "Someday I hope to find a different line of work. But that depends on whether we get out of debt before I meet the same fate." He squelched the note of bitterness creeping into his tone. "Hardly a week goes by that there's not some kind of accident. My next-door neighbor just lost an arm."

"Oh, how awful," Rosa gasped. "Life is not always easy," she added softly. "Even for people who do not work in the mines. As a woman, I may not have the freedom to *choose* my future, my husband. I must follow the wishes of my grandparents. It is our way." Staring straight ahead, her eyes clouded over.

The swiftness at which all pleasure faded from her expression made Ken wonder what distasteful fate Rosa's guardians had in store for her. "Hey," he said, recapturing her attention with a smile of encouragement. "At least I can pray for you, Rosalind. I'll pray for us both, that God will bring about something good in our lives."

"Would He do that?"

"Sure. He wants only the best for those who love and obey Him."

"But what about those who don't even know Him?" she asked, her words barely audible. "Like me."

On impulse, Ken reached over and raised her chin with the edge of his index finger, turning her face so she could meet his gaze. "I think you will know Him soon enough, Rosa."

An eternal moment passed before she looked away. And when she did, her happier expression returned. She shook out the cloth that had wrapped the baklava and brushed crumbs from her skirt. "I must go now."

Ken nodded with reluctance and got up, offering a hand to assist her. His pulse increased as she placed tentative fingers in his. "Will I see you again sometime, Rosa?" he asked, drawing her easily to her feet.

"I cannot say." Her hand lingered a heartbeat within his grasp, until she looked down and gently slipped free. "No one knows I am here."

"Would your people hate me so much?" he asked, searching her face.

A caustic smile curved her lips. "About as much as your people do mine."

He expelled a weary breath. "I see what you mean. But it's not right, you know. We are all the same in God's eyes."

"My grandfather once said that same thing to me," Rosalind said, her eloquent eyes troubled. "Strange, is it not? That people can know something inside, yet not act that way."

"I think that will change one day."

"Perhaps. But I do not believe it will happen in our lifetime. We are from two different worlds."

Ken's gaze captured hers and held it, and he fought the impulse to touch her soft cheek with the back of his fingers. "It has to start somewhere, Rosa. With two people. Like us."

Moisture pooled in her eyes, and she turned to leave. "I must go now. Thank you for the Bible. I will treasure it." She gave a shrill whistle, and Maloof came running.

Ken could not trust himself to speak as he watched the girl and her faithful dog walk away and disappear into the thick growth of trees.

Two people. Like us.

It took all the determination Rosalind possessed to hold back the tears as she and Maloof left the thicket. Ken did not understand that things could not change so easily. She should never have gone there today.

But as her fingers closed around the New Testament in her skirt pocket, she acknowledged how happy she was that she had.

Was he right? Would the day come when individuals from two different cultures could meet openly? Actually be seen together without fear of what people might say or do? At this point, that dream seemed an utterly impossible one.

Rosa tried to envision herself walking glibly up to Grandmother and Grandfather Azar with a smile. "I have met someone. A man..."

No. The very thought was insane. As insane as meeting Ken Roberts again. Ever.

Despite all her reservations to the contrary, Rosa found the young man incredibly fascinating. He was so different from anyone she had ever known. From earliest girlhood, she had grown up feeling inferior to men. Subservient, with no purpose other than to serve and obey a man's every command. That had been Sultana's fate, and it would be her own as well, should Grandfather give her to Nicholas Habib. *If not worse.* A shudder wracked her frame.

Ken, on the other hand, treated her with utmost respect and reverence. . .as if he considered a woman a person of honor, one to be cherished and protected. Perhaps that was the reason she ignored the dangers involved in her clandestine meetings with him and continued to go into the forest to places where she knew he would be.

It would be impossible now to turn back the clock and live as if she had never met him. And even if their friendship could exist only in secret, shady places, she could at least dream that one day they might be able to walk together in the sunshine, for all the world to see.

He had made no overtures regarding anything more than friendship—and perhaps he never would. She had not really thought beyond that point herself. It was all so new. But Ken stirred feelings deep inside of her that she never knew existed. And even if those were all she could ever have, she wasn't ready to give them up entirely.

And she would die before becoming a wife for Nicholas Habib.

The tears Rosalind had thought she'd banked a few minutes ago broke through her resolve, and she didn't bother to hold them inside any longer.

Chapter 6

The trees rimming the encampment were throwing long shadows by the time Rosalind returned from the forest. The late afternoon breeze caught at her skirt with each step and whipped strands of hair in front of her face, annoying distractions in her present state of mind.

Philip, sitting outside his parents' home, looked up and saw her coming. He put aside the whistle he'd been carving and met her halfway.

Rosa attempted a smile as he came to her side, but her cousin's ebony eyes missed nothing. He knew her too well. "You have been crying."

"Only a little," she lied.

"What is wrong?"

"Nothing!" Appalled at the sharp tone of her voice, she emitted a rush of breath. "Forgive me. I should not have spoken harshly to you."

But the young man continued to regard her, his concern maddeningly evident.

The keen perusal made Rosa nervous. Her hand flew to her eyes. "I hoped no one would notice. I tripped over a root and bumped my head. It hurt. I did not want to be thought of as a baby, so when I finished crying, I washed my face in cold spring water. I am better now. That is all."

His mouth lifted in a wry grimace.

"What?" she demanded, halting where she stood.

"You have never been a baby, Rosa. You never cry when you fall—even the time you fell from my pony and broke your arm, you did not shed tears."

Rosalind averted her gaze to the ground.

"And you always look at me when you speak," he went on.

"Look into my eyes and tell me again of this fall that made you cry. Show me where it hurts."

A warm flush climbed her neck, and she shook her head. "I cannot."

"Then what is it? You have always been able to confide in me. All our lives there is nothing we do not tell each other."

Rosa moistened her lips and met his gaze. "I cannot speak of this, even to you. I am sorry. But even you would not understand."

"Something has hurt you enough to cause tears—you, the person I love like a sister—and I would not understand? How can you say this?"

The pain in his expression made her insides ache. Curly-haired Philip had been closer to her than any of her girlfriends had ever been. Their two families had sailed the ocean together, come to Pennsylvania together, lived next door to one another forever. She had trusted him with things she never told anyone. But this. How could she speak of this?

Still, she longed to tell someone. . . . Did she dare reveal her secret to him? And if so, where and how to begin? She opened her mouth to speak.

Grandfather Azar stepped outside just then on his way to the barn to tend the horses. Seeing her and Philip, he waved. "Good. You are home, Rosa. Your grandmother waits for you to help with supper."

A great sense of relief washed over her at the reprieve. She shrugged a shoulder at her cousin. "I. . .will talk to you soon, Philip."

Looking none too pleased at having been put off, he nevertheless stared at her in resignation. "I will hold you to that, you know."

She smiled thinly. "I know. Soon. I promise."

But Rosa had no idea when she would be ready for that.

Ken jabbed the walking stick he'd picked up along the way onto the ground every other stride, scarcely aware of his actions. He could still see the anguish in Rosalind's eyes when she'd revealed her lack of control over her own fate, could still hear her melodious voice whispering across his heartstrings as she expressed the hope of one day coming to know the Lord. And he breathed a prayer that God would speak to her tonight as she read the New Testament he'd given her.

Unlike many of the young women he knew, she was completely devoid of the silly feminine wiles he found so irritating. There was no batting of eyelashes with her, no forced laughter over every witticism he made, no sidling up to him as a few unattached gals at church tried to do at the various socials he'd attended over the years. On the contrary, Rosa seemed utterly sincere and real, and she possessed a fresh innocence—vulnerability, even—that made him want to protect her from harm. She was like Hannah in many ways, which also weighed heavily in her favor.

Yet Rosalind was wise enough to discern that their friendship would stir up trouble—in both their families.

Ken had no idea how his ma viewed the occupants of the Lebanese settlement. She did hold strong Christian beliefs and all his life had lectured him and his siblings about treating others with kindness and generosity. But so many folks looked down on and even feared the "gypsies" on Larksville Mountain. How about Ma?

Maybe it was time to see how far her Christian love reached.

Typical supper smells drifted from various houses along his street as Ken walked home. The Donatelli family would be having spaghetti, kielbasa at the Kryszkas', stuffed cabbage for the Jessups. But nothing compared to the chicken and dumplings he detected at his own back door. His favorite dish. He grinned and went inside.

"It's about time!" Tim griped. "Hey, Ma! Ken's home!"

"Oh, good," she said, untying her apron strings as she came into the kitchen. "Hannah, you can pour the drinks now, and we'll eat."

Ken washed his hands at the sink while the others saw to last-minute details, then he joined them at the table. "Smells great, Ma. We celebrating or something?"

"No, I just thought it might taste good for a change. Hannah made baked apples for dessert."

"Man, I think I died and went to heaven," Ken said, his hand over his heart.

"Could we cut the baloney and eat?" Tim chimed in. "I'm starved."

After a brief blessing, everyone filled plates and dove in.

"How did you make out today, Hannah?" Ken asked. "The rich matrons work your fingers to the bone polishing silver again?"

"No, beating rugs. I never saw so much dust."

"Ha. You should come to the breaker," Tim challenged. "That's nothin' compared to what I see every day."

"Oh, right. I forgot about that. I did have a little help, though. Mrs. MacNamara's son took pity on me and came to help. He's. . . um. . .well, nice."

Noting the faint tinge of pink creeping over his sister's face, Ken watched her toy with her food while he took a second helping. "A kid, like Timmy?" he finally asked.

Hannah didn't quite meet his eyes as she darted a glance at him. "No. Actually he's—" Reaching for her lemonade, she inadvertently bumped the glass, spilling the contents. "Oh, how clumsy of me!" She sprang to her feet and dashed to the kitchen for a towel.

It had been some time since Ken had seen his normally poised sister so flighty and nervous. He'd let it pass for now, but next time he was over in Wilkes-Barre, he'd go by the MacNamara mansion, see if he could spot that only son whom Hannah mentioned now and again.

Oblivious to the undercurrent in the room, Tim helped himself to another plateful of food.

"Say, Ma," Ken said, breaking into the silence, "know anything about the folks who live in the camp on Larksville Mountain?"

"Why?"

"Just wondered."

She blotted her lips on her napkin and replaced it on her lap. "I don't think anybody knows much about those people."

"The gypsies, you mean?" Timmy's eyes grew round. "They give me the creeps. Jimmy told me they almost stole Pete's little sister right outta her own yard. All they have to do is look at you with their 'evil eye' and you go all funny."

"That's nonsense," Ma said, shaking her head.

He made a face, then resumed eating.

"Ever meet any of them personally?" Ken probed. He took a sip of his drink.

"Not me. But some ladies at church have had dealings with them. The Ladies Aid took some canned food to the settlement once, but they refused it."

"How odd," he said thoughtfully.

"Mrs. Wright's sister out in Huntsville buys things pretty regularly from an old peddler who comes around," his mother continued. "She says he seems fair and carries good quality wares. He usually has a young woman with him in the wagon. A grand-daughter, I believe the lady says. Kind of pretty, in her own dark way. But nobody really trusts them as a whole. I don't know if I would myself."

Ken maintained a casual expression.

"Quite a few of those people run small shops downtown," Hannah offered, referring to the city. "They're all over Wilkes-Barre. And there's a couple of young girls from the camp working at the silk mill, too. They stay mostly to themselves. Of course, most everybody sort of gives them a wide berth. They're just so *different*, or something, all those bright clothes and dark eyes that always look like they're holding secrets from us."

"Why do you ask?" Ma repeated.

"No reason. I just happened to meet a young woman from

the camp one day. She was pretty timid but didn't come across as strange, as Hannah put it. I wondered if anyone you knew had any information about them."

"I'm afraid not, other than what I already told you. Maybe they're fine enough at a distance, but I don't think I'd want one living next door."

"You might change your mind if you met the young woman I did. You'd see that she's sensitive and thoughtful, a lot like Hannah, and not in the least scary." He directed the last part of the statement to Tim.

"I doubt it," she countered. "And I'd still rather keep my distance, thank you just the same."

Hiding his disappointment, he gave a nod, then turned his attention to his sister. "Well, did I hear somebody mention baked apples?"

She wrinkled her nose. "Coming right up." And with that, she stood and began gathering plates.

"Oh, Son," Ma cut in, "one of the Jessup kids brought over some books Mike said he wanted you to have. They're on the buffet."

"Thanks. I'll take them upstairs when I go."

Absolutely stuffed by the time he finished feasting on supper and dessert, Ken retired to his room early, study books in hand. He'd only worked summers, as a breaker boy, and later, a nipper. But having quit school in ninth grade to help add to the family's income, he would forever be glad his parents insisted he attend continuation school one night a week until he'd completed high school studies. Likely most of the algebra formulas and equations would come back to him, and he foresaw no problem understanding the engineering and surveying books. No doubt some night classes at the high school would help, too. Hopefully it wouldn't be long before he'd be able to take the state test for his foreman's papers.

But after such a pleasant day, the last thing he wanted to do was bury his nose in some dry textbook. He kicked off his shoes and lay on his back atop the chenille bedspread, hands laced together beneath his head.

Hannah had seemed in a strange mood at supper—distracted, barely picking at her food, knocking over her lemonade, getting flustered over nothing. Ken hoped his sister wasn't dumb enough to form a crush on some rich guy. She'd be sure to end up with her heart broken. No young man of means would deign to court a girl whose family made their living cracking coal. They moved in entirely different circles.

Two worlds, as Rosalind would say.

Like the moon rising over the treetops, thoughts of Rosa drifted to the surface of Ken's mind, crowding out sisters and coal mines and study books. He wondered if she had gone to her room to read, just as he had.

He tried to imagine what her life must be like, wondering if she lived in a shack or a house wagon, a tent or something more permanent. Did she even have a room of her own? She hadn't revealed much about herself, except that her parents were deceased and she lived with her grandparents, one of whom was a healer, the other a peddler. The vivid clothing she wore seemed of good quality, not threadbare, and the earrings and bangle bracelets that gleamed enchantingly against the rich hue of her skin appeared to be pure gold.

It struck Ken as ironic that Mrs. Wright, from church, had a sister who probably dealt with Rosa's grandfather and might have even spoken to Rosa herself. The lady at least appreciated Rosalind's exotic beauty. But then, no one could deny something so obvious.

Ma hadn't been quite as broad-minded as he'd hoped concerning Rosalind's people. Most likely her proper upbringing would ensure her politeness if they came around, but she was leery about having one living in close proximity. The fact that she didn't trust them could have more to do with rumors and never having dealt with any personally than anything else.

He'd just have to ease her into a different frame of mind, that's all. If he went slowly enough, she probably wouldn't even catch on. After all, there was nothing between him and Rosa except a sweet friendship—and unless the two of them shared a spiritual fellowship as well, there could never *be* anything more to it. One thing his pa had drilled into all of them was the warning in 2 Corinthians chapter 6, about unequal yokes. Not that he'd begun considering any sort of a permanent commitment. The extra money Tim earned was helping to bring down the level of debt hanging over their heads, but it would still be awhile before he was in a position to think about starting a home and family of his own.

Reaching over to the bedside table, he switched the radio on, then turned the dial in search of something to occupy his wandering thoughts.

Tim happened into the room just then. "Any games on? The Giants or the Yanks?" He flopped onto his bed, one arm dangling over the side, feeling around on the floor for some comic books one of his pals had loaned him. He found three on the first try.

"I think this one's from Yankee Stadium, but I don't know what other team is playing."

"Who cares?" his brother asked. "A game's a game, isn't it?"

"I suppose." With a wry grin, Ken lay back down, wondering if Rosalind had a radio to listen to. And if the encampment even had electricity at all.

How precious little he really knew about her.

Chapter 7

"You should try this," Rosalind said, hiking the hem of her skirt a bit higher as she stepped from one smooth stone to the next in a gurgling mountain stream not far above the camp. "The water is wonderful." She traced small arcs in the ripples with the toe of one foot, enjoying the cool rush of the current against her skin.

Sitting with his back against a tree and one arm propped on his bent knee, Philip nodded patiently. "The daylight will not last much longer, you know."

"Yes, I know."

On the climb up the hill in the balmy evening, they had chatted lightly about his job and some current happenings at the settlement, but now that those safe topics had been covered, Rosa knew she had to get to the one he was waiting for. Sobering, she glanced homeward to make sure no one would overhear their conversation. Then she waded out of the brook to join her cousin, dropping down to sit beside him, her feet stretched out in front of her to dry.

"What I have to say you must promise not to repeat," she said earnestly.

Not even looking at her, he tossed a flat pebble into the stream. It landed with a soft plop. "I have kept a lot of secrets for you, Cousin, as you have done for me. I would never betray you."

Rosa felt encouraged by his statement, but a long moment passed before she could bring herself to speak. "I think I am. . .in love," she finally murmured.

"Oh?" Philip's dark brows rose higher, and he smiled. "You mean, with someone besides me? Who is the lucky man who has won your heart?"

Rosalind slowly wagged her head. "He is. . .not of our people."

Her cousin's smile vanished. "What?"

She met his gaze and held it. "It is someone I met in the forest some weeks ago. A man from the mines."

Philip's jaw dropped, but Rosa gave him no chance to say anything.

"We met by accident. Once. Then again. And then we began to meet on purpose, eat together, talk. . . . Now I have come to have feelings for him. Feelings I have never felt before."

"Rosa, Rosa," Philip moaned, "this is not good. Do you have any idea how much trouble it will cause if you continue this relationship with an outsider?"

She nodded miserably. "But I cannot help it. I did not plan it. I was seeking only a friend. You are always busy, Sultana has a new life with her husband, and Julianna moved away more than a year ago."

Emitting a whoosh of breath, Philip ran his fingers through his curly hair. "You must end it, Cousin. That is all I can say."

"No. Do not tell me that. I cannot. I will not. He is so nice, so kind. He treats me with the utmost honor."

"But he is an outsider, not one of us. What will you tell your grandparents?"

Rosalind could not answer.

"And what about his people? How do they feel about their son being with you, a *gypsy*, one who possesses the *evil eye*? That's what those coal diggers think of us, you know, they and everybody else around here."

She shrugged. "We do not talk about those things."

"Well, you should. As the old saying goes, 'A bird and a fish may fall in love, but where would they live?'"

Rosalind had never seen her cousin's features so hardened, his jaw so rigid that a tiny muscle twitched. She found it difficult to look away. "But this is America. Times are changing."

"Not for us, Rosa. We will face scorn and prejudice for who knows how many generations before our people earn the respect given so freely to others."

"But it has to start somewhere, with two people. Him and me, perhaps."

Philip's ebony eyes flashed with anger, and he got to his feet. "I doubt that. This can only bring trouble to you and to our people. You are foolish if you think otherwise." Without even waiting for her, he stalked away.

"Wait, Philip," Rosa cried. She grabbed her shoes in one hand and hurried to catch up. Reaching him, she latched onto his sleeve. "You will not tell, will you?"

"I told you I would not," he replied between gritted teeth.

"So then, will you, too, hate me? Shun me?"

Exhaling in a rush, he stopped walking and turned to face her. His demeanor softened, and he reached out and drew her into a hug. "I do not hate you. If we were not cousins, I would offer for you myself—even though you are older," he added teasingly. Then he grew serious again. "But some things we cannot change, Rosa. I fear for you, that you are going to be hurt. Bad. And there is nothing I can do to help."

"Yes, there is," she assured him, easing out of his embrace. "You can believe in me. Still be my best friend. I will need someone to side with me."

He smiled thinly. "Then, for all the good it will do, I will side with you, Cousin."

"Thank you. That is all I ask." Forcing a smile of her own, Rosa slipped her feet into her shoes, then put an arm about his waist, and they walked the rest of the way in silence.

✑

Ken finished the last of a dozen complicated equations on the page and added an exuberant period with his pencil point before turning to a clean sheet in the tablet. He'd always enjoyed math problems, and the more intricate the problem, the more determined he was to figure out the correct answer.

"Whoopee!" Tim yelled from the parlor, where he had the

radio console tuned to a ball game. "The Babe just hit a grand slam! The Yanks are ahead of the Athletics four to one."

"Great," Ken hollered back, smiling as he went on to the next algebra problem.

"I thought you might be thirsty," Hannah said, coming into the dining room with two glasses of lemonade. She placed one in front of Ken, then took a chair opposite him.

"Thanks, Sis." After taking several swallows, he grinned at her. "Hits the spot, as always."

"That looks hard," she commented, eyeing his work. "I never did care for math. Even when I could figure the problems out, it took me forever."

"Oh, I don't know. Seems once a person gets a handle on all the rules, it gets easier. Myself, I love the challenge."

She nodded. "Would it bother you if I work at this end of the table?"

"Doing what?"

"Sewing. I was going to make some pillowcases."

"Running short of them, are we?" Ken chided.

Pinkening delicately, she pursed her lips, then gave into a smile. "Actually, they're for me. For my hope chest."

"Ah. When did all this start?"

"The day I turned sixteen and Ma gave me the china tea set she had when she was a bride," she replied evenly. "The two of us have been adding to it ever since. Doilies, tea towels, pillowcases. . .you know. Girl things. Pretty stuff."

He gave a thoughtful nod.

"Of course, since Pa and Matt were killed, there hasn't been much money for such luxuries. I just thought it was time to get busy again."

"Well, hey," he said, gathering his books and notes into a neat stack. "Use as much of the table as you like. I'm almost finished with algebra anyway. The rest only need to be read and studied."

Hannah smiled and got up to take her empty glass to the

kitchen. She returned with some yard goods and scissors and began laying out the material. "When do you think you'll be ready to take the state test?"

"Couple of weeks, maybe. I figure the extra money I'll earn as a foreman will help a lot."

"I hope so."

Watching his sister as she worked, measuring out the amount of material needed, then cutting carefully along the pins she'd used to mark the size, Ken couldn't help but notice how capable she was. As far back as he could remember, she'd done things just so. Though it was hard to imagine life without her smiling presence around, he knew that one of these days some young man would be captivated by her winsome beauty and ability to keep a nice house. After all, at nineteen, going on twenty, she was only two years younger than he, and that day could come sooner than he imagined.

"Hannah?"

"Hmm?" She met his gaze.

"Is there someone special you've got in mind?"

She merely shrugged a shoulder, but a playful spark twinkled in her blue eyes. "A girl has to have some secrets, doesn't she?"

"I guess. It's just. . .well, hard to think of you ever getting married, moving off somewhere."

"Relax. I'm in no hurry. But don't you plan to find a wife yourself someday?"

"I don't know. I've been so busy trying to get us out of debt, I haven't had time to think about it." *Until recently,* he nearly added. "I guess I thought life would keep on the way it is, indefinitely."

"Yeah, I know what you mean. Sometimes it feels as if we should still be kids, out playing ball and jumping rope. Time goes so quickly." Coming to the end of the first pillow slip, she made a last cut, then folded it and put it aside. Adjusting the material, she started cutting the second. "Other times I feel like I'm thirty already. Like when I look around and see the kids I used to watch as babies already going to school, growing up."

The back door opened, and their mother returned home from next door. She carried a bag in each arm as she came through to the dining room.

"What's all that?" Hannah asked.

"Oh, Aggie insisted I take some of her preserves and things. She doesn't want to cart them to New York. I just feel so bad about their leaving."

"Me, too," Ken piped in. "But they'll make out fine, living out on a farm. I kind of wish it was us."

"You would," she returned good-naturedly. "But since it isn't, how about taking these down to the cellar for me and putting them on the shelves with the other canned things."

"Gotcha," he said, and went to do her bidding. He really did hate to part with such good neighbors as the Jessups, and something told him Hannah wouldn't be far behind. But for him there was Ma and Tim to look after. And the debt. He wondered if he would ever get far enough ahead of his responsibilities to ever be able to consider a family of his own. And Rosa.

❧

Not even the gathering clouds could darken the day when Rosalind came into view; she was breathtaking in her violet skirt and an ivory blouse embroidered with purple. Ken stood to his feet by the log and waved, and she smiled and returned the gesture.

"I wondered if you would come today," he said in all honesty. He glanced apprehensively at the sky.

"Do not worry, it will not rain for awhile," she said. "Grandmother is always right about such things. But I cannot stay long."

"Have time for a walk?"

"A short one, maybe."

"Good." Ken offered a hand, and when she placed hers in it, he schooled himself not to clutch too tightly, to keep things light. "There's something I wanted to show you."

"What is it?"

"You'll see." They walked side by side through the trees and undergrowth until they came to another trail. Obviously less traveled, the ferns and brush had begun to grow over it in places, but it was still quite passable and meandered away from Ken's haven. With his free arm, he pushed tree branches aside so they could pass.

"Where are you taking me?" Rosa asked. She seemed puzzled, but her beautiful eyes showed only trust.

"To another nice spot. It's not much farther."

Gradually the dense forest growth became thinner, and a short time later they emerged into a tiny clearing ringed on three sides by trees. A huge granite formation jutted up from the ground, and a few feet in front of it, the forest floor fell away in a steep drop.

"There's an unbelievable view from the top of the rock," Ken said. Letting go of Rosalind's hand, he climbed up first, then reached down to help her.

"Are you sure of this?" she asked.

"Of course. Come on, I'll help you. See for yourself."

Frowning slightly, she again took hold of his hand and he tugged her up to the flat, smooth brim, amazed at how feather-light she was.

Ken grinned as she beheld a panoramic view of Edwardsville, the mine, and beyond, to Kingston and Wilkes-Barre, where the tranquil Susquehanna River glistened in all its splendor. Despite the cloudy sky, the rolling hills on the opposite side of the valley provided a gorgeous backdrop.

"Ohh," she breathed. "How beautiful."

"Yes, but that's not all." Hopping down, he raised his arms up to assist her. His breath stopped as she leaned into his hands, her slender waist in his grasp. She smelled of wildflowers and mountainsides, and as she raised her lashes to meet his gaze, he had to force himself to let go.

He cleared his throat. "Here's the best part." Capturing her hand once again, he led her to an almost undetectable, narrow path that curved around the base to the front of the rock formation, where a small cave, entirely hidden from view on either side, cut into the hillside. "I got caught in a downpour out here once and found this place by accident. I don't think anybody else even knows it's here."

For the briefest of moments, apprehension widened her eyes, and Ken sensed her uneasiness about being here alone with him, so far from everyone. He immediately reassured her. "Don't be afraid, Rosa. I would never do anything to harm you."

She let out a slow breath and relaxed as she glanced around the interior, green and soft with moss. "It is wonderful," she murmured, her eyes shining.

"I just wanted to show it to you. I thought you might like it."

Her rosy lips spread into a tremulous smile—and they were so close as she gazed up at him. So close.

Inhaling a ragged breath, Ken grazed the curve of her fine cheekbone with the back of his finger. "There are lots of other incredible places around here. I'd like to take you to all of them."

"I—"

"Yes, I know. We'll have to wait for another time. I'll take you back now."

Neither of them spoke for several minutes as they began the return trip. Finally Rosalind turned to him.

"You are so different. I have never known anyone like you."

"Nor I you," he replied, smiling gently.

"With my people, a woman is property. A possession. She must do always as her husband tells her. But you make me feel special, not like that."

"Because you are special, Rosalind. I knew that the first moment I saw you."

She favored him with a shy smile. "How is it with your people? I mean, when a man and a woman marry. Does the wife become her husband's servant, his possession?"

"No. Not at all. We believe that God created men and women as equals, but that He assigned them different roles. The Bible says man has the responsibility of being the head of the household, but he is to love and cherish his wife. A wife who knows she is loved by her husband submits to his authority voluntarily, not because she is forced to do so. And together, as they serve and obey God, they receive His blessing."

"I have been reading the Bible you gave me, but I have not yet come to that part. I would like to read it for myself."

"You'll find it in the Book of Ephesians, chapter 5, I believe. It's not hard to understand."

"This is new to me, being considered equal to a man. I will have to think about it."

"I come across lots of interesting things to think about when I read the Bible," he said. "I'm sure you will, too."

Noticing the thicket up ahead, Ken brought Rosa's hand to his lips and kissed it. "I will leave you now. Take care. 'Til next time. . . ."

" 'Til next time." Stretching to tiptoe, she brushed his cheek with a kiss, then hurried away.

A possession, he thought. *How could any man treat someone so beautiful and sensitive as a servant? No wonder I can see no evidence of joy in her eyes.*

His heart sent another prayer aloft that one day Rosalind would know true joy. And deep, abiding love.

Chapter 8

The storm clouds that had been building all that day let loose as the family gathered around the supper table.

"Aw, fiddlesticks," Tim muttered. "Rain. Now we won't get to go to Kirby Park an' see the Fourth of July fireworks."

"I think we'll live through it, Runt," Ken cajoled. The family always looked forward to the annual event held at the Kingston Armory, but somehow the disappointment seemed of little importance today. Claiming his chair, he silently thanked God for the time he'd spent with Rosalind.

Before their paths had crossed, a rainy Saturday meant only that he wouldn't be able to hike up the mountain. Now, wet weather shut out the possibility of seeing her, visiting with her. He wasn't sure exactly when he'd started counting on her presence and eagerly looking forward to the next encounter. But somewhere along the way, the enchanting gypsy had danced right into his heart, making Saturday the high point of his week.

"Would you ask the blessing tonight, Timmy?" Ma asked, her voice drawing Ken back to the present.

Trying unsuccessfully to focus on the prayer, he heard scarcely more than a few words before the kid uttered the amen. He gave himself a mental shake.

Accepting the platter of fried chicken that Hannah passed his way, he noticed something different about her. Very different. Heightened color on her cheeks, a smile that wouldn't quit, shining eyes. She must have had an unusually good day housecleaning! "So, Hannah," he probed. "How was your day?"

She rested her forearm on the table, fork in hand. "Quite good. The MacNamaras gave me a nice bonus for what they termed 'exceptional work.' I think they were afraid I'd quit on them and they'd have to train a new girl in my place."

"I would imagine it's hard to find loyal, trustworthy help these days," their mother said. "Everybody's looking for greener pastures elsewhere."

"Well, I enjoy working for them," Hannah replied. "Mrs. MacNamara does like things done a particular way, but she isn't fussy and hard to please, like Mrs. Hughes often is."

"Is that the reason you kinda...glow?" Ken quizzed in brotherly candor. "Or is there somebody else in that house who finds you pleasing?" He took a healthy bite of his drumstick.

She stopped chewing and swallowed as a full-fledged blush beautified her delicate features. "Well, actually, now that you mention it. . ." She switched her attention to her mother. "Ma, David MacNamara would like to meet you all. I've...invited him to Sunday dinner next week."

"What?" she gasped. "Here?" In sharp contrast to Hannah's rosy flush, her own complexion paled to chalky white. "A MacNamara from that fine estate in Wilkes-Barre, having dinner in a coal patch house?" She swept a frantic gaze of disbelief over the plain, almost stark, furnishings of the dining room. "That's out of the question. Completely out of the question."

"Oh, Ma," she pleaded. "David is really very nice. He isn't concerned with material things—"

"And why should he be," she countered, "when he has all the material advantages a person could ever hope for?"

Ken, taking a sip of hot coffee, had yet to get past the "David" part. In his mind, he'd envisioned Hannah almost curtsying before her employers, eyes downcast, murmuring, "Yes, Sir. Thank you, Sir." When had things progressed to first-name basis with the son and heir? And for that matter, moved beyond even that, to a social occasion? Idly, he glanced at Tim, whose face bore a complete lack of concern while he reached for the bowl of mashed potatoes.

But Hannah managed to retain her composure, her coloring having returned to its more natural state. "I knew it would take a while for you to get used to the idea, or I'd have invited him for tomorrow."

Completely ruffled by that announcement, Ma shoved her barely touched meal away and sat back against her chair, arms folded. "And what do you suggest we serve His Highness? I'm afraid pheasant season ended a few months ago, to say nothing of what any of us might wear in his presence."

"David doesn't care what we serve," she replied evenly. "In fact, his favorite dish is chicken and dumplings, same as Ken's. And if it mattered to him how we dressed, I'm sure he'd have chosen to have dinner with a flapper from his social circle. In the time I've grown to know him, I've realized he's the opposite of how we view wealthy folks. It's not his fault his parents have money, and if we judge others by that rule, we are the snobs, not them. David is a committed Christian, one who has a real heart for God, a desire to help others."

"Oh," Ma grated, her tone flat. "So we're a charity case then, is that it?"

Hannah sighed and looked to Ken in frustration.

Straightening in his seat, he cleared his throat. "What do you say we give the guy the benefit of the doubt, Ma? What's one meal? We can all brush up on our Sunday manners so we don't act like a bunch of clodhoppers. Then if he doesn't approve of us, he'll probably go his way and leave us to go ours." He shot a small grin of encouragement to his sister.

"I sure wouldn't mind more chicken and dumplin's," Timmy added. " 'Specially if there's chocolate cake to go with 'em."

The heavy breath Ma emitted revealed her gradual acceptance of a matter already beyond her control. She drew her plate toward herself and picked at the cold food with her fork. "Well, I suppose the lace tablecloth will do, if I mend the tear in the edge and turn it to the good side."

Hannah's beautiful smile put dazzling rainbows in her eyes. "Thank you, Ma. You'll love David, I just know it."

As you do? Ken wondered. He'd figured a day like this would come sooner or later. Whatever else might be said about David MacNamara, one had to admire his taste in women. Hannah would be a prize catch for any man—assuming this guy wasn't merely toying with her affection. Next Sunday would provide a great opportunity to check him out.

Ma's apple pie, still warm from the oven, rounded out the meal. Surprisingly little chatter took place during dessert, however. Ken could almost see the wheels turning inside his mother's head, already planning the Big Event a week away. Hannah's secret smile revealed pleasure and anticipation, while nothing fazed their kid brother, wolfing down whatever food was placed before him.

Mulling over his ma's reaction to entertaining someone from the wealthy side of the tracks, Ken could only wonder what she would say when he invited Rosa to come for supper.

✍

No one spoke as the cage creaked its way to the top. By the end of a shift, all the jokes had already been cracked, the small talk exhausted, and weary men wanted nothing more than to shower and get home for supper. Lunch pails in hand, the dust-blackened group stepped clear and headed for the shiftin' shack.

Just then, an ominous explosion came from below.

The men stopped *en masse* and turned, their hearts in their throats as they waited for news of what had happened and where. No one speculated, no one uttered a sound as they gravitated back to the shaft they'd just exited and joined other groups of grave-faced miners already clustering there.

Soon enough, word reached the surface from the bottom men manning the shaft in which the mine cars ascended and descended. A cave-in on level three. Eleven miners trapped.

At once, the huge steam whistle sounded the alarm—heart-stopping blasts that would draw family and neighbors to the mine to wait helplessly until they learned the fate of their loved ones.

In the desperate frenzy that followed, Ken ran to the shiftin' shack and snatched a white helmet from one of the hooks. Then he dropped to his knees and pleaded for the lives of the men below and the welfare of those whose job now lay in rescue and recovery. He knew his mother and Hannah would be frantic, not knowing if he was all right or had met the same fate as his pa; but as a member of the safety team, his main concern now was seeing to the trapped men. He rose and surged forward with other white-helmeted rescuers waiting their turn to go down to help.

Below, they found the amount of fallen rock, shale, and crushed timbers blocking the gangway staggering. But the work-weary men labored tirelessly to save their fellow laborers, knowing that time was of the essence and that one day others might have to do the same for them. High-powered fans aboveground sent increased air through the ventilation shaft to aid the safety team in their grim task.

☙

Rosalind and her grandfather had just pulled into the encampment after having made his rounds when the alarm at the mine shattered the stillness. He sent a curious glance in that direction but wasn't too concerned. "I see to horses," he said, stopping at the house while she hopped down.

"I'll see if there are any berries left up on the mountain for dessert," Rosa offered. Without taking time to grab a basket, much less determine Nicholas Habib's whereabouts, she grasped her skirt in either hand and darted up the hill.

She passed right on by Ken's special thicket, winded and gasping for air as she sought the path they'd taken yesterday.

Thankfully, she found the route easy enough to follow; and when she came to a fork in the trail, she bit her lip and chose the one to the right. It brought her to the granite formation he'd shown her. She scrambled up to the top, her chest heaving, and peered down at Hudson Coal Company.

Something horrible must have happened. Hordes of blackened miners milled about the dreary structures like so many ants. But picking Ken Roberts out of a mob of dust-covered miners was impossible. Even if she went down there and stood on the sidelines, she couldn't be sure she'd find him.

Sinking to her knees on the rocky surface, she clasped her hands together and squeezed her eyes shut. "Dear God in heaven, Ken told me You are his friend. If that is true, please watch over him. I don't know what has happened at the mine or if he was involved. But he trusts You. Please, please, make it turn out right." Not knowing what else to ask or if she'd said the proper words, Rosa gave a last look below and started for home. Never had she felt more helpless in her life.

❧

Additional members of the safety team descended periodically to relieve those below; and as each one reached the point where he could do no more, he would go above and find hot coffee and the tears of relief from waiting loved ones. By the time Ken reached his limit and came up top, he could hardly utter his name to the men who helped him exit the cage. Daylight had all but faded, but floodlights provided circles of illumination for the families and others standing vigil. As his name was announced, a small cry issued from the crowd, and his dear ones flew to his side.

"Thank the Lord, you're alive," Ma breathed, hugging him so hard he could scarcely draw breath.

"Hey, I'm a little dirty," he said in an attempt to lighten the moment. Hannah cried openly, the tears coursing down her face, while Tim, still filthy from the breaker, thumped his back for all he was worth.

Someone handed him a cup of coffee. "Go home and get some rest, Roberts. Likely we'll need you again in the morning."

Too tired to protest, almost too tired even to pray again for the victims, Ken leaned heavily on his kid brother, who looped an arm around him and began leading him toward home. He didn't want to think about how much more digging needed to be done—or that not even so much as a rapping had come from the other side. Thankfully, his family knew better than to ask him any questions just yet.

Ken awakened before daylight, still bone weary, but eager to get back to the mine. He dressed as quietly as possible without disturbing Tim, who would be up soon enough himself. Even with underground work suspended temporarily, the breaker would still be in operation. Heaven forbid the coal company should lose a nickel merely because a few workers got trapped or killed.

Forcing aside the caustic thoughts, he tiptoed downstairs, where Ma had hot coffee and breakfast already waiting. He worked up a smile.

She merely squeezed his shoulder while she filled his cup, but after she dished up his pork chops and eggs, she bent to hug him without a word. The hot meal fortified him for the day that lay ahead. That and prayer.

That afternoon, while Ken took a break and came up top for coffee, the first body was brought to the surface. With the announcement of the man's identity, an almost inhuman wail issued from the miner's widow, and she collapsed beside his remains sobbing uncontrollably. Others gathered around to offer what little comfort they could. Ken had witnessed similar heart-wrenching scenes too often, each one bringing back the day he and Ma had knelt and wept over his pa and Matt. All he could do was lift the poor woman up in prayer and hope for the others still below.

By the end of the day, another nine bodies had been carted to the surface, two of them crushed beyond recognition. But amazingly, one man made it out alive. Horribly injured, he was transported immediately to the nearest hospital to be treated, his relieved family members resolved to accept his future no matter what it involved.

Having known several of the victims personally, Ken needed time to work through his own private grief. He didn't have it in him to talk much at supper, and the family wisely refrained from intruding. When they left to attend a prayer meeting at church for the victims' families, he took a walk in the waning daylight.

When his thicket came into view, a bright spot of color met his eyes. His heart took a joyous leap. Rosa! He should have known she'd be there. He quickened his pace until she caught his gaze and jumped up. . .and the two of them ran the rest of the way.

Ken's arms opened of their own volition, and Rosalind flew into them, tears streaming down her cheeks. "I was so afraid. So afraid for you."

He held her close, stroking the shiny hair he'd never imagined could be so silky, lacing his fingers through the glorious curls. The sensation of feeling the surge of her heartbeat against his own awed him and stole his breath.

"I prayed that God would keep you safe," Rosa said, drawing back a little to gaze up at him.

"Thank you. That means more to me than you know."

She continued to search his soul. "But something else is wrong, is it not? You have lost friends."

With fresh grief rising to the fore, he could not trust himself to speak. He nodded, blinking away the burning behind his eyes.

Rosalind moved once more into the circle of his arms and hugged him, having nothing to offer other than the comfort of her presence.

Ken tightened his embrace, inhaling the scent of roses in her hair. It felt so wonderful to have her in his arms, he might have stayed forever—only he was all too aware that night would soon be upon them.

"I'd better let you get home," he managed to say, albeit with reluctance. "Or we'll both be tripping over brush in the dark."

She nodded, apparently not much more eager to leave than he. "Will you come again on Saturday?" she asked.

"Sure will. . .if you'll be here."

"I will be here."

Simultaneously, their fingers still entwined, they took a step in their opposite directions. Then Ken squeezed her hand.

Rosalind turned back, gazing up to him, her beautiful eyes aglow, her rosy lips slightly parted.

With a smile and a soft moan, Ken tugged her near once more and lowered his face to hers, their breath mingling for the briefest instant before their lips met. Time stood as still as his heart for that moment. But at last it, too, had to come to an end.

Rosa smiled at him and touched his face with her soft fingertips, then slowly walked away.

Just having been with Rosalind for those few precious moments buoyed Ken considerably on the trek back to the house. And he vowed that if he lived long enough to pay off the debt at Murphy's store, he would find another line of work as soon as the opportunity presented itself. With that determination in mind, he pored over the textbooks Mike Jessup had given him until his eyes could no longer focus on the words.

Chapter 9

The dawning of a glorious weekend cheered Ken considerably after the sadness of the previous days, especially knowing for certain that he'd be with Rosalind again.

With David MacNamara's expected appearance scheduled on the morrow, Ma assigned a few extra morning chores, like nailing down the loose porch step, replacing the missing post in the railing, beating the parlor rug, and getting extra clutter out of sight in the yard and the main part of the house. After that, she seemed only too eager to have him out from underfoot so she could scrub the place spotless.

He packed a lunch, then got his Bible and engineering book and set off for the thicket, where he relaxed against his reading log and lost himself in concepts of how much steel and concrete it took to support so many feet of bridge, the angles of various spans and how one differed from another. The more he studied, the more fascinated he became.

His stomach was about to growl when Maloof suddenly bounded from the undergrowth, his long pink tongue hanging out. He came close enough to sniff the area near Ken, his shoes, and the log.

Although Ken appreciated the dog's friendliness, his attention centered on Maloof's enchanting companion, just coming into sight. He closed the book and got up to greet Rosalind, a vision in turquoise and silver. "Hello," he managed to say past the lump in his throat.

"And to you," she said with a misty smile. "I am glad you are here."

"Not as glad as I am to see you," he said teasingly. "I was about to starve to death, waiting."

With a light laugh she took her usual spot and produced some fresh peaches from her pocket while he sat next to her. "What are you reading?" she asked, eyeing the big book he'd set atop the log.

"Oh, this? Just some stuff on building bridges and other structures. It's pretty interesting, though. Hungry?" He handed her a sandwich made from leftover pork roast.

"Yes, and thank you." She waited for him to ask grace, then opened the waxed paper and took a bite of her sandwich. "Are you feeling better today?"

He nodded but could not prevent a small twinge of sorrow at the reminder of the friends he'd lost. "Some days it's all I can do to go to work," he confessed aloud for the first time in his life, "wondering if my number will be up next."

"Do not say such things," Rosa said, her slender brows dipping into a frown. "It is bad luck."

He tipped his head and thought for a moment. "I don't set much store by luck, actually. I can only trust the Lord that He'll help me through whatever is part of His plan for my life. Even if that does mean my number comes up. That's faith. I have no fear of death itself, because I know I'll be with the Lord after I die. But trying to imagine how my family would get along without my help, that's the hard part."

"You know you will be with God? For certain?"

With a gentle smile, Ken nodded. "I'll be with Him because I obeyed what He laid out in His Word. I admitted that in myself there is nothing good and that it took the death of His Son on the cross to pay the penalty for my sins and purchase my forgiveness. That's all it takes. He said it, and I believe it."

"I have been reading such things in the Bible you gave me. But I would think much more than that would be required."

"Earn our way to heaven, you mean? Build a bridge of good deeds from us to God, as so many people strive to do? Even if that were possible, how would a person ever know when enough had been done? He would never find true peace that way."

Rosalind made no reply, but he could still detect confusion in her eyes.

"What God required was the shed blood of a perfect sacrifice. His own Son was the only One who could meet the qualifications. So God Himself bridged the gap *for* all mankind, with the cross. Jesus became our sacrificial Lamb and shed His blood for our sins. It was for that reason He came to earth. That's how much He loved us. But it's up to us to accept that sacrifice for ourselves."

Her features eased into their natural beauty again, and she ate more of her sandwich in thoughtful silence. Then she raised questioning eyes to his. "How is it that you have no wife, a man like you? I should think women would line up at your door."

"Yeah, sure," he said, chuckling. "I have so much to offer." He finished the remains of his own meal and brushed the bread crumbs from his hands.

"You do, you know," Rosa said. "Such kindness, such concern for others. Even for me."

"What do you mean, even you? I happen to think you are incredibly special."

She smiled, then swung her gaze off into the distance. "And your family. . . Would they share your opinion of me?"

He took a few seconds to formulate an answer before he spoke. "I have to be honest, Rosalind. I don't really know what they'd say if they knew I was courting a beautiful little gypsy girl."

"Is that what you're doing? Courting me?" she asked, cutting him a sidelong glance. "I thought that was a custom your people have to prepare for marriage." She chewed the last bit of bread and swallowed.

He reached over and caught her chin with the edge of his finger, then turned her face toward his. "I know it has to do with marriage, Rosa. And I know it's way too soon for either of us to be considering a permanent commitment. Sure, my family would probably have to be eased into knowing about our relationship. But then, you haven't exactly taken me to meet your grandparents, either. Do they know you've been meeting me up here every week?"

"They do not," she admitted miserably, looking down at her hands. "They would have my head."

"Well, see? That's why we have to take things slowly. I do plan to tell my family about you, have you come to the house for dinner, but not until the time is right for both of us. But don't think my intentions toward you are anything but honorable. I am growing to love you, Rosalind Gilbran. And if God allows it, I would consider it the greatest honor to ask you to become my wife one day. But we have to wait to see what the future holds." Leaning toward her, he gave her the most tender of kisses.

Rosa could hardly breathe as Ken's declaration sunk in. He actually loved her! Suddenly the forest became a magical place, where only happiness and peace abounded and nothing bad could intrude. She got up, and in a playful mood, brushed the crumbs from her hands. . .right onto Ken's head.

"Oh, so you think you're gonna be smart, eh?" he said, scrambling to his feet. He reached for her, but she managed to elude his grasp and darted off, laughing, with him in close pursuit. She knew the forest well and dodged around trees with practiced ease, keeping just ahead of him.

Until a protruding root caught her heel and sent her sprawling.

"Ouch!" she cried out, as a sharp pain shot up her leg.

Ken, only a few steps behind her, came and knelt at her side. "Are you okay?"

"I–I think I did something to my ankle." Wincing, she rubbed the throbbing joint, trying to ease the discomfort.

"Oh, no." Expelling a pent-up breath, he stood and whisked her up into his arms.

"What do you think you are doing?" she demanded, even as her arms looped about his shoulders.

"Helping you. Someone has to see that you get home, right?"

"No. Yes. Oh, I do not know. But you cannot take me there, Ken. Please, say you will not."

He halted where he was. "Well, how do you expect to get there on your own? Can you put weight on your ankle?"

"I have not tried. You did not give me a chance."

"Hey, far be it from me to keep both of us in the dark." He set her down gently on her good foot, but supported her with both his hands.

Rosa gingerly put her other foot on the ground, then shifted her weight. "Ow. No."

"See?" Ken challenged.

"But this is not good," she moaned. "You cannot take me home. Not yet."

"Too bad your dog isn't a little bigger," Ken quipped. "You could whistle for him and ride him home."

She pouted up at him, but it quickly turned into a smile. "Yes. Too bad."

"So what do we do now?"

"There is a stream not far from here," she said, thinking aloud. "Perhaps if we put a little cold water on it, I would be able to walk soon."

"It's worth a shot, I suppose."

By the time they got to the creek, however, her ankle had swollen considerably. "Not good," she murmured almost to herself. "This is not good."

Ken, holding her injured foot in one hand, cupped his other hand and drizzled water over the swollen ankle. The coolness felt soothing, but Rosa had seen a few sprained ankles in her travels with her grandmother, and she could tell this one was serious.

She could tell that Ken recognized it as well.

He finally looked up and met her gaze. "You do know, don't you, that I am going to have to carry you out of here. Unless you plan on rolling yourself down that hill."

Rosa had to smile. But not for long. "What if you take me only partway?" she suggested. "I could hop the rest of the way myself. Truly."

He gave her a dubious look, but filled his lungs and swept her up into his arms once more.

She draped her arms loosely around his broad shoulders and rested her head there, marveling at his strength.

"Too bad," he muttered.

"What is?"

"Here I have the most beautiful girl in the area in my arms, and she's in too much pain to enjoy it. Then I have to put her down and desert her, wondering how she's going to make it the rest of the way."

"But I am enjoying it," she said, kissing his ear. "And it is not your problem to get me home."

When they came barely within sight of the encampment, Rosa stiffened. "You must put me down now. This is far enough."

"It's nowhere near far enough," he objected.

"Please. You must put me down here. I will be all right."

"I don't know about this, Rosalind. You still have a way to go."

"And I will do it myself. Please. No one must see us together."

"Okay, but I hope you know what you're doing. I feel like a clod, leaving you like this." He set her down, but refrained from kissing her. He ran a fingertip down her nose instead. " 'Til next time, huh?"

" 'Til next time." How she managed to smile, Rosa would never know as she stood there on one foot, the other one throbbing no matter how she elevated it, and watched the man who loved her walk away. She whistled for Maloof, then sank down into the tall grasses to wait for him.

"My, my, my," came a gloating voice, and Nicholas stepped into view from a nearby stand of white birch trees. "What a touching scene. I am sure Abraham will appreciate hearing that his precious granddaughter is consorting with a coal cracker."

𝒢

Her people couldn't be that callous, Ken told himself as he returned to the log for his books. *Surely they couldn't fault a girl for accepting help to get home when she'd been hurt. Even from a miner.* He had serious doubts Rosa would even get home by herself. How fortunate that her grandmother was a healer, though. No doubt she'd have some kind of herbal remedy for that ankle. And next Saturday he and Rosa would laugh over the incident.

Reaching the thicket, he picked up his books and the uneaten peaches they'd forgotten about, then started for home.

He'd spoken truly to her as they ate lunch. He did plan to invite her to dinner soon. One of these days when Ma was in a particularly good frame of mind, he'd tell her about his and Rosa's relationship.

What could happen?

⟡

"What?" Grandfather bellowed as Nick deposited Rosa unceremoniously onto the davenport.

"I said," Nicholas repeated, "that this granddaughter of yours has a lover. From the mines. They meet secretly in the woods."

"He is not my lover," Rosalind cried in her defense. "He is a friend. I met him some weeks ago by accident. We have done nothing. Nothing but talk."

Her grandfather's dark eyes hardened beneath their shaggy eyebrows, and his mustache bulged outward as he pressed his lips into a thin line. "You will not leave this house alone again," he declared in a tone of finality, the fury in his glare shriveling her insides. "I will have no granddaughter of mine keeping company with an outsider."

"But you would not say that if—"

"Silence!" he yelled, and smacked the table so hard with his palm that a glass toppled over and crashed to the floor, scattering broken shards in every direction.

"I told you she needs a husband," Nick said, pressing his advantage. "One who can control her foolishness."

Rosa looked beseechingly to her grandmother, but found only disappointment and uncertainty in her lined face.

"I must think about this," Grandfather announced. "She is home now. We will deal with her foolishness, Eva and I."

Rosa didn't know which hurt more, her ankle or the shock in her guardians' expressions as they escorted Nick to the door and closed it behind him. She fought tears as the loudest silence she had ever experienced filled the house like a smothering fog.

Ken had to admit, David MacNamara was nothing like the concept he'd had of rich folk. Tall and resplendent in a suit that likely cost as much as all their furniture put together, the young man had no superior airs about him. Rather, he seemed at ease in the church service, even taking part in the songs and congregational responses as if he'd always belonged here. His blond wavy hair and patrician features were a fine complement to Hannah's, and the two of them looked. . .right, as they stood together sharing the worn hymnal. During the sermon, he'd shared his Bible with her, an elegant gold-edged version whose pages bore a goodly number of underlined verses and handwritten notes.

Afterward, he brought them all home in his motorcar, which delighted Timmy to no end.

Ma's nervousness was apparent as they neared the house. "Welcome to our humble dwelling," she said self-consciously, trying hard to appear at ease.

David barely gave the place a second look while he helped her and Hannah step out onto the ground without getting grease on their Sunday dresses. "A house is a house. A place to keep the rain off your head. What makes a home is what's inside."

Ken waited for her to elaborate on how the inside wasn't all that much better, but surprisingly, she kept silent as they went in the back door and on through the kitchen, as always.

Hannah had set the table before they'd left for the service, and it looked nicer than it had in a long time, with Ma's only good dishes, the "company" ones. And nary a chip marred the place setting where the honored guest would sit. Fresh wildflowers sat atop the lace tablecloth, and though the napkins didn't match each other, they were crisply ironed and rested beneath shining dinner forks, with knives and spoons positioned properly to the right of the plates.

"Something sure smells good," David commented. "Looks pretty, too."

"And we'll have everything ready in a few minutes," Hannah told him. "Have a seat in the parlor, won't you? We'll call you when it's time to eat."

Tim led the way to the front room, and the three of them sat in silence for several minutes, Ken tapping an index finger on one knee and David smiling politely whenever their gazes happened to collide.

Ken finally thought of something to say. "Has your family lived in Wilkes-Barre long?"

"Yes, actually. All my life. My grandfather built the house we live in now. It passed to us when he died."

"That's sure a swell automobile," Tim remarked.

"Thanks. It's been handy to have around."

"Do you mind if I ask a personal question?" Ken ventured.

"I was wondering when you'd get around to it," David replied good-naturedly.

His attitude brought a grin, and Ken relaxed a fraction. "I was just wondering why you're paying attention to my sister. I mean, you must have your pick of girls with. . .means."

"Perhaps." He met Ken's gaze straight on. "One or two of them might be almost as beautiful, another might be nearly as kind and sensitive, and now and then I find one who loves the Lord and lives selflessly. But only Hannah is all of those things and more. I think the world of her."

"And your parents. Do they approve?"

He shrugged. "They like her a great deal. As far as approving my choice, if you call Hannah that, I need only remind them of our own background and what it took our forebears to provide us with the life we enjoy today. They will respect whatever decision I make."

"I just don't want my sister to be hurt."

"Then, let me lay your concerns to rest, my friend. I have no intention of doing anything to hurt Hannah. I think far too much of her to do that."

Ken gave a nod. "That's all I ask."

Before he probed further, Hannah's smiling face peeked around the doorjamb, the roses in her cheeks the same fragile pink as her dress. "Dinner is on." She reached out a hand to David as he got up, then took him to the dining room, indicating which chair would be his. "Next to me," she added.

He smiled and seated her first, then took his place while the rest of the family did the same.

"We hope you don't mind plain home cooking," Ma said, her nerves getting the better of her again.

"Are you kidding?" David said, a teasing lilt in his voice. "There's nothing finer. If Mother knew her way around a kitchen, we'd have never had to hire someone to do it for us. And your lovely daughter promised chicken and dumplings, my very favorite."

She seemed more secure after that, and as soon as the blessing had been offered, everyone dove in to the tasty fare.

Ken had to admit that David MacNamara acted genuinely fond of Hannah, and he was swiftly wrapping Ma around his little finger, too. The possibility of losing his sister to someone as decent as he suddenly didn't seem so bad after all.

If it ever did come to that.

And when Rosalind came to share a meal with them, would Ma go to the trouble of making everything special and pretty for her, as she had for David?

Chapter 10

The mine buzzed along in full swing on Monday, as if nothing of any importance had occurred the previous week. But the funerals and wakes for the ten unfortunate miners had left a pall hanging over the town. Here and there, black crepe draped a doorway, or a black wreath framed the brass knocker on the front door, and housewives clustered together in hushed conversation, mopping leftover tears with their handkerchiefs.

Still, life would remain constant. New men would be hired to fill the vacant jobs. The sorrowing families would move away and be forgotten.

As Ken walked home after his shift, the smell of the lye soap the women used to do their week's laundry hung heavy in the air. The bluing from discarded wash water mingled with the gray of stove ashes as it trickled along either side of the dirt street. He wondered if life at the Lebanese encampment was so regulated. Wash on Monday, iron on Tuesday... Seems he remembered Hannah in her girlhood jumping rope to a rhyme with those words.

Hopefully, Rosa's ankle had improved by now under the tender ministrations of her grandmother. Despite the extra prayers he'd uttered on her behalf, Ken needed to see for himself that Rosalind was okay. Saturday seemed ages away.

♋

Rosa reclined on her bed amid a pile of stockings to be mended, a chore she detested—just one of several mundane tasks pressed upon her to do while sitting with her foot propped up. Compresses Grandmother had applied to the injury had helped somewhat, but the ankle remained tender to walk on. Her guardians had scarcely spoken a dozen words to her since Saturday, and even if she could have gotten out of the house, she was forbidden to do so. Embittered over that, she clenched her teeth together while she sewed.

At least they had not restricted visitors. This evening Philip came over to chat and keep her company after supper, and their conversation stayed on a general course until Rosa's grandparents went for their nightly stroll on the grounds.

Once the older couple was out of earshot, he lowered his slim frame to sit on the bottom corner of her bed. "So, how are you?" he asked. "I mean truly."

"Miserable. They do not talk to me, they do not even look at me. It is as if I have some disease, and they do not want to become unclean by coming too close. Sometimes I even see them whispering to each other. Secret things they do not want me to hear."

He raised a shoulder. "I hate to say I told you so, Cousin. But you should have expected them to react as they have."

"But they will not let me tell them anything," she said, the pitch of her voice unnaturally high from frustration. "Ken and I did nothing wrong. He was just being my friend."

"The fact that he is an outsider made it wrong, Rosa. You are a young woman now. And very beautiful. One to be desired. It is dangerous for you to stray from our people and be influenced by someone who does not know our ways."

Rosalind closed her eyes with an exasperated huff, then opened them again. "Our ways. Always our ways. Do you know how tired I am of hearing those words? They make my head hurt."

He shrugged, his brown eyes soft with empathy. "How would you like me to go and talk to your grandparents? They still listen to me."

"What good would that do? They are as stubborn as mules when it comes to me."

"Maybe it would help, maybe not. But would you have things continue as they are forever?"

Expelling a tired breath, she shook her head.

"Someone needs to remind them that you love them deeply and have always been loyal to them. That you would never purposely do something to cause them hurt. . .and that they are choosing to take the word of a man who would deceive them to suit his own purposes over the word of their own flesh and blood."

"Do you truly think they will listen?"

He smiled then, his most irresistible of smiles. "How could they not? Why would they not believe their granddaughter's most charming relative? I have not done anything to cause disgrace to my parents."

"Ouch," Rosalind said, narrowing her gaze.

"But neither have you," he went on without missing a beat. "I will make them see that. Somehow."

Rosa continued to look at him while she considered his words. Maybe her cousin really could help. After all, she only needed for her grandparents to give her a chance to explain. She would tell them part of the truth. They weren't ready to know all of it yet. She refused to believe they never would be. "Fine," she said at last. "Do what you can. I trust you, Philip."

He got up and leaned over to kiss her cheek. "For you, Cousin, I would go to the moon and back. I will try to catch your grandparents now, before they finish their walk."

Rosalind hesitated to get her hopes too high, but after Philip left, she put on a more cheerful face and resumed her mending. At least her guardians would see that the quality of her work had not suffered from her *foolishness*.

While she waited, her thoughts drifted to Ken, as happened so often in moments of solitude. Rosalind knew he must be worried sick about her, wondering how in the world she managed to get home on her own. There'd been no way to get word to him. All she could do was think over some of the things he'd said before she'd gotten hurt.

I have no fear of death. I know I will be with the Lord.

What would it be like, not to fear dying? Having lost both her parents before the end of her childhood, Rosa had always viewed death as a cruel enemy, something to dread. She purposely avoided all thoughts of it. But oh, to have the kind of peace Ken displayed.

Setting aside the darning egg with the partially finished stocking, she reached for the New Testament he had given her. Normally she kept it under her pillow, out of her grandparents' sight, so as not to have to explain where she'd gotten it. But Rosalind had already read it through twice, and sometimes as she immersed herself in its passages, she sensed that the peace she yearned for was almost near enough to grasp. She opened to the Gospel of John and read again the fourteenth chapter, meditating on the verses that caught at her heart:

"Lord. . .how can we know the way?"

"I am the way, the truth, and the life: no man cometh unto the Father, but by me."

Rosa then turned back pages to the third chapter and the story of the Jewish ruler who learned that he needed to be *born again.* She focused on verse 16:

"For God so loved the world, that he gave his only begotten Son, that whosoever believeth in him should not perish, but have everlasting life."

Everlasting life, she mused. *There would be no need to fear death. I would like to have such peace. And it says "whosoever." That must include me.* As the light of truth dawned at last in her heart, Rosalind bowed her head and thanked God for sending His Son to die for her sins. And she asked Him to take her to heaven when it was her time to die.

A peace beyond any she had ever experienced flooded her being, and Rosa knew beyond all doubt that she had been born again.

Surprisingly, she no longer wanted to deceive her guardians with half-truths. If they gave her the opportunity to explain her actions, she would tell them what they should know. She would tell them. . .everything.

She did not have long to wait.

The familiar sounds of Grandmother and Grandfather Azar's return drifted to Rosalind as she continued working on the task they'd given her. She heard them exchange quiet words, none of which she could make out.

After a peculiar silence, they came into her room.

Rosa could tell nothing from their demeanors.

Grandfather cleared his throat. "We have not been. . .fair to you, my Rosa. Such anger filled our hearts, such. . .fear that you would betray us, betray our ways, we could not think. Philip is right. You should speak to us, tell us what you wish."

She switched her gaze to her grandmother and received a nod of assent.

"Thank you," she whispered. "Thank you both. I, too, have been angry and afraid. Afraid that you no longer loved me or wanted me. And I love you so much. You are the only family I have known. I would never wish to hurt you."

Her grandfather gave a grudging nod. "Then you will tell truth to us. What you have been doing up in forest, where no one sees."

Rosa put down the stocking she'd been working on and took a cleansing breath to fortify herself. Where to begin? "It has always been my place to go looking for the herbs and plants you need, Grandmother, for your healing shelves. And that has been my purpose each time I have gone there. Have I not returned with whatever you requested and other things besides?"

"This is true," she agreed.

"And I was happy to please you. But one day my path crossed that of a man I did not know, a man from the mines." Noting how her guardians immediately tensed, she forged on, her tone even. "I wanted to run at once, but he told me not to be afraid, he would not harm me. He had only come to the quiet place to read."

"You should have run anyway," Grandfather cut in.

"Perhaps," she consented, "but I did not. He told me his name. Ken Roberts. And I told him mine. And he said he hoped that one day we might meet again."

"That is all?" her grandmother asked, a wave of relief easing the lines in her weathered face.

Rosalind shook her head. "That was the first time. It was by chance."

"So there is more," Grandfather probed, unease adding gruffness to his voice.

She nodded. "I saw him again another day, in a different place from before. And again he had come to read. He had some food with him, and he offered some to me. . .and I was hungry, so I accepted it. And for a short time we talked. Talked of nothing. And this meeting, too, was by chance."

"Then, this is all," her grandmother said, obviously ready to welcome the end of the story.

"Not quite," Rosa confessed. "After that, even if we did meet by chance, we ate together, we talked, and we laughed. We have become friends. He is not like other outsiders. He does not look down on our people. He talks to me about God." Sensing from the pair's granite expressions that they already had enough information to digest, she decided not to elaborate further just yet regarding the progression of the sweet friendship she and Ken now shared.

"And last Saturday," Grandfather said, "when Nicholas saw the two of you together, he saw nothing wrong?"

"No. Nothing. I had fallen and could not walk. Ken wanted to carry me home to you. I was the one who told him no one should see us together. Nicholas must have heard that, and he drew his own conclusions."

"And this is truth," her grandfather reiterated, his stance revealing nothing.

"It is the truth," Rosalind assured him. "Ken is my friend, and I am his."

His gaze never wavered from hers. "I am glad you told this, my Rosa. And I am glad you have done no wrong. But—" His tone turned chilly, and he jabbed his finger into the air to punctuate each phrase. "You will not again go into forest alone. This man did no harm, and I am glad. But he is still outsider, not of us.

You will make friends among our people."

"But—"

"That is all, Rosa. Your grandmother and I have talked. We think maybe time has come for you to marry."

Rosalind's heart thudded to a stop as her guardians exited her room without another word.

They cannot mean it. They just need time to think.

But inside, she knew that instead of making things better by being open and honest with her grandparents, she had just cooked her own goose.

⸎

Ken read another whole section in the engineering textbook as he waited for Rosalind to arrive at the thicket. Noon had come and gone, and there'd been no sign or sound of her or Maloof. He'd finally given into the urging of his stomach for food, saving the second sandwich for her. But it wasn't like her not to show up at all—unless her ankle had been hurt more seriously than either of them realized. He'd expected her injury to heal quickly and not give her further problems.

The sun was well on its downward path now. He glanced at his watch, wondering how much longer to hang around.

Heaving a sigh, Ken closed the study book and switched to his Bible. He hadn't read his daily Scripture yet or had his usual prayer time. He'd take care of those while giving Rosalind a little more time to get here.

But even after reading and meditating on the chapters for the day and praying for Rosa's ankle and everything else that came to mind, he accepted the fact that she would not be along at all.

There were any number of reasons for that, he decided, preferring not to be a pessimist. And no sense letting perfectly good food go to waste. Standing to his feet, he picked up his books and left the thicket, munching Rosalind's sandwich as he walked home.

But he could not ignore the niggling suspicion that something was terribly wrong.

Chapter 11

Rosalind's fledgling faith offered little comfort during the restless days and nights after her grandparents made their intentions known. She could not accept knowing they planned to marry her off. And soon. A gnawing dread deep inside told her that with but one available bachelor in the settlement, it would not take them long to make their choice.

When Philip had gone out to extol her virtues and make peace with them, why had he not also informed them of the things they did not know about Nick? The man's hot temper was known all over camp, but only she and Philip had ever glimpsed the cruel streak he kept so well hidden and the way he delighted in torturing small animals. Even Maloof knew enough to give him a wide berth.

If her guardians cared at all about her happiness, surely they would not subject her to a life with such a man. How long could it be before she began to endure his abuse? She grimaced. The torment would begin immediately, because there was no way on earth she would allow him to claim his husbandly privileges. She would die first.

Her grandparents at last retired to their bedroom and put out their lamp, and soon their faint snores were the only sound in the house other than Rosalind's breathing.

In the dim light of her own bedside lamp, Rosa wanted desperately to pray for help, for guidance, for deliverance, but no words would come. She picked up her New Testament and pressed it to her breast with both hands, hoping that the God who knew all things would make sense out of the rantings of her mind. She belonged to Him now, and He looked after those who loved Him. Perhaps He would protect her, just as He had protected Ken during the explosion at the mine.

A soothing peace began to flow through her as thoughts of Ken pushed aside all morbid fears. He loved her. He hoped to take her to meet his family soon—and if heaven smiled down on them one day, he dared to hope they could make the ultimate commitment.

Recalling the words she'd read in Ephesians regarding God's plan for husbands and wives, she imagined the joy it would be to have a kind husband who would treat her with respect and consideration. It would be a taste of heaven on earth.

The infinitely precious vision wrapped around her like a warm shawl, and her mind filled to overflowing with love for her Welsh miner.

A tangle of phrases began to take shape in her head, and she felt overcome by the need to put them on paper. Somehow she would get it to him. If worse came to worse, and things did not work out as they hoped, at least he would know she loved him. She removed a pencil and tablet from her bedside stand and let all her wishes, hopes, and dreams flow onto the page in a poem of love. The words poured from her heart with scarcely a pause:

To Walk with You in Sunshine

To walk with you in sunshine,
To never have to hide. . .
    To wear displayed upon my face
The love I feel inside;
    To have my hand entwined with yours
For all the world to see. . .
To let it show, how proud I am,
    To have you there with me;
To say your name out loud, my love,
    For anyone to hear. . .
To have my family know and love
    Those things that make you dear

To be there when you need someone
  To listen or to laugh. . .
To share the joys of being whole
  Instead of only half;
To lavish all my love on you
  As long as life shall last. . .
To know a present strong enough
  To blot out all the past;
To let myself be lost inside
  The wonders of your kiss. . .
To fall asleep within your arms—
  I often think of this;
To know at last the warm glow of
  Your body next to mine. . .
To bask in all your gentleness
  Until the end of time;
Such priceless joys, and yet I ask
  Above all else in life,
To walk with you in sunshine,
  To love you. . .as your wife.

When the final line had been completed, Rosalind added a note of regret for not being there to see him and folded the paper, tucking it under her pillow with the New Testament. Then she laid her head down and listened to the night sounds while she waited for sleep.

Awakening later than usual after many sleepless hours, Rosa found the mood in the house to be one of guarded politeness. Gone was the anger, but also missing was the sense of warmth that had been such a part of her life. She felt as if she were a visitor. "May I help with breakfast?" she asked her grandmother.

"There is no need. We are done. Your grandfather is gone already with the wagon."

"He left without me?"

She didn't even look up, but one shoulder beneath the straps of her bibbed apron moved up and down in a shrug. "You were asleep."

Rosa said nothing. She cut herself a slice of bread at the table and spread it with butter and peach preserves, but the first bite tasted like sawdust. When her grandmother's back was turned, she slipped outside and broke the rest into chunks for the birds. After a quick trip to the outhouse, she went back into the cabin.

"Is there something else you would like me to do? Anything you need from the forest? I have been cooped up for days, and my ankle is much better now."

The older woman turned with a look of incredulity and planted a fist on her hip. "You think I would send you up there again? Ever?"

"Not by myself," Rosa replied, "and I understand that. But I thought maybe Philip could come with me when he comes home from his job. We would come right back, I promise."

Surprisingly, her guardian turned to peruse the herb shelves. After thinking for a moment, she relented. "I do not have any more elecampane for fever. If you could find some, that would please me."

Rosa smiled. "As soon as Philip returns, I will look for some, Grandmother." And she rounded the table and gave her a hug. Then, without being asked, she got the broom from where it stood in the corner and swept the house, shook out the rag rugs, and dusted the furniture, anything to keep busy through the long hours until it was time for her cousin to arrive.

At last she saw him get off the wagon he and the others used for traveling to and from their jobs in Wilkes-Barre. She looped the strap of her tote over her shoulder and hurried to meet him.

Philip caught her gaze and waved, his boyishly handsome face breaking into a grin.

"I hope you are not too tired from work," she blurted in a breathless rush, falling into step with him. "Grandmother needs

115

something from up on the hill, and I am not allowed to go alone."

"Oh, so they are speaking to you again," he said. "That is good."

"They are speaking, yes. And thank you for that. But it is not good—at least, not as good as I had hoped."

He searched her face, then placed a hand on her arm and gave a comforting squeeze. "Well, you can tell me all about it while we climb the hill."

"Thank you, Philip. I have always been able to count on you."

As always, others milled about the camp, tending gardens, seeing to afternoon chores. But no one paid Rosalind and Philip any mind as they strolled the length of the grounds and started up the rise.

The late afternoon breeze ruffled through the vegetation in rolling waves, turning it into an ocean of green. Philip plucked a piece of timothy grass and put the end of the long stem into his mouth, then turned to her. "So what is the bad news?"

"My grandparents want to marry me off."

"They have spoken of it before."

"Not like this. I have never seen Grandfather so determined."

"What have you told them about. . ." He gestured questioningly with his hand.

"Ken and me? The truth. That we met by accident a few times and had become friends. Of course, that made Grandfather furious. I am forbidden to see him again."

"Well, I don't see how you could expect otherwise," Philip chided.

"Yes. But I thought if I was honest, they would understand."

"I am sure they *understand,* Cousin." Taking her hand, Philip drew her to a stop and turned to face her, his sable eyes gentle. "Your grandparents love you very much. You are all they have. Hearing that you have become friends with a miner has put fear into their hearts, and they want to protect you from being hurt. You must see that."

Rosalind gave a grudging nod. "But it is not being with Ken that would hurt me; it is keeping me *from* him that causes pain. And I have fear in my heart, too—that they will force me to marry a man I do not love. How could I endure such a life?"

"You would not be the first," Philip said, his tone consoling. He began walking again.

"But I want something better than that," she insisted. "If I am to share my whole life with a man, I want it to be one who will not treat me as his possession, his servant. I want someone who will be tender and loving. Someone who will respect me."

"Then I wish you luck."

Rosa turned to look at him. "Will you respect and honor the woman you marry?"

"To tell you the truth, I never thought much about it until I started listening to you. I would hope to love my wife, as some of my friends at the warehouse love theirs, and not just expect her to keep our home and bear my children. I know that as a man, I have more control over such matters as finding a bride. When I find a woman I have strong feelings for, I will be the one to make the offer. For the women of our people, that is not always the way, I know."

The conviction that her cousin did not hold out much hope for her happiness was more than a little unsettling. "I need to go to the place where I meet Ken," Rosa said, halting him in his tracks.

"What?"

"Do not worry; he will not be there. I have written something for him and want to leave it where he will find it. He must wonder what happened to me, why I have stayed away."

Philip expelled a worried breath. "I hope you know what you are doing, Cousin. Leaving secret messages is not much different from secret meetings." Nevertheless, he went along with her.

The secluded thicket seemed especially charming in late afternoon, with filtered sunlight slanting through the treetops and speckling the ground in spots like golden coins. The sight caught at Rosalind's heart, knowing she would not be there to enjoy sweet times with Ken, and she had to bite the inside of her lip to keep back tears. Reaching into the pocket of her skirt, she took out the folded paper containing the poem and note she'd written and tucked it into the hollow interior of the old log. *I will always love you,* her heart added silently.

"There," she said, straightening to her full height. "He will read it and know that if I could be here to meet him, I would. Now I must find the elecampane Grandmother needs. Help me look. It has a yellow flower."

By the time they found the proper plant and headed home, supper smells floated enticingly on the breeze.

"Food!" Philip said on an exaggerated moan. "I'm famished."

"So am I." Rosalind quickened her pace to match his, and they swiftly covered the remaining distance. She knew her grandmother would be pleased that along with elecampane, she had found a supply of two of her other most used herbs.

"So, Cousin," Philip said, giving a jaunty wave as they reached her house. "I'll see you later, or tomorrow, or whenever."

"Yes. Thank you for coming with me. I—"

The door opened just then, and Nicholas Habib stepped out, a huge smile of triumph on his face. "Ah, the lovely Rosalind, back from her stroll. And just in time to hear the good news."

"What good news?" Rosa asked, dread rising to the fore.

Philip came to stand behind her, his hands on her shoulders.

"Why, the best news of all," he gloated. "I am to be married. And so are you. Your grandfather accepted my offer at last."

Rosa felt all the blood drain from her face.

Chapter 12

Since not having seen Rosalind at the thicket the previous Saturday, it seemed to Ken that the next several days dragged by at a maddeningly slow pace. His mind was so occupied with all possible reasons for her absence and the hope that she'd come to his haven on the weekend, that he had to reread the same text in the engineering textbook a dozen times before it sunk in. He finally gave up and closed the book.

Hannah's light rap on the bedroom door couldn't have been more welcome. "Supper's on," she announced in her airy way.

"Be right down." Ken stood and stretched the kinks out of his back and shoulders, then descended the stairs two at a time and entered the dining room.

Timmy came in through the squared archway from the kitchen at the same time, freshly scrubbed, his white-blond hair slicked back. He grinned and claimed his chair. "Boy, oh boy," he exclaimed hungrily, rubbing his callused, banged-up hands together in anticipation. "Beef stew. Hope it has lots of potatoes."

"That and everything else," Hannah said, bringing in a plate of thick-sliced bread, while their mother set a pitcher of lemonade on the table. They both took their places and bowed their heads for the blessing.

"How'd work at the breaker go today, Runt?" Ken asked after the prayer. He waited for the womenfolk to serve themselves, then pulled the tureen a few inches closer so he and Tim could dish out their portions.

"Same as yesterday, 'cept Andy Demko snitched on two of the other guys for throwin' grease balls. They got 'im back, though. Somebody nailed his lunch pail to the floor, an' when he picked it up, he only got the top half!" He sputtered into a guffaw.

"How terrible," Ma said, frowning.

"That was only part of it," Tim went on. "Somebody else tied his street clothes into knots an' nailed 'em to the wall."

"Tsk, tsk, tsk. Such behavior." Her head wagged back and forth.

His grin sobered. "Well, nobody likes a rat, an' that's what a snitch is."

The story revived some of Ken's own experiences in the breaker, but rather than venture further into that area, he opted to change the subject entirely. "What about you, Sis? Same old grind at the silk mill?"

"Not quite," she replied. "We had an incident there, too. Seems an embossed compact disappeared from Susie Rowland's purse while we visited the lavatory at the lunch break. Nobody saw it happen; but as we were gathering our things at quitting time, the compact fell out of a Lebanese girl's skirt pocket. Of course, the supervisor fired her on the spot."

Ma stopped chewing. "Isn't that just the way with those people? Gypsies have always been nothing but thieves and ruffians."

"Ma! I can't believe you said that," Ken retorted. "Lumping a whole group of folks together and judging them by one individual's actions. And here I thought we were supposed to love our neighbors, as the Lord instructed. Isn't that what you always preached to us kids when we were growing up?"

She had the grace to flush. "Well, some neighbors are easier to love than others."

But Ken wasn't about to let her off so easily. As the oldest son, he was now the man of the house and knew he should speak up. He did his best to keep his voice at a respectful level, however. "You told me you've never personally met any of the folks from Lebanon, isn't that right?"

"Yes, but—"

"Well, I have. In fact, I believe I already mentioned the young woman I met from the encampment on Larksville Mountain. Her name is Rosalind Gilbran. Our paths have crossed several times since that first day, and I've found her to be intelligent, thoughtful, wise, beautiful, and a whole bunch of other things you'd admire. She and I have become good friends. . .and at this point I'm ready to consider taking our relationship beyond mere friendship, if that's in the Lord's plan for us."

Ma's hand flew to her throat. "You can't be serious."

"Actually, I am," Ken said, his tone softening. "What I'm saying is that no one can judge an individual from a distance, without giving her a chance, getting to know her. Just because someone's ancestors come from a different place in the world, that doesn't automatically make him or her worse than anyone else. And the Lord sure doesn't measure us by our roots."

"And you would actually become. . .involved. . .with—with a *heathen,*" she said, her face devoid of color.

"Not *would,* Ma. *Have.* And Rosa is far from being a heathen. She has a very inquisitive mind when it comes to anything pertaining to the Lord. She and I have had many lively discussions about Bible passages. One day soon I hope to bring her to meet you all. I wanted to lead up to this gradually, get you used to the idea, but now that it's out in the open, I guess it's for the best."

For several minutes, no one spoke.

Hannah reached over to give his arm an understanding pat. "Well, except for the Lebanese girls at work, I've never gotten close to a gypsy myself. But I know you, Kenny. You've always been a good judge of character. If you say this girl has all those good qualities, I believe you." Her lips curved into a smile. "And if she's attracted to you, no one can fault her for her taste in men."

Tim remained silent, his gaze moving from Ken to their mother and back.

But Ma's expression never warmed. She just sat rigid, her arms folded across her bosom.

Ken's optimism plunged like a mine cage. He had really believed the tough part would be getting Rosa's grandparents to accept *him.* Now it appeared he would have to win his mother over as well. And that meant he had his work cut out for himself.

Rosalind lay in bed on her side, listening to the supper sounds while her grandparents feasted on delicious-smelling *Fatayr Bi Sbanaka*. But not even for those tasty spinach pies would she emerge from her self-enforced confinement. She had not eaten for two days, despite the protesting of her empty stomach, and had not spoken a word since uttering her refusal to marry Nicholas.

Equally stubborn as she, her guardians had immersed themselves in plans for the wedding. Grandmother declared that a marriage should be performed at the full moon to ensure good luck. Already they were spreading the word and accumulating all the food and wine needed for the celebration feast. But though Nick came by to pay the final amount of money he and Grandfather had agreed upon, Rosa would not leave her room to see him.

There had to be a way to escape her sorry fate, she mused. . . but how to do it when her grandparents never left her alone? Then it came to her. While they were sleeping, before the first light of dawn, she would run away. After all, she knew the surrounding area better than any of her people. No one would know where to begin looking. She wouldn't even be missed for hours.

Rosa remained fully clothed beneath the light blanket and coverlet on her bed. And though she tried to stay awake the whole night, she nodded off several times. But the third time she jerked awake, she cocked an ear and listened to the snores from her grandparents' room. Then, satisfied that they were sound asleep, she stole silently from her room, a rolled-up blanket under her arm. She took a loaf of bread from the bread box and some apples from the basket on the table and tiptoed to the door.

Outside, Rosalind smiled with relief. But she knew she still needed to get away without rousing Maloof or any of the other loose camp dogs that roamed at will and slept wherever they curled up. She scarcely breathed as she moved stealthily away from the settlement and started up the hill. By the time the sun sent its shafts of light over the land, she would be well within the confines of the forest—and from there, she could fly free.

She could barely make out Ken's special place in the dimmest of morning's light when she passed by. But remembering the cave he'd shown her, she concluded that it was the perfect place to hide. No one except the two of them knew it existed—and best of all, she might even spot Ken from there.

It became easier to pick her way through the undergrowth as the light gradually increased. In preparation for her hiding place, she unrolled her blanket and gathered whatever dry leaves and evergreen branches she could find, then bundled them up.

When at last she came to the granite rock, she followed the shallow shelf of land around to the front of it. Just in case some forest creature was using it for a den, she made extra noise. But nothing stirred. So she crept inside the small cavern and set about preparing her bed. She'd forgotten to bring along a container for water, but with so many streams and springs running through the mountains, she figured that to be a minor problem. The main thing was that she had managed to escape. And she would never go back, no matter what.

ℐↄ

Ken showered to wash the bulk of the coal dust off himself in the shiftin' shack at the end of his workday, then hung his dirty clothes on one of the chains suspended from the structure's high ceiling before changing into his other clothes.

Nearby, fellow miner Sandy MacNeil stepped into the coveralls he wore to and from the colliery. "Sounds like we had a wee bit of a close call today," he commented, "on level four."

"Yeah, but at least it was small enough that no one got hurt this time," Ken replied. "It just took them longer to get out."

"Have ye been hearin' the rumors I have, that some o' the guys are robbin' pillars so they don't have to work so hard to fill their buggies?"

Ken nodded. He knew that mine regulations required a

number of pillars of uncut coal to remain in place to support the roof throughout each level. Cutting them too close presented even more hazards to the workers. "I'm just hoping that nobody actually walks off the job, as they're threatening to do. Feelings are still pretty bad over that last explosion and the loss of ten men. What we don't need right now is another strike."

Recalling the hardships his family and others suffered during previous strikes, Ken held out hope that things would not come to that. The old debt at Murphy's store was finally getting within the possibility of being repaid, now that Tim had started bringing in a regular wage and Hannah was receiving those surprising bonuses. A walkout now would put them back where they started.

"Well, Preacher, I guess ye can take the matter up wi' the Lord. Maybe He'll keep us all goin'."

"Right. I'll do that." Plunking his cap on his head, Ken waved and exited the building. After this long day, all he wanted to do was get home and take a real bath. But as he turned, from the corner of his eye he caught a distant blur of color in the woods—a distinctive shade of green that didn't quite fit in. He blinked, and it was gone. *Must have been my imagination,* he decided. Then it appeared again. Someone was up there. *It couldn't be. Rosalind?*

He glanced down at his still grimy hands, the grubby clothes he put on just to come to work and go home in, and he grimaced. He wasn't exactly dressed to go calling. But he sensed that if that truly was her up there, she must have a good reason. He'd better go and check it out.

Knowing that hiking up there from this angle would be no easy task, he angled around to a gentler route. Even though it would take him awhile, at least he wouldn't have to scale that sheer rock drop-off. That would be impossible.

After a lengthy climb through the thickly wooded hills, he finally came within sight of the massive granite formation. "Rosalind?" he called softly in disbelief.

Her head peeked out from the little cave at the base, then the rest of her, and she came running to him like a gazelle. "Ken! I prayed you would come."

He held a hand out to stop her just when she would have thrown her arms around him. "I'm a little dirty at the moment." He looked closely at her, noting dark circles under her eyes. "What are you doing here?"

"I have run away."

"From your grandparents? What on earth for?"

Rosa's arched brows tipped into a frown, and she pouted. "I could not stay there any longer. I. . .want to be with you."

Entirely confused now, Ken kneaded his chin in thought. "Then why didn't you come last Saturday? I hung around the log waiting for you all day, and you never showed up."

"I could not."

She dropped to the ground and sat with her emerald skirt pooling around her and waited for Ken to join her. "My grandparents have forbidden me ever to be with you again," she said, her sable eyes troubled. "And I could not stand that. What is worse, they are arranging for me to marry a man from the camp. Nicholas Habib."

Ken felt as if someone had just punched him in the stomach. Still, he had a strong conviction that he had no right to interfere with the customs of her people.

"Nicholas is mean and cruel," Rosalind continued, "with a violent temper. He was married once before, and his wife died suddenly. No one knows how. I think he is cruel enough that even if he did not cause her death, she would have wanted to die."

Ken took a few minutes to digest this revelation. In his wildest imaginings he wouldn't have come up with something like the tale she had just told him. But what to do? He scratched his head in thought, his cap moving up and down with the movement of his fingers. Then he expelled a ragged breath. "There's only one thing to do."

"What is it?" Rosalind raised her lashes and looked at him, her face shining with hope.

"You have to go back."

"What?" She jumped to her feet. "You would have me go back there? I cannot believe it." Jamming a fist on either hip, she stalked back toward the rock. "I thought you would be glad to see me. That you cared. I thought you would help me."

"Oh, Rosalind, I am glad to see you. You can't know how glad. I've been worried out of my mind, wondering what happened, if your ankle got worse, or what else was wrong."

She stopped and slowly turned back. "But you will not help me."

Ken went to her and cupped her cheek lightly in his palm. "There is no way I *can* help you at the moment, Love. And even if I could, I wouldn't want us to get together this way. It isn't right. It would mean you had to choose me over your own family. They must love you. . .and now they're worried about you, just as I was, wondering what happened, if you're okay."

"But they want to force me to marry Nicholas," she cried. "And I cannot. I will not. He is not kind, as you are. He does not care about the ways of God, as you do and as I have learned to. I could not bear to be with him."

"I know," he said gently, wishing he and his clothes were cleaner so he could draw her into his arms. But since he could not, he focused on the part of her statement that had sent a bolt of joy through him. "You said you have learned to care about God and His ways. If that is true, then you must know He would not want you to dishonor your guardians."

He raised her chin with his index finger. "You have to trust Him now, Rosa, more than ever before. Let Him handle it. He's promised to work our lives out according to His plan. I know He wouldn't want you married to an unbeliever."

"But you do not know just how determined my grandparents are, and they are not listening to the Lord."

Seeing her misery, he sought a way to add comfort. "Try to remember He's promised never to bring us more than we can bear."

She raised her misty eyes to his with a small smile. "Then I will trust Him. I cannot bear to marry Nicholas, so God will have to prevent it. It is His promise. I will do the right thing and go back."

Ken gave an encouraging nod, hoping he wasn't making the worst mistake of his life—and that Rosalind wasn't, either.

Chapter 13

"I'll go with you part of the way, if that will make it any easier," Ken offered, taking Rosalind's hand and walking by her side. Carrying her blanket roll under one arm, she turned her head, and the lashes that masked her eloquent eyes swept up to reveal her trepidation at the thought of facing her grandparents.

Ken felt his own spirit flagging and had to remind himself to be strong for her. He squeezed her tapered fingers. "I'll be praying for you all the time. I promise."

"Thank you," she murmured. "And I will pray also."

He pushed aside some young branches barring their path, and they continued through the tangle of underbrush that so effectively hid the trail. "Did you really mean what you said back at the cave, about learning to care about the ways of God?"

She nodded, but her gaze fell to the ground. "I believe what I have read in the Bible you gave me, and now I, too, have peace about death. And if I am forced to marry Nicholas," she added almost inaudibly, "I would almost wish for it."

The depth of her misery stabbed at Ken's heart. "Please don't say that, Rosa. If I didn't have every confidence that God would take care of you, I wouldn't be encouraging you to go back there."

Her sidelong glance showed no less pain, but she plodded doggedly onward.

When they reached his special thicket, Ken didn't have to tell her they'd come to the parting of the ways. He drew her to a stop, tugging her gently to face him. Their gazes met and held, and for a timeless moment, Ken felt himself drowning in the rich chocolate depths. He had to struggle to breathe.

"Would you. . .hold me?" she pleaded softly. "Just once? In case. . ."

Ken cast a look of disdain at his soiled clothes, his barely clean hands, knowing that if she returned with traces of coal dust on her clothes, it could only make things worse.

"I will wrap in my blanket," she said, as if reading his mind.

The suggestion provided just enough strength for him to muster a smile. "I wish we'd have thought of that before. Look at all the time we've wasted."

Never once releasing his gaze, she shook out the woolen folds and threw it around herself like a shroud, then took the tiny step remaining between them.

Ken enveloped her soft, willowy form in his arms and cradled her there, and his heart melted as her shoulders shook with silent sobs and her tears dampened his shirt. For a heartbeat or two, he racked his mind for reasons to make her go through with this insane plan, when he could just grab her hand and run. They could go someplace far away, where there were no coal mines and no debts and no relatives who refused to understand.

But soon enough, his more rational side won out.

As if she'd sensed the change, she eased from his embrace and offered a brave smile, then turned and walked away, folding the blanket as she went.

Ken sank down onto the log and put his head in his hands, unable even to pray that God would give them *both* the strength to face whatever lay ahead. How long he sat there, he had no idea. But gradually the realization dawned that his family would think he'd gotten hurt if he didn't show up at least by the time Timmy came home from the breaker.

He put a hand down to push himself to his feet, and his eye spotted something white protruding from the hollow part of the log. He bent and picked up the creased paper, then carefully opened it up.

My dearest Ken. . .these are the deepest wishes of my heart.

His legs folded beneath him as he glimpsed the awesome beauty of Rosalind's heart in the poem she'd written him.

To walk with you in sunshine. . .to never have to hide. . . .

He read every line through once, then again, lingering in places that especially touched him.

To let myself be lost inside the wonders of your kiss. . .to fall asleep within your arms—I often think of this. . . .

He felt overcome that she had somehow managed to capture his own unspoken hopes and dreams and express them in every phrase. Truly the two of them were kindred spirits.

But even as the poignant thoughts and phrases sang in his ears, the utter hopelessness of their love taunted him with cruel finality.

In all likelihood, Rosa was lost to him. . .forever.

Grandmother and Grandfather Azar glanced up from their supper, forks poised midway to their lips, as Rosalind came into the cabin.

"Where have you been?" her grandfather demanded, his tone far more gruff than she'd ever heard it in her life. "We have been out of our minds with worry, your grandmother and I."

"I am sorry," she murmured, refusing to be cowed by his fury. "It was wrong for me to run away. That is why I have come back."

"I will inform Nicholas that we will not have to get men together for a search. He will be glad to hear you have returned."

Rosalind moistened her lips and took a deep breath for courage. "I have not come back to Nick. I have come back only to you. I will not marry him. Ever."

Her guardians' mouths dropped open, and their eyes rounded in shock. She had never defied them before.

But Rosa plunged on without giving them a chance to respond. "You can punish me as many ways as you wish, and I will bear it. But I will never be that man's wife. He is mean and cruel and would only hurt me all of our days. You cannot expect me to go willingly to such a life. Not if you love me."

"But we have contract," Grandfather stated flatly.

Rosa held her ground. "I do not care about the contract. I asked you many times—begged, even pleaded—that you would not force me to marry him. But you still went ahead with your plans, with no regard for my wishes. I thought you loved me and wanted my happiness."

"We do, Child." Her grandmother stood and moved to get another plate. "You must be hungry. Come and eat. We will tell you reasons for our choice."

"Nick is good man," Grandfather added. "Has much money saved. He will give you fine home. Make good life for you."

Casting a gaze to the ceiling, Rosa shook her head. "You do not hear me. It is not money I want. It is not the fine home he might give me. It is not Nick I love." And having said that, she decided to get the rest out in the open as well. "I have been reading the Bible and learning about God. I have become a Christian, just like the missionaries who once came to our people in Lebanon.

"I know you are my elders, and I must respect you. But God has even more power and authority over me now, and He says a believer must not marry one who does not believe. Nicholas does not believe in God, nor does he have regard for His ways. If he had, he would be kind and loving, and we would see peace in his eyes. My friend, Ken Roberts, is a Christian, and my heart belongs to him. I am in love with him. . .and if I cannot marry him, then I will stay a maiden all of my life. I will grow old alone. With you or by myself. It does not matter."

"You do not know what you are saying," her grandmother chided, even as she set utensils and a cup at Rosa's place. "This man—this coal digger—has filled your mind with dreams. But he is not of our people. He does not know our ways. Your life with him would soon turn sour." As if they were in the middle of a discussion regarding the weather, she gestured for Rosa to take her chair and eat.

The food looked tempting enough, as always, and to be truthful, the bread she had taken with her had barely seen her through the day, even though she'd found some dried tea-berries near the cave. But with the thought of her uncertain future, the loss of the man she loved, Rosa feared the first mouthful would stick in her throat and choke her. She made no move toward the table.

Her grandfather expelled a heavy breath. "We will give you a few days to change your mind. A young girl thinks her heart will guide her in right way. Soon you will see that we choose what is best for you. I will go tell Nick that you have returned."

Rosalind looked from one of them to the other, astounded by their stubbornness, yet knowing that her own was a perfect match. "I will never change my mind," she said evenly. "Never. I belong to God now, and I shall obey His instructions. You can tell that to Nicholas when you see him." She threw her hands up in disgust and flounced into her bedroom.

As she sank to her bed, she could feel all her dreams crumbling. They would never understand. She would not let them force her to marry Nick. . .but Ken was as good as lost to her, and she to him.

Ken cast a look of despair toward the clouds gathering in the sky, building up to yet another summer storm. The day had been unbearably hot as it was, and the added exertion of climbing and descending that steep hill to see Rosalind after work caused the sweat to pour down his back all the way home. But with all the other rotten circumstances of his life, the added discomfort fit right in. He'd gotten here before the breaker closed down for the night. . .but no bath would wash away the sadness of giving up Rosa. It made his insides ache.

"Hi, Big Brother," Hannah said cheerfully as he went inside. "You're a bit late, aren't you?"

"A bit. Where's Ma?"

"At the store. I found a note on the icebox when I got home. It says she's going by to take some chicken soup to Mrs. Llewellyn on her way back, too. She should be in soon, though."

"No problem. I'll go take my bath so the tub will be free for Tim."

His sister nodded. "Kenny?" she said, stopping him before he got too far. "Could we could talk later? The two of us?"

"Sure, Sis. Anytime."

After supper ended and the dining room and kitchen had been set to order, Ma took her mending basket and sat in the parlor rocking chair, while Tim absorbed himself in the latest stack of comic books he'd borrowed from a friend. Hannah caught Ken's eye on her way to the front porch, and she motioned with her head for him to go with her.

Rain pattered the porch roof and the dirt street as they took seats on rickety wicker chairs that had been in the family forever. Intermittent flashes of lightning turned night to day, a low rumble of thunder shortly following each one.

"What's up?" Ken finally asked.

She breathed in and out for a moment, as if collecting her thoughts. Then she met his gaze. "David asked me to marry him."

Ken leaned forward and relaxed with his elbows on his thighs, his hands dangling between his knees as he watched a jagged fork of lightning in the distant sky. "I kinda thought that's what might happen, eventually. I didn't figure it would be this soon, though. Have you told Ma?"

"Not yet." She laughed softly. "Can't you just see her planning a society wedding, inviting all the high-and-mighty town officials to celebrate her daughter's nuptials?"

He smiled wryly. "I see what you mean."

"For her sake, David thinks we should keep it a small, family affair. Perhaps an evening candlelight wedding on the grounds of his family's estate."

"Has he told *his* parents yet?"

"Yes. They weren't all that surprised, actually. When he began mentioning my name every other paragraph, they began to suspect we were developing feelings for one another." She paused. "Of course, they weren't too thrilled at the prospect, at first. . .the son and heir to the family fortune marrying the daughter of a poor coal miner. But he told me he was prepared for that and lectured them on how their forebears started out in this valley with nothing, even living in a tent. And that it was their honest, hard work that enabled them to succeed and provide the life he and his parents now enjoy. I can just hear him making that speech. . . it's so like him to stick up for the underdog."

Listening to her speak and rejoicing inwardly for her, Ken couldn't help thinking of how much harder it would be for the rest of the family to get by without his sister's income. But he wasn't about to put a damper on her happiness. He'd just take his foreman's test sooner rather than later and hoped that would help make up the difference. After all, he'd pretty well conquered the books Mike Jessup had given him. There was no reason to put it off any longer.

After a few more rumbles of thunder, Hannah spoke again. "I told David that perhaps we should have a long engagement. . . thinking to myself that I didn't want to leave you and Ma and Timmy high and dry. But David had already thought that through, too, bless his heart. He wants to have a little cottage built on the same grounds as our home for Ma and Tim. That way, Tim will be able to go back to school."

Ken realized how much lighter it would make his own responsibilities, not to worry about providing for the rest of the family. He knew there was no way he could hope to offer them such a promising future just now. The thought of God's indescribable goodness humbled him. . .yet one could not overlook his mother's pride. "How do you think Ma will feel about that? Taking charity and all."

Hannah sighed. "Well, I've done some thinking of my own. You know how she's always loved planting flowers and things. And nobody in the world is a better cook. I'll probably need help running a big house and looking after a flower garden. She'd really be helping *us*. And Timmy could keep up the grounds for us. Anyway, David says there's no sense in having money if you can't do something good with it. I think Ma will come around."

"Put that way, I'd say you're right. . .but I'd still take it slow if I were you. Give her a chance to get used to the idea a little at a time."

Nodding, his sister smiled. "God has blessed me beyond my wildest dreams," she murmured. "I never would have imagined when I applied for that housecleaning job, that one day the boss's son would sweep me off my feet and propose to me. Funny how things happen."

"Yeah. I'm real glad for you, Sis. Couldn't be happier." *Really, I couldn't,* his mind added as a pang of sadness at the thought of Rosa assailed him.

A brilliant flash of lightning barely faded before a thunder crack rattled the house.

"Things are getting a mite close," Ken said, getting up. "I think we'd better go inside."

"I think so, too. But thanks for letting me ramble. I needed somebody to talk to."

"Anytime, Sis. Anytime."

"What were you two doin' out there?" Tim asked as they came in from the porch. "Tryin' to get fried?"

"Just watching the storm, is all," Ken told him. "Tomorrow it won't be so hot out."

"That'll be a relief," Ma injected.

Ken nodded, then flicked a glance around the room. "Well, it's been a long day, and I'm kinda tired. Think I'll turn in now. 'Night."

"Good night," the others said as one.

Slowly climbing the stairs to the back bedroom, Ken marveled over how the Lord had worked things out for Hannah by bringing a really decent Christian guy into her life. David not only loved her, but he would provide an easier life for her—and none of them expected that. But it was hard to figure which one would be getting the better end of the deal, her or David, because Hannah was a prize in her own right.

Oh well, he thought as he undressed and changed into pajama bottoms, at least someone in the family would be finding happiness. Right now he didn't hold out much hope of it ever being him, unless something happened to soften the hearts of Rosalind's grandparents.

Chapter 14

At the cost of a day's work, Ken got the approval from his boss to go to Scranton, eighteen miles away, to take the state test for his section foreman's papers. He hadn't had time to attend more than a handful of the night classes offered in engineering, algebra, and surveying, but with Hannah's upcoming marriage to consider, he couldn't see delaying taking the test any longer. He'd studied hard at home and felt confident that he'd do well.

Dressed in his Sunday suit and tie, he caught the trolley into Wilkes-Barre. From the train station on Pennsylvania Street, he took the Laurel Line to the bustling city of Scranton. There, official state buildings housed the government offices regulating the labor and mining industry.

Yesterday's rains had intensified the lush greenery along the route, adding incredible beauty to the panoramic vistas beyond the train's windows. But even with his mind occupied with factors, formulas, and diagrams, Ken appreciated the opportunity to observe new sights.

Hours later, the intensely detailed test behind him, an optimistic Ken returned home to wait for his test results to be processed. Assuming he'd passed, an official certificate would be issued in due time, and then he'd be available to step into the next opening for a section foreman. That would mean a much needed increase in salary. But somehow, even a victory such as that seemed lusterless if he couldn't share it with Rosalind.

He had to wonder how she had fared with her grandparents, how they had responded to her return. . .and what the outcome would be regarding Nicholas Habib. Even as the train sped toward Wilkes-Barre, he offered another prayer that something would soften her guardians' hearts.

The next morning, quite rested after the extra day off, Ken left for work earlier than usual. On his approach, a loud commotion near the motor house drew his attention. He didn't give the matter too much importance, since an occasional difference of opinion between workers sometimes resulted in a minor scrap that ended about as quickly as it began. Nevertheless, he gravitated over to watch.

Elbowing his way through the cheering throng of onlookers, however, he realized it was more like a heated brawl than it was a mere fist fight. "What's going on?" he asked a familiar face.

A string of colorful words that shriveled Ken's ears preceded his answer. "Some bloke tried to blow the place up."

"What?" Ken gasped.

"But we got the coward good," the man went on. "A couple of guys lit into 'im and took 'im for a ride. Now they're finishing the job. That should teach 'im not to mess with us."

Relieved that the plan had been thwarted, Ken still pitied the guy. A newcomer who mouthed off or got too big-headed for his own good would be shoved into the cage, and the operator would then send it on a drop so fast, the poor soul's feet wouldn't touch the floor until the contraption stopped just before it hit bottom. Usually it scared the offender half to death. It also resulted in a rather swift change of attitude.

"Serves the jerk right," another voice added. "Dirty gypsy. They're all a bunch of tramps and thieves."

"Gypsy?" Ken asked in alarm. He knew of no men from the encampment who worked for Hudson Coal Company, yet for some unknown reason one of them had come to sabotage the mine. This was no meaningless little tiff. The miners were out for blood.

He pushed through to the fray. "Hey, you guys. That's enough," he hollered above the melee and began yanking men one by one off the bloodied offender who lay writhing and moaning and nearly unconscious at the bottom of the heap. "Come on. Let up.

You've made your point."

"Aw, Preacher-boy, we were just gettin' started," one of the last attackers groused. "He was out to get us. Who knows how many mighta been killed?"

"Yeah, well, it looks like he didn't get to do any real damage. There's no need to murder him."

"He's right," someone else said. "No sense gettin' the police involved. It'll be a cold day in Hades before the wretch shows his ugly mug around this place again. Let's get to work, or we'll never get our cars loaded."

The mumbling crowd quickly dispersed to the shiftin' shack, the key shack, the motor house, and other job sites, until only Ken remained at the injured gypsy's side.

He went to see about borrowing the ambulance wagon and brought it around. Then, since no one had stayed around to help, he hefted the battered man's dead weight into the wagon bed himself. After covering him with a much-used blanket, he headed for the Lebanese camp, keeping the horse's pace as slow as possible so as not to cause further pain. Even so, the most insignificant rut in the road caused agonizing moans.

Some children playing on the outskirts of the settlement were the first to give the alarm as Ken and the wagon approached. By the time he reached the entrance, dozens of wary-faced inhabitants had gathered to see what was happening. He nodded to them and halted the horse. "I'm looking for your healer. I have an injured man in back."

A dark-skinned man moved to peer inside. "It's Nicholas Habib!" he informed the others. "Go and get Eva Azar."

Ken recognized the victim's name immediately, and suddenly an understanding of his motive became obvious. Habib's intended attack on the mine was revenge for his own involvement with Rosalind Gilbran. It had to be. Nothing else made sense.

A small crowd milled about, many of them talking among themselves in their foreign tongue. Ken remained in the wagon seat, his eyes searching the faces. Then he saw her. Rosalind, helping an older woman hobble down the lane from the cabin farthest away. His heart leapt, but he schooled his expression to remain calm. He didn't want to do anything that might cause problems for Rosa.

She met his gaze at the same time and drew her lips inward, as if restraining a smile.

"What is wrong?" the gypsy woman asked when she and Rosa arrived at the wagon. She lifted the blanket to assess the extent of Nicholas Habib's injuries.

Ken kept his voice even. "Somebody caught him trying to set off a charge of dynamite at the mine. It, uh, kind of upset some of the men."

"Bring him to his cabin," she said. "I will tend him there."

"Yes, Ma'am," Ken said, and clucked the horse into motion as bystanders led the way.

The short distance to the ramshackle dwelling took only another minute or so, and there was no shortage of help to carry the culprit to his bed, with Mrs. Azar rattling off a list of instructions the whole time. Once he was inside, she turned her black eyes up to Ken. "It was. . .good of you to bring him to us. Few of your people would have done so. Thank you." She then gave a nod of dismissal and started to turn away.

Rosalind stayed her by putting a hand on her arm. "Grandmother. . .I would like you to meet Ken Roberts," she said softly, chin high, her sable eyes luminous.

Ken held his breath as the old woman's graying eyebrows hiked in surprise. For the briefest second, her guarded expression softened as she looked astutely from him to her granddaughter and back.

"Ken, this is my grandmother, Eva Azar," Rosa continued. "She knows of your name."

Ken relaxed a notch and gave her a reserved smile. "It is my pleasure to meet you, Mrs. Azar. I've heard of your wonderful gift for healing. I'll pray for your friend, that he'll be well soon."

"I will do my best," she replied. "Thank you again for bringing Nick to us." With a gracious bow of her head, she turned and shooed Rosalind toward home, then went inside Habib's cabin.

Ken caught Rosa's secret smile as she acquiesced to the wishes of her elder and started up the incline to their dwelling.

And for just a second, he felt God smiling down on both of them.

Except for the brief trip her grandmother made to their home for healing herbs and other items she needed, Rosalind hardly glimpsed the older woman for two days. As an unmarried girl, she was not permitted to aid in the tending of a seriously injured man. . .nor would she have attempted to go to Nick's cabin for any other reason.

Finally, at suppertime on the third day, her guardian returned and put her medical supplies back into all the proper places. Rosa said nothing, despite her curiosity, but quietly set three places instead of two. After putting out coffee cups, she brought the fried fish and browned potatoes she had cooked to the table.

Grandfather was the first to speak when he came in to join them for the meal. "You are home, my Eva. How is Nicholas?"

She cast a glance to Rosa and on to him. "Doing better now. His eyes are no longer swollen shut, but still black. His ribs will take time to mend. He is missing two teeth and has many other cuts and bruises. Everywhere."

With a nod, he sliced into his fish and sampled it, withdrawing a fine bone from his mouth.

"It was a foolish, wicked thing he tried to do," Grandmother continued. "Nicholas is pigheaded as always." She wagged her graying head in disdain. "And I am beginning to believe what I have heard about his temper."

Grandfather shrugged a shoulder. "A man must do as his honor tells him."

"Honor!" she huffed. "What honor is there in setting out to kill others who do not even know him? It is no wonder our people have no respect from outsiders. What Nicholas did was criminal."

He made no reply.

"Ken Roberts showed great mercy to bring him here," Rosa ventured.

"And I have many thoughts about that," her grandmother admitted. "Other miners would not care if Nick lived or died. I wonder what they think when one of their own showed kindness to a man who would destroy them?"

"I told you Ken is not like the rest," Rosa said evenly. "He loves God, and he has love for others also. He does not judge a man by the country where he was born." Neither of her guardians interrupted, so she plunged on. "He is kind and thoughtful…and a hard worker. He has a mother and two others in his family to support. His father and older brother died in the mines."

"It was good thing, that he sees Nicholas got home," her grandfather conceded. "I have respect for outsider who would do that."

"See, Grandfather?" she said sweetly. "Not all outsiders are bad. Maybe we could invite him to supper and thank him."

But she could tell from his expression that she'd best drop the subject and go back to eating.

☙

Ken got up from his knees after his nightly prayer and climbed into bed. Since seeing Rosalind for those few moments at the Lebanese camp, a seed of hope had taken root. It had been four days since he'd delivered Nicholas Habib to his people. And tomorrow, his day off, he would go there and inquire after him. Surely they would not fault someone for showing concern for another man.

The next morning, bright and early, he gulped down his breakfast and rushed through the chores. Then, not bothering to take a lunch, he hiked up into the woods and down into the encampment, approaching it from the high end this time. He'd seen Rosalind and her grandmother exit the topmost dwelling just before coming to Nicholas Habib's aid. He'd try there first. After all, Habib wasn't the person he most wanted to see.

Striding around to the front door and finding it open, he tapped lightly on the frame.

Rosalind answered. "Ken!" she choked out, her eyes huge, her mouth gaping.

"Hello, Rosa. Is your grandmother at home?"

"Yes. Wait there. I will get her."

Ken could tell from the tightness of her voice that she was more than a little surprised and nervous. But he maintained what he hoped resembled calm confidence.

In seconds, the old woman appeared at the door.

"Good day, Mrs. Azar," he said. "I hope you remember me. Ken Roberts. I've come to ask after your friend, Mr. Habib. Is he well?"

"He is doing better," she replied, "but not well enough for a visit."

"That's fine. He probably wouldn't want to see me anyway. I just wanted to find out how he's doing. I've been praying for him, as I said I would."

"That is. . .nice. You are kind, for a. . . ." She closed her mouth, leaving the sentence unfinished.

"A miner?" he supplied optimistically.

"Yes. A miner."

Rosalind moved up to her guardian. "Grandmother, it is very warm today. Should we not invite Ken in for a cool drink of water?"

She appeared to consider the suggestion momentarily, and then her demeanor softened. "We will do better than a drink of water. It is noon, time for dinner. If you would join us, you would be welcome. My husband will also be here."

Ken took the last comment as a warning but concentrated

on the invitation. "I would be honored to eat with you and your family."

She stood aside while he entered, then gestured to the sofa. "Be seated, please. My granddaughter and I will put food on."

Delectable smells already permeated the interior of the small cabin. Seated in the tiny parlor, Ken glanced around at the homey furnishings, the interesting rows of jars on the wall shelves in the kitchen. . .and beautiful Rosalind, whose face positively glowed with hope and barely contained happiness as she worked. Her every movement was like that of a graceful dancer. Now and then she would steal a look his way with a shy smile.

When her grandfather stomped his boots on the outside mat and came in, Ken stood to his feet.

The old man paused at the sight of him and narrowed his eyes.

Rosa quickly came forward. "Grandfather, this is Ken Roberts. He has come to ask after Nick."

"And *I* invited him in," her grandmother added purposefully.

At that news, his stance eased slightly.

Rosa let out a barely discernable breath of relief and turned to Ken. "Ken, I would like you to meet my grandfather, Abraham Azar."

"It's a great honor to meet you, Sir," Ken said, extending his hand. "Some of my friends have told me of the fine goods they have purchased from your wagon."

After a slight hesitation, the peddler grasped his hand and shook it politely.

"The food is ready," his wife said. "Come to table now."

Rosa indicated which chair Ken would be using, and after seating her, he took his own, while her grandparents took their seats.

"Ken likes to pray before he eats," Rosalind announced. "If that is all right." She looked from one guardian to the other.

"Is fine," Mrs. Azar said, and they bowed their heads.

"Our dear Father in heaven," he began, "we thank You for Your wondrous goodness and love for us all. Thank You for this loving home and all who dwell here. Please bless this food You've provided and the hands that prepared it. May Your blessing rest upon us all this day. In Jesus' name, amen."

"Amen," came Rosa's whisper.

"This sure looks delicious, Mrs. Azar," Ken remarked, observing the attractive assortment of food before him.

When Rosa passed the garden salad, their fingers touched. . . followed by their gazes. Then they quickly broke eye contact.

A platter of roast chicken came next, and after that, some cooked greens Ken didn't recognize. He took some anyway and found them to be tasty. Sliced fresh peaches and warm bread came last of all.

Mr. Azar cleared his throat. "Do you work long in mines?"

"Seems like forever," Ken admitted. "My father was a miner, and when he was killed, I had to step into his shoes. But someday I hope to work in a different field."

"Which field is that?" Rosa's grandmother asked.

Ken smiled. "I've been studying engineering lately. And the more I read, the more challenging it sounds, to build roads and bridges and design buildings. The coal mines won't last too many more years, since many people are converting to gas and electricity for heat and fuel. All the miners will need to find different work then."

Mr. Azar, regarding Ken intently throughout the meal, merely nodded in thoughtful silence.

After clearing his plate, Ken barely had room for the baklava that Rosalind served while her grandmother poured strong coffee into each of their cups. But remembering how much he'd enjoyed those honey pastries, he gladly took one and smiled his thanks.

All too soon the meal was over, and Ken knew it was time to take his leave. He stood and offered Mrs. Azar his hand. "I thank you, gracious lady, for the delightful meal. It was so kind of you to invite me to have dinner with you." His glance included all of them. Then he held out his hand to Mr. Azar and was relieved that there was no hesitation this time before the man clasped it warmly.

"It was good. . .your help for Nick," the old peddler said.

"May I see Ken to the door, Grandfather?" Rosa asked.

He nodded, but not without reservation.

She kept her distance as they crossed the room. "I am glad you came," she murmured as he stood in the opening. Her sable eyes said far more than that, but their message remained unspoken. "Take care."

"You, too, Rosa," he said, his chest burning with words that could not be spoken. "God be with you."

Ken's hope went up another notch, and his spirit overflowed with silent praises as he left the dwelling. But before he got very far, he sensed someone following him. He glanced around. Abraham Azar. Ken halted and waited for the old man's approach. "Sir?" he said politely.

The peddler's bearing indicated he had something to say, but it took a moment before he spoke. "It was good of you to care about Nicholas. We do not condone his act. Any of us. But. . .it would be better if you did not come back again."

Ken's spirit deflated and plummeted to his feet. He retained just enough composure to nod. "As you wish. God be with you and your family." Without another word, he pivoted and left the encampment.

And Rosa.

Chapter 15

Two weeks later, Ken brought home a paper that had been sent to the Hudson Coal Company office and presented to him by his boss. He handed it to his mother and waited for her to read it.

"You've made assistant mine foreman on the first try?" Ma's face beamed as she perused the official certificate with its gold seal and dignitaries' signatures. "We'll have to get a nice frame and hang this on the parlor wall."

"Yeah," he said, trying not to look too proud. "As a section foreman, I'll have forty or fifty guys working under me, once an opening comes up. Not to mention a nice raise. Our bill at Murphy's will be history pretty quick after that."

She shook her head in wonder. "I don't know what to say. For so long we've barely had two nickels to rub together, and soon...I know your pa would've burst his buttons. We'll have to celebrate. While you take your bath, I'll run down to the store and get some ice cream for after supper. Sound good?"

"Sounds great, Ma." He bent and kissed her cheek. The only thing that would have crowned the day would have been to share the good news with Rosa. But the only possible way now would be to leave her a message in the log, come Saturday. The thought brought little consolation as he headed down to the tub.

The weekend arrived at last. Ken couldn't remember a more glorious mid-August day. Quickly getting his chores out of the way, he whipped off a quick note to Rosalind and tucked it into his pocket. Then he set off for the woods, not bothering with books or a lunch. It would be a short trip. Even his haven had lost its charm now that he had to spend his time there alone. One of these days he'd seek out another nice spot, one that didn't make his heart ache just being there. The only thing that kept him going back was the slim hope that he and Rosa could maintain some semblance of contact by way of messages. But her poem had been the only attempt she'd made. He wondered how long it would be before she'd find the note he'd leave today.

He hoped things had changed for the better for her since he'd delivered Nicholas home after the mine incident, and he wondered if her grandparents were still adamant about marrying her off. If so, perhaps the rascal's despicable conduct would compel them to use more caution in choosing a possible husband for their beloved granddaughter, at least. . .even if it had to be some other Lebanese man.

Ken appreciated the hospitality they'd shown him when he'd called to inquire after Nick. If only he could have gone back a few times, showed up often enough to give them a chance to get used to him. . . . He let out a ragged breath.

Preferring not to dwell on life's disappointments, he focused instead on the good things happening in his life. His new job responsibilities would start in the near future. Hannah was planning a late September wedding, and soon Ma and Tim would have an easier life. He'd imagined the house would seem empty without his sister, but if her plans for Ma and Tim panned out, he'd be the only one left at home. That would take some real getting used to. Funny how things worked out.

Just outside his thicket, Ken almost stepped on a young rabbit in the path. He stood still and watched the timid little creature hop away into the brush, its little white tail bouncing.

When he turned his attention forward again, his heart lurched.

Rosalind sat on the log, her violet skirt draped over its contours, an incredibly dreamy smile on her lips. "Hello."

"I wasn't expecting to find you here," he said inanely, trying to gather his wits.

"As I recall, that was my line not too long ago," she said teasingly, a glorious light sparkling in her eyes.

He glanced around them, toward the encampment, not wanting to cause her any trouble.

"It's all right," she said, her gold bracelets tinkling as she fluttered a hand. "I have permission to be here."

"Maybe. But. . .with me?"

She nodded. "You made quite an impression on my grandmother. So much so, that she took my side against Grandfather for the first time in my whole life. She's been your champion ever since. He finally gave up and tore the marriage contract he made with Nicholas into shreds. He has agreed to allow us to be friends. And more than that. . .if you still care."

"If I still. . ." With a smothered moan, he reached for her, and she rose into his open arms. "My beautiful Rosa," he said huskily, crushing her to himself. "Even with all my prayers, my faith was too weak to believe this would ever happen."

"Mine was not," she said, smiling up to him. "I would have waited forever for you. I am just glad it did not take quite that long."

Those luscious lips were far too tempting to resist. Ken leaned his head down and claimed them, and his heart soared higher than the tallest trees. When he finally drifted back to earth, he cradled her face between his palms. "Then we have only one bridge left to cross. Tonight you will have supper at my house."

"Are you sure?" she asked, her expression doubtful.

"Absolutely. We'll let your grandparents know first, though, so they won't worry. I sure don't want to start off on the wrong foot."

❦

Rosalind sensed more than a few inquisitive gazes as she and Ken walked hand in hand down the length of his street. She had no idea which house was his, but when he turned at the next to the last one on the left, her heart hammered in her throat. Would his family receive her with at least half the warmth with which her guardians had welcomed Ken this day? Such a miraculous change. Her heart swelled at God's power to turn things around. She hoped and prayed He had been at work in Ken's family, too.

She closed her fingers more tightly around the bouquet of wildflowers she'd picked along the way and checked to see that the gathers of her embroidered blouse looked neat. His encouraging squeeze came just at the moment she would have taken flight, and it eased her disquiet as she accompanied him to the back door.

Rosa tried not to gawk too much at the interior of the kitchen as they entered, but couldn't help noting how tidy and efficient it was, how modern. And such a lovely stove. How Grandmother would love it.

A fair-skinned young woman of slight build looked up from cutting biscuits. She wore her hair in a fashionable loose topknot, and her face bore a close resemblance to Ken's. Her eyes, however, were not the silver-gray of Ken's, but azure like the sky. . .and friendly.

"Hannah," Ken said, "I would like to introduce Rosalind Gilbran. Rosa, this is my sister, Hannah."

She brushed her floury hands on her half apron and smiled as she reached out to Rosalind. "Please forgive me for being such a mess. It's nice to meet you, Rosalind. I've heard quite a lot about you."

"Thank you," she murmured. "I am glad to meet you, too."

"Where's Ma?" Ken asked.

"She just went upstairs. She'll be down in a second."

The words were barely out of Hannah's mouth before an older woman of similar build came in from the next room. Seeing Ken and Rosa, she blanched and stopped dead, her blue eyes wide with shock.

"Ma," he said, unperturbed, "I've brought Rosalind Gilbran to meet you. Rosa, I'd like you to meet my mother, Elen Roberts."

Rosa swallowed, then hesitantly offered the colorful bouquet. "I am honored to meet you, Mrs. Roberts."

Ken's mother swept a quick glance over her, then equally reserved, accepted the flowers, her demeanor gradually taking on gentler lines. "Thank you."

She reached into her skirt pocket and drew out a small packet. "I have also brought some mint sprigs for your tea. And my grandmother has made an embroidered cozy for your teapot."

She accepted the gifts with the graciousness Rosa had hoped and even seemed pleased at the beauty of the intricate design Grandmother had stitched so carefully. "Why. . .thank you. That's very nice of you. Both of you."

"You are most welcome."

"I've invited Rosa to have supper with us, Ma," Ken announced. "We'll be in the parlor." And with that, he led her through the dining room and into the larger room at the front of the house, where comfortable chairs and a large upholstered sofa faced each other from opposite walls. Rosa admired the floral-patterned rug occupying the center of the wood floor, then turned her attention to framed photographs on the walls and lamp tables.

"Pretty wild-looking bunch, huh?" Ken said teasingly.

"Not at all. Your family looks. . .kind."

He nodded. "They are, too, for the most part. Even Ma. So don't worry so much, just be yourself."

"Are you sure she will not hate me?"

"Quite. You're just, well, different. She takes awhile to get used to the unfamiliar. But once she does, nobody in the world will change her mind." He turned the radio on and twisted the dial to one with quiet music, then dug out another album of pictures and brought it to Rosa. "This is a picture of my pa, and next to him is my older brother, Matt, who died with him. . . ."

When Hannah called them to supper half an hour later, Rosa saw that a lace tablecloth had replaced the checked oilcloth she'd seen earlier in passing, and china dishes with blue flowers sat at each place. A glass vase in the center held the bouquet she'd brought. She met Mrs. Roberts's eyes and smiled shyly, receiving one in return.

Ken introduced Rosa to Tim, who looked a little frozen in place as he uttered a quiet hello. Then Ken seated her and asked the blessing on the food and their gathering. His calm voice instilled her with badly needed confidence. And the meal began.

"Ken tells me that during your visits, the two of you talked about the Lord, Rosalind," Mrs. Roberts said, dishing out some mashed potatoes and passing the bowl on to Hannah.

"Yes, that is true. I did not know much about God until I met your son. His strong faith and his kindness made me want to come to know the God he loved. After Ken gave me a Bible and I read about Jesus for myself, I became a believer. I am still amazed at the peace inside me."

"And your. . .family? I believe Ken said you live with your grandparents."

She smiled and nodded. "I am still working on them. I think Grandmother will soon come to know God. Grandfather is much more stubborn. But he has a good heart and a good mind. I am praying that in time he, too, will understand and believe."

"It didn't take the two of them long to realize what a prize chap I am," Ken said with a mischievous grin, and everyone laughed.

Rosalind was amazed at how quickly the conversation warmed after that, as Tim related some amusing experiences at the breaker and Hannah related plans for her upcoming wedding. Rosa finished her peas and carrots, then enjoyed another sip of lemonade.

"Would you care for more roast beef?" Ken asked, passing the platter.

"No, thank you. I cannot eat another bite. It was very delicious, Mrs. Roberts. I have often enjoyed your cooking."

"How is that?" she asked, her face questioning.

"Ken shared his lunch with me when we visited."

She chuckled. "I wondered where he was putting all that food."

Another laugh made the rounds.

Despite her reluctance to eat more, Rosa managed to sample a small portion of the delicious strawberry shortcake Hannah made with the sweet biscuits she'd been working on at their arrival.

"Well," Ken announced at last, "daylight's fading pretty fast. Time I take my beautiful lady home."

Rosa stood and bowed her head graciously at Ken's mother. "Thank you so much for allowing me to enjoy a meal with your family. I enjoyed meeting all of you, and I wish you God's best blessings."

"It was nice to have you here, Dear," Mrs. Roberts said sincerely. "And from what our Ken tells us, we'll be seeing a lot of you from now on. That'll give us all a chance to hear more about you and your life before you met Ken."

The walk home to the encampment never seemed shorter. Ken switched on a flashlight when the path became too dim to see their footing, but Rosa knew she couldn't have tripped over anything. Not with Ken's firm grip on her hand.

"Do you really think she liked me?" she finally had to ask.

"Ma? Oh, yeah. But how could she not?" Sliding an arm around her waist, he kissed the top of her head. "Now me, on the other hand. . ." He stepped in front of her and wrapped his other arm about her. "I will always love you, Rosa Gilbran."

"And I love you." She raised her lips to his and reveled in the tender reverence of his kiss, one that deepened as they clung together for a breathless moment. "Mmm," she sighed as they drew apart and continued walking. "It is as I wished, but hardly dared to dream."

"What is?"

"To let myself be lost inside the wonder of your kiss. . ."

He smiled, hugging her against himself. "I hope you know

that I intend to make the rest of your beautiful poem come true, too, my love. That is. . .if you truly will do me the honor of becoming my wife."

"The honor will be mine," she murmured. "The answer is yes. I could ask for nothing more." She rose to tiptoe and kissed him with more abandon.

When they eased away, Ken's expression turned serious. "You know, even though our families may be ready to accept the thought of our being a couple, not everyone we meet will be so gracious. But with the Lord's help, we'll face them, you and I. Our days of hiding in the shadows are over. From now on, we'll walk together in the sunshine, for all the world to see."

She raised her trusting eyes to his and smiled.

And once again, as he took her hand, Ken felt God smiling down on them.

Sally Laity has written both historical and contemporary novels, including a coauthored series for Tyndale House, numerous Heartsong romances and Barbour novellas, and a coauthored series for Barbour. She considers it a joy to know that the Lord can touch other hearts through her stories. She makes her home in Southern California with her husband of over fifty years and enjoys being a grandma and great-grandma.

The Train Stops Here

by Gail Sattler

Enjoy Your
Bonus Story

Chapter 1

L ouise Demchuck pulled her sweater tighter and wrapped her arms around her body to protect herself from the chill of the spring wind as she stood beside the set of parallel tracks. She stared down the metal lengths, searching for the familiar sight of her father sitting on the front of the jigger while the section gang seesawed its double handles, propelling them toward the station. The never-ending lines extended into the distance until they disappeared with the miles. Not detecting any motion, and since the storekeeper's children were not playing outside today after their return home from school, she strained her ears for a hint of sound but heard only the rustling leaves, singing birds, and chirps of the crickets.

She gathered her skirt and ran back to the house. "I don't see Papa or the section men, Mama."

Her mother stirred the soup and sighed. "I suppose the jigger was switched onto the siding, and they'll wait until the train passes. How long will this one stop?"

Louise hurried into the dining room to her father's desk. She ran her finger down the paper with her father's notes of the daily train schedule, which lay in the middle of the desktop, then glanced up at the clock on the wall. If the section gang didn't have enough time to return to the station and get the jigger off the track before the freight train came, then they would have to wait until the train departed before they could return home.

"The 6:15 is a freight train today, so it won't be leaving again until 7:00. I wonder if there will be any hobos on this one."

Even from her papa's desk at the front of the dining room, Louise heard her mother's spoon land with a clatter against the metal top of the cookstove in the kitchen. As she knew would happen, her mother's footsteps approached. Louise turned to the doorway between the kitchen and the dining room, and as expected, her mother soon appeared.

Her mother stood glowering at her, arms crossed over her apron. "We do not call them hobos. They are people—people whose lives have met with grave misfortune—from all walks of life, some older than your father, and some the same age as you. They are not traveling for pleasure, or they would be on the passenger train, paying their fare. These are desperate men, Louise. I pray that our family will never be faced with whatever terrible things forced those men to abandon their families and head for parts unknown in the faint hope of finding food and lodging."

Louise's throat tightened. It was true. Many people were out of work. Even for those who maintained their jobs, everyone was spending less money on everything, including food.

With Papa being the section foreman for the railroad, their family had been provided with a comfortable home. Their family maintained the most stable and largest income in their small community.

"You are right, Mama. I hadn't meant to be insulting. It's just that everyone calls them hobos. Even Pastor Galbraith. I didn't mean anything hurtful or mean to speak poorly of anyone."

Her mother shook her head. "It's easy to pass them off by speaking of them in such a way, but the city people don't see the suffering in their eyes like we do. Not even Pastor Galbraith."

Louise nodded and turned to look out the window. The train was due in seven minutes, and without doubt there would be homeless men hiding on it. Some would be riding on top of the cars to avoid being seen from the ground, but once the train stopped, the brakeman would leave the caboose to make his rounds and clear the obvious hiding places. Then, when the shipment for the store owner was unloaded and everything checked and in order, the brakeman would return to the caboose, and the train would start moving. All the hobos would scramble back on, and the procedure would be repeated the next time the train stopped.

A single, long whistle sounded in the distance.

Her mother's words interrupted her thoughts. "It's coming. I can hear it."

Low rumbling and the shaking of the ground signified the train's approach to the station, which was next door to their house.

Knowing her father would not come until after the train departed, Louise hurried up the stairs to her bedroom, where she peered into the distance to watch it, as she had done countless times since childhood. From her window on the side of the house, she watched the big black engine puff out its billow of smoke as the train slowly rolled up to the station.

She could also see the school to the left of the train station, and beside it, the church. On the other side was the bunkhouse for the section gang, which was across the tracks from the station.

Louise smiled. If she went into her parents' bedroom, she could look out the back window and see the entire town of Pineridge. Of course she didn't have to. If she closed her eyes, she could picture every single building, burned into her memory. Including their house, the community consisted of only eight buildings. Directly across the main road behind their house was Mr. Sabinski's general store, and to the west, the home of Mr. Johnstone, the bus driver. Next to that was the service station, owned and operated by Mr. Tolson, who often spent more time out on the farmers' fields fixing the tractors where they had broken down than in his own shop in the town.

Besides those and the homes of the teacher and principal, all else around Pineridge was farms. The only reason tiny Pineridge could support those few businesses was because very few families besides theirs owned an automobile, and even fewer could afford rail tickets into the city on a regular basis, where prices were cheaper. Since her family received free rail passes, her father went to the city every second weekend for fresh vegetables and meat, and the entire family traveled to the city once a month to shop and visit relatives. Louise appreciated that their family could take advantage of such luxuries.

Louise watched the train as it squealed to a stop. This time, she didn't see men on the tops of the boxcars, but as usual, a few ran from between the cars where they had been hiding on the hitches until the train slowed. One man ran out of a boxcar to hide in the trees before the brakeman began his rounds to clear the train. As section foreman, it wasn't her father's job to evict the hobos from the trains, but if he did see them hiding, he was required to remove them as well, even though they had nowhere to go, especially in Pineridge.

She didn't know those men, but her heart ached for every one of them.

Often, they were so hungry, not having eaten for days, that they came to the house begging for food. Some simply took what was offered, but others asked to work in exchange for the food, even though there was no work for them to do. Of all the men who came to the door begging, none were turned away. Sometimes, when their clothes were so tattered and worn that they could no longer give sufficient protection from the cold nights, her mother gave them pieces of her husband's clothing.

In the summer it wasn't so bad, but for now, even though the last of the snow was gone, the spring temperatures continued to drop sharply to barely above freezing some nights. At this point in the season, her mother had given away most of Papa's warm clothing. Besides his parka, her father now only had one sweater left to his name. Both Louise and her mother knew they would be busy knitting all summer, preparing to give away everything they made to those in need when the colder weather began again.

Whether it was herself, her mama, or her papa who gave the men food or clothing, they always stopped and prayed with them. Most of the time the men listened politely out of obligation for receiving something, but every once in awhile, Louise thought their prayers touched someone's heart. For that reason, she knew that for as long as their family had food to eat, they would share with those who were less fortunate.

She wished she could give away Bibles, but there simply was not enough money to do so. Even if there were, these homeless men could not carry any belongings with them, not even items needed every day. They only had the clothes on their backs. Nothing more.

And week after week, month after month, more and more destitute men passed through the small community of Pineridge on their way to their last hope, a job in some big city, wherever these tracks could take them.

Louise stayed in her room until the train was gone, then went downstairs to find something to do until her father returned, and they could begin eating their dinner.

☙

Elliott Endicott wiped his mouth and curled into a ball as he lay on the cold wooden floor of the boxcar. He had given up trying to make himself comfortable. It had been so long since he'd last eaten that he'd been sick, except there was nothing left in his stomach to expel. There hadn't been for days. Because he had been on the move for so long and the trains stopped often, he also couldn't remember the last time he'd had a proper sleep.

The whistle sounded and the movement of the train changed, indicating they were approaching and stopping at another station. This time, he would wait until the train was almost at a stop before he moved, because he didn't think he could get up twice. He had never been so weak or felt so ill in his life. He also wanted to move as little as possible because of the filth in the empty boxcar.

His eyes burned from lack of sleep as he watched the movement through the crack in the boxcar door. The train slowed, and he could see he had no choice but to get up and ready himself to jump. As he stood to the side, preparing himself for the right moment, his knees wobbled like rubber, making it necessary to grasp the door frame of the boxcar for support.

The train continued to slow, and Elliott glanced up ahead to see where they were. He could see the train station and across the road what appeared to be a school.

As he neared the set of buildings, Elliott squeezed his eyes shut, trying to block out what had become of him, of his life, and of his dreams.

The second the train stopped, he jumped. He stumbled as he landed, skinning his knuckles, and ran into the trees. If he didn't find berries, he hoped at least to find water to quench a thirst so harsh his throat hurt when he breathed.

Instead of staying close to the station, Elliott wandered down the track and into the bushes, staying out of sight, hoping that if he ventured farther from the main area, he would indeed find berries untouched.

He had sold his watch long ago and therefore didn't know the time. From the position of the sun, he guessed it to be shortly after six in the evening.

Dinnertime. His stomach grumbled painfully at the thought.

Not for the first time, he wondered what would happen once he arrived at his friend Edward's home in British Columbia at the end of his journey, provided he lived to make it. Good or bad, no matter what awaited him would surely be better than this.

Hopefully, he could find something to eat before this train left again. He'd learned the hard way that generally the freight trains traveled in the same direction approximately ten hours apart. The next one to go by would be in the middle of the night. Since this was such a small community, the train wouldn't stop. Elliott calculated that the next train to stop wouldn't be along before noon tomorrow. That being the case, the night promised to be a very cold one with no shelter if he missed getting back on this train. For this moment, he didn't care. He had to find something to eat.

As he wandered farther along the tracks, he recognized the wild strawberry bushes. The bare bushes told him he had not been the first person to discover this patch. However, because of the size of the patch, his heart quickened in the hope that there could be more nearby that had not been consumed by other men riding the freight trains. Elliott made his way farther into the trees, not caring if he came face-to-face with a bear. The bear would have to fight him because whatever he found, he planned to eat.

He hadn't gone too far into the trees before he met with success. Behind an outcropping of rock, he discovered a mother lode of strawberries. Many were green, but others were tender and juicy and begging to be eaten. In the distance, he heard the train beginning to pull away from the station, but he didn't care how cold he would be tonight. He had food.

Elliott sank to his knees in a short prayer of thanks to God for the bounty before him, then grabbed for the berries. At the first bite, he closed his eyes to savor the flavor. They were only wild berries, but he'd never tasted anything so wonderful in his life. They were sweet and tangy and delicious.

He shoveled the strawberries into his mouth as fast as he picked them. One after another, he ate as many as he could, as quickly as he could, not caring that the dark red juice dribbled into his beard. He had over a thousand miles and many days to go before he reached his destination, and he knew he would be much worse for wear by then. Berry stains in his beard would be the least of his worries.

As he reached for more, Elliott's hand froze. From the same direction he'd come, he heard someone else approaching.

For a second, he didn't want to share his prize, but then he chided himself for being greedy. God had provided, and if God desired, God would take away.

"Papa? Is that you?"

It was a female voice.

The foliage parted. "Papa?" A young woman of about nineteen appeared. She wore a dark green dress that would nearly have blended her into the background if it weren't for her blond hair, as bright as the sun in the dark surroundings. In her hand she carried a dull metal pail.

The second the young woman saw him, her green eyes widened and she backed up a step. She gasped and covered her mouth with one hand, still holding the pail in front of her with the other.

Elliott sprang to his feet. "Excuse me, Miss. Please, don't be frightened. I'm only here to eat these berries and nothing more."

"You were on the last freight train! And it's gone!"

He cringed. He knew it was obvious how he'd arrived, but he was still ashamed. He hadn't seen himself in a mirror recently, but he could guess at his appearance. Neither did he want to think what he smelled like.

Today, for the first time, he had taken the risk of sleeping in a boxcar because the train was in motion. Until only a few hours ago, he had heeded the other men's warnings about the dangers of going into the boxcars. For days he had traveled by scrambling over countless greasy hitches between the cars. He'd ridden many miles from atop the boxcars, which were always heavily laden with dirt and dust, not to mention the gifts from countless birds.

He didn't want to think about the other unmentionables he'd had to deal with inside the boxcar. Without a doubt, in all his twenty-five years on God's earth, he had never been so disgustingly filthy, not even as a child. At least when he was a child, it had been good, clean dirt. However, he'd been so desperate for sleep and protection from the weather that he had taken his chances and actually gone inside when he'd discovered a boxcar with an unlocked door.

He'd never had a beard in his life, and he hated the feel of it. The rough whiskers had grown long enough to be in the bristly stage. Even if it had been long enough to be a cultured beard, he still would have hated it. And, as long as it'd been since he'd bathed or shaved, it was equally as long since he'd combed his hair. No doubt it was matted with things he'd rather not think about.

In addition to everything else, his right shirtsleeve had ripped, and he had no new shirt to change into. His trousers and shoes were grimy, but so far, intact. His shirt pocket had also been ripped when another man had tried to rob him as he slept, leaving a gaping hole.

Unfortunately for both of them, he had nothing the man could steal.

Elliott backed up a step. The last time he'd combed his hair had also been the last time he'd brushed his teeth. "I think I'll find another patch of berries elsewhere."

The woman cleared her throat and also backed up a step. "Are you hungry? Would you like something to eat? My family and I will be eating dinner soon, and you're welcome to join us. I was about to pick some strawberries for dessert."

He opened his mouth to turn down her generous offer but couldn't force out the words "no, thank you." While the berries were tasty, they were no substitution for a real meal.

If God had found a way to give him a decent meal, Elliott would not turn Him down.

"Thank you for your generosity and kindness. I would appreciate that more than words can say."

Her shaky smile warmed his heart, and something went to war in his battered stomach. "You're quite welcome."

"My name is Elliott Endicott, and I'm on my way to where hopefully a job awaits me."

She smiled again, this time with more confidence. "My name is Louise Demchuck. My father is the section foreman here in Pineridge."

Elliott bowed his head. "I'm pleased to met you, Miss Demchuck."

"Please, call me Louise. We are not formal here in Pineridge.

But before we go back to the house, I do need to fill my pail. I think there are plenty of berries here for both of us—for me to pick, and for you to eat."

Elliott had been prepared to help the lady pick, but he discreetly glanced at his hands and decided against it. He could only guess that Louise would not want him handling food she would eat. If he hadn't been so hungry, he wouldn't have eaten food touched with his hands.

The young lady didn't speak as she picked, but instead, she began to hum. Elliott nearly dropped the berries from his hand when he recognized it as "Rock of Ages," his favorite hymn. If he wasn't eating, he would have joined her with a harmony. Then his better judgment reminded him that he was only one of countless, desperate men passing through her town. As such, he was not in a position to develop a friendship with this woman. He probably should not have even spoken to her.

But it didn't matter. Before this time tomorrow, he would be gone on the next freight train.

Chapter 2

I think I have enough strawberries in my pail now. It's time to go back to the house. Papa should be arriving back very soon, and then it will be time for dinner."

Elliott didn't know which held less dirt, his face or his clothing, but he couldn't stop himself from wiping the berry juice from his mouth onto his sleeve when Louise turned her head. The strawberries had filled a void, but he anticipated dinner like no other time in his life.

"Thank you," he said as he rose and followed Louise through the bushes until they emerged from the trees. She slowed her step for him to catch up, but he hesitated, not wanting to walk beside her in his present condition. However, neither did he mean to insult her, especially considering her generosity. Elliott quickened his pace and walked beside her at what he hoped was a respectable distance, downwind, toward the house beside the train station.

"I won't tell Mama you've eaten your dessert first." She turned to smile at him, and Elliott forced himself to smile back. He'd never felt less like smiling. While he knew she was probably only trying to lighten the moment, it didn't make him feel any better. He'd always said he would rather die than accept charity from a stranger. Now his lofty ideals had been reduced to exactly that—accepting charity versus the harsh reality of dying of starvation. And he'd never considered the possibility of accidental death from the often dangerous predicaments he'd been forced into while riding the freight trains. He would never again speak such words lightly.

Instead of going in the front door, he followed Louise around to the back of the house.

"Please wait here, so I can tell my mother we have a guest."

Elliott's heart sank. A guest. He wasn't a guest. He had been reduced to begging. He was a vagrant. A bum. Or, as the new

167

term dubbed him and other men in his situation, a hobo.

Living as he had been recently gave him an entirely new perspective on what was needed as the bare minimum to survive. He'd been given many lessons in pride and humility like he'd never experienced. Never in his life would he have thought he would be surviving only through the help and sacrifice of anonymous strangers.

While he waited, he tried to figure out where he was. Louise had said they were in a town named Pineridge, but he'd never heard of the place. However, as he'd passed through the countryside, he had also learned a lesson in geography such as he'd never been taught in school.

He'd traveled through countless cities, towns, and communities of varying sizes, but this one had to be the smallest he could remember. From where he stood at the rear of the Demchucks' house, he could only see a handful of buildings—eight total. He surmised that this small outcropping was the hub for the local community of farms in the area.

He found himself staring at the school. Quickly, he turned his head. He didn't want to think about schools. It was only a reminder of what he couldn't have.

Louise stepped outside once again. "Please come in. Mama is heating some water. You can wash up before Papa comes back." She stepped back inside, indicating that he should follow.

In his present condition, he didn't want to go inside their house, but he wouldn't insult her generosity and turn down her invitation. Still, he would much rather have eaten outside than carry his dirt into their home. Elliott inhaled deeply and followed her through the doorway.

As soon as he stepped into the kitchen, the delicious aroma of a fragrant stew caused his stomach to make an embarrassing sound. He automatically covered his stomach with one hand and tried to think about anything other than food.

To distract himself, he glanced around the room. The

Demchucks' home was modest but pristine and well cared for. The linoleum floor shone brightly with the sunlight peeking in through the lace-curtained windows. Beside him to his right, just inside the door, stood a small wooden table with a white enamel basin and a bar of soap in a matching dish on top. A colorful floral printed curtain hung from the tabletop to the floor, hiding what was likely a pail beneath. Above the table, a framed mirror hung on the wall.

To his left a woman in her fifties, an older version of Louise, stood beside a large cast-iron cookstove. She wore a dress very similar to Louise's, but the front was covered with a cotton embroidered apron. She turned and smiled at him. "Greetings. Welcome to our humble home."

He forced himself to smile back. "Thank you for having me."

Louise smiled at both of them. "Elliott, this is my mama, Anna Demchuck."

He closed his eyes briefly as he bowed his head in greeting, grateful for the distance between them, because he didn't want her to see how disgusting he was. "Ma'am. Thank you for your invitation. If there is anything I can do for you to return your kindness, please ask."

"Nonsense. God has provided for us well, and all we are doing is sharing it with others in times of need. One day you can return the favor to someone else. I think the water has finished heating. The basin is there beside the door if you'd like to wash up."

There was no if about it. He'd never welcomed soap and water so much in his life.

Without waiting for his response, Mrs. Demchuck brought the basin to the cookstove, ladled some warm water into the basin, and returned it to the washstand.

Elliott stepped back to let her pass. While Mrs. Demchuck settled the basin, he noticed what appeared to be a pump on the floor next to the washbasin table. He tried to be discreet in peeking outside through the window.

An outhouse sat in the corner of the property, confirming the full scope of the Demchucks' lifestyle in a community far away from any metropolitan area. In addition to not having running water, they didn't have indoor plumbing.

In Katona Falls, most homes, although not all, had running water and flushing toilets. He knew that most farms still did not have this convenience, but he had never thought about the smaller communities that weren't quite farms but weren't really a city, either. Now he knew.

Unable to stop himself, he glanced quickly around the room to see what they did have. Next to a large wooden table set with three chairs and covered with a brightly colored oilcloth, he could see a large stand-up lamp, which confirmed that the Demchuck home had electricity. He also noted a china cabinet, the washbasin and stand, and the large cookstove, but no refrigerator or icebox.

Still, compared to what he'd seen and done over the past week, their quaint home felt like a palace.

Louise's voice beside him brought his attention back to where it should have been in the first place. "I brought this for you."

Elliott blinked and shook his head slightly. Lack of food and lack of sleep had distracted him from good manners, which was inexcusable. He hadn't noticed Louise leave the room, but now she stood beside him, smiling, holding a clean towel toward him.

"Thank you," he mumbled. Part of him could hardly wait to wash for the first time in longer than he cared to think about, but part of him dreaded it. Now he had to face the mirror and see what he had become.

Mrs. Demchuck removed her apron and slung it across the back of one of the chairs. "Come with me, Louise; there is something I need your help with in the living room."

In the blink of an eye, the two ladies left the room, and a curtain slipped closed in the doorway leading to the rest of the house. With their departure, everything became so quiet all

Elliott could hear was the crackling of the wood in the cookstove.

He suspected they really had no reason to leave the room except to give him some privacy while he did his best to wash. What he really needed was a bath, but he was in no position to do that, especially in the middle of their kitchen at dinnertime. Most important, Louise's father would be returning shortly to find a stranger in his house. Elliott did not want to step any more beyond the bounds of propriety than he already had. Therefore, he decided to hurry to do the best he could to clean himself with the hand soap and small basin of water provided.

Slowly, Elliott turned to the mirror. The man who looked back at him was a stranger. His hair was no longer than it had been a week ago, but in addition to the natural oils of a week of not washing it, it was so dirty it was the wrong color—not his usual neutral brown, but instead, dark and clumpy. He didn't think he'd lost more than a pound or two after eating nothing other than berries for the better part of the past week, except that he hadn't had any extra to lose to begin with. He could feel the difference in the way his clothes fit, but now he could also see it in his face.

He blinked back at himself and looked into his eyes. The mixture of the brown and green that made the hazel color had faded to a dull brown. No doubt because of the lack of sufficient sleep and horrid conditions under which he'd lived, the sockets of his eyes were hollow, yet puffy underneath. He couldn't tell the exact color of his skin; however, his face appeared pale beneath the layer of grime and soot, when he should have had a tan after spending most of his time outside.

He didn't think it was possible, but he looked even worse than he felt.

He squeezed his eyes shut for a second, then stared at himself again as he ran his fingers over his chin, something he'd done countless times over the last week. He'd felt his whiskers grow from harsh stubble to longer, softer hair. The unkempt length disgusted him.

As a teen he'd been proud to be able to sprout a beard quickly, but conversely, as an adult, it now meant he was the first to appear untidy. And now, he noticed as he turned his head, to his dismay, in addition to the dirt, his beard wasn't the same color as the rest of his hair.

The face of the stranger in the mirror made Elliott wish he had access to a razor, but if the best he had was soap and water, he was more grateful for that than words could say.

He worked up a lather in his hands, then rubbed it not only on his bare skin, but into his beard, and then over his hair to get out what grime he could. The blackness of the water turned his already upset stomach, telling him if that was what came off, then he was still very dirty. Trying not to drip water onto the floor, he opened the back door and dumped the dirty water outside and returned the basin to the cookstove to ladle out more warm water, just as he had seen Mrs. Demchuck do. He walked slowly across the room with the second basin of wash water and washed his hands and face again, this time with better results.

Voices on the other side of the curtain warned him of Louise and her mother's return, so Elliott quickly dried his face and hands. Not knowing what to do with the towel, he draped it over the back of one of the chairs, then froze. Despite having washed twice, he had left smudges of dirt on their nice towel.

Before they returned, he dumped the water into the pail hidden beneath the table, barely having straightened as the curtain opened.

"I'd guess you must be feeling much better?" Mrs. Demchuck asked, smiling so warmly he immediately relaxed.

"Yes, Ma'am. Thank you."

"My husband must be in the middle of a big job that they can't leave, because they're usually back by now. I think we'll begin eating dinner without him today." She picked up the apron and fastened it behind her, and both ladies turned toward the stove.

Elliott wasn't sure what he was supposed to do. If he were a true guest, he would have sat at the table to chat with the man of the house while the women set the food on the table, but he wasn't a guest.

"Is there something I can do to help?" he asked.

Louise carried a loaf of bread and a large knife to the table while Mrs. Demchuck scooped the stew into a porcelain bowl and brought it with her to the table. "This is all there is. We're ready."

He remained standing and pushed in the ladies' chairs to seat them, then sat himself down.

Mrs. Demchuck folded her hands on the table in front of her. "We always give thanks to the Lord for the food we eat."

"As do I, Ma'am."

Her eyes lit up. "Would you like to pray, then?"

He'd never in his life felt more like praying. "Yes, Ma'am. I would."

Elliott cleared his throat, bowed his head, and closed his eyes. "Dear heavenly Father, I thank You for this day and for this wonderful meal before us. Your timing and Your grace is sufficient, as always. I thank You for the bounty which You have provided, for the kindness and generosity of strangers. Today I ask for a special blessing on the Demchuck family as a special thank-you for their willingness to share with a stranger." Elliott paused to clear his throat, which had become tight with a rush of unaccustomed emotion. "Also I ask a special blessing on all the men who have been forced onto the trains, and all people, everywhere, for all their struggles and hardships in these difficult economic times. I pray that You touch every one of them with Your hand of mercy, that they, too, can be provided for, day by day. I ask this in the name of our Lord and Savior, Jesus Christ. Amen."

Silence reigned over the table for a few seconds. Mrs. Demchuck quickly ran the back of her hand over her eyes. "As you can guess, we see many homeless men on the trains. We try to do everything we can for all who ask."

"I can assure you that in the days I have been traveling, I have never met such gracious people as you, Ma'am. I can hardly wait to meet Mr. Demchuck." Elliott paused to smile, and for the first time in a long time, his smile was genuine. "I must admit, I do feel somewhat nervous. After all, he works for the railroad, and I'm not exactly a paying passenger."

Louise pushed the bowl of stew to him, encouraging him to help himself, while her mother began slicing the bread.

Elliott didn't wait for the bread. He spooned out a large but reasonable portion of stew and immediately began to eat. At the first delicious mouthful, he closed his eyes to savor the rich flavors of the meat and gravy but didn't stop chewing while he did so. Ignoring his manners, he spoke as best he could around the food in his mouth. "This is delicious. Thank you, Ma'am."

Mrs. Demehuck smiled and nodded in response. "You're more than welcome."

"Where are you headed, Elliott?" Louise asked as she pushed the plate of sliced bread toward him, along with a bowl of butter.

He tried to swallow quickly, but before he could, Mrs. Demchuck spoke.

"Louise! Let the poor man eat some before bombarding him with questions."

Elliott swallowed. "It's okay. I'm on my way to British Columbia, where hopefully a job in the logging industry awaits me."

"Then you still have many days' travel ahead of you."

"Yes. It took me five days to get here, but now that I've become accustomed to the schedules, and other men have shown me some of the tricks, the rest of the way should be quicker."

Louise grinned. "I can tell you a lot of tricks to riding on the trains, too."

"Louise!"

Louise's mouth quivered. She bit her bottom lip for a second then lowered her head and whispered to him, "I'll tell you later."

"If you still have many days' travel ahead of you, especially if you are going through the mountains, I can assure you that you will be cold. I assume you have no jacket or coat?"

Elliott tried not to cringe as he spoke. He had begun his journey with a good coat and two suitcases full of clothes and his personal effects. Now, all he had left were the clothes on his back, which were tattered and filthy.

He couldn't help himself. He lowered his head and pushed at a carrot on his plate, unable to meet her eyes as he spoke. "No, Ma'am, I don't."

"Then I can give you a sweater of my husband's to help keep you warm. We often give out clothing to those in need. At the same time, we also try to share the gospel as we share food and clothing with the men off the trains. This time, it does my heart good to see you already know the Lord. For you, I especially want to help."

"I don't know what to say. Thank you, Ma'am."

Fortunately, conversation turned to other topics than his personal necessities. If he weren't moving on soon, he would have liked to get to know them better. Besides their generosity in helping him when he needed it, he simply liked them as people. Now, more than ever, he anticipated meeting Mr. Demchuck.

As they talked about mundane, normal topics, the two women encouraged him to eat another helping of stew, which he appreciated from the bottom of his heart.

After they finished their meal, Elliott didn't know what to do. In Mr. Demchuck's absence, it would have been proper for him to thank them for their generosity and leave, but he had nowhere to go. Even if the next freight train that passed through actually stopped, that wouldn't be until nearly sunrise. There were only two places he could spend the night and not be seen by the residents of the area. He could sleep in the forest alongside the track, where he would be exposed to the cold. Or he could hunch down in the doorway of the train station.

Neither held much appeal, but he didn't have a choice. The

sweater would offer some warmth from the cold night but not enough to be close to comfortable. The spring temperatures still dipped quite low after sundown, and the sun was already starting to set.

Something else he had not previously considered—Mrs. Demchuck's kind donation of the sweater forced him to think of the trip through the mountains, where there would probably still be snow on the ground. He didn't want to think of how cold that portion of his journey would be. First, he would worry about tonight. He would worry about what tomorrow would bring tomorrow.

Since the meal was done, Louise and her mother stood. Due to the continuing absence of Mr. Demchuck, Elliott did the same. "Ma'am, I know I've said this before, but thank you again for your generosity. Before I leave, please, is there anything I can do for you?"

She smiled at him as she slipped the apron back on. "Yes, Elliott, as a matter of a fact, there is."

Elliott smiled back. He wanted so much to do something for these kind people. More than anything, he hoped that whatever she was about to ask would in some way be of benefit to the ministry they provided for other men in his situation. "Anything, Ma'am. Just name it."

"You can stop calling me 'Ma'am.'"

"Yes, Ma'—uh—Mrs. Demchuck."

They smiled at each other.

"That's better. Now if you'll excuse me, I am going to go heat the rest of the stew. I think I finally hear the jigger coming. Louise, why don't you take Elliott into the living room, and you can listen to the radio until your father has finished eating."

Chapter 3

Louise tried not to let Elliott see her shock at her mother's request to invite him into the living room. Never before had one of the hobos been invited into their home past the kitchen. Some were too awkward to come inside at all, and some were too dirty. Those who did come inside only stayed as long as it took to eat the food given to them, and they never went beyond the kitchen. The men left quickly and quietly once their physical needs were taken care of, hiding until the next freight train came by, and then they were gone from Pineridge forever.

Secretly, it made Louise happy that Elliott had been invited into their home and not encouraged to leave immediately following dinner. Of the countless men riding the trains for whom her family had provided food and clothing, he was not the first to be a Christian. However, beyond his faith, Elliott seemed different than the others, although she couldn't define why.

The majority of the men she'd met who came off the trains had seemed like honorable people. They weren't lazy, nor did they expect free handouts or figure they were owed something for their misfortune. Even though they had fallen on hard times, most of them were riding the trains because they had some specific destination in mind, usually a large city, in the hope of finding a job.

Elliott, it seemed, did not just hope to find a job. From his comments at the dinner table, it sounded as if a job awaited him—he only had to arrive at his destination. She didn't question why he wasn't traveling as a paying passenger if he had a prospective job.

Louise led him through the doorway from the kitchen into the larger room, half of which served as a dining room, the other half as the living room. His eyes widened as he quickly glanced over everything, taking in the fine furnishings and her mother's beautiful doilies, lace runners, and embroidery scattered throughout. His attention lingered first on the piano in the corner and then on the framed photograph of her family, taken before Louise's sister had married and left Pineridge.

As her mother had suggested, Louise approached the radio. While Elliott studied the family portrait atop the piano, she discreetly swiped off a little dust from the polished wood just above the dial that she must have missed earlier. "Please, sit down. We might be able to catch the 'Jack Benny Show.' Do you listen to Jack Benny where you come from?"

He turned and briefly studied the couch, then turned back to her. "Yes, I do," he said as he smiled. "But if you don't mind, I think I'll stand."

Louise turned the radio on, then turned to face him. During dinner she had noticed the exhaustion apparent in his face. Of course, she had never ridden the trains any other way than in the comfortable passenger cars, but from what her father had told her about how the hobos had to travel, she doubted Elliott had seen comfort since he left home, wherever that was.

"Please," she said, extending one arm toward the couch. "Don't be nervous. Consider us your Christian family and relax. Papa isn't going to lecture you about how you got here. None of the railroad employees like to see people ride the freight trains in such a way, but they also know there is no way to avoid it, so it's going to happen. You look so tired. Please, sit down. I'm sure Papa would love to talk to you once he's finished eating."

He rammed his hands into his pockets. "I do appreciate your hospitality, but I don't want to sit down because I'm so dirty. I don't want to ruin the fine fabric of your couch or leave a mark that will remind you of my presence long after I'm gone."

Louise's throat clogged, and a strange burning sensation began at the backs of her eyes. She didn't know where he came from, but his words made her wonder what horrible situation had caused a man of such a caliber, who would be concerned about soiling their furniture, to be reduced to such means. His concern made her ashamed that her family was doing so well in these troubled times.

"You're so kind to be concerned," she ground out through the tightness in her throat. "I'll be right back."

Quickly, Louise scurried into the kitchen, where her mother was stirring the stew. "Mama, I need a blanket or something for Elliott to sit on. He doesn't want to soil the couch with his dirty clothes. I don't know what to say. He seems so different from the other men who've come through in the past few years."

Her mother nodded. "I know. He seems like an extraordinary young man of good faith and strong character. Your father seems to have been so discouraged lately. I thought that speaking to Elliott would be good for him." Her mother smiled. "I knew you were wondering why I'd invited him in like this."

Louise nodded. "Maybe a little." Abruptly she slapped her hands over her mouth, then shook her head. "I mean, no! I knew you had a good reason."

"Hush, girl. Take the blue blanket from the dresser in your bedroom and throw it over the couch for him."

Louise ran upstairs for the blanket, and she had just returned downstairs as the thumping of the jigger sounded from outside, signifying the return of her father and the section men.

A loud banging sounded on the front door, causing her to nearly drop the blanket. Very aware of Elliott standing not far away, she ran to the door and opened it. Frank, one of the men from the section gang, stood in the doorway, wringing his hat in his hands. "Miss Demchuck, where's your mama?"

Louise's knees turned to jelly. As she wavered, she grasped the frame of the doorway for support. "Papa. . . . Is he—?"

Frank shook his head. "No, he's just hurt, but it's bad."

Louise turned to run into the kitchen, but her mother was already running toward the front door, a dish towel clutched in her hand. "What happened? Where is John?"

"We're going to be bringing him in, Mrs. Demchuck. We think his leg's broke. You're going to have to take him to the hospital."

Frank disappeared outside, and after a few agonizing minutes, Frank returned with Henry, slowly bringing her father to the door. Louise and her mother stood aside as Frank and Henry carried her father to the couch, where they laid him down.

Louise had never in her life seen such pain on a person's face, not even when Richard Sabinski fell off the roof of his daddy's store and broke his arm.

"If you need us, just call. We'll be at the bunkhouse."

Without another word, the two men left.

Louise watched as her mother bent over and reached out one hand in readiness to touch his wound but then jerked her hand back. Instead of touching him, she wrapped both arms around her own waist. "How badly does it hurt? Is it really broken?"

He squeezed his eyes shut, pressed his open palm against his lower right leg, then winced in pain. "Probably. A bundle of new ties fell on me. A split second sooner, I might have been killed. Praise the Lord for strange miracles."

Louise watched the change in her father's expression, recognizing the exact moment he realized that a stranger was amongst them.

"Who are you? What are you doing here?"

"My name is Elliott Endicott, Sir. I'm here passing through on my way to British Columbia. Your family invited me in for dinner. I have been waiting for your return so we could talk, but this isn't the meeting I had anticipated. Is there anything I can do for you?"

"You wouldn't happen to be a doctor, would you?"

"Unfortunately, I am only a barber. But I can drive you to the hospital, if you'll give me directions. I'm assuming you own an automobile?"

"Yes."

Her mother glanced nervously between the two men. "What about your lead hand, Robert?"

Drawing in a deep breath, her father turned to her mother, wincing with the movement and scowling at the same time. "I caught Robert drinking some moonshine when he was supposed to be working. I don't know how I didn't notice sooner, but I guess it's because we were busy. By the time I noticed, he was quite drunk, so I fired him. We were at the end of the shift, getting everything ready so we could leave a bundle of new ties for the section we have to do Monday morning, when Robert tripped and knocked the stack of ties off the jigger and onto me. I couldn't get out of the way fast enough."

Her father turned back to Elliott. "Robert's not going to be driving me anywhere. Are you a good driver, Mr. Endicott? These are all dirt roads here, and it's going to be getting dark soon. The clay is slippery to drive on if it rains, and the clouds are coming."

Elliott nodded. "I assure you, I am a cautious driver, even though most of my driving has been within the city. It's not dark yet, which is good. I don't know where we are or how far it is to the nearest town with a hospital, but I'll gladly do what I can for you. It appears the good Lord set me here at this time for a reason."

Her father started to smile and opened his mouth to speak, but then his smile turned to a grimace, and he sucked in a deep breath of air.

"Can I help you to the car, Sir?"

As soon as her father nodded, Elliott wrapped one arm around her father's chest. Bracing both of them by pressing his other hand into the top of the couch, he then pulled her father up. While leaning on Elliott and balancing on one leg, her father positioned one arm over Elliott's shoulders. In response, Elliott repositioned his arm tightly around her father's waist, and they started moving.

Louise stood in one spot and watched as her mother ran for

the keys, while Elliott and her father very slowly hobbled toward the front door. Despite his slim build, Elliott supported her father firmly as they made their way down the steps.

Louise couldn't imagine either herself or her mother trying to move her papa. She and her mother were the same height of five foot two. Her father was a big man, nearly six feet tall, towering over Elliott by a couple of inches, at least. In addition to being so tall, because he worked hard every day, her papa was muscular and, therefore, heavy. She didn't even know how Elliott managed to support her father, but she had a feeling that the fine meal they'd fed him had helped provide the strength required.

While Elliott very carefully helped her father down the front steps one at a time, Louise mumbled a prayer of thanks for Elliott being with them today.

Her mother ran past her, speaking quickly. "I'm going to go to the hospital with them. Take dinner off the stove before it burns. I don't know when we'll be back."

Louise stood on the top step and watched Elliott and her mother make sure her father was able to support himself on one leg while leaning against the railing. When they were assured he wouldn't fall, Elliott ran to the garage, opened the door, and slowly backed the car out. He turned around and drove as close as he could without driving over her mother's flowers. They helped her father into the car, trying to position him so he would suffer the least amount of pain and discomfort, and drove off.

Louise stared blankly down the road long after the cloud of dust settled. The drive to the hospital in Beauséjour would take close to an hour. She didn't know how long it would take to set her father's leg and do the cast, and then the trip home would take them much longer in the pitch-black of the night, so she had no idea when they would be back.

Absently, she gazed skyward and prayed for a cloudless night and that what little light the moon provided could help keep their journey a safe one.

A bang from beside the bunkhouse made Louise flinch. She stopped studying the sky and watched Robert and the men of the section gang carry out a suitcase, a bedroll, a pillow, and a few personal items and throw them into the trunk of Robert's car.

Louise wrapped her arms around herself to ward off the cooling night air, continuing to watch as Henry and Frank struggled to load Robert's heavy radio into the passenger side of the car.

Swaying as he walked, Robert opened the driver's door. He hopped in and the motor roared to life. Robert drove off so fast that his spinning tires created a cloud of dust so thick she couldn't see the bunkhouse while he disappeared down the road leading to the highway.

She thought of Elliott driving her father's car and of both her parents with him. She'd been on that road countless times, and the road was barely wider than one car. She didn't know if Elliott really was a good driver, despite his assurance. However, she did know that Robert was a poor driver, plus, in addition to being angry, he was drunk.

Her stomach clenched so tightly it hurt. The possibility existed that in his angry state, Robert might not care if he ran his former boss off the road.

She squeezed her eyes shut to say a quick prayer for their safety.

Needing to distract herself from the possibilities of her father's car lying in a ditch somewhere, Louise returned inside the house, removed the pot of stew from the stove, and tidied up the kitchen. When all was done, she returned to the living room. Rather than stand and look out the window, she turned off the radio and sat down at the piano to occupy her mind and soothe her fears. It was too early to worry. If morning came and they hadn't returned, then she would have the right to panic.

Alternating between her favorite hymns, Bach, Mozart, and other classical pieces, Louise played until her eyes were sore from concentrating on the paper in the yellow light. She averted her gaze to rest her eyes, but that only drew her attention to the photograph, on top of the piano, of her family, which only served to remind her of their absence.

Louise closed her books, tucked them into the bench, then crossed into the dining room, stood in front of her father's desk, and looked up at the clock hanging above it.

It was nearly midnight, and Louise had never been alone so late at night or for so long. She tried to calm her fears by telling herself that she'd lived here all her life and Pineridge was a safe community. She knew everyone here well. The three men of the section gang were the only changing faces here. Except for Robert, who would not be returning, Frank had lived in the Pineridge bunkhouse for nearly six months, Henry was the last person in the community who was new.

As she had done earlier that same day, Louise went upstairs to her bedroom window and pressed her fingers to the cold glass. She watched out the window, looking for something, anything, to tell her that she was not the only soul still awake in Pineridge.

The only sources of light were the two streetlamps, one in front of the train station, the other in front of the school. Then, a glow appeared in the distance, along with a low hum. Louise smiled and ran downstairs to the door.

They were home. All was well.

Chapter 4

W here's Papa?"

Her mother smiled wearily, pushing her hair back from her forehead. "They decided to keep him overnight. We'll have to go back tomorrow to get him. At least the drive will be easier in the daytime. Your father hates that road, and now I remember why we seldom go anywhere at night."

Elliott pushed his fists into the small of his back. "No, it wasn't a pleasure trip, that's for sure. But Mr. Demchuck is being taken care of properly, so that's what's important."

Louise glanced up at the clock, although she didn't know why. "I guess we can ask Mr. Pollack to drive us to Beauséjour tomorrow when we have to pick Papa up."

"We all talked about it, and Elliott is going to stay with us tonight so he can drive me to the hospital tomorrow and bring your father home."

Of course she was glad that Elliott would be driving the car for them, but her relief went far beyond the simple need of transportation for her father.

Ever since the men started riding the freight trains, she had been told of the dangers. The evening freight trains stopped at their station, but the early morning trains only slowed as they passed through their small burg, some well before daybreak, making it very dangerous to climb aboard as the cars moved. She knew that despite the risk involved the men still did it.

Over the past few years she'd watched men who'd wandered away from the tracks in search of food when they missed the evening train. Most of them hid in the trees until the next train came. Of those who came begging for food, it was usually her mother who gave them something, so she didn't often get to meet them. However, the early morning freight trains didn't stop. Her heart had missed many beats watching men falter or stumble while trying to jump onto the moving boxcars. A number of times she had been positive that when the train rolled away she would see a man sprawled across the tracks, dismembered or crushed by the huge steel wheels after missing his mark. So far, that had not happened in Pineridge, but fatalities did occur when men rode the freight trains.

Plus, there were other less obvious but still very real dangers besides being hurt jumping on and off. She'd heard many instances where men were unintentionally locked in the boxcars which were detached from the trains and left in the train yards. The men inside had died because no one could hear them calling out for help.

While she always had been concerned for the safety of the men, they were still strangers and her worries had never been personal. Now that had changed. In the short amount of time since she'd met Elliott, she'd come to know him a little bit as a person—he was no longer a nameless entity passing in the night. She didn't want to think of the many risks he was taking as he made his way to his final destination.

Because her father was a railroad employee, her family received a free rail pass to be used anytime they wanted to travel. Therefore, she couldn't offer him a ticket, because she had none. However, she'd managed to save a small amount of money from working occasionally at Mr. Sabinski's store. Since Elliott wouldn't be leaving until Saturday evening, this allowed her the time to buy him a ticket, although she had a feeling that for his help in driving her father to the hospital and back, her parents would instead be the ones purchasing it for him.

In addition to wanting to be assured of his safety, the delay would give her more time to talk to him, and she dearly wanted to talk. Or, if the last passenger train left before they arrived back from Beauséjour, then he would have to stay until Sunday afternoon. That meant not only would she have another day with him, but he could attend church with her family.

Louise smiled at him, hoping she wasn't being too forward or that he wouldn't get the wrong impression of her words. "That will be nice. It will be good to have you as our guest so we can thank you for doing this for us."

Elliott nodded. "It's not a problem. I didn't give my friend a specific date as to when I would arrive, although admittedly it has taken me much longer than anticipated. If I've calculated correctly where we are, I'm only halfway to my destination. I'm wondering if I could trouble you for some paper and a stamp to write and tell him I'll be there later than my last letter stated. I don't want to further jeopardize the job he's offered me, but at this point all I can do is to send the letter to my brother and have him forward it. I don't have Edward's address memorized, only the directions on how to get there, and I can't put those on the letter."

Out of the corner of her eye, Louise caught her mother attempting to hide a yawn. "I think we should start getting ready to retire for the night. Elliott, I hope you don't mind sleeping on the couch. We can get you a blanket and a pillow."

He smiled, and Louise thought it was a lovely sight.

"Compared to where I've slept in the last few days, your couch is pure luxury."

Her mother smiled back. "But first, and I'm sure you won't argue with this: You, Mr. Endicott, need a bath."

His lovely smile faded, and even beneath the untidy beard, Louise could see his blush. "Yes, Ma'am, I believe I do."

"And one more thing, Mr. Endicott. And I've asked you this before."

"Yes, Ma'am?"

"Please. Stop calling me 'Ma'am.'"

☙

Elliott followed Louise into the basement. He'd never seen anything like it in his life. Instead of a trapdoor in the kitchen floor leading down to a dugout, the doorway to the basement was wide open and had a set of real stairs going down, just like the stairs going up to the bedrooms. This basement ceiling was low, but the room itself was as large as the house. Instead of a dirt floor, the floor and walls were concrete.

The large room was far from empty. Straight ahead he could see a huge round metal tub, and beside it, a smaller metal tub with a washboard inside. To his right as they walked down the stairs, were shelves filled with preserved fruit, and next to the shelves, piles of boxes. To his left sat a large furnace, and next to it, a large woodpile consisting of both logs and broken-up old railway ties.

"There's the washtub."

He nodded and lifted the tub, which was more awkward than heavy. He slung it upside down over his back, and once he got to the top of the stairs, rolled it sideways through the door. He carried it in the same manner all the way to the kitchen, where he put it down near the cookstove.

Mrs. Demchuck straightened from beside a pump on the floor near the back door, where she had just finished filling a pail. She then carried it to the cookstove and dumped it in a large oval container that covered half the top of the surface.

Bathing in a metal tub in the middle of a stranger's kitchen would in no way compare to the relaxing experience of a nice warm bath at home. However, between the late time and his disgusting condition, he couldn't complain, nor did he have the right to compare. Even though he had been born and raised with the conveniences of the city, he thought he remembered a similar tub as a young child. When he was ten, his family had updated to a stationary tub with running water at the same time as the rest of the neighborhood. He appreciated all the work the Demchuck family was doing for him, sharing their best and seeing to his most obvious need, which was to clean himself up.

During the drive to the hospital, he had been embarrassed to think of what it had been like for them to be enclosed with him in the confined quarters of the car for such a long period of time. When they had arrived at the hospital, he'd tried to wait outside since he was far from sanitary, but Mrs. Demchuck insisted he stay with them, as if they had belonged together.

The odd situation had moved him more than he cared to admit. After the death of his parents five years ago, the only family he had left was his brother and his brother's wife and their children. As close as he felt to his brother, he still felt like an outsider when it came to family affairs. Without words, a bond he couldn't explain had developed with the Demchucks. Even if all he could do for them was to drive their car, he would do anything they asked him, simply because of the way they had opened their hearts and home to him.

"Can I carry that pail for you? You must be tired; it's been a long day for you," he said, trying to stifle a yawn of his own, after watching Mrs. Demchuck's yawn. It had also been a long day for him. It had been over twenty-four hours since he'd last slept, and that sleep had not been long or comfortable. He felt himself start to sway at the thought of lying down for a much-needed sleep on their comfortable couch.

Even though he was thoroughly exhausted, the work of carrying the bucket and filling the tub helped to keep him awake, but at this point, he doubted anything could keep him alert.

Louise changed places with her mother at the pump, and Mrs. Demchuck left the room.

"Tell me about where you come from. Is it a big city?"

Elliott could barely think straight, but he tried to describe what he thought were the most interesting aspects of Katona Falls to someone who would never go there. She laughed when he explained that there really was no waterfall there. Often the residents conjectured about how the name of the town came to be, yet they came up with no answers.

Once the washtub contained a few inches of water in the bottom, Louise walked to the cookstove and ladled the water from the oval container into the pail, then dumped it into the tub.

Mrs. Demchuck returned with an armful of clothing. "Here is a clean towel for you, and I've brought you the smallest of what I could find of John's clothes." She laid the pile of neatly folded clothing on the corner of the table. "The soap is on the table with the basin, and I've also brought you a facecloth. If that water is warm enough, we'll leave you alone now."

Louise dipped one hand into the water. "Yes, I think it's fine. Please call us when you're done."

Before he could say anything more, they quickly left the room, and the curtain between the kitchen and dining room slid closed.

He'd never been in such a situation in his life, but he suspected that they were feeling as awkward as he was to have a strange man bathing in their kitchen. He marveled at their trust in him in the absence of the man of the house. No matter how quickly his exhaustion claimed him, Elliott vowed to say a special prayer for them tonight and perhaps every night for the rest of his life.

He quickly removed his soiled clothing and stepped into the tub. The warm water tempted him to relax, but considering the circumstances, he bathed as quickly as he could. By the time he left the tub, his eyes were nearly closing of their own accord.

He discovered the hard way that Mr. Demchuck's clothing was at least two sizes too big for him, but it was clean and warm. Mrs. Demchuck had no doubt compared his frame to that of her larger husband, because in addition to the clothing, she had also supplied a belt and suspenders.

He toweled his hair dry and joined the ladies in the living room. They both lowered their knitting to their laps at the same time.

"Should I assume that the water gets dumped outside?"

"Yes, a few steps beyond the back door we have a small ditch where we dump all the used water."

"You ladies go to bed; I'll do that. I don't know how I can ever thank you for your hospitality."

"Consider it our pleasure. I've left a pillow and some blankets here for you. Sleep well, Elliott."

He nodded. "And you, Mrs. Demchuck, Louise."

Through weary eyes, he could see the hint of a smile from Mrs. Demchuck when he called her by name, instead of "Ma'am."

When the ladies climbed the stairs, he returned to the kitchen and dumped the water in the ditch as she'd explained. With this task accomplished, he aimed himself for the soft, comfortable couch. Once down, he didn't bother to cover himself properly, and he fell into a deep, exhausted sleep.

Elliott slowly became aware that the world was shaking. A rumble that grew to a loud roar tried to separate him from his dreams, but what finally pulled him out of his sleep was the heavenly aroma of frying bacon and fresh coffee.

With a start, he sat up, discovering himself tangled in blankets, on a couch, in a living room he didn't recognize. As the world came into focus, he realized that the shaking and the roar was from a train going by.

He blinked, and slowly the events of the day before played over in his head like the script of a movie, except that everything was in color.

As quickly as he could, he gathered his thoughts and folded the blankets. He wasn't sure where he was to leave them, and as he looked around the room contemplating the best place, he spotted a man's jacket hanging over the chair next to the desk.

Elliott smiled at Mrs. Demchuck's thoughtfulness. He slipped on the jacket, exited the house, and walked around to the back of the property to the outhouse. Over the past few days he thought he'd become used to the cold, but after only one night in a warm house, the morning air chilled him to the bone. Never again would he take indoor plumbing for granted.

Once he returned inside, he draped Mr. Demchuck's jacket

over the chair and entered the kitchen.

"Good morning, ladies."

Mrs. Demchuck turned to him. "And a good morning to you. Did you sleep well, Elliott?"

"Yes, I did. Thank you, Ma'—Mrs. Demchuck."

At his near slipup, Louise made a strange sound, covered her mouth with her hands, and turned away.

Elliott couldn't look away. Yesterday, since he had been so tired, he had poured all his concentration into trying to help them. By the time they'd arrived back at the house, he could have fallen asleep on the hard wooden floor, but instead, he'd had to take a bath. He'd been so tired he had barely been able to keep his eyes focused. He didn't remember making it to the couch, but obviously he had.

Today, he felt like a new man. Most of all, he could think clearly.

The first thing that popped into his mind was that he hadn't properly dealt with Louise. Yesterday everything had happened so fast, and, before he knew it, he was waking up on their couch.

In too short a time, the next freight train would be pulling away from their little burg, and he hadn't yet properly expressed his thanks for all Louise and her family had done for him. If he and Louise had met any other way, he would have liked to get to know her better. But, since he was in the middle of nowhere and would never pass this way again, developing any sort of relationship, even a simple friendship, could only lead to hurt and disappointment. When the time came for them to separate, it would be forever.

Still, if all he had was until dinnertime when the next freight train passed through, he wanted to make the most of it.

"What time is it?" he asked.

"It's nearly ten o'clock. You've apparently slept in."

Mentally, he counted on his fingers. By the time they ate, then drove to the hospital and back, it would be midafternoon.

He didn't know if the freight trains kept the same schedule on the weekend. Actually, the more he thought about it, he really wasn't positive that this was the weekend. Something deep inside hoped that today's schedule would allow him more time to stay, even if it meant a colder ride due to a later hour.

"Dare I ask, what day is it?"

Louise's eyebrows quirked up. "Today is Saturday."

Mrs. Demchuck turned from her place at the cookstove. "Breakfast is almost ready. Would you like to have a seat?"

He glanced quickly to the table, which was already set for three. Elliott lowered himself into one of the chairs and waited while Mrs. Demchuck brought the frying pan to the table and portioned the food onto the plates.

"Checkout time at the hospital is noon, although it won't take nearly as long to get there as it did last night."

Elliott looked up to the clock on the wall. "What time should we be leaving, then?"

"Actually, if I have to go this time, I won't have enough time to prepare dinner. Since everything is under control and he's now coming home, I thought that I would stay here, and Louise can go in my place to give you directions to the hospital. I doubt you'd remember your way after that awful trip in the dark." She turned to her daughter. "Louise, do you mind?"

Chapter 5

Elliott backed the car out of the garage, then got out and ran around to open the passenger side door for Louise. She smiled hesitantly at him as he held the door open for her and slid in, carefully tucking her skirt beneath her before he pushed the door closed.

He quickly ran back around, grinning as he made a point of glancing at the only road in and out of the small burg. "I don't think I need directions to get out of Pineridge," he said as he began the trip down the long, narrow dirt road.

She grinned back. "No, I don't suppose you do. I guess where you come from is much bigger than this. Cat—something Falls, where there are no falls?"

He smiled. "Katona Falls. Because it was dark and we were in such a rush, I didn't see much of the city on the way to the hospital. I think Katona Falls is much bigger than Bows...uh...I really can't remember what it is, much less pronounce it."

Louise laughed, and it was a delightful sound. She pretended to tie a bow tie at her throat. "Bows. Now think zees." She pointed to her lower lip, letting her mouth open wide as the next syllable came out. "Zuh." Lastly, she pressed her teeth together at the same time as pursing her lips, the last syllable coming out between her teeth. "Zhure. Beauséjour. It's a French name. I don't speak French, nor do I know what it means, but I can pronounce that one word." She grinned widely. "After a little practice, mind you."

They laughed together as she continued to coach him with the correct pronunciation until he got it right. As they continued on, they talked about many things, yet nothing in particular for the length of their journey. Elliott couldn't remember the last time he'd enjoyed himself so much.

He also couldn't believe how soon they reached the town

limits, compared to the grueling expedition the previous evening. While the trip would have taken longer at night, he knew the companionship had made the difference. He found himself very disappointed that within minutes they would be at the hospital, and his time alone with Louise would be over.

As soon as he parked the car, he ran around to Louise's door and opened it for her. She turned to enter the small hospital building, but he touched her arm, stopping her midstep.

"This probably isn't the best time to ask, but since this will likely be the last time we will have alone together, I want to ask if I may write to you once I'm settled into my new job? Within a few hours I'll be gone, and I feel there is so much more we have to say to each other."

Her eyes widened, making Elliott think he had never seen such pretty eyes. Her cheeks darkened, and she lowered her head and stared at the ground. "Yes, I think I'd like that. Our address is very simple, just Pineridge, Manitoba. Everyone knows everybody else, and the post office is at Mr. Sabinski's store. We don't need to use the addresses or anything like that."

He escorted Louise to her father's room, where they found him perched on the side of the bed talking to a nurse. Mr. Demchuck smiled as soon as he saw them enter the room.

He held up a pair of crutches. "This is harder than it looks."

The nurse crossed her arms over her chest. "We wanted our patient to stay another day, but he insists on going home."

Mr. Demchuck shook his head. "I have work to do. I don't have a lead hand to take over for me. No one will have done the track inspection this morning, and I can't leave it unchecked another day."

The nurse tapped her foot, her arms still crossed. "I'm sorry, Mr. Demchuck, but I'm afraid that's impossible. You won't be doing any work for awhile. You might be up more in a week when you get used to the crutches, but even then, you'll find movement quite exhausting. And if you fall. . ." The nurse shook her head. "I don't want to see you back here with a broken arm in the next few days. You'll heal best if you rest. Do I have to call for the doctor?"

"I can only rest once the track is taken care of and I'm at home. Louise, did your mother give you the money to pay for everything?"

Louise pulled an envelope out of her purse and handed it to her father. Mr. Demchuck counted the money inside and nodded. "We'll be leaving then."

The nurse scowled, but at the same time, one corner of her mouth crooked up, and she cleared her throat.

Elliott leaned closer to Louise so he could whisper. "Is he always like this?"

She nodded very slightly. "Yes, but it's not what it seems. We've been here before when members of the section gang have been hurt, and most of the nurses know Papa. This is the first time he's been hurt, so it's a little different this time. They know he likes to tease, but they also know when he is being serious."

"He's being serious, now?"

She nodded again. "Yes. With Robert gone, there isn't anyone to oversee the track if Papa isn't there, and it's crucial that the inspections be made daily."

The nurse helped Mr. Demchuck into a wheelchair, and Elliott and Louise walked beside him as they proceeded to the front desk, where Mr. Demchuck paid the bill. The nurse pushed the wheelchair until they were all the way to the car. When Mr. Demchuck was steady on his crutches, she reluctantly allowed him to dismiss her and wheeled the chair back toward the hospital.

Elliott opened the passenger door, then helped Louise's father steady himself beside it before he ran around and climbed inside. Elliott crawled across the seat on his hands and knees, and as best he could from the awkward position, he helped Mr. Demchuck to lift himself inside. At first Mr. Demchuck appeared to be doing fine by himself. He pulled himself into the car backward, keeping one hand on the back of the seat. He braced his other hand on the dashboard, while maneuvering his leg. The heavy cast made the task awkward at best. He had almost pulled himself up enough to slide the rest of the way on the seat when he bumped his bare toes on the metal car door. Mr. Demchuck recoiled from the pain, causing him to lose his grip on the back of the seat. He frantically tried to right himself, but he began to slide down.

Louise dropped her purse on the ground and raised her arms, as if she could do something to prevent him from falling. The vision of Mr. Demchuck falling on Louise and both of them being hurt flashed through Elliott's mind.

Without thinking, Elliott lunged forward and grabbed Mr. Demchuck under the arms, then half pulled and half dragged the poor man all the way onto the seat.

Mr. Demchuck swiped his arm across his forehead. "I still seem to be a little dizzy. Those painkillers must have affected me more than I thought. Thank you, Elliott. That was a close one. I had no idea it was going to be this difficult, but I have to go home today. Waiting won't make it any better tomorrow."

"No, Sir, I don't imagine it will."

Once her father had properly positioned himself, Louise climbed up into the seat and squeezed into the small remaining space. She tucked her legs in so she wasn't touching her father's cast, then pulled the door closed. "I'm ready. We can go home now."

Elliott drove as carefully as he could. The roads in town were fairly smooth, although there were many winter potholes to maneuver around. The highway, being concrete, allowed him to reach a good speed of 30 mph to make the journey in as little time as possible. Very little was said as they traveled along, and the silence started to make Elliott uncomfortable.

He cleared his throat. "This is a fine car, Sir."

Out of the corner of his eye, he saw Mr. Demchuck nod once and smile. Immediately, Elliott relaxed.

"Yes, it's a 1932 Ford Cabriolet with one of those new eight-cylinder block engines. I suppose you have noticed how smoothly it runs."

"Yes, Mr. Demchuck, it does. Shifts easily, too."

"It has a 65-horsepower engine, and I only paid $610 for it, brand-new."

Elliott checked the odometer. "It doesn't have many miles on it for a six-year-old car."

"No, generally the only place I drive is to Beauséjour, and that's not very often. We take the train to Winnipeg twice a month to do our shopping. Other than that, there really isn't anyplace to go. We don't even have to drive to church; it's right in Pineridge. However, it's too small to have our own minister, so one minister travels around to many such community churches around the farming areas. Some services in the area are Saturday, but we've been blessed to actually have our service on Sunday at two in the afternoon. Do you have to travel far to your own church?"

Elliott forced himself to smile. The stock market had crashed when he was only sixteen. He'd been old enough to remember better times, but too young at the time to realize why they could no longer buy the things they had when he was younger. As he grew into adulthood, the economy continued to worsen and unemployment steadily increased. Instead of following his dreams, which included going to university and owning a car of his own, he had to work at his family's barbershop. Because he couldn't afford a car, he'd bought a motorcycle. Then, as times continued to worsen, he'd had to sell the motorcycle, among other things he'd valued, just to have enough money to pay for his food and other needs. Lately, the only time he drove, versus walking, was when he drove his brother's car when they needed supplies for their shop.

He faced straight forward as he spoke, concentrating more on the road than he needed to. "At home, I attend services at a church within walking distance from home."

"Louise plays the piano, so she plays the organ at church. She plays well."

"Thank you, Papa. You know I enjoy it."

They continued in silence until Elliott slowed to turn down the road that led to Pineridge.

"Elliott, while you're here, I was wondering if you could do something else for me. I hate to ask this, but I'm stuck. I need someone to inspect the track."

"Inspect the track, Sir?"

"Yes. It is my duty as section foreman to inspect my thirty-mile section of track every morning. It's also critical that I check and test every switch, every day."

"I'd be glad to, but I'm not sure what to do."

"You'd look for loose or broken spikes and ties that have split or become deteriorated. Then you'll have to mark those for the section gang to replace the next day. Any dead animals or debris must be cleared immediately, because any debris could cause an accident or derail the trains. Switches must be checked to be sure they are operating perfectly, including filling up the indicator lights with coal oil. When I do the inspection on my own on the weekend, it usually takes only a few hours."

Elliott had seen a clock on the wall at the hospital, and he estimated the time to now be about half past noon. He tried to calculate when they would arrive back at the house, then how much longer for him to receive adequate instruction for such a task. If the job took an experienced man a few hours, he didn't know how long it would take him, when he wasn't sure what he would be looking for. He suspected it would be much longer. Still, he couldn't say no, not in light of the present circumstances. "I'll do my best, Sir."

"I know what you're thinking. You're trying to figure out if that will give you enough time to hop back on the next freight train, and it might not. I want you to forget about that. For your trouble, I want you to spend the night with us again. Come to church with us tomorrow, and then I'm going to buy you a ticket on the passenger train for your kindness in helping us. Anna tells me that you have a job waiting for you on the coast. You'll get there faster with a paid ticket, even leaving a day later, than riding the boxcars."

"I don't know what to say, Sir."

"Well, there is one thing you can do."

"Yes, Sir. Anything."

"This is Pineridge, not the city where you came from. You can stop calling me 'Sir.' And don't call me Mr. Demchuck, either. My name is John."

Elliott bit his lower lip. Out of the corner of his eye, he saw Louise trying to hold back a giggle. Today, he was alert enough not to make the same mistake as he'd made with her mother. "Okay. . ." He nodded once, slightly. "John."

Upon their arrival at the house, Elliott drove the car as close as he could to the door and did his best to help John climb out. Elliott knew that even long after he left their home, he would always struggle to think of the man by his first name, as he hadn't been raised to address men old enough to be his father in such a manner.

Rather than have either of the women help John up the stairs, Elliott hurried to park the car in front of the garage, then jogged back to help John balance with the crutches up the three steps and get into the house. Once inside, he followed John to the couch and helped lower him as gently as he could until John was seated as comfortably as possible. Even still, John was short of breath for a few minutes.

"I'm not going to be able to do much, but I figure if we can do the inspection today and all is perfect, it should go smoothly tomorrow. We never miss a day of inspection unless it's an emergency, but both Frank and Henry are gone for the weekend, and Robert is gone for good. Monday they'll be back, so I can make arrangements for them to help until I'm out of the cast. For this weekend, I don't have a choice but to ask you to help. Usually, when I'm with the section men, we use the jigger, but since I can't put the speedster on the tracks, you're going to have to."

Elliott had no idea what a speedster was, but in the back of his mind, he could vaguely picture what a jigger looked like. He'd occasionally seen them, but he'd never been up close to one. He knew jiggers had wheels large enough to fit on the train track, and that in structure a jigger was basically a platform on wheels with some kind of double-handled pump in the middle, which was used to propel the unit. He didn't know what a speedster was, but if it was anything similar to a jigger, he had to assume it also would be constructed of mostly metal, and therefore, it would probably be heavy.

"Put it on the track? Has it fallen off?"

"No, no." John shook his head. "During the day, when we're working, we have it on the siding, but we can't store it on a siding when it's not in use."

"Siding?"

"That's about a half-mile section of track which runs parallel to the main track. It's operated by a switch, and one train uses it to park to allow another train to pass by. We also use the siding to park our jigger while we work. I do the same with the speedster when I'm alone."

"Oh. Then where is this speedster now if it's not on a siding?"

"It's in the toolhouse around the back of the bunkhouse. The railroad doesn't put in a length of track just to move the jigger, and especially not the speedster, so we pull it off the track at night and push it into the toolhouse."

Elliott tried to picture the procedure and couldn't. "Can this be done by one man?"

"There are ties laid out so it can be pushed on a solid surface, like a bridge, if you will. That way it won't sink into the ground. From the shed to the track is about fifteen feet. At the end, we've got the ties parallel to the track, so we only have to lift it sideways and put it on the track from beside. I do it myself every weekend."

For now, Elliott sat eye-to-eye with John, but since he was wearing John's clothes, he knew exactly how much bigger John was than himself. John had to outsize him by three inches in height and a good thirty pounds in weight. Of more importance than the difference in physical size, by trade Elliott was a barber. He knew he was too thin, but more so, he didn't do much in the way of physical labor. He didn't want to embarrass himself by being unable to do the task.

He cleared his throat. "I'll do my best, but I will need instructions."

"I can go with you. I figure if I can get into the car, I can get onto the speedster, which is lower than the seat of the car. We'd have more room on the jigger because the speedster is only meant for one, but one man can't move the jigger. And if we're going to do it, we should do it now. We have to keep the schedule in mind, and we can't afford mistakes. They could be deadly with a train coming on the same section of track."

Elliott stood. This wasn't something he was looking forward to doing, but putting it off wasn't going to make the situation go away.

John lifted one arm to brace himself on the back of the couch, stiffened, but didn't push himself up. "Louise, did you by any chance get the schedule today?"

"Yes, Papa, I did." She turned and walked to the desk, picked up a piece of paper, and returned with it, handing it to John, who relaxed and skimmed it.

He rested the paper in his lap, then lifted his head to face Elliott. "Every morning at seven o'clock they give everyone down the line the daily schedule by phone."

Elliott turned his head slightly toward the desk and felt his cheeks heat up. It wasn't realistic to expect any degree of privacy in the middle of the living room of such a small house, but it embarrassed him to know that Louise had been in the room with him, on the phone for quite some time only fifteen feet away. Even if she hadn't meant to, she couldn't have helped but watch him as he slept. He'd been so exhausted he wondered if he slept with his mouth open or, worse, if he snored. "I didn't realize I was that tired. I didn't hear the phone ring."

Louise shook her head and smiled. "It doesn't ring. The phone is only hooked up between the dispatch office in Kenora and the other section houses along the rail line. We have to be at the desk to listen at precisely seven o'clock every morning. It's difficult to hear clearly at times, but we have to be accurate in case there is a change in the schedule. Papa has to be sure the section gang and the jigger are off the main line and that they don't have a tie pulled out without a replacement at the time the trains are scheduled to pass by. He also needs to know if the trains are stopping, as time has to be allowed for the mail to be transferred and passengers to get off or board. After all, with only one store, the freight trains don't stop here that often. Nor do we often have passengers stopping."

Elliott couldn't imagine a community so small that the trains wouldn't necessarily stop, but it was so in Pineridge. The town, if he could call it a town, was no different in the daylight than it was in the dark. He'd counted exactly eight buildings here, and that included the train station.

John lowered his head to read the paper. "There's going to be a passenger train going through in about ten minutes, then the next train won't be by for three and a half hours, which is a good time to do the track inspection. We should go now and start getting ready to move the speedster." Once more, John braced himself against the back of the couch, but this time, he actually rose. Elliott stood in front of him, prepared to help if required.

When John was standing and leaning properly on the crutches, he turned and called out to the kitchen. "We'll be back in plenty of time for dinner, Anna. If you wouldn't mind, can we take those sandwiches you made for lunch with us? I believe Elliott and I have a lot of work to do."

Chapter 6

Not caring that her mother could see what she was doing, Louise stood at the kitchen window to watch Elliott and her father as they slowly made their way to the toolhouse. Her heart clenched to see how carefully Elliott helped her father position the crutches in order to make his way across the tracks. She could only imagine how difficult it would be to maneuver over the rails and not have the crutches slip while going over the ties, to say nothing of going over the loose rocks that surrounded the tracks. Watching how Elliott diligently did everything he could to help her papa nearly brought tears to her eyes. She didn't want to think that by this time tomorrow, he would be gone. Her only consolation was that he had promised to write. For anyone else, she would have questioned the sincerity of such intentions after such a short time spent together, but for Elliott, she knew he would keep his word.

Her mother's voice behind her made Louise jump. "I'll miss him, too. He seems like a fine young man."

Louise felt her cheeks burn with the realization that her mother knew what she was thinking. "Yes. I hope I will be able to sit beside him in church tomorrow."

"I don't see why not. Your father appears to like him."

The long whistle sounded, announcing the approach of the passenger train, right on time. Her mother joined her at the window, and together they watched the Transcontinental, which never stopped in a place as small as Pineridge, go by, momentarily blocking their view of Elliott and her father.

After the train passed, they watched as the men continued to make their way past the bunkhouse and to the toolhouse.

"He says he's a barber, Mama. I could tell he didn't know what Papa was talking about."

Her mother nodded. "I know. And he's so thin. I don't know how your papa expects that Elliott will be able to move the speedster by himself."

They watched at the window in silence as Elliott pushed the speedster down the row of ties, then struggled to lift it onto the tracks.

"I think he's going to need some liniment tonight."

Louise nodded. "Yes."

She remembered back to the previous night when he had offered to do some work, any work, in order to pay them back for providing a meal for him. She doubted he had any idea of the kind of work they did here to maintain the track. In a way, she wondered if Elliott was sorry he'd asked, but the more she thought about it, she doubted that he had any regrets, no matter how sore she knew he would be in the morning.

"Look, Louise! He's done it!"

She also caught him pressing his fists into the small of his back when her papa wasn't looking.

Next, they watched as Elliott braced himself, allowing her papa to use him for stability to push himself up onto the speedster. Struggling with the crutches, her father half pushed and half lifted himself onto the small seat; and Elliott hopped onto the back of the speedster's platform, barely managing to stay on, as the small unit was only made for one person. Her father pointed to a few things on the control. Elliott nodded, then pushed down hard on the handle to get the speedster moving.

Very slowly, the speedster began to inch forward, then pick up its pace. Louise and her mama watched as it disappeared down the length of track.

"I think we've done enough dillydallying, Louise. It's time to start cooking dinner. Can you fetch some meat from the outdoor cellar? I think today we'll have a nice roast beef and mashed potatoes."

Louise slipped on her boots, then her sweater, and went

outside to unlock the trapdoor beside the garage. She fastened the buttons to her neck, then descended the steps into the outdoor cellar. She saw that since more of the snow which she had packed down in the winter had melted with the warmer weather, she needed to lower the strings on the pails containing the meat, as a few were now more than a few inches from the snow-packed floor.

From one of the hanging pails, she selected a nice-sized roast beef that her father had purchased on his last trip to Winnipeg and quickly ran back up the stairs, outside, and back into the house where it was warm.

As she deposited the roast on the table, her mother laid an armload of clothes on one of the kitchen chairs.

"While they're gone we can get the ironing done. Since I had to wash Elliott's clothes while you were gone to Beauséjour, I also washed some of your papa's things. You can start ironing, and I'll go fix the holes in Elliott's shirt, now that it's dry. Plus, I also have some other mending to do."

Louise rested the iron on the cookstove to heat it, then brought the ironing board up from the basement to begin her chore. While she ironed, she listened to her mother work the treadle of the sewing machine, which was in the dining room under the window.

She could tell the difference between ironing her father's trousers and those belonging to Elliott. Still, she realized that even with the difference in size, Elliott's smaller-sized clothing didn't fit as they were meant to. She wished there were some way to send food with him. She also hoped that when he left he would take full advantage of the fine food on the dining car during his long trip to the coast. It made her heart ache to think that it wasn't simply because he was single that he didn't cook properly for himself. The reason he was so thin was because he couldn't afford enough food.

"Mama," she called out, "are you going to cook lots of extra potatoes since we have a guest?"

Her mama appeared in the doorway, Elliott's shirt in her hand. "Yes, Louise. It breaks my heart to see him so thin. I only wish he was staying longer."

"As do I, Mama, but to wish that way wouldn't be fair. He does have a job to get to, and he's been so kind to stay and help us."

The daily track inspection didn't take much longer than usual, and the men returned with plenty of time before dinner. However, instead of sitting in the living room as Louise expected, they both went to her father's desk.

Elliott pulled one of the dining room chairs to the desk, positioning it so her father could have his casted leg extended. Her papa's left leg was tucked partway under the desk, giving him access to the desktop if he leaned sideways in the chair. Louise didn't want to think that he was as uncomfortable as he looked. The doctor had told them he would be in the cast for eight weeks, and they would be long and miserable weeks. Of that, she had no doubt—not only for her father, but likely for the rest of the family as well.

Elliott sat at the regular desk chair off to the left side, also straddling the desk on his own side. With his right leg under the desk and his left leg sticking out, he didn't look comfortable either, but the strange position allowed both men access to the small desktop at the same time. As her father talked, Elliott made notes. They frequently stopped to read from the paper, talk about it, then continue on with her father talking and Elliott writing once again. At times, they stopped talking and writing entirely and examined other leaflets and books her father used for the railroad's records and schedules.

Louise finished the ironing and then began preparing a cake, which would go into the oven as soon as the roast was removed, so they could have something sweet for dessert. They had decided Louise would make her favorite—a special honey cake, made with honey purchased from one of the farms in the area.

Instead of staying in one spot to iron, she now could only sneak peeks at Elliott and her father as she walked back and forth while she did her baking.

Elliott and her father continued to mull over the papers at the desk. She strained her ears to hear what they were saying, but she could hear only the muffled murmur of low male voices, since they were facing the wall as they worked. Occasionally, she could make out the odd familiar word while they discussed the daily track inspection, but yet, the conversation seemed to be more detailed than she ever remembered when she overheard her father discussing the same things with the men from the section gang or even Robert, his former lead hand.

"Louise, I think we're going to eat in the dining room today, since we have a guest and this is the only time we'll have the opportunity to seat the four of us together for dinner."

Louise smiled. She could barely believe that only one day ago Elliott came into their lives as a hobo off the freight train. In that short space of time, she'd come to know him as a man of character and fine upbringing, regardless of the method of his arrival or his current situation. Also in that short space of time, he'd earned a special place in her heart, something he would never know.

Just as she entered the dining room to begin setting the table, Elliott and her father rose. Instead of going into the living room, Elliott followed her father outside. He stood on the steps and allowed her father to support himself by leaning on him as they hobbled down the steps together. Side by side, the two men made their way to the outhouse.

Her heart ached to see her father require assistance with such a simple thing as going outside and wished it didn't have to be so. She knew what it was like to have indoor plumbing from when they visited friends and relatives in the cities. Now knowing more about where Elliott had come from, it embarrassed her to think of how primitive their lifestyle appeared to him.

More than the simple necessities, seeing her father's difficulty with the few steps in the front of the house brought to the fore-front of her mind how difficult it would be for him to climb the stairs in the house to go to his bedroom.

The more she thought about it, the more worried she became that neither she nor her mama would be able to do everything necessary for him, even the simple tasks of helping her father move around their own home.

As Louise set the dining room table, she tried to close her mind to the problems of the future. She stopped all her motions and quoted Matthew 6:34 in her head, only letting her lips move, with no sound coming out as she prayed. "Take therefore no thought for the morrow: for the morrow shall take thought for the things of itself."

Before she opened her eyes, she heard the clunking and banging of the men coming back up the stairs, reminding her to add a thanks to God for the blessings they had received in having Elliott with them for the past day and especially for his willing-ness to help. Elliott may have thought they were helping him, but so far, he had helped them more than he could ever know. She only hoped Elliott knew how much his help and presence had come to mean to them.

As soon as the door opened, her mother walked through the doorway from the kitchen, wiping her hands on her apron as she spoke. "Please go straight to the table. Everything is ready now."

Louise helped her mother bring the food to the table, her father prayed over their food, and they began to eat. During the mealtime, Elliott and her father bantered back and forth good-naturedly about the track inspection, and Elliott playfully groaned out loud when her father reminded him that they would have to do the same thing the following morning, only this time, they would do it early in the morning, at the time it was supposed to be done.

Elliott first laughed at her father's joke about being awake and ready at seven o'clock to listen to the daily schedule on Sunday morning, but then suddenly, his laughter and his smile faded.

"Wait. Are you saying that you also must do this on Sunday?"

Her father also lost his smile, and suddenly the house became very quiet except for the distant crackle of the wood in the cookstove.

"It's necessary to inspect the track every day, including Sundays. The trains never stop running. Either a passenger train or a freight train comes through every few hours, every day, even Sunday. Therefore this is for the safety of hundreds of people who will be on the trains on Sunday. I liken it to a farmer, who must do certain tasks every day in order to keep the farm running and the animals healthy. Only that which cannot be left is done, and the rest of the day is set aside for the Lord's Day."

"I see."

A silence remained over the table, until Elliott cleared his throat and continued.

"Unfortunately, in our modern society, there are many things that must carry on, even on Sundays. Times are changing, and after being with you for only the one inspection, I understand what you mean about things that cannot be left. You said that your worship service in Pineridge is in the afternoon. That does allow you to put aside the majority of the day for our Lord to the best of your ability. I'm sure God honors that."

Her father nodded. "This job is one of few that gives us daily opportunities as a family to be able to help others who are less fortunate. We see homeless people every day. Even though it's only one stop and one day in their journeys, I like to think that the good we do for them can make a difference. Without this job, the home, the good wage, even down to the wood the railroad provides for us, we couldn't do that."

Elliott's cheeks darkened below his beard. "Yes. I'm a testimony to that."

Louise remained silent, but her mother spoke up. "We'll never know if the one thing we do for those who ask will help lead a lost soul to salvation, but we trust that this is what the Lord would have us do."

Briefly he turned his head, making direct eye contact with Louise. She froze, her fork lifted halfway to her mouth, and stared back. His gaze remained fixed as he spoke. "Only the Lord knows what my stop here has meant to me." He paused for a few seconds, then turned back to her mother. "You truly do have a wonderful ministry here, both for the Christian and the nonbeliever."

Louise thought her heart might pound out of her chest. She wanted to say that she also knew that this time was special in a way she still couldn't figure out, but she didn't want to say anything in the presence of her parents and especially not at the dinner table.

Fortunately, the conversation continued with Elliott sharing some of his experiences while riding the freight trains. His tales were fascinating, but at the same time they drove pangs of sadness into her heart to hear of such heartbreaking testimonies. Elliott mentioned many men he'd met. Though times were difficult, they all shared an underlying thread of hope—hope that when every man arrived at his destination, wherever it might be, he would also find a job and the means to a better life.

As soon as everyone was done, before anyone left the table, Louise rose, scurried into the kitchen, and returned with the cake she'd made.

Elliott stared at it as if he'd never seen a cake in his life.

Louise smiled from ear to ear. "This is my favorite cake. I hope you like it. It's a honey cake."

"I don't know what to say. I can't remember the last time I had a piece of cake. Saying thank you doesn't seem like enough for the way you've opened up your home and welcomed me like a friend."

Regardless of the fact that her parents were there, or perhaps because of it, she allowed her fingertips to rest lightly on his arm. "We're welcoming you as a Christian brother, as well as a friend."

He looked up at her, and all thoughts of cutting the cake fled Louise's mind. Not even when they helped her father at the hospital and not even when they were alone together in the car had she been so close to him. This was the first time she truly looked closely at him, and she was mesmerized. She couldn't see most of his face because of his beard, but his eyes were beautiful—brown, flecked with green, but they held a sadness, as well as something else she couldn't define. Mindless of all else, she continued to stare, until her father cleared his throat.

Louise blinked and tore herself away, totally ashamed of herself. She'd only kissed one man in her life, but she had at that moment been wishing her parents were elsewhere so Elliott could have kissed her now. And that was wrong.

By this time tomorrow, he would be gone. She knew he had promised to write, but writing wasn't the same as developing a personal friendship. Despite the best of intentions, she knew that soon, when he settled into his new job and his new home, that he would faithfully write, because he had promised. Then, as tended to happen, he would write less and less often, until one day the letters would simply stop. It would perhaps take a period of time, but in the end, Elliott would be one more of the countless homeless men who passed as a shadow, never to be seen again.

The thought crushed her heart like a vice.

Louise picked up the knife, and willing her hand to stop shaking, she began to cut the cake. "Who gets the first piece?"

Chapter 7

Elliott tried not to groan at the jangle of the alarm clock on the floor beside the couch. The ringing meant it was now a quarter to seven in the morning. He had fifteen minutes to wake up and prepare himself to take notes on the daily schedule, as John had instructed him to do.

His eyes burned from lack of sleep. He tried to rub it away, but the contact only made them water.

He sat up, but then flopped his head back and stared at the ceiling in the early morning light.

He didn't remember it being this way the previous night, but then he'd been so exhausted he would have slept through an earthquake.

But then, an earthquake would have been quieter. Every few hours, all night long, another train rumbled past. Not only did the trains shake the house, and therefore the couch, but the noise would have awakened the dead.

Not that he was dead, though. And with thanks to the Demchuck family, he wasn't likely to be dead soon. He hadn't realized until he'd actually begun to travel just how dangerous riding the freight trains could be. Knowing now what he didn't know then, the promise of a ticket was more than an answer to prayer.

Once more, he blinked hard, then stood, stretching his arms over his head, trying to wake himself. Slowly, he moved his head from side to side to work out the kinks in his neck, when he spotted the same jacket he'd worn the day before hanging over the back of the chair at the desk. He smiled and slipped it on and, as quietly as he could, made his way out the door. Indoor plumbing was nice, but the trip to the outhouse in the cold morning air would serve to wake him up like nothing else, including the all-night trains.

When the time came for him to pick up the phone and take notes, he was alert and ready. Exactly as he had been warned, the reception was poor. Every once in awhile he heard banging and other noises, probably made from the other people in their various sections along this rail line as they, too, listened and made their notes.

Out of curiosity, he continued to listen after the clerk in the faraway dispatch office in Kenora finished reading the schedule. Some of the men made reports that they needed rails replaced, and therefore required special equipment; others mentioned particular supplies they needed. One mentioned a problem with a switch, and then the clerk in Kenora confirmed that all things mentioned would be handled by the main office.

Overall, Elliott found the procedure fascinating. He couldn't imagine the organization or the teamwork for all those section gangs to keep the line running perfect with no downtime, yet they did. He wondered if the section foremen down this line ever got together for social activities or if their association was strictly business, at precisely seven o'clock every morning, seven days a week.

Unfortunately, he would never find out. Today, after the church service, he was leaving.

The house was quiet, although he couldn't imagine how the Demchuck family managed to sleep through the racket of the trains.

Elliott continued to sit in the chair, reading the schedule. While straining to hear, he had written as quickly as possible, not paying attention to actual content or meaning. He only wrote numbers for the sake of accuracy. Now, he could put all his notes into perspective.

It was with sadness that he read that the train he would be leaving on would be departing at half past four. He laid the paper down and counted on his fingers. Nine short hours.

He wanted to spend those nine hours with Louise, but he

couldn't. Soon John would need help down the stairs and outside. Following that, they would do the morning's track inspection, which would take them to lunchtime. After lunch they would attend the Sunday worship service, and then Elliott would have less than an hour before the freight train arrived. It would stay for a short ten minutes, then depart.

Elliott suddenly froze as he found himself unconsciously stroking his beard. Now aware of what he was doing, he paid attention to what his fingers were telling him and once again touched his chin. The hair had grown soft and was no longer completely untidy, but he still didn't like it. As a barber by trade, Elliott frequently shaved other men. By the nature of his job, it was of utmost importance that he not be in need of a shave himself and that his own hair was always well trimmed.

If he shaved, he would be properly groomed for exactly one day, because he had no means to shave again until he reached his destination. Therefore, he had no alternative but to keep the beard while he traveled. When Elliott received his first paycheck, the first thing he would buy besides clothing would be a new razor.

Still, Elliott wished Louise could see him as he really was, not as an unkempt vagrant off the freight train. After he arrived at his destination, provided the job was still available, he wondered if he could get his picture taken and enclose it with a letter, telling Louise how much he missed her.

Abruptly, Elliott stood in order to rid his mind of such foolishness. He'd only had a few hours alone with Louise and known her for under two days. He could only reason that his odd attachment was in some way related to the circumstances he now found himself in.

Under normal conditions, he would have had more time to get to know her better, perhaps even court her as she deserved to be courted. However, conditions were not normal. He had no job, no assets, and no home.

His thoughts were interrupted by voices at the top of the stairs, followed by the gentle thuds of John's crutches and the heel of the cast echoing on the floor.

Without waiting to be asked, Elliott bounded up the stairs and removed the crutches from John's hands. Very slowly, one stair at a time, he guided John down while John held the handrail with one hand and supported himself on Elliott's shoulder with the other.

Once he was at the bottom and properly balanced on both crutches, John turned to Elliott. "Praise the Lord, I'll only have to do that once a day."

Louise and Mrs. Demchuck slipped behind them without speaking and scurried into the kitchen.

"Let me help you down the steps outside, and I'll wait for you."

Upon returning to the house, Elliott could already smell bacon and eggs cooking. He sat in the kitchen with John to go over the daily schedule while the women busied themselves making breakfast and setting the table.

Elliott glanced up at the clock on the wall. "According to this, we have three quarters of an hour before the next passenger train. Then we will have two and a quarter hours to do the inspection before church."

John nodded as Mrs. Demchuck and Louise set the plates on the table in front of them and poured the coffee.

Since they were in no rush, Elliott found it pure pleasure to be able to linger over their breakfast and enjoy their time together. It had been many years since he'd shared such a time with his own family, and it served as a pointed reminder of how much he missed it.

Mrs. Demchuck leaned forward on her elbows, cradling her coffee cup in her palms. "Please forgive me for asking, but we've all been so curious about you. All we know about you is that you're a barber by trade and you come from Katona Falls in Ontario. Do you have family somewhere? Of course, we're happy that you have a job to go to. What kind of job is it that you have to travel so far?"

Elliott forced himself to smile as the unspoken question hung in the air—what was he doing riding the freight trains?

Mrs. Demchuck's question was reasonable and expected. He'd stayed with them two nights; he'd eaten their food. Mrs. Demchuck had even washed and repaired his clothing. It seemed wrong to be in this situation, being treated this way by an employee of the railroad after essentially stealing a ride on the train to get there. However, not only did they welcome him as their guest, they welcomed him as their friend.

So far, he'd successfully avoided giving them the more personal details of his life, even fooled himself into believing he could get away with it. Now, he could no longer avoid their curiosity.

He stared into his coffee cup. He would have preferred to share his hopes and dreams with these fine people, not the details of his failures.

"I'm not sure where to start. My father owned a barbershop in Katona Falls. Our house caught fire in 1933 when I was away at university. Both my parents died in the fire."

Mrs. Demchuck lowered her cup to the table, and rested her fingers on his forearm. "Oh, Elliott. . .I'm so sorry to hear that."

"Thank you for your concern," he muttered. "It's been five years, and I still miss them, but as Christians, they're in a better place than I am." He paused, snapped his mouth shut, and cleared his throat. "I'm sorry; that came out wrong. Being here with you now is wonderful."

Louise and her mother smiled at him.

"That's okay, Elliott," Mrs. Demchuck said, patting his arm as she spoke. "I don't think our small home in the country could in any way compare to the golden gates of heaven."

John quirked up one corner of his mouth and nodded. Immediately, Elliott relaxed, feeling better about his poor choice of wording.

Elliott cleared his throat. "Unfortunately, like so many other people, in order to cut back on expenses my parents had canceled the house insurance. I was only twenty years old and had just entered university. When they died I had to quit school. First, I couldn't find a job to support myself while I continued my schooling. Also, with our dad gone, my brother Ike needed a partner for the barbershop. So, I left school and started working with him. Since I had nowhere to stay and the house was gone, and since I'm obviously single and don't need a lot of room, we converted the storage area in the attic of the barbershop to living quarters for me. We made it into a one-bedroom suite, which suited my needs, as long as I didn't mind sharing my living room with the supplies."

His cup had long since been empty, but Elliott swirled the last few, cold drops around in the bottom and then drank them. "Ike is a few years older than I am, and he's married and has a family to support. Business for the barbershop continued to drop off, and then a couple of months ago the bank foreclosed on Ike's house. Since he needed a place to stay, he and his wife and their two children moved into the suite with me. As you can guess, it became very crowded very fast, with three adults and two children living in a one-bedroom suite above the barbershop."

They all nodded.

"We can only imagine," Mrs. Demchuck mumbled.

"By then things were so bad, we were forced to admit that the shop couldn't support all of us. Ike wasn't going to kick me out or dissolve the partnership, but then I received an answer to prayer. A letter came from an old friend, saying that if I was interested he could give me a job in a logging camp in British Columbia. He said the work would be hard, but. . ." Elliott paused to grin weakly and shrugged his shoulders. "He said that the wages were good. For now, any steady work would be good, regardless of the amount. So I wrote him back to tell him I was on my way. I'd already sold most of my furniture. I gave what was left to Ike, packed everything I owned in two suitcases, and left."

He could see their eyes widen at the thought that he could carry everything in the world he held valuable. Even he had struggled with it when it came time for him to pack. Once he'd laid everything out on the bed, he couldn't believe that everything he owned, except for a couple of pieces of furniture and a few other small items, could fit into two suitcases. As it was, he had to sell his watch in order to have enough money to pay for the bus and train tickets.

With the promise of a job, he'd considered the opportunity a new start, even though he had mixed feelings about moving away from the only place he'd ever known to live in parts unknown. In a way, he felt like one of the three little pigs out to seek his fortune. He had hoped that in the end he would liken to the little pig whose house was made of bricks.

"I bought my ticket for the bus to Ottawa, where I planned to buy a train ticket to Vancouver. The plans were that once I arrived in Vancouver, I was to contact a friend of Edward's, who would in turn contact Edward up at the logging camp, and then Edward would come and get me. But, on my way from the bus depot to the train station, a gang of men attacked me and robbed me, leaving me with nothing except the clothes on my back."

Louise gasped, and her mother covered her mouth with her hands. "That's horrible! Were you hurt?"

He rested his fingers on his neck. It didn't take much imagination to still feel the cold steel of the knife blade pressed to his throat. Fortunately, the tender spots and bruises from the beating they had given him were now healed, although his left arm still hurt when he moved it a certain way. "I wasn't badly hurt, no. But I had to decide if I should go back with nothing, knowing that Ike could barely support his own family, never mind having an extra mouth to feed. I prayed about it, and rather than take the food out of the mouths of my brother's children, I decided to carry on. And here I am. Apparently, the Lord does provide our needs, just as I was taught in Sunday school."

Silence hovered over the table and John spoke first. "That's quite a story, Elliott."

"Actually, my story is not much different than many of the men I've met along the way. Traveling like this is quite lonely. When you have time to talk to someone else in the same situation, there's an instant bond. I've always found it easy to talk to people, and this last week has been no exception. I've spoken to many men who needed the hope that you can only have with Jesus Christ in your heart. I only pray that my words have had a lasting impression on some of those men. Unfortunately, I'll never know, because I'll never see a single one of them again."

He only meant to glance up quickly, but his attention became glued to Louise. Her eyes opened wide and she appeared to be staring at a blank spot on the wall behind her father. Her eyes became strangely glassy, then she swiped her hand across them before turning to him. "We've felt that same way when we've given food or clothing to the men who pass through Pineridge. A few will listen openly to what we try to give as a message of hope, but most of them only listen to be polite because we're giving them something. We'll never know which of those we've spoken to will ever receive the message of hope and eternal salvation."

Elliott opened his mouth, about to say he understood perfectly, but a long whistle sounded in the background.

Mrs. Demchuck rose quickly. "Goodness! How the time has flown! You'd better get outside, because the train will be through in a few minutes and you have to get that inspection done quickly. We'll have a quick lunch when you're done. We don't want to be late for church."

John turned toward him. "We should try to make it across the tracks before the train arrives. We have to get the speedster out of the toolhouse."

Elliott rose, wondering if he should have been trying to help John stand. He hated to see the man struggle, but he didn't want to continuously offer help when none was required. He wanted to allow John to retain as much dignity as possible in a difficult situation. Instead, he thought about the work involved in pushing the speedster out of the toolhouse and lifting it onto the tracks. He could still feel yesterday's efforts in his back.

"I must say that speedster is a strange contraption, but it seems quite efficient for its purpose."

"Yes. But as you no doubt found the hard way, it's meant to seat only one person."

Elliott nodded. He'd barely managed to stay on the unit, and the two of them had jostled for position, both of them being quite uncomfortable for the entire time it took to travel down the tracks to do the inspection. He'd also seen the larger jigger in the toolhouse, which would have been more appropriate for more than one person. However, John had told him that it took four able-bodied men to put the jigger on the tracks every day, implying those four men were accustomed to hard work. One look at the huge jigger told him it was not a task for a man with one leg in a cast and another man whose heaviest lifting job until then consisted of occasionally lifting boxes of shampoo.

By the time they were ready to move the speedster, the train had already passed. As Elliott pulled the unit out of the toolhouse and struggled to line it up on the tracks properly, he thought about how difficult the next few hours would be.

It wasn't the track inspection he was thinking of. The track inspection was a new experience, even if it did mean a rather uncomfortable journey on the speedster. However, compared to riding the boxcars as he had been, trying to maneuver around John on a unit that was really meant for one couldn't compare. On the bright side, as different as it was from what he was used to doing, he found the experience rather interesting.

As for attending church with the Demchucks, he very much anticipated going. He tried to think of what their service would be like and couldn't. He'd always attended the same church at home, a grand old stone building with polished oak pews and ornate stained glass windows. He couldn't imagine a church service being conducted in the small wooden building where the entire structure could have fit into his own church's Sunday school room.

Regardless of the setting, the purpose of getting together was to worship God with other believers, and that was exactly what he planned to do. While trying to imagine the order of the service, he wondered if Louise would be playing the organ. Part of him hoped she would, because he wanted to hear her play, but part of him didn't. He didn't want to participate with her from across the room, no matter how small he knew it would be. He wanted to worship God with her at his side.

Suddenly, the reason for his apprehension about leaving hit him with the force of a tornado.

The reason he didn't want to leave was because he didn't want to say good-bye to Louise.

Chapter 8

L ouise stood at the window, watching her father and Elliott start off down the track on the speedster.

"It was good of him to stay one more day, wasn't it?" her mother said from behind her.

"He'll get to the coast faster with a ticket, even leaving one day later," Louise muttered, continuing to stare down the track, even though the men had disappeared from sight.

"Did you tell him he doesn't need to know the address, just Pineridge?"

Louise spun around so quickly her skirt billowed around her knees. "Mama!"

Her mother didn't even have the grace to blush. Fortunately, she didn't comment further.

"I think we should do the dishes and make lunch; then I'll change into my good dress." Without needing instructions, Louise pushed the plates to the side, took the basin down from its hook on the wall, carried it to the cookstove, and filled it with warm water.

"For lunch, we're going to use the rest of yesterday's roast beef for sandwiches. The bread should be ready to come out of the oven in a few minutes. I was also thinking we might make some donuts for dessert."

Louise nearly dropped the basin of water on the floor. "Dessert? At lunchtime? And donuts? Before church? Doesn't that take too long?"

This time, it gave Louise great satisfaction to see her mother's cheeks darken.

"Hush, Girl. We'll have time if we hurry. You carry that water, and I'll go get the flour and sugar out of the cellar."

Louise chatted very little with her mother as they worked to complete their tasks. The long periods of silence allowed her to think. She could tell her mother liked Elliott. She couldn't help but like him, too. However, Louise suspected there was more to her mother's words than had been said aloud. She deemed this was her mother's unstated approval to keep in contact with him.

Aside from Mr. Farley's son, Johnathan, and William McSorbin, one of the local farmer's sons, there were no other young men in Pineridge. The only times she had opportunity to meet other young men her age was when their family traveled to Winnipeg every month and stayed at the homes of friends or relatives in the city.

So far, she had not met anyone specifically to her liking beyond a simple friendship. However, at nearly twenty years of age, it was time for her to start thinking of her future and getting married. Louise would have liked to take the time to see if Elliott could have been that special man God had chosen for her, but she would never know. Later that day, he would be gone and living over a thousand miles away.

Just as she finished frying the last donut, she heard the squeal of metal wheels on the track in front of the house.

"They're back, Mama!"

"Quickly, Louise. Go change your dress now, and I'll finish putting the donuts on a plate."

Obediently, Louise ran up the stairs and quickly selected her favorite dress and, along with it, a hat with lace bows that her mother had made to match her dress. She picked up the hand mirror from atop her dresser, appraised herself quickly, adjusted one of the bows, returned the hat to the dresser until it was time to go, and ran back downstairs.

Since the men had not yet come inside the house, Louise slipped her apron back on to protect her good dress and poured the coffee into the cups already on the table.

Behind her, the door closed with a bang. "Wow. Something smells great!"

"Mama made donuts."

Elliott's eyebrows raised, and one hand settled on his stomach. "Homemade donuts? Wow."

Louise smiled. "You've never had homemade donuts?"

"Never."

"Mama makes the best donuts in Pineridge." She beamed.

"Hush, Louise. You can make them just as well as I can."

Across the table, Elliott remained standing while her papa inched his way toward his chair and slowly began to lower himself, leaning on the crutches for support with one hand and steadying himself with his other palm on the tabletop. "I must be getting old. I'm so tired, and we haven't even had lunch."

Without warning, the crutches slipped on the linoleum. Her father's eyes widened as his unsupported weight on the edge of the table caused it to shudder, and suddenly, as his side of the table started to go down, the other end started to go up.

In her mind, Louise pictured all their dishes and their lunch, hot coffee and all, flying through the air, and her father crashing to the floor. She sucked in a deep breath to scream, but before a sound came out, Elliott pushed all his weight on his corner of the table to steady it. With the table held firm, her father regained his balance, half leaning and half hanging onto the edge of the table.

The dishes clattered and settled. Some dribbles of coffee ran over the surface of the table, but the cups all remained upright.

Her father dropped himself into the chair and covered his face with his hands. "I'm sorry, Anna. You can't believe how difficult this is."

Her mother turned away and busily tucked the sandwiches back into good order. "Hush, John. I know it's hard. The nurse told me when we left you for the night that little mishaps would happen, and she was right. It will take time to become accustomed to moving around on crutches, plus she said your balance will be off. Now, everybody, let's eat. We don't want to be late for church."

This time, Elliott prayed over the food, and because of the late hour, they ate more quickly than at breakfast.

"Thank you for a wonderful lunch, Mrs. Demchuck."

"Hush, Elliott. I haven't done all this by myself. Louise has done more than her share. Louise is a very good cook, isn't she?"

Louise stiffened in her chair. "Mama!" she hissed quietly, then quickly turned to force a toothy smile at Elliott.

He blinked twice and stared back. "Yes, she certainly is. I've never in my life eaten so well as these last two days."

Thankfully, instead of saying more, her mother rose. "If you'll excuse me, I must change my dress before church. John, I've left a clean shirt for you by the washbasin, and Elliott, I've taken a few tucks in one of John's shirts, so you can also have something to wear, although I'm afraid your own trousers will have to do."

"Thank you, Mrs. Demchuck. I appreciate everything you've done for me more than words can say."

"And we appreciate all you've done for us as well. Now let's hurry, or we'll be late."

Louise ran upstairs to fetch her hat, but before she set it on her head, she ran her brush through her hair to fix it and applied a thin coat of lipstick to her lips. She'd never much cared for such things, but today she wanted to look her best.

She waited in the living room with her mama while the men washed and changed their shirts. Even though it wasn't far, walking down the dirt road on crutches would be too difficult for her father; so she and her mama walked to the church and Elliott drove her father with the car, since only three people could fit inside.

"Mama, you can go join Papa and Elliott. I have to talk to Mildred for a minute."

Before her mother could protest, she ran off to speak to her friend, then returned as quickly as she could to be with her family.

Rather than stand around to talk, they escorted her father up the two steps and helped him take a seat inside where he could talk to people who were curious about his cast and his accident.

When the service began, Pastor Galbraith welcomed all present. He extended a special welcome to her father for coming in spite of the cast and then reviewed the community announcements.

Mildred walked to the organ, and the congregation stood.

"Louise," her mother whispered in her ear, "why is Mildred playing the organ?"

Louise turned to whisper back. "I asked her to trade with me. I wanted to sit in the congregation today."

Her mother's one raised eyebrow told her that she knew it was a specific visitor in the congregation with whom she wanted to sit. Ignoring her mother's telltale smirk, Louise flipped through the hymnal to the correct page and began to sing with the congregation.

She nearly choked on her words when Elliott began to sing beside her. Not only did he sing in a lovely baritone, but he sang in perfect flowing harmony for every song. The rich blend of his voice, combined with the deep bass of Mr. Sabinski, the only other man in the congregation who could also sing a harmony, profoundly affected everyone present during the time they worshiped the Lord with their songs.

Elliott sat with rapt attention for the entire length of the sermon and mumbled an enthusiastic "amen" each time Pastor Galbraith made a good point.

After the close of the service, many people approached them to talk, first, because having a visitor to their small congregation in the country was rare, but mostly, Louise suspected, it was because Elliott's fine singing had created a stir.

Mildred was the first person to approach him. "Was that you singing like that? Praise the Lord for your lovely voice!"

In the bright sunlight, Louise could see the color of Elliott's checks darken, even beneath the beard.

"I love to sing, especially for the Lord on Sunday."

"I hope your home church has a choir, and that you are in it."

"Yes, I am. I'm also a member of a barbershop quartet, which is a lot of fun. Actually, I get teased a lot about that, because I really am a barber."

He smiled fully, showing a beautiful set of teeth, in addition to his beautiful smile. It made Louise long to see that same smile more often, but she felt the minutes ticking away, reminding her that their time together was running out.

As much as she didn't want him to go, she didn't want him to miss the train, either. "Elliott, you stay here with my friends. I'm going to find Papa and see if he's ready to go. I'll tell him you'll be at the car shortly, but I know it will take him longer to get there than you."

His answering smile made her foolish heart flutter. Before he noticed that she was acting strange, Louise walked away, in search of her parents.

Since she didn't see them outside talking to anyone, Louise walked back into the church. Not finding them there either, she stood still and crossed her arms, wondering where they could have gone. Then, she heard what sounded like her father's voice coming from the doorway leading to the Sunday school classroom.

Because she was in the Lord's house, Louise didn't call out to them. Instead she approached them, meaning to speak to them at a respectful volume.

Her feet skidded to a halt on the polished wood floor when she heard her father mention Elliott's name.

"John! Are you serious?" she heard her mother whisper to her father. Even though she couldn't see her mother's face, Louise well imagined her expression. Surely she would be standing with her arms crossed and her head tilted to one side. Any second, Louise expected to hear the tapping of her mother's shoe on the hard floor.

Her papa replied, his voice also hushed. "I know what you're thinking, Anna, but listen to me. I know he doesn't know what he's doing. I'm not sure that he's very mechanically minded, but you should have seen him out there. He has a real eye for detail. More so, he's humble, and he's teachable. He's young, but he's an honorable man, and that combination makes him more suitable than anyone could ever be."

"Do you know what you're asking him to do?"

"I'm not asking him to turn down the other job. He told me that he doesn't have a specific starting date; his friend's letter said whenever he got there. I want to ask him if he could get in touch with his friend and ask if the job would still be his in eight weeks. If he has to go, I'll certainly understand, but I really believe the Lord has placed Elliott in our path at this time for a reason."

"I don't know, John."

"I've prayed about it, and I have my answer. It's up to Elliott now."

"You'd better ask him quickly, then. Doesn't the train leave soon? You're not giving him much time to think about it. This is a big decision for him. And what about Louise?"

"What about her? I don't think it will be that much more work for her if we have to feed an extra person for a couple of months."

"You don't understand. Louise has taken a shine to him. And rightly so—he seems to be a fine young man. But this presents a problem."

"How so? I believe that he feels the same way about her, so why would that be a bad thing?"

"As her parents, we must make sure they aren't left open to temptation. But more than that. What about when he leaves? She's my daughter, and I don't want her to be hurt."

"Anna, she's not a little girl. She's nearly twenty years old, old enough to be married. Nothing will happen if she knows he'll be leaving again."

"I don't know...."

"She's a sensible girl, and you said it yourself; Elliott is an honorable young man. Come on. We have to find him so I can take him aside and talk."

Louise didn't need to hear anymore. As fast as her feet would go without taking the chance of making noise on the hardwood floor, she hurried across the room. Once outside, she ran the rest of the way.

She found Elliott alone, leaning against the flagpole. He straightened as soon as he saw her coming.

"There you are. I was wondering where you went and what was taking you so long. I wanted to talk to you about something privately."

Louise's throat tightened. She didn't know what to think. Of course, she would have loved him to stay so she could get to know him better, but if that meant risking his job, then such thinking was selfish. "There's something I have to tell you, too."

"Please, let me go first; this is difficult. I'll be leaving soon, and this is my last chance."

"But—"

He held up his palms to silence her. "No, please, let me finish. This is difficult. I know I've said I would write, but I should have asked you first if you would like to exchange letters with me, rather than expecting you would want to. For my lack of manners, I apologize."

"Elliott, listen to me." Quickly, she turned her head from side to side to make sure her parents hadn't caught up to her yet. "We may not be exchanging letters."

"Oh. I'm sorry. I should have realized there was already someone else in your heart. Now if you'll excuse me—"

"Hush, Elliott," she whispered and reached forward to touch his sleeve, halting him in his tracks. "It's not that. I heard Mama and Papa talking. Papa is going to ask if you'll stay here and be his lead hand until he's out of the cast and back to work."

"Lead hand? But I know nothing of maintaining the track

other than what little your father told me over the last two days."

Louise nodded so fast her hat wobbled on her head. She reached up with her free hand to straighten it and kept talking. "I know. I'm only repeating what I heard. He trusts you."

"Well. . .I'm honored. I don't know what to say."

"Of course, he knows you have another job, but he says from the sound of it, you don't have a specific start date."

"I'm not entirely sure of that until either I get there to speak to Edward or somehow find a way to get a letter to him."

She glanced behind her to see her parents advancing slowly.

"I probably shouldn't have told you, but I couldn't help myself."

One side of his mouth quirked up. "I'm glad you did. Today while we were out, your father asked me some rather strange questions. I thought I had done something wrong, yet he assured me that wasn't the case. It all makes sense now."

"What are you going to do?"

"There's only one thing I can do. I have to think about it and pray. But I suppose I shouldn't do that until your father talks to me and gives me all the details and tells me all my options."

Once again, Elliott got the car to drive her father the short distance home, leaving Louise to walk with her mother.

"Let's walk slowly. Your father has something to talk to Elliott about, and they may be awhile."

Louise inhaled deeply, then let all the air out in a whoosh. She couldn't look at her mother as she spoke. "I know. I'm sorry, Mama, but I heard you and Papa talking."

"Did you tell Elliott?"

"Yes. I'm sorry."

"It's okay. You've never been good at keeping secrets. I suppose it's foolish of me to expect that you could start now."

Louise didn't know what to say, so she said nothing.

When they arrived at the house, instead of joining the men in the living room, they went in through the back door and immediately started making preparations for dinner. Louise brought a roast pork out of the outdoor cellar, and they peeled potatoes to tuck inside the roaster before it went into the oven.

Although she could hear the murmur of their voices, Louise couldn't hear their actual words from where she was. After a rather lengthy conversation, a long silence followed. Louise suspected that they were praying for wisdom for Elliott's decision.

Even though he'd met with hard times, Elliott Endicott truly was an honorable and godly man. One day, he would make some lucky woman a wonderful husband.

She nearly dropped the potato onto the floor, startled with pangs of jealousy for a woman who so far didn't exist.

Louise and her mother continued to make dinner, not knowing if Elliott would be staying or leaving with the passenger train that was due shortly. Louise didn't want to think about it, so she struggled to think of other things while she did the worst job she'd ever done of slicing carrots.

The carrot she'd been peeling dropped to the floor when her father and Elliott entered the kitchen.

"Anna, Louise. I hope you're setting a fourth plate at the table. Elliott has agreed to be my lead hand for eight weeks."

"That's wonderful!" Louise and her mother said in unison.

Louise wanted to run to Elliott and throw her arms around him but couldn't do so in front of her parents, especially after what she'd heard them discussing about watching her interaction with Elliott during the time he was there.

"We're going to name his position officially as lead hand, but really his duties will be mine, and he will act as substitute section foreman. For at least the first few weeks, after the daytime work with the section men is done, I'll have to teach Elliott the rest of the job in the evenings, since that is the only way he can be properly trained. Because of that, he can't be staying in the bunkhouse with the section men. We've decided that he's going to continue sleeping here on the couch. This way he can take the scheduling call every morning at seven, and he'll be here for me when I need help as well."

Louise clasped her hands together. "I'm so glad, Elliott! And that means you'll be making a good salary, too."

"Until he gets his first paycheck, he's going to borrow whatever of mine he needs. Anna, you're going to have to help him, since I can't. In fact, I think I'm going to go lie down on the couch until dinner is ready."

Louise stood in silence as her father hobbled into the living room.

Her mother wiped her hands on her apron as she spoke. "I'm going to enjoy having you here, Elliott. I can show you where everything is now that dinner is cooking and Louise is doing the vegetables. What's the first thing you want to see?"

Elliott ran his hand over his chin and smiled from ear to ear. "A razor."

Chapter 9

Louise didn't know which was less proper, to go into the living room where her father was trying to sleep or to stay in the kitchen and work with her mother while Elliott shaved.

She'd occasionally been in the kitchen when her father had shaved but only when it couldn't be avoided. Besides, her father was family, which allowed them to bend the rules of propriety somewhat.

Elliott wasn't family. He could have been loosely considered family as a Christian brother, but already in her heart, he was much more than that. She'd become quite fond of him, but that didn't mean she wanted to watch him shave. It would almost be like. . .Elliott watching her pluck her eyebrows.

As nice as the houses were that the railroad provided to the families of the section foremen, their house was small. Besides the living and dining rooms or the kitchen, her only option would be to go upstairs to her bedroom where she had nothing to do. She couldn't do that, because she had plenty of work in the kitchen helping her mother prepare dinner. She still had to finish preparing the carrots and potatoes, and they still hadn't finished cleaning up the extra mess from making the donuts.

Mostly, going up to her bedroom would be cowardly.

She finished peeling and slicing the carrots while Elliott pumped some water into the kettle and placed it on the cookstove.

As he continued to gather up the shaving supplies, Louise couldn't help but watch him out of the corner of her eye. She wondered if a professional barber would shave differently than her father.

He leaned close to the mirror and ran his fingers through the beard. "May I trouble you for some scissors? My whiskers are too long for the razor."

Her mother left the room and returned with her sewing scissors, which Louise knew were the best scissors in the house. He stared at them as her mother placed them in his palm.

"I know they're not like the barber scissors you're used to, but that's what I use to cut John's hair."

Louise bit her lip when she saw the slight movement of Elliott cringing. Her mother returned to the cookstove, and without speaking, Elliott leaned close to the mirror and snipped away as much length as he could. He then laid the scissors on the table beside the basin and poured a little water into the shaving mug, whipped up the soap into a fluffy lather, and set it aside.

He smiled as he pulled the blade of her father's razor out of its slot in the handle, then gently ran his thumb along the cutting edge. "I suspect this will have to be sharpened when I'm done. Do you know where John keeps his strop?"

"If it's not there, then I'm not sure. I'll ask him later."

From where she stood, even though his back was to her, Louise could see his face in the mirror. She watched as Elliott patted his face with warm water, then brushed on a thick layer of lather. Slowly, and in small sections, he scraped the razor along his cheeks and under his chin, but she couldn't watch as he shaved under his nose.

When he was done, he bent at the waist and rinsed his face with the water in the basin, then stood as he patted his cheeks dry with the towel.

Just as he was about to remove the towel from his face, their gazes met in the mirror. Elliott froze, his eyes widened, and Louise couldn't force herself to look away. Almost in slow motion, he turned, not lowering the towel from his face.

When he spoke, not only was his voice muffled from speaking through the towel, but there was also a husky quality Louise had not heard before.

"I don't want you to be disappointed, but nothing is going to

GAIL SATTLER

change me now. This is what I really look like."

Slowly, he lowered the towel from his face. Instead of his smile being warm and friendly, it looked like he was trying too hard to smile for a photograph.

His eyes were the same, but everything else seemed different. Even his nose without the mustache beneath it seemed somehow changed, and his hair appeared lighter than before, although that didn't make sense.

While she wouldn't have called him handsome, he was by no means ugly. Without the beard, all his features seemed thinner. His cheekbones were more prominent and his nose seemed longer. His forced smile showed thin lines beside his mouth, although she suspected they would fill out after her mother's good cooking put more meat on his bones.

She'd never paid notice to a man's chin before, but even with his thin features, he had a strong jawline. Though it was forced, he had a lovely smile without all the dark hair surrounding his mouth.

Louise grasped both sides of her skirt, smiled, and curtsied. "Pleased to meet you, Mr. Endicott. Although I'm sure we've met before."

Something in his smile changed. The lines softened and the start of crow's-feet appeared at the corners of his eyes, and this time, a genuine smile lit his face. He rested one arm in front of his stomach with the towel still clutched in his hand and slid the other behind him as he bowed politely. "Ma'am."

Louise lifted both hands to her mouth. "Ma'am? Didn't you promise not to say that?"

"I only promised your mother. Now I think I should clean up the mess I've made, and you'd better get finished with those carrots before your mother becomes angry with me for distracting you."

After waiting for John to sit first, Elliott sank onto the couch.

He'd never been so tired in his life. Beyond the overtiredness due to the lack of sleep while riding the freight trains, this was different. This was simple and complete exhaustion. He hurt all over. Even his hair hurt. Well, maybe not his hair, but certainly everything else did. He had sore muscles where he didn't know he had muscles.

John had told him that it took four men to lift the jigger, although it could be done in a struggle with three. He should have put this into perspective. John moved the smaller speedster with little effort. Doing the same thing, Elliott felt like he'd put his back out and strained every muscle in his entire body.

The heavy-duty construction of the recessed handles used to move the jigger also should have given him a hint of the physical exertion required. Once they actually started to lift the heavy unit, without John being able to help, Elliott didn't think he and the other two section men were going to manage. After much struggle, they finally did wrestle the beast onto the tracks, although he didn't know how.

Fortunately, it was not quite as difficult to get it off the tracks as to put it on.

This was a daily part of the job.

Compared to him, the other two men possessed the strength of Samson—before the haircut.

Since they were missing an experienced man, he'd pitched in to work replacing ties, just as the regular lead hand would have done, rather than just stand by and supervise. Even though Frank and Henry were older than him by ten years, so far it appeared that they had accepted his position of leadership without question. Just to be safe, John had warned him not to tell them of his inexperience or how he'd come to arrive there until he felt confident of his ability to lead the section gang without John present.

Hopefully, soon he would know what he was supposed to be doing beyond the basics, and the unaccustomed demands on him physically would build his strength quickly. Until he could perform the duties of the section foreman without assistance, every evening would be spent with John teaching him what was involved in maintaining thirty miles of parallel railroad tracks.

Except, Elliott didn't know if he'd be able to stay awake.

If he had been at home, he would have ignored the rest of the world, ignored his aches and pains, ignored everything going on around him, and crawled into his bed. He wouldn't even have eaten dinner, because he was more exhausted than he was hungry. But here, he and John and Mrs. Demchuck were sitting on his bed.

The only person missing was Louise. According to her mother, Louise had gone on her bicycle to a nearby farm and had not yet returned.

He'd thought of her often during the day. Whenever they'd finished removing a tie, sliding in a new one, then driving in the spikes to hold the new one in place, they could take a short break until the next train passed. After a short time, they would pack their tools and the tie they'd removed and move to the next location he and John had marked on the weekend. In those slower moments, his thoughts drifted to Louise.

Now, when the bright spot of his long, hard day would have been seeing her, she wasn't at home. He thought it odd that she would run such an errand and be late for dinnertime, but Mrs. Demchuck had told him that they'd unexpectedly run out of eggs because they had been doing more baking during the day. Louise was due back any minute, and upon her return, they would serve dinner.

Elliott let his eyes close as he wondered what delectable treat they had made for dessert today. He'd never eaten like this in his life. He suspected that after the eight weeks were up, John's cast was removed, and he would be on his way, he never would eat like this again.

He sighed deeply, allowing himself to relax a little more, without opening his eyes. Louise's honey cake was great, but the donuts were better. He'd never tasted anything like them. But then the strawberry and rhubarb pie they'd made yesterday at dinnertime had been great, too. Now that he thought about it, before he and John had left that morning, Mrs. Demchuck had mentioned during breakfast that they were going to make a walnut cake and how important it was that they had fresh eggs. He didn't know that an egg being laid a few days ago versus that morning would make a big difference in a cake, but he chose not to voice his opinion. After all, she knew all about delicious baked goods, and he knew nothing except that Mrs. Demchuck and Louise cooked food like he'd never had in his life.

Elliott sank deeper into the couch, and his head flopped over to the side. If they kept this up, he might get very spoiled, very fast.

The murmur of John and Mrs. Demchuck's voices droned on, and a Glenn Miller tune came on the radio. In the background, he heard a small bang but ignored it. He would open his eyes in just a minute. . . .

"Elliott? Are you sleeping?"

His eyes sprang open and he sat up with a jolt. With a slight shake of his head, the world came into focus and, with it, the sight of Louise standing above him.

Elliott rubbed his eyes. "I'm sorry. I guess I was more tired than I thought. Please forgive me for being so rude."

He thought his heart was pounding from being startled, but it only seemed to get worse with Louise hovering above him.

"That's okay. I know you're tired. I didn't think this would take so long. Apparently, you created quite a stir in church yesterday. Everyone is talking about the stranger with the lovely tenor voice in our midst. I had nearly made it out of the McSorbins' house when Dorothy started asking about you. Do you remember her? She wore a hat with a yellow ribbon to church."

He remembered meeting a number of young women yesterday, but no one particularly stuck out in his mind. He had accompanied Louise, and since at the time he'd thought he would only have a few hours left with her, he hadn't paid attention to much else, especially other young ladies. "I don't really remember. Sorry."

She rested her fingertips on his shoulder as she spoke, and his heart continued to beat far too fast. "Don't worry. I told her simply that you were a friend of the family and that as a special favor, you were going to be staying on as part of the section gang until Papa's cast is removed."

His throat constricted. He hadn't yet thought about what his relationship to Louise or her family was to be. Considering the short amount of time he had known them, he thought it an honor to be counted as their friend. However, he wasn't sure that friendship with Louise was exactly what he wanted.

At twenty-five years of age, it was time for him to settle down—to find a wife and raise a family. So far, he had not met a woman who interested him in such a manner. Until now. In only a few days, he'd become quite fond of Louise. He couldn't stop thinking about her, to the point of wondering if, as they got to know each other better, their association could go past friendship and perhaps into a courtship.

Suddenly, her fingers moved off his shoulder, and Louise hurried into the kitchen.

Mrs. Demchuck followed Louise, but Elliott remained seated. He was in no position to think of courting Louise or any young woman. The only reason he had a job for the moment was because her father had given it to him, not because he deserved it, neither had he earned it. John had only given him this job because John was desperate, and Elliott had happened to be in the right place at the right time, by God's timing. This job was temporary. He still didn't know for sure that the job promised to him at the logging camp would come to pass, which was the main reason he'd accepted John's offer.

Under such circumstances, he had no security to offer a woman, especially Louise. Her father possessed the most secure income, if not the largest, in the community. Even the business owners in town were at the whim of the economy. Elliott, on the other hand, had no real permanent job and no assets. He didn't even have a home to live in, rented or otherwise. For now, only because God had provided, his home was the couch in the Demchucks' living room.

If Louise wanted to think of him as a friend, and friend only, she obviously had more sense than he did.

Friends, it would be, and it would never be any other way.

And then, in eight short weeks, he would be gone.

"Papa! Elliott! Dinner is ready! Come into the kitchen."

Elliott pushed himself up, offered his hand to John, and accompanied him into the kitchen.

✑

Louise removed the basins from their hooks on the wall and set them on the table while her mother filled the kettle to heat the water to wash the dishes. Today was Louise's turn to dry and put everything away in the hutch on the other side of the kitchen. Usually she preferred to wash, but today, she had changed her mind.

She hadn't thought about it before, but every time she walked back and forth from the table to the hutch to put the clean dishes away she could look through the doorway between the kitchen and dining room and watch Elliott and her father sitting at the desk.

She didn't mean to eavesdrop, but she couldn't help looking every time she walked past.

As they had every other time the two men sat together at the desk, Elliott sat to the left with his left leg sticking out to the side, her father to the right with his casted right leg extended on the outside of the desk. Beneath the small desk, Elliott's right leg and her father's left almost pressed together as they sat side by side.

She slowed her pace every time she walked past the opening. At varying times, Elliott nodded as her father talked while referring to different papers on the desk. Once it appeared her father had attempted to draw a picture and pointed to it as he explained something.

Every time Louise walked past, she noticed Elliott's posture sagged a wee bit more and he sat a little less upright. From behind as she walked back and forth, often she could see his complete profile as the two men faced each other. Elliott's eyes progressively became less and less bright, and his expression began to dull from the combination of exhaustion and information overload.

Her mother's voice from behind her nearly made her drop the plate from her hands.

"Louise, if you want to put the plates and cups away one at a time, that's fine with me. But if you think you are going to continue walking back and forth with every single piece of cutlery, you had better think again."

Her cheeks burned as she hurried to the hutch, tucked the plate onto the stack, and shuffled back to the table, where she picked up a handful of the clean cutlery. Louise opened her mouth, intending to defend herself, but her words caught in her throat. Her mother was nibbling on her lower lip in an attempt not to laugh.

"It's not funny, Mama. He's almost falling asleep in the chair and Papa is still talking. You saw him at the dinner table. I was surprised he didn't nod off while we were eating."

Her mother's grin faded. "Of course, you're right. We know he's not used to this pace or this much work. Perhaps it's a good thing that cake didn't make it into the oven until so late. If it's done, this is a good reason to interrupt them."

Louise nearly ran across the room as she dried the handful of cutlery and closed the drawer.

"The walnut cake does smell done. Do you remember what time we put it in the oven?"

"No, I only remember that it was when we called Elliott and your papa for dinner and that it was late."

Louise picked up the pot holders and opened the oven to remove the cake. As the heavy door swung open to the right, she stepped to the left to avoid the rush of heat. She bent at the waist to examine the cake before lifting it out. Since it was nicely rounded in the center, she reached inside, lifted the cake out, and set it on the flat surface of the cookstove. Gently, she pressed her finger into the center of the cake and smiled when the indent she made bounced back. "It's done, Mama." Today, she would not wait for the cake to cool before she cut it.

She walked to the doorway between the kitchen and dining room and stopped. "Elliott? Papa? The cake is done. Would you like to stop and have a piece?"

Her father raised his arms over his head and stretched his back, while Elliott arched his shoulders and moved slightly from side to side. Her father then pushed the papers to the back of the desk and laid down his pen. "I think that's enough for one night anyway. Let's have that cake, and maybe we will call it an early night."

Without her father being able to see him, Elliott looked directly into her eyes, mouthed a thank-you, and stood. Louise knew she had done the right thing.

"I can hardly wait to taste that cake. It's been teasing me as it cooked. If you keep this up, by the time eight weeks go by, I'm afraid I may become very spoiled and very fat."

Louise smiled. Not that she wanted to make him fat, but he did need to put on more weight for his height. "Nonsense. Now come and have a piece of cake. Mama is cutting it now. It's my favorite recipe, and it's wonderful when it's warm."

Chapter 10

"Good-bye, Papa! We'll be back in time for dinner."

"This will be a good time to catch up on my reading. Have fun shopping."

Louise waved to her father, who was standing on his crutches in the doorway and watching Elliott back the car out of the garage. Her mother gave him a quick peck on the cheek as she moved around him. Louise and her mother hurried to the car and got in while Elliott closed the garage door, and they were on their way.

"I can't say how much I appreciate this, Mrs. Demchuck."

"Nonsense. I simply don't have time to have to wash the same clothes so often."

Louise smiled at Elliott's grace in not saying more. All week long they had no choice but to have him wear the only set of clothes he'd arrived with, and when they became soiled, her mama had loaned him some of her father's clothes, which fit him poorly. A shopping trip was exactly what he needed to purchase some shirts and trousers of his own, in addition to a few personal items.

They hadn't discussed it, but she was perfectly aware that Elliott was not comfortable borrowing her father's personal things, but he had no choice. Unfortunately, because he'd only worked for the railroad for a week he'd missed the pay period. Because of that, her parents offered to give him enough money to cover a few necessities. Elliott had been awkward about accepting their money. He'd made it clear that this was strictly a loan which he would repay promptly out of his first paycheck.

"When I went to Nick's store, I saw a few shirts and other items that I could have purchased instead of going all the way into Beauséjour."

"Hush, Elliott. Nick's prices for clothing are outrageous. Why, the same shirt that he charges a dollar and a quarter for, we can get in Beauséjour for a dollar. We could probably get it for ninety-five cents in Winnipeg, but that would involve making arrangements to stay overnight, as it's simply too far to do in a day. Besides, since you haven't worked for the railroad long enough, you're not entitled to free rail passes, as we are. We shop at Nick's store on the odd weeks we don't go to Winnipeg. His food items are reasonable, but he charges far too much for the clothing and sundries."

"Yes, I had noticed that much of his merchandise was fairly high priced."

Elliott slowed the car, and Louise almost asked what he was doing when a doe stepped out onto the road. However, the noise from the car frightened it, and it disappeared back into the trees quickly.

Elliott turned his head to stare into the bush where the deer had disappeared as he drove past, then once again faced forward. "That was beautiful. I don't see a lot of wild animals in Katona Falls. I suppose that out here you must see a lot of wild animals."

"Yes. Sometimes I think I see more animals than people in Pineridge because very few people ever come off the trains. We're so far away from a city that even the iceman won't come by. I suppose you've noticed we don't have an icebox."

He smiled as he drove, glancing only quickly toward her before returning his attention to the dirt road ahead of him and all its hazards. "Yes, I did notice that. I suppose that's why you don't have a telephone, either."

"I guess you noticed that the phone is only connected to the other section houses, and the district office."

"Yes, I did notice that. This area is very remote. Do animals ever come right into the town of Pineridge? It's not what I'd call a bustling metropolis."

Louise giggled and told Elliott about the time a family of

skunks made themselves at home under the porch at Mr. Tolson's repair shop and the ensuing disaster trying to remove them once their nest was discovered. Every drop of tomato juice had been purchased from Mr. Sabinski's store that day.

They were still laughing when they finally arrived at the main street of Beauséjour. They parked the car near the first general store on Park Avenue, then walked to the smaller store on Second Street for a better selection of the cotton yarn her mother needed to make sweaters to give away to the homeless men who passed through. Her mother made Elliott stand next to the bin of yarn while she selected her colors, which told Louise without words that the next sweater her mama made would be for Elliott.

Next they took Elliott through the few stores in town. He graciously accepted her mama's assistance in choosing the best styles and colors for the trousers and shirts he picked, although they allowed him the privacy to select his more personal clothing items alone.

Once Elliott paid for his selections, they walked to the drugstore. He held the door open for them to enter, but when Louise stepped inside, her mama stopped.

"I have a list of things to get. I'll meet you back here."

Without waiting for Louise to respond, her mama turned on her heels and nearly ran down the walk.

Louise looked up to see Elliott standing beside her, frozen, his mouth open and one finger in the air.

She pressed her hand to her mouth to muffle her sudden case of the giggles, but she couldn't control herself.

"You'll have to excuse Mama," she said between her fingers. "We've never been shopping without Papa before, since he has to drive us. I heard them talking, and he gave her some extra money to spend. She's very excited. She's never been shopping alone before."

"I suppose this will give me more time to buy what I need, then. Do you want to come with me, or do you have a special list, too?"

Louise smiled. She'd never wanted anything more. "Mama has the list, so I'll go with you."

Slowly, she directed him through the store to the men's area, where he began to browse through the selection of razors and other men's toiletries.

While Elliott compared the different razor handles without speaking, Louise stepped closer to him so other shoppers couldn't hear her words.

"I suppose this is all very strange for you."

He let out a very humorless laugh. "You have no idea. I feel like I'm starting all over again, and in a way, I suppose I am."

"Did you lose everything?"

"What I didn't sell before I left, I more or less gave to my brother and his family. Except for stuff like my photo album and a few smaller but heavier items, I packed everything I had left into my suitcases and took it with me. I was counting on things working out enough to the point where it would be a permanent move out of Katona Falls. When I was robbed, it all happened so fast. I certainly didn't expect something like that to happen so close to home. There were at least five men in the group who attacked me. I thought people only got mugged in Toronto."

Louise shook her head. "These modern times are frightening, especially with so many desperate people out there. I've always felt safe around here, but I suppose that will change someday. The important thing is that you weren't hurt. . .or worse."

He raised his hand to his throat, then quickly dropped it to his side as he turned to select a comb. "I suppose it's better to be a live coward than a dead hero." He turned to her as quickly as he'd just turned away. "I've wondered over and over what lesson there was in being robbed like that, and I just can't figure it out. I like to think that I choose my battles intelligently. I believe in my heart I did the right thing by not fighting back because I was badly outnumbered. Plus, they had a weapon and I didn't. The contents of those two suitcases were basically all I had left, but they were not worth fighting impossible odds. I don't think anything but my clothes would be of much value to anyone. Still, I hope that somewhere, someone is reading my Bible and thinking of what the words say, although I suspect that it's just been thrown in a trash bin somewhere. In the end God provided for me, although it's in a way I could never have imagined in my wildest dreams—or nightmares. I don't know what would have happened to me without you and your family."

Louise's throat tightened. She couldn't believe they were having such a conversation beside the men's deodorants. "We would have done the same for anyone in your situation. It's what we feel the Lord has called us to do as a family. Now let's talk about something else. Shopping is supposed to be fun."

His hesitant smile made Louise's foolish heart flutter. "I've never considered shopping fun. I buy what I need and go home."

At the same time, they heard her mother approaching and turned in unison. Her mama's arms were filled with bags, making Louise shake her head and wonder what wonderful bargains she'd found this shopping trip, especially without her papa present to temper her choices.

Louise lowered her voice to a whisper. "Mama normally considers shopping an adventure, today even more so."

Her mother joined them, smiling from ear to ear. "I never knew they carried yarn here. And such a good price! I've never seen these prices, not even in Winnipeg. And such a fine quality cotton! It will take me until Christmas to knit all this, but I look forward to it. Here, Elliott. You can carry these bags for me." Without waiting for him to respond, she emptied everything she carried into Elliott's arms, only retaining her purse. "Have you finished here? I still have a few things left to buy, and we have to be home for dinner. It's a long drive home."

"I've made my selections, but I don't know where they are under everything I'm carrying."

Her mama led Elliott to the counter, where Louise helped

him put all the bags down neatly. He then paid for his own items, and they continued on.

Every time they stopped at another store and her mama made another purchase, Elliott ended up with more packages to carry. He never complained, even though Louise didn't know how he managed to hold everything without dropping something. She did notice his sigh of relief when her mama suggested they return to the car before they continued with the last of their shopping, which was for groceries.

The entire time they were in the grocery store, instead of carrying it or walking to the counter, her mama handed everything to Elliott, who made many trips to pile everything on the counter as they shopped. The entire time, Elliott behaved as a perfect gentleman, being very good-natured and teasing her mama that at least he didn't have to carry everything at once.

By the time they had bought everything on her mama's list, when added to the bags containing Elliott's purchases, the trunk compartment was filled to overflowing. Elliott struggled with some creative rearranging, tucked a few items under the seat, then pressed down on her mama's cotton yarn with considerable force, still barely managing to close the trunk.

He shook his head as he started the engine. "If you can't tell, I've never shopped with women before, and I don't think I will again. This also reminds me, I want to pay for my share of the groceries."

"Hush, Elliott. You are doing work worth more than the cost of feeding you by helping John. I don't know what we would do without you. Right, Louise?"

This time, Louise got the window seat, and her mother sat in the middle. She missed sitting beside Elliott, and her mother's words interrupted her thoughts contemplating how she could ask if perhaps the next time their family needed goods, if she could take the list and go alone with Elliott.

She turned away from the window, nodding as she spoke.

"Yes. Especially on the stairs. I don't think Papa would accept our help, but he doesn't question or complain when you make sure he goes slowly and doesn't fall."

"I'm glad to be of help."

"I hope everyone has worked up an appetite shopping, because when we get home, there is a pot of stew simmering. I hope John has been able to put more wood in the stove like I asked him to. Shopping always makes me hungry. What about you, Elliott? Are you hungry?"

"I'll never turn down your good cooking, Mrs. Demchuck."

"Unfortunately, since we've been out all day, Louise and I haven't made a dessert. Can you believe this is the first time since you've been staying with us that we won't have dessert?"

"But Mama, there are still cookies left from yesterday."

"Yes, I suppose they will have to do."

"You ladies are spoiling me, but I am not going to complain."

Louise watched Elliott smile, and he made no further comments as he continued to drive. The lines on his face weren't so prominent as they had been a week ago, which meant that, despite the hard work, all the extra treats were doing what they were meant to do. She tried to imagine what he would look like by the time he left, with his thin frame more filled out than at present.

And that reminded Louise that the next seven weeks were going to go by much too fast.

Rather than allow herself to dwell on him leaving, she chose to enjoy the rest of the day. Today, she would participate in the conversation inside the car and not dwell on things she couldn't change.

Her mama gasped and pointed out the window. "Look! Another deer! Did anyone see it?"

❧

"Amen," Elliott said aloud with the rest of the congregation at the close of the service.

He stood at the same time as the rest of the people present but didn't file outside. Instead, he waited at the end of the pew for Louise to return from the organ.

In the past week, he'd never once had the opportunity to hear her play. Every evening, a delicious dinner along with a delectable dessert had been ready as soon as he and John arrived back to the house after the day's work was done. Immediately following dinner, he spent at least two hours with John at the desk, learning as much as he could about the specific duties of the section foreman as well as background information and history of the railroad. The knowledge gave him a greater understanding of what happened beyond John's thirty miles of track. As well, it showed him the magnitude of the details the district office had to oversee in order to ensure everything was in perfect order to keep the trains running every minute of every day.

While this was far from his choice of the ideal job, Elliott was grateful beyond thoughts or words to have it. A week ago he'd sent a letter to Ike to advise him of the delay in his planned arrival to the West Coast. He'd asked Ike to locate Edward's address and forward a second letter he'd enclosed. So far he had not heard from Edward, but considering what Ike had to do to forward his letter on its way, he knew he couldn't expect a reply yet. All he could do was hope that when his time working for the railroad was over, he still had the opportunity for employment in the logging industry, which wasn't his ideal choice, either. However, at this point in his life, like countless other men, he would take anything he was offered to provide an income, permanent or temporary.

A pause in the music brought Elliott's thoughts back to Louise and where he was, but she turned the page and played another hymn, filling time until most of the congregation dispersed.

Elliott smiled as he listened to the music. Louise played the organ beautifully, even more outstanding than her mother had promised. He also knew from standing beside her during the service last week that Louise sang as well as she played, despite her protests and denials.

While the music continued, a deep male voice sounded behind him.

"Greetings! Louise tells me you're new on the section gang. I'm Nicholas Sabinski, but everyone calls me Nick. I couldn't help but hear you sing. My daughter Minnie tells me that where you come from you were part of a barbershop quartet. I've always wanted to do something like that, and I was wondering if you would consider helping us start such a group here in Pineridge."

Elliott recognized him as the man in the congregation who sang the bold bass harmony, and he recognized the name as the man who owned the town's general store, if he could call this burg of eight buildings a town.

He stiffened and tucked his hands into his pockets. "I'd love to, Nick, but I'm only going to be here for seven more weeks, until John is out of the cast. And then I'll be on my way to British Columbia. Otherwise, I'd be glad to."

"Would you consider helping us get such a group started until you leave? I've spoken to a few of the men here, and they are interested in doing both hymns for the Sunday service, as well as other numbers just for fun. And as far as a quartet, there are actually five of us if we count you. We'd like to meet every second or third Saturday afternoon."

Elliott couldn't help his smile. What Nick was explaining was exactly what his group back home was like. They had seven permanent members, and a few other men who dropped in and out as time and energy permitted. He glanced over at Louise, who now was slipping her hymnal and some loose music into the bench. He had been looking forward to spending as much of his remaining time as possible with her, especially since so far the only time he'd spent with her was when they sat together at church. While he'd enjoyed their shopping trip yesterday, they'd been far from alone.

Since Nick indicated that only a few hours of his time would be needed, and not every week, the suggestion gained more appeal. "That does sound like it could be fun. Do you have a place to meet? I don't have transportation."

"Pastor Galbraith says we can use this church building, since it's central and has the organ."

"That's great."

As Louise joined them, Nick nodded a greeting but kept speaking to Elliott. "You don't happen to play the organ or piano, do you?"

"I'm afraid I don't."

Nick frowned and crossed his arms. "That's one thing that has been keeping us from doing this. I'm the only one who can read music, and none of us can play an instrument."

Elliott nodded. "I can also read music, but I can't play an instrument, either."

Louise's eyebrows scrunched in the middle, something Elliott so far hadn't seen. He figured she looked absolutely adorable. "What are you planning that you need an organist? Is there something I can do for you, Mr. Sabinski?"

Nick turned to Elliott. "Mildred Johnstone and Louise are the only ones in our congregation who can play the organ or piano." His smile softened, and he turned to Louise. "I couldn't help but be impressed with Elliott's fine voice in church. I'm trying to convince this young man to help us start a men's singing group. We've got use of the organ, but I think a group singing in harmony would require at least someone who can read music enough to show us the notes we're supposed to be singing." Nick returned his gaze to Elliott. "I don't suppose you would happen to have any music with you? Although I would think we would start on the hymns, which of course we have access to. As if we could read anything besides the words." He turned to grin at Elliott.

"Sorry, but I didn't bring anything like that with me." He didn't want to tell Mr. Sabinski the full extent of what he hadn't arrived with into their community.

Louise turned her head and looked at the organ as she spoke. "I could probably help you. There are quite a few songs for groups in the pile of music in the bench. I don't know why, because I don't think our church has ever had a choir. But I suppose we could make some changes so they could be for men only."

Nick smiled, then reached to shake Elliott's hand. "Great. Can we start next Saturday at two o'clock?"

Elliott nodded. It wasn't like he had anything else to do or anywhere else to go. Also, now that Louise had agreed to help, this was a good way to spend time with her in a pleasant environment away from her parents' house, even if they wouldn't be alone. "I think that's a good time. Louise?"

At her answering smile, something funny happened in his stomach, making him wonder if he was hungry.

"Yes, that sounds good. I'll see you then, Mr. Sabinski. I only ask for one thing."

"Anything. Name it."

"Please do not think of singing 'I've Been Working on the Railroad.'"

Chapter 11

Louise sat on a comfortably flat rock as she carefully selected the largest and plumpest strawberries and dropped them into her pail. As she picked, she kept Elliott in view out of the corner of her eye.

Elliott had also chosen to sit while he picked. Never in her life had Louise ever seen her papa pick berries with her mama, but when Mama suggested Elliott join her, he had accompanied her without hesitation.

The first time she'd seen Elliott he had been eating strawberries from this same patch. She didn't know what kind of berries grew near Katona Falls, but these strawberries were among the best early berries she'd ever seen. Apparently, Elliott felt the same, because for every one strawberry that made it into Elliott's pail, at least two went into his mouth.

She studied him in silence. She couldn't help but compare the unkempt and bedraggled man of barely over a week ago to the man before her now. Knowing now what she didn't know then, she could only guess at how hungry he must have been. So far he had successfully avoided saying much about his experiences on the freight trains, but he'd told her much of his life back in Katona Falls.

While she'd come to know him fairly quickly in some ways, in other ways she didn't know him at all. She had hoped if they could ever spend time together without her parents or a crowd around him, they could talk more freely about things that really mattered. She wanted to know more than his history. She knew he was a man of faith, but she also wanted to know his hopes and his dreams, even if at this point his dreams were all he had left.

Louise settled the strawberries in her pail, which was now half full. She couldn't see how much Elliott had in his pail, but she suspected it wasn't much.

"This works better if you eat only one for every other one put in the pail."

In one quick movement, he dumped the small handful of berries from the pail into his hand, popped the whole handful into his mouth, then held the pail upside down and shook it. "Then I think I'll have to start over," he said, doing rather poorly at talking around the berries in his mouth.

Even stuffed with berries, his cheeks were thin but better than they were a week ago. Unfortunately, having cakes and desserts every day was also doing the same for her as it did for him, but she could ill afford to gain much weight. Today, they were going to make a strawberry and rhubarb pie. If she could get enough strawberries.

He turned and began to pick again, and this time, since his mouth was still overstuffed, the entire handful of berries made it into his pail.

"I didn't want to ask you this in front of Papa at lunchtime, but how did your first solo track inspection go this morning?"

"It went fine."

Louise continued to pick, not looking up as she spoke. "I mean really. It's okay. Papa isn't here to listen to what you say. How are you managing with the section gang? I know it's hard work. Even when jobs are hard to find, the men tend to come and go."

"It's hard work, to be sure, but I think I'm getting more used to it. And very honestly, the track inspection went well this morning. I don't think I'll have any problems." He paused for a few seconds, allowing Louise to hear the plunking of the berries as they bounced in the bottom of the metal pail. "So far the hardest part is moving the speedster by myself. That thing is heavy."

"I wouldn't think that being on the section gang was like any job you'd ever thought of doing. You said before that you had attended university until you had to quit. What course were you taking? What did you really intend on doing?"

Suddenly, Louise clamped her mouth shut. She couldn't believe the words had actually slipped out of her mouth. She'd wondered and thought about him so much that she hadn't been aware she'd asked out loud until it was too late.

Unable to face him as she spoke, she turned all her concentration to picking the berries in front of her. "Please forgive me for asking such personal questions. It's none of my business. I have such bad timing. I can only guess at how hard this whole thing is for you." Louise paused for a few seconds and cleared her throat. "How much do you have in your pail? I think we must have enough to make a pie by now."

"It's okay, Louise. I know you're curious. In your position, I'd be curious too."

She could feel the heat in her cheeks, but she raised her head and met his gaze to listen to his words.

"My hope was to become a mathematician and, with that, be a university professor. The way things have gone over the last few years, that's not going to happen now. I'm already twenty-five years old, and I don't see any chance of going back to university in the foreseeable future. Even if I could scrape together the tuition and books, I'd still need living expenses. All I can do is trust in God's will for me and follow the path I believe He's set out. I can't see where that is yet, but I have to trust that one day, I will."

"Is that why you accepted Papa's job offer? Working on the section gang can't compare to being a university professor."

One corner of his mouth crooked up. "Neither is working in a logging camp. For now, I have to go where I can earn an income. I believe in miracles, but I also believe that not all miracles come in the form of handouts. Sometimes, when God provides, what He provides is opportunity, and sometimes it involves work."

"Yes, that is true."

"Tell me about yourself, Louise. You're what, nineteen? What do you want to do with your life?"

"Actually, I'm almost twenty. Since I like to cook, and since it's been so satisfying for me to help people by feeding them, in the fall I'm going to go to college to become a dietician. Papa thinks that's a good idea, as opposed to what my friends would rather do. They want to move into the city and just take any type of job so they can meet someone and get married. Papa says I shouldn't be in a rush to get married; there's plenty of time for that."

"Your papa is right."

"I only want to get married when God places the right person in my path. When that happens, I figure I should know it. Do you think that happens?"

His voice took on a husky edge, making Louise wonder if he'd swallowed something strange with the berries. "Yes, I do. It happened that way with my brother. I'm praying that one day that will happen to me, too."

"Louise! Elliott!" her mama's voice echoed from the distance.

Louise raised one hand to her lips. "It's Mama! She's waiting for these berries! How much do you have in your pail?"

Elliott's cheeks darkened. "Not much, I'm embarrassed to admit. What about you?"

"Coming, Mama!" she called out. Louise dumped a portion of her berries into Elliott's pail and lowered her voice, although she didn't know why. Her mother obviously couldn't hear her from where she was. "Come on. We'd better hurry. I think there's enough to make a pie."

He stared down into the pail. "Louise? What are you doing? I doubt your mama will care that I hardly picked any berries."

For a brief second, she considered taking the berries back. "I don't know. We had better go."

She hurried down the path with Elliott following close behind, until they arrived back at the house and placed both pails on the table.

Her mama stared down into the pails. She remained silent, her brows knotted, and she jiggled both pails slightly.

Behind her, Elliott cleared his throat. "I'm sorry, Mrs. Demchuck. The berries were so good I'm afraid I ate more than I brought back. If this isn't enough, I'll go back and pick more. And this time, I promise not to eat them."

"I suppose this will be enough to make one pie. If you've eaten so much, I do hope that you will be able to eat your dinner. Today I cooked that ham that we bought yesterday. It's such a treat to get a ham that's so tender and juicy; we don't get them often. And as a special treat, I'm making a salad with head lettuce and crisp celery!"

Louise saw Elliott blink. His eyebrows raised, but he didn't comment.

She stepped closer. "Head lettuce and celery are not grown by our local farmers. The only time we can enjoy a nice fresh salad is after a trip to Beauséjour or Winnipeg."

"You mean you can only make a salad once every two weeks, after driving two or more hours to go shopping?"

"Yes. Living here in the country is nothing like living in the city."

Elliott turned back to her mother and covered his stomach with his hand. "I can assure you, Mrs. Demchuck, none will be wasted. Have I told you recently how much you are spoiling me?"

Her mother grinned back. "I think you said something to that effect at lunchtime. Now if you'll excuse us, Louise and I must get busy or no one will be eating."

The soothing strains of the classical music coming from the radio were interrupted by the low murmur of voices when Elliott joined her papa on the couch.

"I was beginning to wonder if you'd been eaten by a bear."

"I'm sorry, Mama. We started talking and I forgot all about picking." She covered her mouth with her hands but couldn't cover up her giggle. "But you should have seen him. He was really funny eating the strawberries. When he caught me looking, he put them into the pail, but when he thought I wasn't looking, everything he picked, he ate."

"I don't know why you're laughing. You used to do that when you were a little girl."

"I suppose I did. I guess I thought I was getting away with it. It must be true that mothers have eyes in the back of their heads."

"Not really. If you don't get busy, dinner won't be ready for a very long time. And I don't need eyes in the back of my head to know that."

⁂

Elliott stood to the side of the jigger to help John support himself while Frank stayed on the jigger's deck to help John balance. John leaned on the crutches, barely staying upright as he watched Elliott, Frank and Henry hoist the heavy jigger off the track and onto the ties. Together they pushed the unit into the toolhouse for the night and said their good-byes.

Elliott joined John, and they slowly made their way over the tracks and to the house, where John nearly collapsed by the time they made it to the couch.

John swiped his sleeve over his forehead and his head fell to the back of the couch. "I hardly did anything today, but I'm exhausted. I don't want to think of what the next seven weeks will be like."

Without being asked, Mrs. Demchuck appeared with a glass of water, which John drank gratefully, then closed his eyes to rest.

Elliott couldn't help but feel sorry for John. While just as he said, John didn't do much, Elliott could see the difficulty involved in any movement with the cast. The weight of it alone was daunting.

Last week, John had remained on the jigger while he and the section men went about their duties. Today, at John's insistence, they had helped him down off the jigger when they arrived at the particular tie that needed replacing. They could see John was getting bored with staying in one spot for so long and, even though he wouldn't admit it, he was starting to become irritable.

Today they were working on replacing ties, which meant John had been off and back on the jigger numerous times, and the strain showed. Helping him get on and off the jigger wasn't doing wonders for Frank or Henry, either.

Then, John had been so tired that they had packed up earlier than usual, just to take him home.

Elliott hadn't wanted to be at the house at this particular time. Today, the freight train was stopping to unload a shipment for Nick. And that meant Elliott would be watching from an entirely different perspective.

Today, he would be watching the homeless men on the 6:15 freight train not as one of them but as an employee of the railroad.

Technically it was the job of the brakeman to clear the hobos from the freight cars, but when John was in the area, he was also required to as well.

Elliott knew the hard way that even if the men were removed from the train in a place such as this, they had nowhere to go. He also knew that because it was his duty, John went through the motions to remove the homeless men from the trains, as did the brakeman, but everyone knew they would get back on. Neither John nor the brakeman did anything to stop them. There was nothing they could do.

This time, since the train was stopping long enough for a shipment to be dropped off, that meant the men riding the box-cars would be able to wander around until the train departed. Most of them would hide, but some of them were bound to go searching for food.

According to Louise, some of them would come knocking on the door, begging for food. For anyone who asked, none would be turned away.

Just as he had not been turned away.

The women remained in the kitchen preparing dinner and doing laundry, and beside him on the couch, John nodded off to sleep. A long whistle sounded in the distance, indicating the pending arrival of the freight train, followed by a low rumble, increasing in volume. The house only shook slightly this time because the train actually stopped.

When all was quiet, Elliott closed his eyes. He didn't expect to hear much, but he knew what was happening. He had no intention of going outside to clear the train of hobos. Instead, he kept his eyes closed, bowed his head, and prayed for the men, whoever they were, on that train and all the trains across the continent. He prayed for their safety, for opportunity, and for them to find other good-hearted people like the Demchucks as they continued on their way.

His mind went blank when he heard a knock on the back door. Until today, he'd been working or waiting on a siding with the rest of the section gang when the freight trains passed. Today was the first time he was at the house when a freight train stopped.

The knock meant someone had come to beg for food—a man just like him who had come off the freight trains—a man so hungry he had been reduced to begging.

Today it was Louise who answered the door. He listened to the drone of their conversation, and even though he couldn't hear the words, he knew that Louise was gladly giving the man food, sharing a brief message that Jesus loved him enough to die for him, and sending him outside with a plate of food.

He still didn't know why he had been the only homeless man to be invited inside, nor did he understand why he had been chosen to be so blessed by them. Not only did they provide food and lodging and a job, but their actions extended past mere ministry. They welcomed him into their home and even adjusted their own lifestyle to suit him. He could tell they were going to bed earlier than usual in order to give him some privacy as he fell into an exhausted sleep every night on their couch. He doubted they regularly slept nine hours every night, but at this point, he needed to take advantage of their kindness in order to develop his endurance—both to the hard work and to the noise of the trains as they passed, to his dismay, every few hours, all night, every night.

He would never be able to pay them back, but at the same time, he knew they didn't want him to.

Elliott buried his face in his hands, trying to figure out what God was trying to teach him. If he ever in his life was to be able to provide a ministry to others, he wanted to do it like the Demchucks. They didn't set themselves apart. Instead, they followed the example of Jesus and treated the people they helped as equals, not as second-class citizens as he'd so often seen people do.

Part of him wanted to go outside and talk to the men who came off the freight train, even though he had nothing to give, but he couldn't force himself to get off the couch. In addition to accepting their kindness and their food, he'd accepted money from these warmhearted people because it would still be almost two weeks before he received his first paycheck. For now, his wounds were still too raw. However, Elliott made up his mind that as soon as he was able to do so, he would follow the Demchucks' example and help those less fortunate than himself.

"Papa! Elliott! Come for dinner!"

Elliott stood in front of John, waiting. When John became aware of his surroundings and was alert enough to stand, Elliott extended one hand to help pull him up off the couch. At the same time, the train pulled away from the station.

Today, he wanted to be the one to lead in a prayer of thanks. He had a lot to be thankful for.

Chapter 12

Elliott laid the tongs on the ground, then dropped to his knees to help Henry push the new tie into position. When it looked right, Elliott stood back to wipe the sweat from his brow while Frank kicked the tamping bar to set the ballast around the new tie.

"Kick it over a little to the left," John called from his seat atop the jigger, which was pulled off onto the siding.

When it looked good, Elliott measured its distance from the other ties on each side to make sure it was centered and level. "It's good," he called out.

Together, Elliott and Henry slid in the tie plates to support the rails, and John pulled the new spikes out of the box. Frank picked up the spike maul and drove the first spike through the tie plate. He was about to pound in the second one when Elliott raised his palm to stop him. "Wait. Do you hear that?" His heart pounded in his chest to think that a train was coming and they had not completely replaced the tie. He squinted and stared down the parallel lengths of track. "Something's coming, but the train isn't due for half an hour. Besides, that's too small." He also didn't feel the ground trembling, which was always a warning that a train was approaching.

John, Frank, and Henry groaned in unison.

"Not today!" John called out to the sky.

Elliott let his mouth hang open at the sight of a car coming... down the tracks.

"But...," he muttered, then snapped his mouth shut. Suddenly he understood.

If he thought he was sweating before, he was definitely sweating now.

This was it. His first inspection by the road master.

Frank and Henry helped John down from the jigger while Elliott watched a black sedan approach on the tracks. Instead of rubber tires, the car rode on miniature train wheels which set it perfectly and efficiently on the track. The car slowed as it neared the switch, then stopped. A man got out, threw the handle on the railway switch, drove the car onto the siding, got out of the car once again, flipped the switch back, then continued on toward them.

John's voice dropped to a mumble. "His name is Heinrich Getz."

Elliott lowered his voice so he could speak to John without Frank and Henry hearing. "Your supervisor?"

"Yes and no. He's not my direct supervisor, but my supervisor gets his report. Heinrich's comments and opinions of my section affect my supervisor's appraisal of the job performance of my crew, and that affects me."

The car came to a stop a few feet away from the jigger. A tall and rather handsome man a few years older than Elliott exited the car carrying a clipboard. Elliott stepped forward to meet him and stretched out his hand.

"I'm Elliott Endicott, John's new lead hand. Pleased to meet you."

Heinrich's brows knotted as he glanced at John leaning on the crutches. He quickly met Elliott's eye contact and returned the handshake. "Heinrich Getz, road master. Yes, I've heard that John hired a new lead hand." He turned to John. "It looks like you've had a bit of an accident."

"Yes. Nothing too serious."

Heinrich smiled. "Looks serious to me, but it's nice to see it's not keeping you from working." He took a pen out of his pocket, checked the time, and made a few notes on the top page of the clipboard, glanced down at John's cast, then back to the clipboard. "You know the routine, John. Or should I go through this with your lead hand?"

"You can go through it with me. Elliott, you can finish up, and when the train passes, go to the next one without me."

Elliott nodded. As lead hand, he should have gone to oversee Frank and Henry, but his feet remained fixed. John started to make his way to the car Heinrich had come in, which meant crossing the siding tracks to get into the passenger side of Heinrich's car. So far, every time John crossed the tracks Elliott had assisted him, first making his precarious way over the rocks which surrounded the tracks, then finding a firm footing for the crutches on the tarred wooden ties. Also, the process of getting the cast over the height of the metal rails on crutches required considerable orchestration.

To Elliott's surprise, Heinrich smiled and carefully helped John through the rocks, then waited for John to position the crutches on the best spot on a tie. He then slipped one arm around John's waist and allowed John to lean on him as he lifted the cast over the rails, just as Elliott had done for the past week and a half.

He swallowed hard, then turned to Frank and Henry. In John's absence, this would be his first time officially supervising John's section men. He hoped and prayed he was up to the task.

Elliott watched as Frank pounded in the last spike. After checking the tie when all the work was complete and finding everything satisfactory, they shoveled the displaced rocks back into place, packed up the tools, and loaded them onto the jigger.

Out of the corner of his eye, every now and then Elliott stole a glance at Heinrich's car, still parked beside the jigger. Both doors remained open as John and Heinrich discussed what was written on the papers attached to Heinrich's clipboard.

The ground started to tremble. Elliott pulled on the chain attached to his belt loop to draw out the pocket watch John had loaned him. "Right on time," he mumbled.

He climbed aboard the jigger, along with Frank and Henry, and waited for the train to pass. When it did, the engine of

Heinrich's car roared to life. Elliott pushed down on the jigger's handle, and slowly, they made their way to the switch. Once there, Elliott jumped off the jigger and set the switch to allow the jigger to go from the siding to the main track. Once it passed, he reset the switch and they backed up the jigger to sit behind the intersection of track next to the switch. After setting it again, they signaled, and the road master's car passed them and continued on, heading down the track to the station at Pineridge. Elliott watched it disappear into the distance, reset the switch for the last time for the next train to pass straight through, then clambered back aboard the jigger.

"Okay, let's get going," Elliott muttered. "And after the next one's done, we'll call it a day."

The next tie they replaced went as smoothly as the previous one, boosting Elliott's confidence in his new leadership capabilities. This time, he sat on the bench while Frank and Henry pumped the jigger's handle as they made it back to the Pineridge station in plenty of time before the evening freight train.

The road master's car remained parked on the siding at the station, even after they removed the jigger from the track and pushed it into the toolhouse.

Elliott bade good night to the other men, then walked to the Demchucks' house.

When he opened the back door, he expected to see both Mrs. Demchuck and Louise busy preparing dinner, but only Mrs. Demchuck was in the kitchen.

He kicked off his boots and tucked them into the corner of the boot tray, then slipped off the denim overalls and hung them on the hook on the back of the door. After he smoothed some of the wrinkles out of his trousers, Mrs. Demchuck walked up to him and helped him brush the wrinkles out of the sleeves of his shirt.

"You're early, which is good. We've invited Heinrich to stay for dinner, and we have to eat early so he can get to Winnipeg before nightfall, as he's booked into a hotel there for the night."

At the mention that the road master would be staying, Elliott glanced at the kitchen table. Instead of being set for dinner, it was spread with the bowls and utensils Mrs. Demchuck had been using to prepare their meal.

"I know what you're thinking. We'll be eating in the dining room today."

"I guess Heinrich is a special guest."

"Yes, he is. As you have no doubt seen, we don't get many visitors. We like to treat all our guests as special, but I must admit that we give Heinrich better treatment than most. Now you go into the living room, and I'll call everyone when dinner is ready."

Since Louise was absent from the kitchen, Elliott wondered if she had made an unexpected errand to their favorite local farmer again to purchase the ingredients for a treat for the road master.

As he thought about it, he walked into the living room to wait for her return. His feet skidded to a halt when he saw Louise sitting in the center of the couch with John on one side and Heinrich on the other. She was laughing at something someone had said, but when she saw him, her laughter faded.

"Glad to see you here before the freight train," John said. "Bring yourself the chair from the desk and please join us."

Elliott preferred to remain standing, but he wouldn't contradict his host in front of their distinguished guest.

Conversation had not yet resumed when Mrs. Demchuck called them for dinner.

John led everyone in prayer over the food, and Mrs. Demchuck and Louise served creamed chicken. Elliott knew they had no cream in the outdoor cellar, so Louise had made that special trip to visit the local farmer, as he suspected.

Elliott expected conversation would have centered around work-related projects, but instead, Heinrich spent most of his time talking to Louise. At first, Elliott found it strange that Heinrich knew her so well, but then he remembered John telling him that the road master paid every section foreman a monthly visit.

Since Elliott was new and since his method of arrival had been somewhat less than ideal, Elliott chose to add little to the conversation. As the meal continued, Heinrich talked more and more, entertaining everyone with his stories. Elliott found himself laughing with the others at the interesting twists, although it was more than obvious parts of the stories had been embellished for entertainment value.

At the end of the meal, instead of retiring to the living room, John saw Heinrich out the door and to the car on the siding. With Mrs. Demchuck and Louise in the kitchen cleaning up, Elliott made his way into the living room. He sat on the couch to listen to the radio, but he didn't do much listening. Instead, as he sat alone, he did some thinking.

If he looked out the window from his place on the couch, he could see John and Heinrich talking.

Heinrich appeared to be a good man and a likable fellow. For his age, which appeared to be in his early to mid thirties, he carried a job with much responsibility. From the way John spoke of him, he appeared to do it well, and Heinrich had earned the respect of all the section gangs under his jurisdiction. Frank and Henry liked him, John liked him, and even Mrs. Demchuck liked him. Elliott thought that he would have liked Heinrich a little more if Louise didn't appear to also like him.

Elliott watched as John and Heinrich walked to the toolhouse, where they disappeared inside. A few minutes later, they exited the small building, shook hands, and Heinrich walked to his car on the tracks. The engine roared to life and started to pull away. Rather than watch John struggle over the tracks with the crutches, Elliott sprang to his feet and jogged to John, barely beating him to the set of tracks.

In the distance, the road master's car stopped. Heinrich exited the car, set the switch, drove off the siding onto the main track, exited the car to close the switch, and the car began its journey down the tracks.

Elliott stood beside John as they watched him disappear in the distance.

"Will he make it to Winnipeg before dark?"

John nodded. "Yes. He can't go very fast, but you must admit, it's a very direct route."

Elliott didn't look at John as he spoke. "It appears he didn't know about your injury."

"No, I didn't tell him, nor is there really a way to do so, except on the morning scheduling call. My job is only to supervise and guarantee the quality of the maintenance and repairs on my section, but I tend to do extra and often pitch in and do some of the heavy work when necessary. Within reason, of course."

"He didn't say much to me. Is that normal?"

"I think he was surprised to see you join us at dinner. Anna doesn't invite the section men in for dinner, not even the lead hand, when Heinrich comes for his monthly inspection. I have to warn you, though, he did question where you'd come from, because he's never seen you before. Usually the lead hand position is awarded to someone who has been on their particular section gang for awhile, or at least it's someone who has had experience with another section gang."

Elliott crossed his arms, then turned to John. The road master's car had long since disappeared from sight, yet they still stood beside the track. "My being here won't cause a problem, will it?"

"Shouldn't."

John continued to stare down the empty track, his brows knotted.

After a few minutes of silence, Elliott turned toward the house. Even though John would never admit it, Elliott could tell the events of the day were taking their toll on him. "Let's get back to the house. I think it might start to rain soon."

Neither spoke as Elliott assisted John over the tracks. Louise met them at the door, shuffling her feet while she waited for Elliott to help John up the few steps to the house.

"Papa, I was at McSorbins' farm today. They have some chicks ready for me. Can I pick them up tomorrow?"

Elliott blinked. "Chicks?"

John nodded and smiled as he slowly thumped his way across the room on the crutches. Elliott helped John lower himself onto the couch, and then John resumed speaking.

"Every year we get some chicks for Louise from one of the local farms."

Louise smiled at her father. "Can Elliott drive me in the car to go get them when you come back from work tomorrow?"

John turned to Elliott. "Don't ask me. Ask Elliott."

She turned to him and smiled so brightly Elliott had to remind himself to breathe. "Elliott?"

He cleared his throat. "I suppose I can drive you. Where are you going to put them?"

"Mama and I found the crate from last year in the basement. Can you bring it up for me?"

"Crate? You keep chickens in a crate?"

"Of course I don't keep them in a crate. They only stay in it until they're big enough to go outside."

Elliott shook his head. He wasn't sure he wanted to ask the next question, but he had to. "Do you mean to say that you bring animals into the house?"

"They're very young and have to be kept warm. It still gets too cold at night, so we keep them beside the cookstove until they are strong enough. Every year we lose a few, but Mr. McSorbin gives them to me for a lower cost if I buy them when they are this size. He needs the room for his own chicks that his family will keep and sell themselves when they get big enough. They also give me a better discount if I bring my own box to take them home in."

Before he could ask any more questions, Louise had already left the room. He followed her into the kitchen, then down to the farthest corner of the basement to a pile of wood, a reel of wire mesh, a stack of stakes and poles, and an orange crate.

He stood behind her as she bent down, brushed some dust off the orange crate, picked it up, stood, and handed it to him.

"So how was it?" she asked.

"Pardon me?"

"The inspection. Did Heinrich say anything?"

"No, he didn't. Should he have?"

"Not really, but I heard some of what he was asking Papa while they were at the desk. That was before I had to leave to get the cream from the McSorbins. He asked Papa who you were and where you came from and who was doing the track inspections."

Elliott's dinner went to war with his stomach. "Did I miss something or do something wrong?"

"It didn't sound like it. I heard Papa tell him that you had done the track inspection a few times when he wasn't able to. If he hasn't said anything to you, then everything must be fine."

"I know that Heinrich came to do an inspection, but does he usually stay for dinner?"

Louise tilted her head, and one eye narrowed. "Actually, no, he usually comes earlier, in the mornings; and Mama always asks him to stay for lunch, which he does. Now that you mention it, it is a little odd that he came so late and stayed for dinner."

Elliott also thought it was strange that for a supposed business visit, very little of it was actually business. Most of his time was spent talking to Louise.

"Does he always spend so much time visiting with you when he's here to talk to your father?"

She blinked twice and crossed her arms over her chest. "I don't know. He's always been friendly to me. Just today he—"

John's voice drifted from upstairs. "Louise! Come quickly! That cooking program is on the radio! They're talking about that chicken dish you tried before!"

"Oh! I have to go!" Louise turned and ran to the stairs.

Elliott extended the orange crate slightly forward. "Wait! What do you want me to do with this?"

She turned her head and spoke over her shoulder as she ascended the stairs. "Put it outside by the back door. For tomorrow."

With her words, she reached the top of the stairs and disappeared into the kitchen.

Elliott stared at the orange crate in his hands. It was nothing that Louise couldn't have carried herself, and he wondered why she had brought him downstairs.

He shrugged his shoulders, walked upstairs and outside, and laid the crate on the ground, as requested. Before he went back in the house, he stared down into it and smiled, imagining three or four cute little baby chicks inside.

Chapter 13

Louise slipped the cheesecloth over the bushel of grain she'd purchased for feed and carefully tucked in the corners. She stood back to admire her creativeness, then pushed the trunk of the car closed. "That should be it. I don't think any will spill on the way home." She turned to Elliott, who had the orange crate containing the chicks in his hands. "We should go quickly. They won't stay very warm like that."

He stared down into the wooden crate. "How many are in here?"

Louise stood aside and opened the car door. "Two dozen. They're bigger than the ones I had last year. Maybe I won't lose any of these."

Elliott slid the crate into the center of the seat. "Twenty-four chickens...," he muttered under his breath as he stepped aside to allow her to get in. When she was sitting comfortably, he closed the door and walked around the car, giving her enough time to pick up one of the darling little chicks before the driver's door opened and he slid in behind the steering wheel.

Nestled into her hand, the little chick curled into a ball and fell asleep. She gently ran her finger over the yellow fuzz that would soon be turning to feathers, then held it out to give Elliott the chance to pet the chick, too, which he did.

"Isn't she cute?"

"She certainly is. What are you going to do with all those chickens? Would you really use two dozen eggs a day?"

Louise shook her head. "They wouldn't start laying until late fall, but by then, most of them will be eaten."

At her words, he jerked his hand back and his face paled.

"Why are you looking at me like that? You enjoyed the creamed chicken Mama made for dinner yesterday."

"Yes, but I didn't have to look it in the eye before I ate it."

"It's not a dog, and it's not a pet. It's a chicken."

He started the car, not looking at her as he spoke. "Still. . ." His voice trailed off.

Louise couldn't hold back her smile. "You really are a city boy, aren't you?"

He turned and grinned at her, and Louise's foolish heart fluttered. "Yes, it appears I am."

She set all her attention on the chicks in the crate between them. "We must seem so primitive to you. I know when we visit my aunt in Winnipeg and stay overnight, it feels like a trip to a palace. I think the thing I like the best is my aunt's icebox." She felt the heat rise to her cheeks. She wasn't going to say out loud that the real best part was not having to go outside to use the outhouse.

"I know. At home in Katona Falls, the iceman came right to my door twice a week. When I was growing up, all the children in the neighborhood used to love it when he gave us chips of ice to suck on."

Louise smiled, imagining him as a young child. "That sounds like fun. Of course you know we've never had an icebox, just the outdoor cellar. When I was a child, it used to be fun for my sister and me to pack snow in the outdoor cellar, but the older I got, the less fun it became, especially after she moved away. I guess that's probably why I think the icebox is the best part about living in the city. What do you like best about living in the city?"

Elliott grinned. "Hot water." He paused to glance at her, then turned his attention back to the road. "A few years ago, when business was still good, Ike installed a tank, kind of like a large boiler that keeps the water warm all the time so we don't have to keep filling up the kettle on the woodstove at the barbershop, especially in the summer. Since I lived in the suite upstairs, we ran a pipe upstairs. My friends loved to come over just to get hot water from the tap."

Louise turned her head and stared out the window, no longer interested in the chicks. Not that she was dissatisfied with her life in Pineridge; she enjoyed the simple lifestyle here, but she didn't want to appear uncivilized in his eyes. Not only did Elliott have running water, he had hot running water. Even her aunt didn't have hot running water, although Louise heard that the newer homes in the city did.

"I know what you're thinking, Louise. I don't mind having to pump the water and then wait for it to be heated. Aside from not having a few newer conveniences, your parents have a lovely home. Most of all, they're wonderful people. They've been so kind and gracious to open their home to me, a stranger."

Suddenly, Louise felt ashamed of her jealous thoughts. While it was true her home had none of the luxuries Elliott's home had, in reality Elliott no longer had a home. He owned nothing but one set of clothes. Everything else he had was borrowed from her father or purchased with money he'd borrowed. Worst of all, he'd had to rely on the charity of other people, for now her family, even to eat. His life had come to the point that if it weren't for her family, he wouldn't be eating now.

In the end, it was not material goods or the luxuries of modern conveniences that mattered. Elliott had lost everything he'd ever held dear and was left to rely on God's grace and the charity of strangers for his very survival. Because of that, Louise could see that underneath all the things that could hide a person's true self, Elliott Endicott was a man of faith and fine character.

Louise cleared her throat. "I suppose I would be safe to assume that you've never raised chickens before."

"I've never had the opportunity to raise any kind of animal before."

"Then you're in luck. Every spring Papa gets a pig. We fatten it up all summer and then slaughter it in the fall after we have enough snow in the outdoor cellar and it gets cold enough to keep the meat frozen until it's used up. Maybe this year, you can get the pig for Papa and take care of it for him until he gets the cast off."

"I think I'll pass. I'd probably name it and teach it tricks like a dog. I couldn't bear to know that it would soon be coming to an untimely end. Everything I eat I've bought from the store, ready to cook without having to do anything else first or know any of the gory details, and I like it that way."

As Elliott stopped the car, Louise realized they had arrived at home. She hadn't been aware of most of the journey. Before she figured out what he was doing, Elliott had slipped out of the car, opened her door, and he stood to the side to allow her to get out. When she stood beside him, he leaned inside, reaching for the crate of chicks. "None of them are going to jump out on me, are they?"

"They're not frogs. Baby chicks do hop a little bit, but they certainly don't jump that high at this age."

"I don't know about that. All I know is that they're bouncing now."

As he backed out of the car while steadying the orange crate in front of him, he bumped into her from behind. He straightened quickly, and the sudden movement caused the chicks to cheep loudly. Automatically, Louise reached to steady the crate, and as she did so, her hand brushed his. Their gazes met, and he slowly brushed the back of her hand with his thumb.

Suddenly, Louise's heart started to pound out of control. "City boy," she muttered.

His hand covered hers completely. "Apparently," he mumbled, his voice unusually low in pitch.

Louise's throat clogged, and she couldn't respond with him touching her. She didn't know what happened, but something just had.

Without speaking, she yanked her hand away and ran into the house, leaving Elliott to carry the chicks by himself.

"May I see some identification, please?"

Elliott stiffened. "I'm sorry, I don't have anything. My wallet has been stolen, and I haven't received my replacement driver's license or anything yet."

The bank teller paused, read the front of the check, then put it to the side. He picked up a form and his fountain pen. "Since you're opening an account, we can use a letter from another financial institution to verify your identity."

"I don't have anything like that. I'm new to the area, and I don't have anything set up yet. That's why I'm here. To open a new account."

The young man tapped the top of the pen to the counter. "Your address, then?"

Elliott shuffled his feet, wondering how many banks there could possibly be in Beauséjour. "I, uh, don't have an address. I'm staying with friends. In Pineridge. That's not too far from here. Would you like that one?"

Elliott gritted his teeth and forced himself to smile, hoping against good sense that the clerk wouldn't ask for their address because he didn't know it. No one used it, apparently not even the post office.

The clerk laid his pen on the counter, picked up Elliott's paycheck, read it again, turned it over to examine Elliott's signature, then folded his hands on the countertop. "Let me get this straight. You have no identification, no letters, no address, no other accounts in town, and you want to cash this check?"

"Yes, I do. It's a railway check. It's good."

"I'm sorry. I'm going to have to call for the manager. Please have a seat."

Elliott's stomach took a nosedive somewhere into the bottom of his shoes. It wasn't until he had the check in his hand that he'd realized he might have difficulty cashing it. He hadn't, however, expected this.

He left the teller's window and walked to the waiting area, where he stood beside Louise.

"What's taking so long? Why are we standing here?"

"They won't open an account and cash the check without seeing my identification, and I don't have any. Nor is there any local establishment they can contact to confirm I am who I say I am or that has my signature on file. Until I get something in writing, I'm stuck."

"What about asking your brother to send something? I hope your birth certificate wasn't in your wallet."

"No. That's the one thing that wasn't, but I'm hesitant to send the only identification I have left in the world through the mail, in case something happens to it. Besides, my birth certificate doesn't have my signature on it."

The teller returned. "Mr. Endicott? This way, please."

"I'm going with you," Louise whispered beside him.

He opened his mouth to tell her that wasn't necessary, but she was already ahead of him.

The teller ushered them into a private office. The manager leaned over his large wooden desk to shake Elliott's hand, waited for Louise to sit, and both men sat as well.

The manager folded his hands on the polished desktop. "I understand we have a bit of a problem."

It wasn't "a bit" of a problem. He had finally received his paycheck for his first week. Until he had the check in his hand, he hadn't known what his salary was to be. He'd heard the railroad paid well, and he found that to be true. After he cashed his paycheck for $16.89, he would have enough money to pay back what he owed the Demchucks from his last shopping trip. Then he could do more personal shopping, send some money to his brother, and have some for the offering at the church. He might even be able to buy himself a new Bible. He'd thought of buying himself a new wallet, but after all his expenses were taken care of, he doubted he would have anything to put in it. Therefore, that expenditure would wait for two weeks for his next shopping trip, when he would actually need a wallet. Still, he'd never made so much at the barbershop in one week, not even in two.

Elliott cleared his throat and faced the manager. "My wallet was stolen, so I have no identification. Also, I'm from out of town, so I have no local references."

"That's not true," Louise said, her voice causing both men to freeze. "I have an account here, and I can give him a reference. My name is Louise Demchuck." She started digging through her purse. "Here is my bankbook; I believe this is everything you'll need."

The bank manager smiled as he accepted it. "That will be fine, thank you." He stood, then leaned over to shake Elliott's hand once more. "I'll tell Randolph to set up that account for you. Good day, Mr. Endicott, Miss Demchuck."

As soon as the teller saw the door open, he appeared. The manager gave him Louise's bankbook and instructed him to set up the account.

Louise accompanied Elliott to the same grated window he'd been at previously and waited beside him while the teller filled out the information from Louise's file. Elliott stepped to the side when the teller directed her where to sign on the form, and he then continued to open the account.

He flinched when Louise touched his arm. "See? Everything is fine."

"Yes. Thank you." Elliott tried to smile, but inside he was numb.

It wasn't fine. A woman had to vouch for him. His ability to conduct financial transactions was in the hands of a woman who wasn't even legal age.

A few weeks ago, a man he had never met before had offered him a job, and he'd accepted it. He was now living in that man's house, sleeping on his couch, and driving his car.

That man's wife was feeding him.

Even their church and community had welcomed him when he had nothing to offer.

Elliott felt like a flea living off the blood of a friendly dog. He was a parasite.

"You have to leave some money in the account to keep it open. How much shall I leave in, Mr. Endicott?"

"Whatever is the minimum."

The man counted out the money. "Thank you, Sir. I hope to see you again soon."

"Yes," Elliott mumbled. "You will. In exactly two weeks."

Louise was nearly skipping beside him as they walked down the main street. "Isn't it wonderful to have your own money, finally?"

He forced himself to smile. "Yes."

For longer than he cared to remember, Elliott had thought that all he needed to be happy was a job with a good income. Now he had it, but the hole in his soul seemed larger than ever. Eight weeks of a good salary didn't mean he was set for life, but for the near future, especially with no expenses beyond replacing the necessities and a few items for work, the money he earned would go a long way. In the end, though, it didn't make him as happy as he thought it would.

"The co-op at the corner of Derwent Street has the best prices for the overalls you'll need. And you can buy the boots at the co-op on Tarlton Street."

"Okay." His future was still hollow and uncertain. He'd never been shy for adventure, but Elliott didn't want adventure. He longed for the time he could spend his day at work, then spend his evenings at home in the good company of the woman who would be his wife and not have to worry about what the next day would or wouldn't bring.

"Mama gave me her grocery list, plus I have a couple of things to buy at the drugstore. What do you want to do first?"

"Makes no difference to me."

"I also want to buy Papa a good book. He's getting so bored and frustrated when all he can do is sit around all the time, and he's read everything in the house at least twice. Those two days it rained and he stayed home all day while you went to work, well, I've never seen Papa so restless. Can you help me pick out a good book for him?"

"Sure." He wondered what John liked to read, then thought he would have liked to buy John a book as a gift. Elliott felt his face tighten as he walked. He could well imagine John's reaction to his gift. Despite his best intentions, Elliott knew his host would not accept a gift from him graciously. John had made it more than clear that he didn't want Elliott to ever think of trying to pay him back. Even though he worked hard all day, the railroad paid well for that. When he accepted the job and all that went with it, Elliott had not foreseen how strange he'd feel about receiving free room and board. All his meals and needs were taken care of, merely for escorting John around the house and property and helping Mrs. Demchuck with tasks that John temporarily couldn't.

It unsettled Elliott to know he wasn't doing enough to reciprocate their kindness. Yet, when he managed to put the uneasiness aside, he felt happy at the Demchucks' home. The same bond existed between John and his wife that Elliott had seen between his own parents. As a young boy, he hadn't understood completely, but now, from an adult perspective, he did. He saw in the Demchucks' marriage the things he wanted for himself. As well as the love between husband and wife, they were best friends, something he didn't see very often. Just as his own parents were, John and Mrs. Demchuck were comfortable together, as well as apart.

He'd seen many of his friends fall in love so intensely that they couldn't bear to be separated, and then when they were together, they behaved as if they were walking on eggshells, afraid they would do or say the wrong thing. Elliott didn't think that was the way love should be, but since he'd never experienced it personally, he simply didn't know.

"Look, Elliott, here's the barbershop. Is yours like this one?"

The shop had only one customer, who was in the chair and covered by a cape while the barber snipped at the man's sideburns. He wondered if this barbershop did any better than his brother's in Katona Falls and if this one earned enough income to support a man with a family, even if it could never earn anything close to what a man's father-in-law might make.

He nearly stumbled at his own thoughts, but he kept walking as he spoke. "I guess they're pretty similar," he mumbled, quickening his pace.

"Elliott? Where are you going?"

He stopped abruptly to discover that they had arrived at their destination, which was next door to the barbershop.

"Is something wrong? You're being so quiet."

"No, nothing's wrong. I was just thinking."

"About what? Or should I not ask?"

He gazed into Louise's beautiful green eyes as she spoke, wondering what it would be like to come home to Louise after a hard day at work, sitting on the couch while she made dinner and little children played at his feet.

Abruptly, he looked away, back to the barbershop, whose only customer had just left. "I was thinking about things that will never happen. Now let's get that shopping done. Your mama will be unhappy if we're late for dinner." He covered his stomach with his hands and sighed, remembering the delicious roast pork Louise's mother had made last night. She'd made sandwiches with the last of the meat for their lunch today and used the most fragrant, mouthwatering bread he'd ever tasted, which he knew Louise had made. "I don't know how your family manages to stay so thin. I've never eaten so well in my life. I fear my new clothes won't fit me by the time I leave."

Louise shook her head so fast her hair flopped on her shoulder.

"I doubt that will happen. But you are right. I don't want Mama to be angry, and I think she might need some items on this list for today's dinner. We had better hurry."

Elliott forced himself to put his thoughts of the future and what could never be out of his head. For the rest of the day, he would be alone with Louise, and he intended to enjoy it. Although Mrs. Demchuck said she was too busy to go with them today, Elliott highly suspected she merely wanted to spend some rare private time with her husband.

"Elliott? Are you coming?"

He turned back to Louise. Her lovely smile did strange things to his stomach, and this time, he definitely wasn't hungry.

He smiled back, determined to forget his troubles for the day. "Yes, I'm coming. Now let's have some fun shopping."

Chapter 14

Elliott handed John the crutches at the top of the stairs and watched John hobble into the bedroom. Elliott closed the door behind him, then made his way down the stairs and joined Mrs. Demchuck and Louise on the couch.

Besides the pleasant music of Glenn Miller, the clicking of their knitting needles added to the homey atmosphere.

"John was so tired," Mrs. Demchuck said as she turned her knitting and started another row. "But it's his own fault for insisting on walking to church. I told him that he should have let you drive him."

Elliott nodded and leaned back, letting his feet stick out straight in front of him as he linked his fingers behind his head. "I know. I told him he was going to be sorry."

Louise smiled, not missing a stitch as she spoke. "You know Papa. Once he makes up his mind, it's nearly impossible to get him to change it."

"I meant to ask you at dinner but didn't get the chance. How did your men's choir practice go?"

"Mama!" Louise laid her knitting in her lap. "It's hardly a choir. There were exactly five men. And it's called a barbershop quartet."

"But there were five. A quartet is four."

Louise resumed her knitting. "They still call it a barbershop, regardless of the number of men. It's the style rather than the number of people that determines the name."

Elliott smiled as Louise and her mother continued to banter back and forth. As the conversation progressed, he found he didn't have to say a word. Louise was doing a fine job without him, telling her mother everything that had happened, from figuring out the participants' vocal ranges, to selecting the music, to trying to show Stan Pollock when to go up and when to go down with the music in front of him.

All in all, it had been a long time since he'd enjoyed himself so much. Nick Sabinski had been correct in that he was the only one able to read music. However, that hadn't stopped the men from putting together a simple but melodious version of "Amazing Grace" in four-part harmony. Because Elliott was the only one experienced with group dynamics, they had looked to him for leadership, but it had been Louise who had held the group together with her skills on the organ, as well as her patience when they started doing more joking than singing.

As the two women continued to argue playfully over the clicking of the knitting needles, Elliott closed his eyes to think about everything that had happened that day.

At church this morning, he'd met more people, all of whom welcomed him like he belonged there. Everyone had accepted him as a friend of the Demchucks. He'd received a tentative invitation to dinner to the McSorbins' home, the family Louise had purchased her baby chickens from. Because the McSorbins had four children, the oldest of whom was Louise's friend Dorothy, he had been hesitant to accept. However, they had assured him he was welcome and they wanted to get to know him better, even though his presence in their community was temporary. The only thing he'd found odd—and realized too late to change his acceptance—was that he'd been invited without Louise.

"Hush, girl. I think he's sleeping."

He opened his eyes and smiled at Mrs. Demchuck, not moving from his stretched-out position. "No, I'm not sleeping, but I am relaxing. I was just thinking that all these years I've lived alone, I didn't know what I was missing."

Both of their mouths dropped open, and for the first time that evening, the room was silent. They'd even stopped knitting.

Elliott couldn't hold back his laughter. He sat straight and ran his fingers through his hair. "I was just teasing you. Honestly, spending a quiet evening like this is quite pleasant. I've lived alone for five years, and it's difficult to describe what it feels like to hear the sound of movement and voices around me when I'm used to only silence inside and the noise of the city outside. That changed when my brother and his family moved in with me two months ago. It's kind of relaxing, in a noisy sort of way." At the same time as he thought about his words, he also thought that listening to the sound of Louise's voice was far more pleasant than listening to the sounds of his brother back when his own family was still together under one roof.

The clicking resumed, and this time Elliott joined them in conversation as they discussed what they'd heard at church as the latest happenings in their community.

Before they knew it, it was time to go to sleep. Over the last few weeks, Elliott had learned the hard way that the seven o'clock phone call often came far too early.

⟳

Louise burst in through the door, not caring that it slammed on the wall as she ran inside. At the sudden noise, the chicks in their crate beside the cookstove cheeped louder than usual. "Mama! Elliott is going to be so pleased! A letter came for him from his brother!"

Her mama smiled and wiped her hands on her apron. "Yes. He's so far from home. Do you know it's been three weeks since he's arrived? It's always good to hear from home. I remember when your father and I moved here to Pineridge, so far from our families. It was always so special to get a letter from home, but at least we had each other. Elliott has no one."

Louise was about to say that he had her but stopped. They had come to know each other quite well in the last three weeks. As well as being together every evening until bedtime, they were together almost every waking minute of every day on the week-ends. Still, as much as they tried to make him feel at home with them, Louise could tell he felt awkward at times and sometimes even sad. Nothing could replace news from his family.

"Do you think he's happy here, Mama?"

Her mama rested her spoon on the cookstove. "I think so, most of the time. I suppose you've noticed that at times he seems to disappear into a world of his own."

"Yes."

"You must admit, his life has been difficult. I only hope and pray that when he leaves things will go better for him. I wonder if his brother managed to contact that friend on the coast and if there's also a letter about his other job."

Louise looked at the letter in her hand, suddenly feeling ashamed of herself. She had already been tempted to feel the thickness of the envelope to try to guess if the envelope held one letter or two, but it hadn't been a letter from his future employer she'd been thinking about. She had been wondering if there was a second letter in the envelope from a woman—a woman who would have been missing him, and conversely, a woman whom Elliott would be missing.

She laid the letter on the table as fast as if it might burn her skin. Until Elliott chose to divulge such information, such thoughts were not her business, no matter how much they disturbed her and no matter how she was coming to feel about him.

A knock on the back door made Louise glance up at the time. The freight train had arrived before the return of the section gang, and with a freight train came more hungry men.

"You're busy, Mama. I can take care of him."

As usual, Louise answered the door, spoke to the man very briefly, gave him a plate of food to eat outside, and did her best to tell the poor, bedraggled, and skinny man that Jesus loved him. He didn't look like he believed her, but hopefully one day he would remember this act of God's love for him and see that God really did care. For now, his immediate need for food had been met. When the man was done, he returned the plate, thanked her quietly, and disappeared back to the freight train. She continued to stand in the doorway as the man, plus a few others, hopped back on as the train started moving.

Louise turned and walked back into the house, closing the door behind her. "Papa and Elliott should be here soon. What can I do?"

Her mama smiled. "Set the table. As you can tell, we're having a treat for dinner today."

Louise took her time to set the table, then stood to chat with her mama about the things Mildred had told her at the post office until her papa and Elliott arrived.

She waited until she heard the thumping of Elliott helping her father up the steps stop before she opened the door. It was important for her to respect her father and not witness his difficulty, allowing him to salvage some pride after needing to be helped with the simplest things.

As soon as the door opened, her papa smiled. "Does that smell mean what I think it means?"

Elliott's brows knotted and his nose wrinkled. "Has a skunk made its home under your porch, too, now? I didn't smell it outside."

Louise laughed at Elliott's joke, then began putting the food on the table as Elliott slipped off the boots, removed his overalls, and both men washed their hands.

After they paused for a word of thanks for their meal, her mama set the rest of the food on the table.

Her papa took his portion and passed the plate to Elliott. Elliott held it for a few seconds, spooned a very small portion on to his own plate, and passed it on, as well.

Suddenly it occurred to Louise that Elliott might not have been joking about the skunk-like smell. "It's *studenetz*," she said slowly as she spooned a generous portion for herself, hoping Elliott would take her hint. "This is Mama's specialty."

Elliott looked at it, smiled hesitantly, then poked at the *studenetz* a few times with his fork before lifting a very small forkful to his mouth. With his first bite, his shoulders hunched slightly forward, his cheeks bulged slightly for a split second, and at the same time as he swallowed, he reached quickly for his coffee. Louise was about to warn him that it was still too hot to drink, but he moved too fast and drank it anyway, then flinched when he scalded his tongue.

Elliott's cheeks darkened, and he gave a forced smile to her mama, whose eyes were wider than Louise had ever seen.

"I'm very sorry, Mrs. Demchuck, but what is that?"

"It's *studenetz*. My mother taught me to make it when I was a child. It's a Ukrainian dish."

He looked down at his plate, staring at it, and saying nothing.

Louise leaned forward across the table, lowering her voice. "The English translation is pickled pig's feet."

Not only did all the high color fade from Elliott's face, his cheeks paled to a ghastly gray.

"From the pig we slaughtered last fall. We're using up last year's meat from the outdoor cellar, because soon all the snow will be melted. The weather has been too warm for it to stay frozen in there much longer."

"Pig's feet?" He gulped.

Louise lowered her voice even more. "It's not as awful as it sounds. It's just meat. The pig's feet are cleaned and singed, and they are boiled with a beef shank, onions, and spices for half a day. Then the meat is picked off the bones and put with the liquid to cool, and it turns to jelly."

The continued pallor in his face told her that he thought it was indeed as awful as it sounded.

Her mama rose from the table. "I'm sorry, Elliott. This is a very popular dish in our community, as most of the people here are of Polish or Ukrainian heritage, with some Germans. It didn't occur to me that you wouldn't have seen it before. I'll find you something else to eat."

He stood also, lifted one hand, and made what Louise

thought was a very strained smile. "No, please, Mrs. Demchuck. It's fine. You do so much for me. Please sit down and enjoy it. It's just something I've never seen before. It's good. Really."

Her mama smiled hesitantly, then returned to her chair. Everyone continued to eat their dinner, although Louise noticed that Elliott ate very little.

When the meal was done and everyone had left the table, Louise opened all the windows on the main level of the house, as well as the front and back doors to freshen up the house, despite the cool evening air.

She had almost finished drying the dishes when Elliott stepped into the kitchen. "Louise, it's okay. I didn't mean to be rude, and you certainly don't have to risk everyone catching a chill just because of me. And look at your baby chicks; they're getting cold."

Without waiting for her response, he closed the door and the windows, and immediately the house felt warmer.

"Do you make that concoction, too?"

"Yes, of course."

He opened his mouth as if he were going to say something, then closed it again and shook his head. "I'll see you soon in the living room."

With that, Elliott turned and walked away.

The rest of the evening passed quickly. No mention was made of their dinner, although Louise had a feeling her mama would not be making *studenetz* for a long time.

Since both her papa and Elliott looked tired, they all went to bed earlier than usual, but sleep eluded Louise until the wee hours of the morning. When she finally did drift off, she didn't sleep well, and it only took the sound of a small noise in the kitchen to wake her. Worried that something had happened to her chicks, Louise grabbed her robe out of the armoire and ran downstairs.

Her feet skidded to a stop in the doorway. Elliott, wearing the striped flannel pajamas he'd purchased on their first shopping trip, with his back to her, was fumbling in the dark with something at the kitchen table.

Immediately, she averted her eyes, putting all her concentration on the washstand. "Elliott! What are you doing!" she said in a loud whisper, not wanting her voice to carry upstairs to her parents' bedroom.

At the sound of her voice, the chicks cheeped louder, and whatever was in Elliott's hands clattered to the table. He spun to face her, and she couldn't help but look at him. The faint glow of the streetlamp in front of the train station coming in through the kitchen window was the only light in the room, but it was enough to show his surprise at seeing her. He glanced quickly down at his pajamas, then shuffled backward until he was against the table.

"Louise! I'm sorry. I didn't mean to wake you," he whispered back.

She clutched her robe closed around her throat and craned her neck in a futile attempt to see around him. "Are you looking for something to eat?"

"I, uh, I was hungry."

Louise couldn't contain her smile and covered her mouth with the hand not still clutching her robe closed. She forced herself not to look at his pajamas, so she stared very intently straight into his eyes and nowhere else. "I noticed you didn't eat much at dinner. If you would like, I can find some of the leftover *studenetz* for you."

"Very funny."

She giggled again. "I'm sorry. I've grown up on it. I never thought anyone would find it strange. I don't think Mama did, either. Papa just loves it."

"Does Heinrich love it, too?"

Her smile dropped. "Heinrich? Why would you think. . . ?" She let her voice trail off.

He dragged one palm down his face. "Don't mind me; I don't know if I'm more tired or hungry. Those chickens of yours woke me up, and once I was awake, my stomach wouldn't let me sleep."

"The chickens?" She glanced toward the orange crate, where she could see a few of the chicks hopping after being awakened by all the noise. It was true that they did tend to cheep a lot, but with her bedroom upstairs, the chicks in the kitchen had never disturbed her. She had not considered that their cheeping would carry into the living room and disturb him.

Guilt assailed her. "I'm so sorry about the chicks. Can I help you find something to eat? Mama has some wonderful wild strawberry jam, and there is bread from lunchtime in the bread box."

He smiled, then backed away as Louise walked to the bread box. "Thank you. But don't worry; I can do it. I ate just fine by myself when I was living alone. Please, go back to bed. I'm sorry I disturbed you."

She almost made a comment that judging by how skinny he was when he first arrived she doubted he fed himself very well but caught herself in time. It had not been lack of ability; it was lack of food.

The concept of Elliott having to go hungry almost made her ill.

She turned her head, but he remained backed up against the table.

While she would gladly have sliced the bread to make him a midnight snack, she suspected that more than really wanting to do it himself, she had embarrassed him by catching him in his pajamas.

She smiled, and he smiled back hesitantly. "Good night, Elliott. Sleep well and enjoy your snack."

Chapter 15

Elliott drove the spade into the ground and turned another shovelful of dirt. As he continued to dig, he ignored the telltale shaking of the ground. Today was Saturday. The morning track inspection was done, so he had the rest of the day off, and for today, he could ignore the trains.

He stood and wiped the sweat from his brow with his sleeve. "Is this deep enough?"

Louise leaned forward and looked down into the hole. "Yes, it is. Now come, help me split the root."

Elliott had never done any form of gardening before, but he found he didn't mind the work. It was also a good way to spend the afternoon with Louise.

Together, they tried as delicately as they could to split the large peony into two plants. Elliott was up to his elbows in dirt when a male voice sounded behind him.

"Good day, Elliott. Louise."

Both he and Louise froze and looked upward at the same time.

"Heinrich?" Elliott's head swam. "What day is it? Isn't it Saturday?"

Heinrich smiled and nodded, and Elliott immediately felt some relief, but his heart still pounded. He stood and tried in vain to wipe some of the mud off his clothes and his hands. Rather than extend his muddy hand in greeting, he crossed his arms over his chest. "To what do we owe the pleasure of this visit?"

Heinrich smiled at Louise, then turned back to Elliott, and his smile dropped. "I'd like to say that I dropped by for a simple visit, but, unfortunately, I'm here because I need to talk to you unofficially. Do you have a minute? I also need to talk to John. Do you know where he is?"

Elliott's stomach churned, and Louise's face paled.

Elliott cleared his throat. "He's in the house. I'll go get him."

He hadn't taken more than a step when Heinrich stopped him. "Wait. I think it's best we sit down and talk inside." Heinrich turned to Louise. "If you will excuse us."

As soon as they were out of Louise's range of hearing, Elliott spoke. "Is there something wrong? If there is, I take full responsibility."

"Not exactly," Heinrich replied as they walked together up the steps and into the house. "John. Good to see you."

"Heinrich?" John struggled to his feet, taking a few seconds to stop wavering on the crutches in his hurry to stand. "How did you get here?"

"Since this is an unofficial visit, I used my pass and came by the train."

"Anna! Can you make us some coffee?" John called over his shoulder, but Elliott saw that Mrs. Demchuck had already entered the room.

"Heinrich? What are you doing here on a Saturday?"

Elliott would have smiled if he hadn't been so nervous.

"There is a matter I must discuss with John and Elliott. If you'll excuse us?"

Mrs. Demchuck slipped out of the room in the blink of an eye, and Elliott's stomach flipped over a few times as John and Heinrich sat on the couch. Rather than sit three in a row, Elliott brought himself the chair from the desk.

Heinrich folded his hands in his lap. "I'll get right to the point. First of all, there was nothing wrong with the inspection or the track, so don't worry about that. However, I had to make a note of your broken leg and your new lead hand in my report, and that has drawn the attention of a few heads at the district office."

John raised one finger in the air. "Now wait a minute. I'm authorized to do all my own hiring and firing of my section gang without anyone's permission or collaboration."

Elliott stiffened in the chair rather than let it appear like he was shrinking. Of all the things he'd tossed and turned about at night, being the cause of trouble for John at the district office was one thing he hadn't considered.

"Above everything, my only concern is the maintenance of the track, and your section is exemplary, as always. What I'm about to tell you is confidential, and I won't reveal my sources. However, if you figure it out yourself, well, that's your own reasoning. Let me say that a certain individual who heard that you fired Robert wanted the job as your lead hand. I know you are aware that your current section men get first consideration and that who gets the job is your decision."

"Yes, but nether Frank nor Henry want the job. They don't want the responsibility."

"Yes, and this person apparently knows that. He was going to apply for the job when he heard you had hired someone. Someone who has never worked for the railroad before. Someone with no experience."

"That was my choice, and I have every right to make that choice."

"Yes, you do. But be warned that this person has connections. Quite honestly, he's a good man and a good worker, and he would be an asset to your crew. What I'm trying to say is that this man, as well as others in top positions, can cause you a good deal of trouble. I'm not saying you have to let Elliott go. Considering that Elliott has no experience, I'm surprised everything has gone so well, as I know you haven't been out there working alongside him every day. I want you to consider this a friendly warning that you are going to have trouble behind the scenes, to watch for it, and to prepare yourself. I would hate for you to lose your job over this."

Elliott forced himself to breathe. His brother's letter had been brief, but in it Ike assured Elliott he had immediately forwarded his letter to Edward in British Columbia. But Elliott still hadn't heard from Edward about the logging job. If Elliott didn't hear from him, or if he received a reply that the job was no longer available, Elliott had considered staying on as John's lead hand. When the cast came off and John could manage on his own, he could simply move into the bunkhouse with Frank and Henry and hold down the job, doing as Robert, the previous lead hand, had done. At the end of the eight weeks, he would be free and would no longer have to do everything around the house and property for John, or help John over the tracks or up and down the stairs, or anything else with which he experienced difficulty.

Now, due to extenuating circumstances, this was no longer an option. He was grateful beyond words for the job John had given him, but he couldn't keep it, knowing he was the cause of dissension between John and the supervisors at the district office, who ultimately controlled John's job.

Elliott stood and cleared his throat. "Thank you for the warning, but it's not necessary. As a friend, John and I had made arrangements for me to stay only as long as he is restricted by the cast. When the cast is removed and he's back on his feet, I will be moving on, so the lead hand position will be open."

He heard John's sharp intake of breath.

Heinrich raised his eyebrows. "Really? But this is a good job and an outstanding section. John's section has won many awards in past years." He stood to meet Elliott eye-to-eye. "I know I came with a warning, but I'll be sorry to see you go. Is there another section you wanted to be working with?"

"No. It's a position not with the railroad."

Their gazes met, Heinrich nodded, and they both sat again.

"I'm glad I came. I shall make it clear at the district office meeting on Monday what your intentions are, in order for the parties involved to wind down their plans to make this an issue. How much longer does that mean that you'll be here?"

Elliott didn't need to calculate it. Even though he'd only recently considered the possibility of staying, he had been counting almost to the day his remaining time with the Demchucks. "I have four more weeks."

John didn't rise but extended his hand to Heinrich, who reciprocated it in an unspoken gentlemen's agreement.

"I really appreciate you coming out all this way on your own time to pass on that warning, and I'm glad we were able to defuse this matter before any damage was done. There must be something I can do to thank you."

Heinrich smiled and glanced outside to where Louise was busy planting her peonies. "I must admit, there is another reason I came today. With your permission, I would like to take your lovely daughter to the movie theater tonight."

Louise cast her line into the water. "So the city boy does know how to fish."

He didn't look at her as he spoke. Instead, he bent his head and looked beneath him, past the trestle to the water far below, and swung his feet back and forth a few times. "I do know how to fish, but I must say, I have never had to watch the time so closely while doing it before. Fishing is supposed to be relaxing." He turned his head to stare down the length of track, then pulled her papa's pocket watch out of his pants pocket. "I'm glad this bridge isn't in your father's section," he muttered as he checked the time.

Louise couldn't hold back her giggle. While she enjoyed fishing, she'd never fished for relaxation. She fished to catch a fish. The railway bridge was the best fishing spot, as long as she was careful to be off the bridge before a train came by. Because she knew the train schedule every day, she knew in plenty of time when to get off the bridge. "If you catch something, will you be able to eat it, even after looking it in the eye?"

He grinned, and that funny thing happened in her chest again. "You're never going to let me forget that, are you?"

She smiled back. She would never forget the day they'd gone to pick up the chicks, but soon it wouldn't matter. In under a month he'd be gone.

Something in her stomach went to battle with the lunch she'd recently eaten, and she lost her smile. She wasn't going to fool anyone, least of all herself. It did matter.

Louise turned her head and concentrated on her line in the

water, far below. "Heinrich told me you aren't going to take the lead hand job on a permanent basis and that you will be leaving when Papa's cast is removed."

"That was the arrangement from the beginning."

"I was kind of hoping you'd consider staying on. Papa says you're doing a good job."

"I gave my word to Edward about the other job already. I have to admit that I briefly considered staying here, but really I can't. Besides, I won't be the cause of problems for your father because he's bent the rules for me. He's already done so much. When the time comes for me to move on, I will go—and trust that's the path God has laid out for me."

"Your decision has been made, then?"

"Yes."

There was nothing more she could say, so she remained silent.

"So how did your evening with Heinrich go?"

"Fine." It was horrible. She'd always liked Heinrich as someone her father had to answer to, but as to anything else, she had no interest. As funny as Heinrich was in a group, in private all he did was talk about himself. He was amusing to listen to, but only in the same sense as listening to an entertainer on a radio show. The conversation, what there had been of a conversation, had been all one-sided. However, if Louise wanted to be fair, she had to admit she hadn't made much effort to contribute. Heinrich was nearly fifteen years her senior. She felt the differences in the things he and his friends liked to do in their spare time. The contrast was so clear, she couldn't seriously consider him as a suitor.

Louise preferred to date men who were, and she mentally counted on her fingers, five or six years older than herself.

At first, she'd been so angry with her papa for sending her out with Heinrich that she could barely think straight. It had been so bad that she'd been forced to hold her tongue rather than be rude to Heinrich. And then, when Heinrich told her that it was definite Elliott would be leaving in under a month, she hadn't been able to think at all.

She'd been praying that Elliott could stay. She wanted him to stay on and move into the bunkhouse when her papa was out of the cast. When Elliott no longer lived under their roof, then they could start a real relationship. Until then, Elliott carefully behaved as a perfect gentleman, maintaining a careful distance, even the night she caught him in his pajamas in the kitchen. For now, it was best this way. Still, it didn't mean she had to like it.

She didn't want to be courted by her papa's supervisors. She wanted to be courted by his present lead hand.

She turned her head to study Elliott as he reeled in his line and put a new worm on the hook.

"Aren't you going to ask for more details?" she asked.

He didn't turn his head as he cast the line. "What you did is none of my business."

Louise gritted her teeth. She wanted it to be his business, but all the wishing in the world wouldn't make it so. First she'd heard it from Heinrich, now she'd heard it from Elliott himself.

He really was leaving, and there was nothing she could do about it.

"Louise! I think I caught something. Quick, get the net!"

Louise shook her head. There was something she could do. She couldn't force him to stay, but she could make the best of the time that he was here.

She grabbed the net and helped to contain the fish.

"It's just a perch. You may have caught the first one, but I'm going to catch the biggest."

He grinned at her, then froze. For a split second, she thought that if they hadn't been laden with fishing rods, and if she didn't have a squirming fish in her net, and if they hadn't been precariously seated on the railway bridge above the river that he might have kissed her.

"Is that a challenge?" he asked, but his voice carried the same husky undertone as the day he'd helped her bring home her chicks.

Louise gave him a shaky smile. "Yes." Although she had a feeling the challenge had extended beyond a little fish.

Chapter 16

I t's from Edward."

Elliott didn't bother to sit down, nor did he take the time to remove his boots and overalls. He wiped his hands on the rag he kept in his back pocket, then ripped open the envelope right where he stood in the doorway.

While he ripped the top, Louise stepped closer, smiling. "Mr. Sabinski teased me because this letter actually had our address on it."

Elliott smiled as he pulled the letter out of the envelope. "It was easier to just give Edward the complete address than explain why it wasn't necessary."

Louise opened her mouth, but Mrs. Demchuck's voice cut her off. "Louise! Give the man a moment in private to read his letter."

"Oops. Excuse me." She backed up, but only one small step, and waited.

Elliott skimmed the paragraphs until he found the words he wanted to read. "This is good," he said, unable to stop grinning. "The job I had originally wanted is gone, but there will be another one opening up at the time I will actually be arriving, and Edward has reserved and promised it to me. This is great! The Lord really does provide."

"That's wonderful!" said Mrs. Demchuck.

"I think I'll read the rest of the letter in the living room." He handed the letter back to Louise to hold while he slipped off his boots and overalls, and John hobbled out of the kitchen and into the living room until dinner was ready.

In his prayers before the meal, John extended an extra word of thanks for Elliott's new job opportunity and the letter from his friend.

While the general mood of everyone present was of joy and genuine happiness for him, he also experienced a strange undercurrent of sadness at the same time. It wasn't until they had finished eating that he realized what it was and why.

The news also served as a final confirmation that he would, in fact, be leaving.

He didn't want to go.

Knowing the job was his also solidified in his mind that if the opportunity to stay had arisen, he would have taken it and moved into the bunkhouse and lived as the previous lead hand had done. And that way, he would have been in a position to begin courting Louise.

But that couldn't happen. Heinrich had passed on the warning, which had to be genuine and very serious for him to have come on the weekend to deliver the message unofficially.

Elliott only partially listened as the Demchucks talked about an unfortunate incident with one of the Charumkos's cows.

He didn't want to think of Heinrich, but he had to. Louise apparently had enjoyed herself with him, but then again, he'd expected she would. Not only was Heinrich a good man, but he was considerably young to be holding such an important position with the railroad. That meant Heinrich had a promising future and a very good-paying job, certainly better wages than Elliott could make at the logging camp and certainly with more stability.

He guessed that Heinrich lived fairly close to Pineridge, which meant that Louise wouldn't be too far away from her parents when they got married.

Elliott's mouthful of ham suddenly turned to cardboard. Instantly, he lost his appetite.

"Elliott? I said I have good news for you."

Elliott blinked twice in rapid succession. "Pardon me? I'm sorry. I was thinking about something else."

Louise smiled at him, her green eyes sparkling, and Elliott temporarily lost his ability to swallow.

"I said Mama's going to do the dishes by herself tonight, because it's time to put the chicks outside."

He couldn't stop his smile. It had taken over a month, but he had finally managed to get used to the trains passing at night. He would have been able to sleep through the nights if it hadn't been for the chickens in the kitchen, scratching at the paper and cheeping and peeping at varying times during the night, then rising to full volume at the crack of daylight, which was earlier than he needed to get up.

"Yes, that is good news."

"I'll show you where Papa's cutters and the bundle of wire are."

He blinked again. "Cutters? Wire?"

Louise nodded. "Yes. You'll have to repair the holes in the fence around the chicken coop or they will escape."

"But it's Wednesday night. What about *Burns and Allen?*"

John snickered. "I'll let you know what Gracie is up to this time."

Elliott sighed. He would do anything to get rid of that annoying racket the chicks made at night, even miss his favorite radio program.

The second everyone had finished eating, Louise sprang to her feet, grabbed his arm, nearly dragging him out of the kitchen. It took him several trips to the basement and storage shed in the back of the property, but he managed to collect everything needed to repair the fencing around the chicken enclosure.

He did his best to repair the holes while Louise cleaned out the inside of the old wooden chicken coop.

Their last duty was to lay out the straw collected from the cuttings along the railroad, so the chickens could make their nests and lay their eggs.

Despite the work, Elliott enjoyed her company, even amidst the hay and chicken wire.

By the time they finished, the sun had dipped low in the west, making the skyline glow with hues of pink and purple as the sun fell to the flat prairie ground. Elliott walked carefully along the darkening ground as he carried the orange crate full of chattering and bouncing chickens out to the coop. The fuzzy little round creatures he had carried into the house not that long ago had nearly doubled in size. Now, besides the yellow fuzz, some white, black, and gray striped feathers were showing through. He also thought it was getting mighty crowded in that orange crate.

He gently lowered the crate in the straw, and Louise closed the gate behind them to prevent their escape. One by one, they released the baby chickens into their new home, then stood to watch them peck and run in the straw.

Elliott couldn't help but scratch his arms. He wondered if straw contained fleas or if it was just the dry dirt and pieces of straw that caused the itch.

"You should wash your arms right away. I know the straw can be irritating."

"You can say that again."

He stood beside Louise as her brood of chickens bounced around their feet. It wasn't like having children, but he knew these chicks were the closest he could ever come to that with Louise. He turned to tell her that he looked forward to a relatively quiet night, except for the trains, but when she raised her head toward him and smiled, his words caught in his throat.

"Well, city boy, I guess you're glad they're finally outside."

"Yes," he mumbled, then raised his hand to touch her cheek. "You have something on your face." As gently as he could, Elliott tried to brush the offending dirt, but the feel of her soft skin beneath the roughness of his own fingers distracted him.

He wanted to kiss her. But he didn't have that right.

Elliott quickly lowered his hand and stepped back. "You're right. I'd better go wash up."

And with that, he nearly ran into the kitchen.

Despite the absence of the chickens from the kitchen, Elliott knew it was going to be a long night.

Louise poured the iodine onto Elliott's finger where she'd pulled out a splinter, then gritted her teeth in sympathy when he blinked repeatedly.

"All better?" she asked meekly. "You don't want it to get infected."

He blinked a few more times, then swiped his sleeve over his eyes. "Wow, that made my eyes water. But, yes. Thank you."

"Did Papa not warn you that some of the window frames were rough?"

Elliott stood at the foot of the ladder and gazed skyward, up to the window on the second story of the house. "Yes, he did, but it started to slip out of the clip, and I had to catch it quickly before it fell to the ground and broke. I've never had to take storm windows out and put up screens before. The barbershop didn't have windows that opened."

Louise glanced briefly at her papa, who was busy painting the wooden frames of the storm windows that Elliott had taken off the house while her mama diligently washed the dust off the screens before he put them up. "At least Papa is able to do something. I've never seen him enjoy painting before. I hope he doesn't get too much paint on the cast."

Her mama stood and handed Elliott the cleaned screen for her bedroom window.

Louise held the ladder steady while Elliott scaled it. He fitted the screen into place, turned the clips, then came down the ladder very, very slowly.

She could tell by his unsure footing on the ladder that not only had he not changed windows before, it didn't appear that he'd spent much, if any, time up a ladder, especially one so large. Of all he'd done for them since he'd been there, Louise thought this chore to be the most daunting for him.

Overall, she couldn't help but admire his willingness to tackle without complaint all the jobs given to him. Since he arrived, he'd chopped all the wood they needed for the cookstove, as well as carried it into the kitchen. Then, as the weather continued to warm with the coming of summer, came the weekly chore of cutting the grass.

The last time he'd tended to a lawn had been in his teen years, when he'd lived at his parents' home. Since he moved into the upstairs suite at the barbershop, which had been a space of five years, he hadn't touched a lawn mower because being in the business area of Katona Falls, there had been no lawn. Unfortunately, it showed. Her father had to teach Elliott both how to repair and how to sharpen the blades of their lawn mower. The first time he'd done it, Louise had worried that he might be cut by the twirling blades, but of course, she'd worried for nothing.

Last week, her mama had done her spring cleaning, and she'd had Elliott help move all the furniture, including the piano, so she could wash behind everything.

All through the years, Louise had never realized the tasks her father carried out concerning the house and property, jobs neither she nor her mama could do, especially in the spring. Now, when her papa was unable to do them, she didn't know what they would have done without Elliott.

Her mother appeared at her side as she steadied the ladder for Elliott at her parents' bedroom window.

"This must be very trying for him. I can tell he's never done this before, either. His life must have been very different in the city."

Louise nodded, not letting her attention wander from Elliott, perched high above them. This time the clip to hold the storm window had rusted into place, and he was banging at it with the handle of a screwdriver to loosen it. "I couldn't believe his face when we asked him to fix the roof of the outhouse."

Her mama nodded back. "I know. But it was a job that needed doing."

Louise couldn't help her smile. "I've noticed no hesitation

when we ask him to drive the car. I think driving us around is the only job he finds fun."

"Yes. He will be taking your papa to have the cast removed next Saturday morning. I think Elliott will enjoy the drive, but your papa will enjoy it more."

Something in Louise's chest tightened. Of course, she was happy for her papa that his leg was healed and he wouldn't be so restricted. The past seven weeks had been difficult for him, because as well as the cast being heavy and awkward, the last couple of weeks had been highly uncomfortable for him, just as the doctor had predicted.

Soon the cast would be removed, and there would be no need for Elliott to remain to do her father's chores for him.

Every day the calendar in her head flipped another page.

Her mama moved to the side as Elliott began to descend the ladder, balancing the storm window in his arms as he struggled to keep his footing on the ladder. "Next Sunday his barbershop quintet will be singing in church. I look forward to it. They were so beautiful the other time they sang for everyone."

"It's called a barbershop quartet, Mama."

Her mama grinned. "No, it's not. There are five of them, and that makes it a quintet." With her words, her mama fetched the next screen for Elliott to put up and left it leaning against the house. Louise held the ladder more firmly as it shook with Elliott's movements as he continued to come down.

Once his feet touched the ground, he rested the storm window against the house, picked up the screen, and ran his fingers through his hair, pushing it back off his forehead. "It's getting hot up there. Isn't this weather great?"

Louise looked into his face. Since he'd been staying with them, he'd changed so much. He'd put on some weight, and although he was still thin, he looked good, even handsome. She noticed he smiled more often, and occasionally he repeated jokes he heard, although he sometimes missed the delivery on the punch line.

In many ways, she couldn't believe he was the same man she'd found desperately eating wild strawberries, only seven weeks ago, but in the ways that counted, he was exactly that same man.

Louise felt the burn of tears starting in the back of her eyes. She couldn't let him see her cry. "You look thirsty," she mumbled. "Let me get you something cool to drink."

With that, she turned and ran to the house.

She knew at that moment, she'd fallen in love with Elliott Endicott, and in eight short days, he would be gone.

Chapter 17

Elliott gave the other men the signal for the close of the worship song, and they all cut off the final note at the same instant, leaving an awed silence in the sanctuary. In the back row, he could see Nick's wife dabbing at her eyes and blowing her nose. As he scanned the room, he could see many women sniffling, as well as a few of the men trying to discreetly wipe their eyes.

Elliott's step faltered slightly as he started to walk off the platform to take his seat.

This was it. His last Sunday with this church family. John's cast had been removed on Saturday. John would be using the crutches for a few more days off and on, but he was doing well. Soon he would be completely on his feet unassisted again, and life would be back to normal.

The new lead hand had arrived yesterday. They'd done the track inspection together, and as Heinrich had said, the new man was experienced and a good worker, sure to be an asset to John's section gang.

They no longer needed him. Elliott's work here was done.

Rather than prolong the agony and in order to make a clean break for the new man to start the next day, Elliott had planned not to draw out a painful departure. He would be leaving on the 3:15 train today, not as he'd come, but as a paying passenger.

He inhaled deeply and stepped down from the platform, but as he did, Pastor Galbraith called his name from the pulpit, then addressed the congregation.

"In case any of you don't know, this is Elliott's final service with us. Elliott, would you like to come and share a word with the congregation?"

Elliott's stomach clenched. He'd never spoken in front of a

group before. Even though this congregation consisted of some very friendly people and he'd spoken to everyone individually at some time in the last eight weeks, the fact was that in the present situation, he would be speaking to a collective audience.

He turned around, about to decline, but everyone seated smiled and nodded at him, making it impossible to refuse.

"Hi," he mumbled.

"Speak up!" someone called from somewhere in the middle of the congregation.

Elliott cleared his throat. "I don't know what to say. I suppose I can start by saying what a blessing it's been to be a part of this fine community for the short amount of time I've been here. You've welcomed me as a friend and as a Christian brother when I was a stranger."

He smiled to the congregation, ready to step down, but the smiles and nods of many people kept his feet rooted.

He fixed his sights on a piece of paper on the pulpit and continued. "When I arrived here, I had literally nothing. I lost my job, my home; and the only family I have left has enough troubles of their own without me. I thought I was following the only option I had left, but on the way I was robbed and what little I had left was taken from me.

"I'd never imagined what it would be like to have to accept charity from strangers as a means of survival, with little or no hope in sight. It's not a pleasant place to be. I can now understand the despair and depression that drives some people to the brink of taking their own lives.

"Living off the freight trains is dangerous and difficult, and I was not prepared for what lay before me when I chose that path. In the state I was in, I'm not sure I would have survived if God hadn't placed me in the path of the Demchuck family. They fed me, clothed me, encouraged me, and treated me as their equal. They even gave me a job when I had nothing to offer in return. They gave me the means and the will to carry on when I had nothing left down to the depths of my soul."

He paused for a few seconds to compose himself, and a hushed silence permeated the crowded room.

"John, Anna, and Louise, thank you. I owe you my life."

Elliott swallowed hard, knowing he was about to lose control.

He faced the congregation, so many of whom had become more special to him than words could say.

"God bless you all, as He has truly blessed me."

Without another word, he walked quietly to his seat.

Pastor Galbraith returned to the pulpit. "There is nothing I can say today to add to that. I think I'll save this sermon for next week. If the men's group would like to return to the front for another song of praise and worship, then we'll close the service."

Elliott rose once again, and the men took their place in a row. Louise played a single chord on the organ, and they sang "Rock of Ages." As they neared the close, Elliott had to struggle not to let his voice crack. Not only was "Rock of Ages" his favorite hymn, but it was also what Louise had been humming the first time he'd met her. He found it disquieting to be singing it now, as a reminder that in an hour he would be gone and he'd never see her again.

He barely held himself together, but mustering all the strength and dignity he had within him, Elliott made it to the end of the service and endured a number of teary good-byes before he excused himself to be with Louise.

That not a word was said the entire trip back to the house seemed strangely fitting. He had so much he wanted to say, there wasn't enough time if they'd had all day.

Once they arrived at the house, he tucked his last few belongings into his new suitcase and zippered it closed while Louise watched.

"I can't really believe you're going," she said, her voice far too quiet to be Louise.

"I know. For one of the few times in my life, I'm completely lost for words."

The slam of the back door told him they were not alone. John and Mrs. Demchuck walked into the living room and stood beside him.

"Thank you for everything you've done for us, Elliott. I will always believe it was God's perfect timing to deposit you here, waiting for me, the day of my accident."

"I know. I feel the same. And I don't know how to thank you for all you've done for me, either. The Lord really does provide."

Elliott reached forward to shake John's hand, but when their hands clasped, John pulled him into a quick embrace, still holding one hand and patting him on the back with the other.

Elliott squeezed his eyes shut so he wouldn't make a fool of himself and patted John's back as well.

When he pulled himself away, he turned to Mrs. Demchuck, who was standing beside him with tears streaming down her face.

"Thank you, Mrs. Demchuck. I don't know what else to say. Except that I'll miss you."

At his words, Mrs. Demchuck flung herself at Elliott, wrapped her arms around him, and sobbed. He couldn't make out a word of what she said, so he hugged her back and said nothing. Not that he could have said anything if he wanted to.

"Anna, come with me. Elliott's train will be pulling into the station in five minutes. Let's let him say good-bye to Louise."

Mrs. Demchuck backed up and rested her palm on his cheek. "Write soon and write often. And may the Lord be with you, night and day, Elliott. Now go to the station. You don't want to miss that train."

Elliott picked up his suitcase, and he and Louise began their last trip together to the train station. About halfway there, he felt Louise's hand touch his. She linked her fingers between his, then clasped his hand. Elliott closed his fingers around hers, then gave her hand a gentle squeeze.

The train arrived at the station at the same time as they did.

He lowered his suitcase to the ground, but he didn't let go of Louise's hand.

Her lower lip quivered and one tear rolled down her cheek. "I'll miss you, city boy."

Elliott thought his heart was in a vise. Every beat hurt. He couldn't breathe. His stomach felt like a rock.

If he didn't do this now, he never would.

He let go of her hand and cupped both cheeks in his palms and brushed a few tears away with his thumb. He gazed into her beautiful green eyes one more time, his eyes drifted shut, and he lowered his head until their lips were almost touching. "I love you, Louise," he ground out in a ragged whisper. And then he kissed her with all the love and longing in his heart and empty soul.

When her arms slid around his back and tightened, Elliott thought he'd died and gone to heaven. For a second their lips separated, but he could still feel the heat of her breath on his cheek, and he didn't want to let her go.

"I love you, too, Elliott," she whispered back, and then she kissed him the same way he'd just kissed her.

"All aboard!" the conductor called out.

He struggled to get his next words out. "I have to go."

Louise stepped back. Elliott picked up his suitcase, and she walked with him to the edge of the platform. He handed the conductor his ticket.

"Luggage?" the conductor asked.

"Just one and I'm carrying it with me."

The conductor returned his ticket. Elliott started to go up into the coach but stopped on the first step. Louise shuffled forward to stand on the platform beside the steps extending from the car's entrance. He turned sideways, and with his free hand, he brushed his fingers on Louise's cheek, rubbing his thumb over the line of tears. "I'll write," he muttered, then hopped aboard the train, and took his seat.

The conductor closed the door, which brought up the steps. He pulled the cord to signal the engineer that all passengers were aboard, and the train started to move.

Elliott stared out the window, watching Louise standing on the platform getting smaller and smaller.

This part of his journey had ended, and a new one had begun.

✍

"Louise! You've got another letter from Elliott!"

Louise dropped her bucket of chicken feed, picked up her skirt, and ran to the house. In a single motion, she grabbed the envelope from her mama's hands and tore it open.

"What did he say? He's been gone over a month, yet he still must be sending three letters a week. He's sent your papa another letter this time, too, but you get far more letters from him than your papa does."

Louise only half listened as she read. She broke out into a smile as she skimmed through. "He's asking about the chickens, and he's come up with names for all of them so we won't eat them." Louise lowered the letter and grinned openly at her mama. "Before he left, I could tell he had a few favorites in the chicken coop, almost like pets."

"I suppose I'm not surprised. How is his job working out?"

Louise continued to read. "No different than his last letter. He says it's hard, but it's good, honest work." Louise stopped to giggle and covered her mouth with one hand. "He says he's put on five more pounds, and he doesn't look like a city boy anymore."

"That must mean he's keeping it on. I was worried for a while. This is good."

"Oh! He was telling me about this in his last letter. That ministry he's developing with the other men in the logging camp—he says he's working on starting a small church there. There are also a few married couples living out there, some even with children."

"Really?"

"I've told you that before, Mama. It's a large place."

"Louise! Your chickens are escaping!"

Louise tucked the letter into her apron pocket as she ran to catch her chickens. Already, she had thought of a number of things she wanted to say to Elliott, even though she'd last mailed a letter to him only three days ago.

It nearly tore her heart out every time she mailed a letter to him, because it reminded her of how far away he was. On the other hand, reading a letter from him was almost as good as seeing him in person. They'd been pouring their hearts out to each other in their letters, to the point that Louise knew she had found her soul mate. If only he didn't live so far away.

Just as Louise caught the last chicken and returned it to the coop, the road master's car rode onto the siding, and Heinrich and her papa got out.

Louise's heart sank. She had reluctantly gone out with Heinrich once since Elliott had left, but nothing had changed, and nothing ever would. She felt nothing for Heinrich, regardless of what he felt for her.

Her papa walked inside, and Louise knew he would be getting something out of his desk before the two men went into the toolhouse to check the speedster.

Instead of waiting at the toolhouse, to her dismay, Heinrich approached her.

"Good day, Louise."

She nodded and wiped her hands on her apron. "Greetings, Heinrich."

"I don't have much time, so I'll say this quickly. As you no doubt know, I'm quite fond of you."

She could feel the heat rising in her cheeks. She didn't know what to say, so she said nothing.

"But it is more than obvious to me that your heart is elsewhere. Would I be correct to say it's far away, with Mr. Endicott, your father's temporary lead hand?"

"I'm sorry, Heinrich, that is true. I didn't mean to hurt you."

He sighed. "Such is the way of life, Louise. I know with him so far away, this has not worked out the way you would have wanted it, either, but alas, life often disappoints. I just wanted to thank you for our time together and tell you not to worry. But if one day your feelings for Mr. Endicott do change, please, let me know."

Louise smiled and reached out to touch her fingers to Heinrich's forearm. "Thank you, Heinrich," she muttered. "You are a good man, and one day, with God's blessings, that right woman will come to you."

Her papa's voice from the step stopped Heinrich before he could reply. "Heinrich! I've found that report you were looking for."

Heinrich smiled and nodded once. "Until next time, Louise."

Louise smiled, turned, and ran into the house. She didn't care that she couldn't use her papa's desk; she would sit on the floor if she had to, to write back to Elliott and get the letter away before the next train came through for the mailbag.

꧁

A knock on the back door nearly made Louise drop the potato she had been peeling. She glanced up at the clock, but as she suspected, according to the time, the train that had just pulled into the station was a passenger train, not a freight train. If it wasn't a hobo begging for food, she had no idea who it could be, because anyone who knew them would be knocking on the front door.

Her mama had gone upstairs to get a new apron, so Louise answered the door.

"Greetings."

"Elliott!"

Her head swam as he enveloped her in his arms, kissed her, and twirled her around so fast her feet left the floor. The second her feet touched the floor, he kissed her again.

She wrapped her arms around the back of his neck, not wanting to let him go as they spoke. "What are you doing here? I should be angry with you for not telling me you were coming."

"I did write, but I suppose I'm on the same train as the mailbag."

He grinned, sending Louise's heart into a tailspin.

She grinned back. "We're having chicken for dinner. Are you staying?" She almost blurted out a name for the chicken she had in the oven when suddenly all foolish thoughts left her and her stomach tied into a painful knot. "Why are you here? Did you lose your job?"

Elliott shook his head. "No. The opposite, in fact. I've been promoted to a supervisory position, with the help of a good recommendation from our friend and road master, Heinrich Getz."

"Heinrich gave you a recommendation?"

"Yes. And I'm here to ask you if you'd like a job. Two jobs, actually."

"A job? But Papa wanted me to go to college in the fall, which is coming up in two weeks."

His calloused palms cupped her cheeks, and Louise leaned into his warmth.

"I've already got permission from your papa, but now, I'm going to ask you. First of all, the logging camp is in need of a head cook for the cookhouse, and I was wondering if you were interested in the job."

Louise's heart stopped, then started up in double time. "Me?"

"The homes and conditions out there are a little rough, but in many ways not too much different than this, although I hear talk of improvements happening as they continue to expand. I've experienced your cooking skills firsthand, and I've also seen the work you've done organizing the church suppers and other events for your church. I think you'd be perfect. And most of all, I think you'd enjoy it."

"I don't know...."

His hands slipped to her waist and he pulled her closer. "The second job is the more important one. With every letter we exchanged and every day that went by, I knew I couldn't live without you. My future is stable now, and even though it's not the job I'd dreamed of, it wouldn't matter if I could have something far more important. What I'm asking is if you'll be my wife and come back with me to the logging camp, whether or not you want the job in the cookhouse. I want you to be there with me, at my side, as my helpmate and my friend and the mother of our children. We've got a church together, and it has a real sense of fellowship and community. Louise Demchuck, will you marry me?"

"Yes!" she squealed, then rose up on her toes to meet his kiss.

While locked in his kiss, in the back of her mind Louise heard the front door slam, followed by her papa's voice. "Louise? Anna? Where are you? Someone told me they thought they saw Elliott get off the train."

The echo of two pairs of footsteps stopped in the doorway, and to Louise's dismay, Elliott backed up and released her.

"Papa, Mama. Elliott and I are getting married."

Her mama squealed, ran to her, and wrapped her arms around Louise. "I'm so happy for you, Louise!"

Her papa started to shake Elliott's hand, shrugged his shoulders, then pulled him closer to give Elliott a suitable manly hug, still shaking one hand and patting him on the back with his free hand.

When the hugging was done, Louise backed up from her mother and stood beside Elliott. Her heart fluttered and her knees turned to jelly when she felt his arm slip around her waist. "You do know that this means I'd be taking your daughter away to the logging camp in British Columbia?"

Her mama smiled and sighed at the same time. "Of course we'll miss you both, but I have to think of what our own parents thought when we got married and moved here to Pineridge to follow John's job. You have our blessings."

Elliott pulled her closer. "I have to warn you, the logging

camp has even less conveniences than Pineridge."

Louise didn't care about conveniences. All she cared about was that God had blessed her with Elliott's return. She didn't care if they lived together in the heart of the city or in an igloo at the North Pole. She only wanted to marry him, and she wanted to marry him right away.

"Can we get married this weekend when Pastor Galbraith arrives and then go back to the logging camp together?"

He smiled, and her foolish heart fluttered, something she'd experienced a lot when she was with Elliott. "I think that's a fine idea."

"I'd love to work at the cookhouse at the logging camp. As long as in the spring, I'll be able to raise some chickens."

Elliott sighed. "One thing about that logging camp, it's at least quiet at night. But if it makes you happy, you know I won't say no to a few chickens."

"Even a few dozen chickens?"

Elliott squeezed his eyes shut, then gave her a rather weak smile. "Only if I can name them."

Louise raised her hands to his cheeks and pulled his face down to hers. Just before their lips touched, she stopped and whispered, "I love you, city boy."

Gail Sattler lives in Vancouver, BC, where you don't have to shovel rain, with her husband, three sons, two dogs, and a lizard who is quite cuddly for a reptile. When she's not writing, Gail is making music, playing electric bass for a local jazz band, and acoustic bass for a community orchestra. When she's not writing or making music, Gail likes to sit back with a hot coffee and a good book.